Praise for *The Freedom Broker*

"A fast-moving thriller featuring kidnapped oil tycoon Christos Paris and his kidnap-negotiator daughter, Thea. She's tough, she's smart, she's diabetic. The best scene—and who cares if it's plausible—involves bungee jumping over the Zambezi River. It's worth the price of the book. A spectacular start for what promises to be a great Thea Paris series."

—*Kirkus Reviews* (Starred Review)

"Howe provides nonstop action, believable characters, and a well-researched look at the world of international kidnapping."

—*Publishers Weekly*

"This debut novel generates nonstop suspense, commanding attention from the start and never letting go. Intended as the start of a series, this is a must for thriller fans."

—*Booklist* (Starred Review)

"Razor sharp and full of you-are-there authenticity—a superb thriller."

—LEE CHILD, #1 *New York Times* bestselling author

"*The Freedom Broker* combines terrific thriller writing and fascinating research about hostage rescues. This is fact and fiction at its best."

—JAMES PATTERSON, #1 *New York Times* bestselling author

"Move over Jason Bourne, action has a new name as international kidnapping expert Thea Paris pulls out all the stops to rescue her own father in this clever and gritty debut."

—LISA GARDNER, #1 *New York Times* bestselling author

"Unparalleled storytelling . . . Her characters are memorable and realistic. She has a great talent for description of landscapes, action, and an unerring detail for stealth from the beginning to the climactic end. I wish I could write as well."

—CLIVE CUSSLER, #1 *New York Times* bestselling author

"K.J. Howe is a master at weaving together action and suspense. Her debut is an engaging, fast-moving, spellbinding international intrigue that will leave you breathless. In Thea Paris, Howe has created a smart, complex, kick-ass character that you'll want to follow and root for."

—SIMON GERVAIS, former RCMP counterterrorism agent and bestselling author of *The Thin Black Line*

"*The Freedom Broker* has great bones: engaging characters, nimble pacing, and crackling action."

—KATHY REICHS, *New York Times* bestselling author

"The pulse-pounding excitement never ends in this remarkable debut novel . . . Howe takes the reader on the thrill ride of a lifetime . . . Memorable characters, muscular prose, and a world atlas of fascinating insider details make this a can't-put-down read. I loved it!"

—GAYLE LYNDS, *New York Times* bestselling author of *The Assassins*

"A high-octane debut thriller. Kidnap negotiator Thea Paris is a heroine with brains, martial skills, and true characters, whose own dark and deep family history drive her on as she travels the world bringing kidnapped victims home to their loved ones. Here's hoping Paris returns soon for another outing!"

—MARK GREANEY, #1 *New York Times* bestselling author

"Breathless action, great characters, and convincing details make Howe's *The Freedom Broker* a surefire rocket to the top of the lists."

—LINWOOD BARCLAY, #1 internationally bestselling author

"*The Freedom Broker* opens hot and stays that way. Author K.J. Howe and her protagonist, hostage-negotiator Thea Paris, are off to a high-octane start in this international thriller and series debut. Thea's oil-tycoon father is kidnapped—echoing the abduction of her brother two decades earlier—and it's up to Thea to solve the family's brutal business. A wickedly fast read."

—NEELY TUCKER, author of the Sully Carter series

THE FREEDOM BROKER

K.J. HOWE

Quercus

New York • London

Quercus

New York • London

© 2017 by Kimberley Howe
First published in the United States by Quercus in 2017

Any member of educational institutions wishing to photocopy part or all of the work for classroom use or anthology should send inquiries to permissions@quercus.com.

ISBN: 978-1-68144-310-2

Library of Congress Cataloging-in-Publication Data

Names: Howe, K. J. (Novelist), author.
Title: The freedom broker : a Thea Paris novel / by K.J. Howe.
Description: New York : Quercus, 2017. | Series: A Thea Paris novel ; 1
Identifiers: LCCN 2016027674 (print) | LCCN 2016029866 (ebook) | ISBN
    9781681443102 (hardcover) | ISBN 9781681443034 (ebook) | ISBN
    9781681443027 (library ebook)
Subjects: LCSH: Kidnapping—Fiction. | Hostage negotiations—Fiction. | Rescue
    work—Fiction. | GSAFD: Suspense fiction.
Classification: LCC PR9199.4.H687 F74 2017 (print) | LCC PR9199.4.H687 (ebook) |
    DDC 813/.6—dc23
LC record available at https://lccn.loc.gov/2016027674

Distributed in the United States and Canada by
Hachette Book Group
1290 Avenue of the Americas
New York, NY 10104

This book is a work of fiction. Names, characters, institutions, places, and events are either the product of the author's imagination or are used fictitiously. Any resemblance to actual persons—living or dead—events, or locales is entirely coincidental.

Manufactured in the United States

10 9 8 7 6 5 4 3 2

www.quercus.com

To RJH,
Thanks for being my freedom broker.

Children begin by loving their parents. After a time they judge them. Rarely, if ever, do they forgive them.

—Oscar Wilde, *A Woman of No Importance*, Act IV

Chapter One

500 feet above Kwale, Nigeria
November 1
2:30 a.m.

Thea Paris knew the drill.

If the mission failed, no one would retrieve her body. She'd be left to rot in the jungle, unidentified and forgotten. And that wouldn't do. She couldn't miss her father's sixtieth birthday party.

Her gloved right hand glided over her flak jacket and M4 with practiced ease. Night-vision goggles, flares, grenades, extra magazines—all easy to access. The weapon had been tested, cleaned, and oiled, and it was ready to withstand the humidity of the jungle. Pre-mission checks done.

The hypnotic purr of the resurrected Hughes 500P helicopter set the tone for the operation. Black, in every sense of the word. Sound, movement, light, all kept to a minimum. They were flying nap-of-the-earth: low, utilizing the terrain to stay below the radar.

As operational commander, she'd led her six-man team through endless rehearsals, using a model of the targeted area. Now it was time for execution. Brown listened to Hendrix in his earbuds, his way of psyching up. Johansson stared into space, probably thinking about his pregnant wife, who wasn't happy he'd accepted this mission. Team A, following them in the other retrofitted chopper, consisted of twin brothers Neil and Stewart—native-born Scots—and a wizened former French Foreign Legionnaire named Jean-Luc, who could outshoot them all. She'd handpicked each one from the pool of operatives at Quantum International Security.

Except Rifat Asker, her boss's son.

Who was staring at her. Given their fathers were best friends, she and Rif had known each other since they were kids. Thea respected his combat skills, but the two of them often locked horns on tactics. She traced the S-shaped scar on her right cheek, a permanent reminder of Rif's clash with her brother, Nikos.

She tapped her smartphone screen to call up her glucose reading: 105. Monitor batteries fully charged. Perfect. Nothing could screw up a mission more than low blood sugar. She slipped her phone into the pocket of her tactical vest beside her glucagon kit. Rif was still watching her as she adjusted her vest, and she wondered if he knew. She'd done her best to keep her condition a secret, but he didn't miss much. It probably wouldn't change anything, but she didn't want anyone on the team thinking she wasn't up to the job.

The pilot's voice crackled in her earpiece. "Three minutes to touchdown."

"Roger that. We're green here."

The stormy sky hid the second helicopter from view. Thea wiped her damp palms on her fatigues. Rain rattled on the chopper's fuselage, and the turbulence unsettled her stomach. Flying had never been her strong suit. The poor visibility would allow them to fly in under the radar, but the cloying humidity and heat could degrade the chopper's performance. They'd reduced its fuel load to stay as light as possible, but that left only a minimal buffer if they ran into any problems.

Rif shifted to face Brown and Johansson. "Okay, boys, let's grab this Oil Eagle."

The hostage, John Sampson, a petroleum engineer from Texas, earned high six figures consulting at overseas drilling sites to help increase their output. Sampson had two kids, and his wife taught third grade. He coached Little League baseball every Thursday night, but he'd missed the last ten games because he'd been kidnapped and held captive by an outfit called Movement for the Emancipation of the Niger Delta, or MEND. Seemed every terrorist group had some catchy acronym, as if they'd all hired PR firms to maximize their brand.

This Nigerian militant group wouldn't budge from its three-million-dollar demand; unfortunately, Sampson's kidnapping insurance topped out at one mil. That left a single option: rescue. But the overall success rate for hostage extractions was only twenty percent, which was why Sampson's outfit had sought out Quantum: when a life was on the line, you went to the best.

"Sixty seconds until touchdown," the pilot warned.

Thea slipped on her night-vision goggles and clutched one of the handhold straps anchored to the cabin walls.

"You sure there's no leak?" Black camo paint emphasized the tension in the lines around Rif's eyes.

"Roger that." She concentrated on the positives—always better than bleak thoughts when descending into potential hellfire. They should have the element of surprise, and she'd selected a crackerjack team. Every member would put his life on the line for the others, and their combined combat experience read like the Ivy League of special ops.

The pilot threaded the riverbed using the narrow thermal image provided by the FLIR camera mounted near the copter's skids. Flying into thick jungle on a moonless night was far from optimal, but their intel was time sensitive. They had to get Sampson out tonight.

"Thirty seconds." The pilot's warning was like a shot of amphetamine. They hovered above a small clearing in the triple-canopy jungle two miles from the rebel camp.

A film of perspiration coated Thea's back. Her body tingled. She felt alive, awake, adrenalized.

"Ten seconds."

The pilot raised the bird's nose, then settled onto the ground. Thea nodded to the others, and they exited the chopper post-haste, hit the ground, and rolled away from the clearing, feeling the rain on their skin and the heat emanating from the rotor wash as their transport rose up and away.

A moldy stench flooded Thea's mouth and nose, the residual effect of endless rainy seasons. The team huddled in thick, drip-ping bush while the other Hughes dropped off Jean-Luc and the two Scots. She scanned the area. The roar of the choppers faded into the distance, their faint but peculiar silhouettes briefly showcasing their modifications for stealth.

Normal local night sounds returned: crickets chirping, water gurgling in the nearby riverbed, the ominous roar of a hippo, the splashing rain. She checked her GPS, signaled Rif, and moved forward through the dense foliage. Forty-two minutes to execute the rescue, rendezvous with the helicopters, and get the hell out of there. She circumnavigated the heaviest brush, then froze.

A sound. Scuffling in the bushes. Her hands tightened on her M4. A sentry so close to their launch point?

She glanced over her left shoulder. Rif's large frame crouched two feet behind her. Brown and Johansson squatted beside him, while Team A covered the rear. The shrubbery to their left rip-pled in the brisk breeze.

Silence. A mosquito implanted itself in her neck. She ignored the sharp sting.

Then a twig snapped. Crunching footsteps. A small, shrill cry.

She flicked off her assault rifle's safety. She scanned left and right. Her finger hovered beside the trigger.

Then movement flashed directly in front of them at ground level.

A porcupine scurried across their ingress route, its quills in full attack mode.

Thea exhaled a long breath and gave Brown a half smile. Dammit to hell. She'd almost shot the prickly creature, which would have blown their cover. Brown touched the rabbit's foot he wore on a chain around his neck and nodded. Good luck charms were an operational must. She always wore the Saint Barbara silver pendant her father had given her on her twelfth birthday. It hadn't let her down yet.

The two teams silently traversed the unfriendly terrain, minimizing any disturbance of the bush. Animal sounds punctuated the night, the rainfall a constant backdrop. Thea scouted the path, moving cautiously in the darkness. At the edge of a ridge, she looked down. Faint flames from a fire kicked her heart into overdrive. The outskirts of the MEND camp lurked below.

She squeezed Rif's arm, signaling him to lead Team A down the escarpment. They'd have a rough time of it. The earth was thick, muddy, slick.

Thea remained on the curved ridge. As commander, she needed a bird's-eye view. Brown and Johansson flanked her, positioned to counter any patrolling rebels.

She cloaked herself in shrubbery and settled into her hide. They'd mapped all the major landmarks from satellite images: the rebels' weapons hut perched beside the acacia trees, a large shelter to the west sequestered in the jungle, and five small buildings rooted in the camp's southwest quadrant. Outbuilding "Tango" held their hostage, a quarter mile away.

She waited and watched for what seemed to be an eternity, the rain seeping into her shirt mixing with her sweat, leaving her skin clammy and cold. Her mind went to the weirdest places during missions—she pictured this sodden landscape as an ideal backdrop for a waterproof-mascara ad.

A tiny shiver darted across her shoulders. The world seemed preternaturally still, quiet—as if death had arrived. Twenty-five precious minutes had elapsed since Rif and the others had headed into the camp.

Thea nestled her rifle into the overhang. Her breathing slowed. She scanned the area below her, pursing her lips, the familiar taste of camo grease comforting her.

A soft hiss whispered in her earpiece; then Rif came on. "Going for the Eagle." Team A hovered on the outskirts of the camp.

Muffled laughter echoed in the distance. A few rebels huddled by the campfire, undoubtedly trying to ward off the dampness with some *kai-kai*, the local palm liquor.

"Six hostiles by the fire with AK-47s. You're good to go." Her voice was barely audible. They had to assume MEND had guards posted. Double-crosses dominated the rebels' lives, making them especially paranoid.

Footsteps sounded nearby. She froze. Definitely a human cadence. The soft glow of a cigarette caught her eye. A lone rebel was up on the ridge, headed straight for her.

Time for cocktail hour. She eased her hand into the pack and pulled out the tranquilizer gun, her fingers brushing the ballistic syringe loaded with an immobilizing drug.

The rebel cleared his throat and continued his patrol, oblivious he was walking straight toward her position. She waited, keeping her breath even, her body motionless. The man stepped into range. In one motion, she twisted her body, lifted the tranquilizer gun, and fired. The rebel grunted and swiped at his neck, as if swatting an insect. Seconds later, he slumped to the ground.

She scrambled over to him and poked him with the toe of her boot. No response. She crushed his cigarette into the wet earth and secured his hands and feet with plastic cuffs, slapping a strip of duct tape over his mouth. Her team should be long gone before he woke.

Thea's skin was slick. Rain continued to batter the earth. She glanced at her stopwatch—another four and a half minutes had passed since Team A had entered the camp. Glancing to the southwest, anxious to hear the code word "Gusher" in her earpiece, meaning the hostage had been found, she waited for Rif and his team to either signal or return.

Minutes ticked by, and nothing. Her nerves were tighter than the strings on a Stradivarius.

Her earpiece buzzed. Rif's measured voice came through. "Dry well. The Eagle isn't in Tango."

She sucked in air. Intel from two hours ago had confirmed Sampson's location in that outbuilding. He must have been moved.

"Abort." It killed her to do this, but she couldn't endanger her team members' lives by ordering an exploration of the camp. There wasn't enough time. They'd tried—and failed. The intel was bad. End of story. End of mission.

Silence greeted her. Dammit. Rif was a pro; he knew to respond to her command.

"Abort mission. Confirm." She scanned the camp. A few more rebels had joined the group around the fire.

Rif's voice filled the silence. "Give me three minutes, over."

No way. Three minutes was a lifetime. They needed to leave immediately to meet the choppers.

"I repeat, abort mission, over."

Silence.

Her earpiece finally crackled. "Wait, out." Operator speak for *Bugger off, I'm busy.* Rif had spent years in Delta Force, but this wasn't the US Army. She was in charge of this mission, and he was defying orders.

Before she could respond, gunfire erupted below at the campfire. No more hiding in the shadows. Time to bring it.

"Go active," she commanded her team.

The men from the campfire scrambled for their weapons while Brown and Johansson blasted their M4s from their positions on the ridge. Figures dropped to the muddy earth. Bullets ripped through the night, and the scent of gunpowder flooded her nostrils.

"Brown, take your shot." He was responsible for disabling the rebels' ammo hut with the grenade launcher.

"Eyes shut," Brown warned, protecting the team from the bright lights of the explosion, since they all wore night-vision goggles. Seconds later, the building erupted in a burst of crimson flames.

The sound of metal hitting rock sharpened her focus. Bullets showered the area around her. She pressed her chin into the mud, flattened her body, and returned fire.

A group of rebels stormed toward the cliff, but the team's NVGs made the figures easy targets. Blasts reverberated across the valley as muzzle flashes flared.

"Return to home base, over." Her voice remained calm, but four-letter words ricocheted through her brain.

Where was Rif?

She spotted rebels at the base of the hill, the men cutting off Team A's egress route. Dammit to hell. Well, "all in" was obviously the theme of the day.

"Cover me, Brown." She jumped up and ran down the slippery hillside, her footing uncertain in the muck. Before the rebels could react to her presence, she flipped the M4's setting to full auto and pressed the trigger, rattling off round after round. She slammed in a fresh magazine and kept firing. Several men fell; others ran for cover. She continued the suppressive fire. The egress route was clear. At least now Rif and the others had a chance of getting out.

Her earpiece buzzed. "Bravo Four, hit." Johansson's voice was reedy. He'd been shot.

The northeast wasn't covered, and Rif was AWOL. It was up to her to help.

She pressed the talk button. "Coming, Jo. Brown, watch my back."

Sprinting back up the hill, she traversed the ridge, mud sucking at her combat boots.

Fifty feet. She pushed harder.

Thirty.

Ten.

Bullets peppered the air around her. She dove behind a tree. Her forearms bore the brunt of her landing, the pain rumbling up to her shoulders. She low-crawled toward Johansson. Blood seeped from his shoulder. His face was ashen, his eyes unfocused. She grabbed a QuikClot from the first-aid kit in his backpack and placed it on his wound. "I'm too scared to face your pregnant wife alone, so keep your shit together."

He gave her a weak smile.

She removed the morphine syringe from his front pocket and jammed it into his left quad. He'd be comfortably numb soon enough.

A group of rebels climbed the embankment. Brown maintained his disciplined fire but couldn't keep up. Thea aimed her own M4 at the oncoming attackers and pressed the trigger. Several men fell. She shoved a fresh magazine in.

Figures appeared in the distant mist, the heat of their bodies a hazy green through the night-vision goggles. She counted them. Four. The tallest one, Rif, had a body slung over his right shoulder. Sampson. They'd found him, but she couldn't tell if the hostage was dead or alive.

"Jo, Team A's back. Can you walk?"

His breath was rapid and shallow. "Hell, yes."

She wasn't sure she believed him, given the morphine. She was strong for a buck-thirty but couldn't run while carrying over two hundred pounds. They'd make too easy a mark.

"Stand up, soldier," Thea said.

Johansson groaned. "My wife's going to kill me."

"She's going to have to take a number." She helped him to his feet. He stumbled, unsteady in the mud. She wrapped his left arm around her shoulder, supporting his weight. "Let's get you home."

The faint sound of incoming rotor wash spurred her. They only had a few minutes to reach the clearing.

A burst of nearby gunfire startled her. She looked up, prepared to shoot, but realized it was Rif firing suppressive bursts while sprinting across the ridge. Having handed off the hostage, he joined them behind a massive tree. Rain smeared his black camo paint, giving his face a sinister look. "Team A's headed back to the clearing with Sampson." He slung his rifle across his back and hoisted Johansson over his shoulder. "Cover me."

Thea stormed after them, heart and rifle on full auto. The rebels dove for shelter as she and Brown laid down covering fire. She shouted at Brown, "Chopper!" She wanted everyone in the Hughes before she would jump aboard.

The three of them ran for the clearing as another hail of bullets peppered the surrounding trees. She used a large mangrove for cover and returned fire, giving Rif time to help Johansson board the chopper.

She zigzagged across the open field. Her ride was in a valley over three hundred feet away. The other Hughes carrying Team A and Sampson lifted off into the rain behind her as she ran. Bullets whipped by. A sharp sting flared in her left arm as she plowed into thick underbrush. She ignored the pain and ran faster.

She scrambled down the gorge and dove into the chopper. Johansson, Brown, and Rif were already on board. She ripped off her night-vision goggles and grabbed her headset.

"Go!" she yelled at the pilot.

"Hold tight."

The winds gusted from the east, which meant they would have to power up while heading straight for the barrels of the rebels' AK-47s. The rotor blades strained as the group of armed men ran toward the Hughes. *Come on, come on.* Her fingernails dug into her palms. The chopper plunged into live fire like a flying piñata.

She kept her gaze straight ahead, willing the chopper to reach sixty knots so they could turn. Seconds felt like hours as they finally accelerated and swerved away from the camp. She glanced into the cockpit. The pilot's shirt was soaked with sweat.

Rif glanced at the blood on her sleeve. "You hit?"

"Just a graze." She stared at bullet holes in the fuselage, realizing how close a call it'd been—and how Rif's changing the plan mid-mission could have cost her teammates their lives.

"Is Sampson okay?" After all this, she prayed the hostage was alive.

"He's dehydrated and a bit roughed up, but he'll make it."

"Amen for that." Saint Barbara had done her job again. Thea slumped against the fuselage, grateful the rebels didn't have an RPG. She checked her phone. As expected, the intense stress had sent her blood sugar levels skyrocketing. But rapid-acting insulin would counteract that soon enough.

She inhaled a deep breath. Another hostage safely returned by Quantum International Security. Looked like she'd make Papa's party after all.

Chapter Two

Quantum International Security headquarters, London
November 28
3:00 p.m.

Thea studied the physicians gathered around the conference room table for their pre-travel briefing. If she could prevent just one kidnapping through these educational sessions, then the effort was worthwhile. Every group was different, but she always tried to predict which individuals would fare best if they were kidnapped and tailor the talk to those who probably wouldn't cope as well. She'd been a response consultant—the industry term for kidnap negotiator—for seven years, long enough to understand how different personalities dealt with captivity.

She smiled at the doctors, who were headed to Culiacán, the narco-crime capital in Sinaloa, Mexico, for relief work. "Let's talk a little physiology, which should be right up your alley. Ordinarily, if you're confronted with a traumatic or threatening situation, your hypothalamus triggers a fight-or-flight reflex, which propels your body into a state of hyperalertness, right? Blood surges to your extremities to prime the muscles for action. This makes you want to battle or bolt. But in a kidnapping, either of those actions could be counterproductive—and potentially deadly. And updated research includes a third reaction, which is freezing. Also not good."

The doc in the Zegna suit admiring his manicured nails emanated superiority and boredom. But was that mere bravado, masking fear? Likely. He'd certainly make a perfect target. And Mexican kidnappers would instantly deflate his overpuffed ego with the customary "welcome" battering they deployed to dominate hostages. Strip this guy of his Rolex and other trappings of wealth, and he'd be huddled in a fetal position, begging to go home. People with a titanium core, not a cream-puff center like his, were the ones who survived without permanent damage.

"When you're a captive, you're stuck in an anxiety-ridden purgatory that might last hours, days, months—or even years—with no control over your fate. To survive unbroken, you need to override the fight-or-flight reflex and avoid freezing. Instead, you must summon up survival qualities like patience, optimism, and discipline." Thea indicated a fit, middle-aged woman who sat near the front, her name written on her binder. "For example, Annie here would probably weather captivity well. She chooses sensible shoes over stilettos, which demonstrates practicality, and, judging by the crossword-puzzle book tucked into her briefcase, she has the required mindfulness and patience needed to endure both boredom and apprehension."

Annie gave her a small smile.

"But I hope none of you will have to find out how you'd cope. We're here today to minimize your risk of being kidnapped."

She paced the boardroom. "Most abductions take place on weekday mornings, and seventy-eight percent of them occur within two hundred meters of the hostage's home or workplace. How can you protect yourself? Become a hard target. But what does that mean in practical terms? Don't take the same route to work every day, maintain an unpredictable schedule, and always be aware of your surroundings. Remain alert and attentive. No texting or talking on the phone while in public. Instead, make careful note of any suspicious vehicles or individuals lingering around."

A man with a large handlebar mustache raised his hand. "If someone tries to abduct me, how hard do I fight back?"

"Good question. And there's no perfect answer. The actual grab is a risky time for hostage takers, so they hit hard, immediately asserting their dominance. Expect to be blindfolded, beaten, drugged, or forced into a vehicle's trunk. Under those circumstances, remain calm, and do what they say. Focus on survival. Remember that, to them, you're a commodity, and they'll want to keep you healthy and alive so they'll receive your ransom payment. If you're in a public place and you feel you can escape, it might be worth the risk. But if you are staring down the barrel of an Uzi on a deserted street, it's probably better to acquiesce. Don't be uncooperative or hostile toward your captors. Act like a brat, and you can expect to be punished. These people do not mess around."

"Should we curl up like frightened schoolgirls?" Zegna asked, eyebrows raised.

"The point is not to be difficult." *Asshole.* "If you become a hostage, your job changes. You need to be observant, taking careful note of your surroundings and the schedules of your captors. Also, since you might be held in captivity indefinitely, it will be vital to establish a routine of mental and physical exercise to keep yourself focused and fit."

"I'd find a way to bust loose. From what I've read, most kidnappers are fairly unsophisticated. I mean, they're probably not highly educated," Zegna said.

"You don't need a PhD to put a nine-millimeter round into someone's head. If you attempt an escape, you'd better be damn sure you won't be recaptured. Otherwise, your captors are likely to make an example out of you to keep other hostages obedient. Focus on the endgame, which is your survival. Most kidnappings don't result in loss of life or permanent injury, so it's usually smarter to find a way to endure the captivity and allow the experts to negotiate your release."

Kidnap prevention, negotiation, and extraction were all services offered by Quantum. Sometimes high-risk companies hired QIS to mock-kidnap executives to demonstrate what would be involved in being a hostage, to help the execs develop the skills needed to survive. Zegna could benefit from one of those programs. He was the type of client who ignored any and all advice.

Fatigue clawed at Thea, battling with the caffeine she'd ingested twenty minutes ago. She'd just returned from an intensive stay in Iraq, working a journalist's kidnapping. It'd been a tough one. The ransom cases were often simpler, more direct, than the political ones. Sadly, terrorism, worldwide economic recession, the proliferation of inexpensive weapons, and the globalization of organized crime had all contributed to making kidnapping a billion-dollar-a-year business—and that figure only included the reported cases.

Handlebar Mustache raised his hand again. But before she could field his question, her boss signaled to her through the glass wall of the conference area that he needed her in the situation room.

"Take a ten-minute break, and please help yourselves to coffee and pastries," Thea told the physicians. "I'll be back shortly."

She hurried down the long hallway, the walls covered in breathtaking nature photos her employer had taken during his yearly vacations. His principle used to be that kidnappers didn't take statutory holidays, so neither would he. But when his cardiologist suggested that, ironically, he had become his own hostage, Hakan Asker had started exploring the rain forests of the world, snapping artful photos at his usual workaholic pace.

Thea herself hadn't had a chance to breathe over the past few weeks, jetting off to Iraq right after Nigeria, then returning to the home office in London only two days earlier. Sleep was a luxury in their business, which had no regular hours and operated in every time zone of the world.

And with Papa's party coming up, she still had to finalize his gift.

The situation room's steel entrance door had no windows. She stared into the retinal scanner on the wall, allowing it to map the blood vessels behind her eyeballs. After a sharp beep, a green light signaled she could enter, and concealed hydraulics swept the door aside.

A large electronic display on the right side of the room listed all of QIS's ongoing cases. Some hostages' names had been up there a few days, others a couple of years. Several large video screens covered the longest wall: one showed a news feed; another provided a secure videoconference display for response consultants working around the globe; yet another showcased a map of the world, blinking red dots signifying clients wearing subcutaneous tracking devices.

When clients had to travel on business to dangerous or politically volatile locations—say, Syria or Egypt—they could take comfort in the knowledge that QIS's situation room was manned 24/7. If they sensed trouble brewing while abroad, they could make contact with Quantum agents at any hour of the day or night, and Quantum could instantly muster a network of black-book contacts to reach them anywhere, anytime, with pinpoint precision.

QIS owner and director Hakan Asker was a strong leader with an air of absolute authority that came from twenty-seven years in the field. These days, he spent most of his time in the office, doing research and managing clients. An elite-response consultant's fieldwork demanded the sacrifice of any semblance of a personal life, and Hakan had more than done his time.

Thea smiled at her boss. He was hunched over a workstation, typing quickly, using one of the Quantum encrypted e-mail accounts their analysts had designed. When he saw her, Hakan beckoned her over, his hawkish features narrowed in concentration.

"Give me a sec to finish this e-mail. The CFO of Beltrain Communications just called. One of his guys in the Sudan was grabbed. I put Freddy on the job." Hakan's jacket bore his trademark elbow patches, giving him a mildly professorial air. Still, she'd trust him to watch her six any day.

"Family?" She always asked for the details, even if she wasn't the one assigned to the case.

"Poor bastard has five kids and two ex-wives."

That could make for a complicated case. She glanced at the clocks positioned evenly along the wall, each displaying a different time zone. Whatever time zone—or zones—this guy's relatives were in, their world was about to change forever.

"Hey, when we get a moment, I want you to look at my latest weather-mapping patterns. They show some pretty interesting data when you correlate them to kidnap frequency and location."

The boss was an analytics geek, deeply engrossed in the statistical side of the business. His revolutionary approaches to crunching data had helped them on more than one case.

Thea glanced over her shoulder at the whoosh of the situation-room door opening. *Rif.* It had been a few weeks since the Nigerian operation, but she still smoldered at the memory of his rebellious behavior.

"Ah, the prodigal son returns." Hakan stood up and squeezed Rif's shoulder in welcome.

"More like Rambo," Thea said.

"You're still pissed," Rif observed.

"Insubordination can cost lives."

"There wasn't time for a chat over tea and crumpets. I took the calculated risk for *you* and the team," he replied.

She turned to her boss. "Not much has changed since we were kids and he toted that toy M60 everywhere he went." This time, his audacity had saved the hostage's life, but more often than not that kind of breakdown in discipline could end in disaster.

Rif stepped closer to Thea. "How's the arm?"

"Good as new." The bullet had only grazed her triceps. She'd been very, very lucky. "And John Sampson returned to work yesterday stateside. Certainly a better result than the guy from Equipe

Oil." That man had been found nailed to a pipeline, rats chewing his face. He'd still been alive when he was picked up but barely.

Rif's left eyebrow rose a fraction. "TIA—you know the deal."

This Is Africa. It was a cliché, but, like all clichés, it coiled around a painful truth. Rif had become jaded after his time in the military, and his fondness for reductive comments demonstrated another cliché—there really was no "mercy" in "mercenary."

She was grateful John Sampson had rallied, returning to his normal routine. Still, he would carry emotional scars from his ordeal that would last a lifetime. She knew from experience that, however it turned out, kidnapping transformed you. Permanently.

"I called you out of the session because Rif has critical information about Nigeria." Hakan adjusted his tortoiseshell glasses.

Concern shadowed Rif's eyes. "As you know, Brown hit the munitions hut we had identified, but when I was poking around looking for Sampson, I stumbled on two other huts full of explosives and weapons. I've since traced the source of those munitions. China."

The hairs at the nape of Thea's neck stood at attention. While Chinese AK-47s were ubiquitous, Chinese explosives and detonators were rarely discovered outside of state arsenals. If the Chinese were somehow involved in supplying John Sampson's kidnappers, it could signal a significant change of players in Africa. And it could explain the skyrocketing number of successful abductions in that region.

"Brief our people on the ground in Kenya, Zimbabwe, and Somalia. We need to determine if the Chinese are playing *Lord of War* across the whole continent," Hakan said before dismissing both of them.

Assessing the unsettling news, Thea turned and headed back to the conference room, where the physicians waited.

Chapter Three

Colombia
December 25
4:00 p.m.

Deep inside the FARC camp in the Colombian jungle, the international arms dealer known as Ares studied the dark-stubbled, concave face, shadowed eyes, and grease-slicked hair of the man sitting opposite him at the battered teak table. Ares had been dealing with Carlos Antiguez for seven years—seven years of wasted breath, of endless negotiations. *Guerrillas weren't what they used to be.*

"Coffee?" Carlos offered.

They were long past such niceties. Ares ignored the offer. Never once looking down, he let his deft fingers repeatedly disassemble and reassemble the small music box he always carried, the poignant notes of the song it played—"Tie a Yellow Ribbon"—echoing in the back of his mind.

Carlos droned on. Ares half listened as he considered the latest text he'd received. It said that Gabrielle Farrah, a Fed who'd been futilely chasing the mythically named arms dealer known for kidnappings and arming underdog militias, was about to make a breakthrough. Ares was satisfied—that was all part of his plan.

Carlos's mouth kept moving, but nothing inspiring came out. The bottom line? FARC wanted to expand its territory, and it was on a spending spree. But if the guerrillas really desired success, they'd need more than money.

"Four million for the Kalashnikovs, the RPGs, and the M24s." Ares brushed away a fly hovering over his lapel. He might be wearing Armani, but he felt just as comfortable in the jungle as Carlos.

The Colombian sucked in his cheeks, reflecting his desperation. "Ridiculous. Not a peso over three million."

Ares's gaze drifted to Carlos's nephew, Jorge. The kid couldn't be more than twenty-three, but his intelligent eyes absorbed the subtleties—unlike his uncle. Jorge's talent could be honed, mentored. Young people needed good influences, and Carlos was hardly that.

"The Colombian army recently purchased Black Hawks, missiles, and tanks. If you want to compete, you need my weapons. Four million."

"How do I know that information is accurate?" Carlos rubbed his stubble with his right palm.

"The Ares Corporation has eyes and ears where it matters." He didn't disclose the fact that he'd hijacked the Colombian army's latest shipment to supplement his regular supply of Chinese black-market weapons. Someone had to help the Davids of the world in their rebellion against the bullying Goliaths.

"I've been offered the same product for three million. Your prices aren't competitive."

"Rapier doesn't supply turnkey service, which includes training. Do you want your men battle-ready or left to shoot themselves?"

Carlos's eyes bulged.

It had been a good call getting better acquainted with the nephew, Ares reflected. The inside information he had gleaned from the young man about his competition had just paid off in spades.

"H-How . . . ?" Carlos spluttered.

"You need to work with someone who understands your long-term goals. Rapier's thugs can't help you expand your territory." Usually he shadowboxed a few rounds with Carlos, letting the older man feel that he had landed a solid blow or two, distracting him with a feeling of triumph before outmaneuvering him. Today, he had more pressing things on his mind. "Do we have a deal?"

"You're impossible." Carlos lit an unfiltered cigarette and blew a cloud of smoke straight into Ares's face.

He didn't flinch. "No, I make things possible. Now get the money."

"I need time to find the extra million."

"The weapons will be sold to the customer who pays first." Ares stood.

"You're a hard man."

This from a man who'd killed his own daughter over a kilo of coke. "It's just business, my friend." Ares slipped the music box back into his pocket and strode toward the exit. Carlos undoubtedly had millions stashed inside this compound alone. The narco-bourgeoisie didn't believe in banks.

He'd almost reached the door when Carlos said, "Wait. Jorge will take you to the money. I expect the weapons to be delivered within twenty-four hours."

Ares turned. "You'll have everything you asked for in twelve."

Carlos's nephew scrambled to his feet and followed him out, then led Ares to the outbuilding where the cash was held under armed guard.

"Jorge, it's time. An hour after I leave, my men will arrive with the weapons. You'll make it happen?"

The young man's gray eyes gleamed. "I'm ready." Jorge was eager, intelligent. No doubt he'd lead FARC for years to come. No more meetings with the insufferable Carlos. The thought almost made Ares smile.

Jorge loaded several large black duffel bags onto the helicopter. Ares didn't count the money. The young man wouldn't double-cross his backer—at least, not yet. Not that he wouldn't warrant a close eye in the future. After all, Jorge was betraying his uncle. Was nothing sacred? These days, you couldn't even trust your own family.

Ares shook the young man's hand and climbed aboard the Black Hawk, the helicopter blades coming to life.

Chapter Four

Santorini, Greece
December 25
6:00 a.m.

While most of the island was observing the birth of Christ, Thea would be celebrating her father's sixtieth name day. The family was fully American now, but they still celebrated Greek holidays, especially name days, and Christos's fell on Christmas Day. This tradition brought father, daughter, and son—and their cherished Rhodesian ridgeback, Aegis the Second—together no matter how busy their lives. Every year, Christos and Thea and Nikos flew from wherever in the world they were to Athens and boarded Christos's yacht, the *Aphrodite,* for the hundred-nautical-miles cruise to Santorini, paying homage to Christos's humble beginnings as a fisherman's son. And every year the festivities there expanded, keeping pace with her father's fortune.

Papa's loud voice emanated from the salon. "I don't care if you have to shovel through the tar yourself—get that oil. Stop worrying about the Canadians. I'm sure they'll politely thank you when the oil is flowing."

He was in business mode, accepting no excuses. He could be an unforgiving taskmaster.

Aegis nudged Thea with his snout. The ridgeback needed intense and regular exercise, and Thea was always a willing accomplice. "We'll go soon." She stroked the ridge of wheaten hair that ran in the opposite direction from the rest of his coat. "Come on, let's say good morning to the oil baron first." She walked into the salon as her father ended the call on his BlackBerry.

"*Hronia polla*, Papa. Still a caveman, I see." She enjoyed teasing him about his everlasting attachment to his phone.

"If it was good enough for Barack Obama . . ."

Fair enough. Many prominent people used the outdated phones for security-related reasons. Still, even world leaders would have to find other ways to satisfy their fetish for mobile-communications security and physical keyboards—the Black-Berry Limited had ceased production of the phones forever.

"Three hundred disciples are flying in for your celebration tonight." A large team was already preparing for the party at her father's favorite restaurant, set high on the island's infamous cliffs. "And less than a week until the negotiations in Kanzi. The newspapers are calling it the largest oil discovery since the Ghawar Field in Saudi." The discovery in the African country near Zimbabwe and Zambia could change the political face of oil. She crossed the stateroom and kissed the top of Christos's graying head.

"Athena Constanopolous Paris, those shorts are indecent—you'll be the talk of Firá." His dark eyes were stern, disapproving.

"But I'm about to run the stairs." She tugged her Nike athletic shorts down an inch, then hiked them back up. Nigerian rebels were easier to manage than Papa.

Her father's face broke into a wide grin. "Got you!"

She shook her head and smiled. Fair enough: she'd fallen for it. "I was about to say, that's priceless advice, coming from a man on his fifth wife."

"Ouch. You are your father's daughter. Makes my chest fill with pride."

She laughed. "Espresso?"

"With cinnamon?" Papa rubbed Aegis behind the ears and blew her a kiss.

Caffeine had long been a staple in the Paris family diet, but it was Thea who had started adding cinnamon. She headed to the espresso machine to work some magic. Steaming, toffee-colored liquid dripped into the tiny cups, and a blissful scent permeated the salon.

She carried the espressos back to the sitting area and plunked down on the sofa across from her father, adjusting the insulin pump hidden below her bra line. A quick check of her phone app confirmed that her blood sugar levels were looking good. Growth hormones from her liver increased her blood sugar levels between 3:00 and 7:00 a.m., typical for people with type 1 diabetes. No need to eat anything right now: those numbers would get her up the stairs and then some.

Aegis sat down next to her, the look in his intelligent eyes saying, *Hurry up and let's go already.* The powerful, eighty-four-pound dog had been in their family for eight years now, taking the place of the first Aegis, who'd lived to the grand old age of twelve.

"How were your latest A1C test results?" Papa had taken great care to educate himself on her condition.

"Very good. According to Dexter, no falling off the wagon on the sugar front the last few months." Trying to maintain a sense of humor about her diabetes, she'd named her Dexcom CGM—continual glucose monitor—Dexter.

"You're more disciplined than I could ever be." Christos stared at her through his reading glasses, his expression serious. "On another matter, *latria mou*, I need you to tail Peter. He's up to no good—I can feel it."

"Peter Kennedy is one of the most talented CFOs you've ever had, even if he is a strutting peacock. Is this another attempt on your part to finance my rent? Don't worry—Hakan keeps me plenty busy." Her job at Quantum International Security involved long hours, endless travel, and constant danger—none of which met with Papa's approval.

"Something's off with Peter. The last few weeks, he won't meet my eye."

"Well, you can be intimidating to lesser mortals, Papa."

"But not to you. I wish I could convince you to join me at Paris Industries." Her father's face buoyed with hope.

"This is your special day, so I won't say an outright no. How about I think about it?"

"I understand that your kidnapping work is important to you. But couldn't you just keep supporting that charity that helps former hostages instead of working the front lines?"

"I prefer fatigues to fund-raising." She half smiled. The truth was that she needed to be in the action, making a real difference. When her brother, Nikos, was twelve, he'd been kidnapped in her place. She had a lot of atoning to do.

"I don't tell you often enough how proud I am that you've brought so many hostages back home. But every time you travel to one of these Fourth World countries, I can't relax until you're safe again."

"I'm sorry, Papa. It's the job." She hated causing him stress, but she had to go where the kidnappings were. Countries like Switzerland and Canada weren't exactly hot spots for abduction.

"Paris Industries is growing. I need someone I can trust at the helm—family."

As a young man, Christos had scraped together every cent he'd made working on his own father's fishing boat in Santorini, and he'd traveled to the United States, taking a job as a roustabout on an oil rig. Mopping floors, fixing machines, he'd worked his way to the top from the ground up, learning the ropes along the way.

Using his no-nonsense work ethic to propel himself through the ranks, he had become a foreman. Then he'd proposed a partnership of sorts with a playboy oil baron who wanted someone hands-on to run the business. Papa had brokered deals, assumed incredible risks, and triumphed, becoming the self-made man he was today, eventually taking over the company and renaming it Paris Industries. Now he headed one of the three largest oil organizations in the world. The Kanzi deal would make him number one.

She hesitated, then decided to jump right in. "Well, there's always Nikos. He's done incredible work for our African Sanctuary for Children orphanage, and he certainly has the business experience. Maybe he could help you with the Kanzi negotiations?" Her brother had developed quite a reputation as an import/export guru.

A vein pulsed in Papa's temple. His Adam's apple bobbed up and down three times in quick succession. "We need to have a serious talk about Nikos. But let me have my coffee first."

Nikos's name was like a wet shroud on any conversation with her father. Her older brother came home for most holidays and her birthday every year, but the rest of the time he traveled the globe for work. She missed him, but every Friday he sent her a photo from wherever he was, and they were in touch regularly about the charity they co-chaired in Kanzi.

The thing she wanted most was a united and happy family, but getting her brother and father to relax in the same room seemed like a pipe dream. Thank goodness for Aegis. He was the glue that held everyone together, each family member vying for time with the beloved pet.

"Is Helena flying in this afternoon?" she asked, changing the subject. Papa's latest wife, an internationally successful interior designer was the kindest and most age-appropriate companion he'd had in years. Ever since her mother had died twenty-four years ago, when Thea was seven, Christos had been emotionally adrift, working obsessively and in his free time indulging himself in Scotch, sex, and starlets. She'd worried about him, wishing he could find someone who loved him rather than his fortune. Maybe Helena was the answer. She was a thoughtful, sweet woman; Christos had met her while on a cycling trip in France.

He straightened his tie. "Helena would never miss this special celebration. She just had to finish up a project. But enough about me. When are you going to settle down? You can't be chasing around the world saving people once you're a mother."

With her job and travel schedule, she hadn't had sex, let alone a relationship, in over a year. Immaculate conception was the only way she'd make Christos a grandfather.

Aegis raced to the door and returned with one of Thea's running shoes in his mouth, tail wagging. Saved by the dog. She laughed. "Message received," she told the ridgeback.

She turned back to Christos. "Papa, your special day gets you only so much latitude to pry." She reached into a nearby cabinet to procure the gift-wrapped package she'd hidden there earlier. "Speaking of which, I have something for you."

His face lit up as he peeled back the edges of the wrapping paper with care, unveiling a humidor embossed with a photo of father and daughter taken when Thea was six. Both of them had cigars in their mouths, hers unlit, and they sported million-dollar smiles. He opened the humidor.

"Sixty of the best cigars in the world, one for every year since you were born." She'd been working on this project for more than eighteen months, picking up unique cigars in her travels, as they were Papa's favorite indulgence.

"This is incredible. I don't know what to say." His gaze softened, full of love.

"You don't need to say a thing. Just know that I love you. Let's have breakfast together after I get back."

"Not a second past ten, kóre. I want to enjoy breakfast sooner rather than later—and we need to have that talk about Nikos."

"Aye, aye, Captain." The perpetual feud between her father and brother exhausted her. Maybe the real problem was, the two men were too much alike.

She headed for the door, Aegis rushing past her. Papa used to join her on these runs, but arthritis in his left knee had forced him into taking up cycling and swimming instead. He could still kick her butt in the fifty-meter freestyle, though.

Fueled by caffeine, she planned to sprint the tortuous stairs leading up to the town of Firá in under ten minutes. She glanced at her watch. No, today she'd break nine—give her something additional to celebrate at breakfast.

Outside, the brisk, salty air greeted her. "Morning, Piers." She hopped over the Aphrodite's transom. A former Koevoet operative from South Africa, her father's lead bodyguard was climbing out of the ocean-racing Donzi berthed next to the *Aphrodite*, his shoulders straightening as she appeared, his weather-beaten face breaking into a grin.

"Morning, Ms. Paris. Wager?"

She could listen to his accent all day. "Double or nothing for under nine minutes." The two of them made bets on anything and everything, but no one ever paid up.

"You're on."

She laughed. For her, he always had warmth in his blue eyes. Perhaps because traveling with Christos meant Piers rarely saw his own daughter.

The crisp December breeze raised goose bumps on Thea's arms and legs, but she wouldn't be cold for long. A quick wave to Piers, and she headed for the bottom of the stone stairs leading up to Santorini's capital, Aegis staying in step with her. She was grateful it wasn't the middle of summer, when out-of-shape tourists saddled donkeys to climb the cliffside or created endless serpentines along the wharf waiting for the cable car.

At the base of the steps, an old woman wrapped in a tattered blanket huddled in a corner. She'd obviously spent the night outside. Her face was heavily lined, her skin sallow, but her eyes were bright and aware. Aegis sniffed her toes, then rubbed against her legs.

Thea found the twenty-euro note she kept in her shorts for emergencies and slipped it into the woman's hand. *"Kala Hristouyienna,"* she said, smiling, wishing her a merry Christmas. She'd bring the woman some food from the yacht after finishing her run.

"Efxaristo." The old woman tightened her fist around the bill and scurried down the pier, as if afraid her benefactor might rescind the gift.

Thea stretched her hamstrings, calves, and quads, then did a few squats to warm up while Aegis paced. Breathing deeply, she admired the stunning vista of the crescent-shaped caldera, the craters of volcanic eruptions in ancient times. Today, Santorini was peaceful, the cerulean sky complementing the dark sapphire waters.

The *Aphrodite*'s sleek lines and brilliant white fiberglass hull blended well with Santorini's low-lying, whitewashed architecture. She gave a little salute toward the tinted windows of the yacht's upper deck. No doubt Papa was standing behind one, setting his own stopwatch to verify her time.

"Lead the way, Aegis." While the ridgeback rocketed forward, Thea clipped her phone to the back of her shorts, pressed the start button on her Garmin stopwatch, and zoomed up the wide cobblestone steps, her eyes focused slightly ahead of her feet. The uneven surfaces presented a challenge for every footfall.

The stench of the donkey droppings barely registered. She flew past a few restaurateurs sweeping their verandas, preparing for the day's celebrations. Already, her lungs seared, her calves burned. She negotiated the switchbacks, lunging upward. Her legs were metronomes, her heart a jackhammer.

She reached the halfway point and glanced at her Garmin.

4:38.

Gotta move faster.

The air thinned. Her feet skimmed the cobblestones, barely touching before lifting off again. Moisture dampened her chest. Her long, dark hair matted against her neck. Her body begged her to slow down, but Aegis spurred her on. He led by several steps, as always. Damn, that dog was in great shape.

6:12.

Her cell buzzed against her spine. Whoever it was could wait three minutes.

The final leg of her climb would present the toughest challenge, the cobblestones worn and slick. She bore down. In spite of her intense concentration, a familiar face sprang to mind. Rif. He'd be at Papa's party tonight. Was he the one calling?

She wasn't exactly in the mood to see Rifat Asker, but she'd get over it. Apparently he had uncovered more information from their African contacts regarding Chinese-manufactured weapons floating around the continent. That could be interesting to hear firsthand.

Her thoughts distracted her, and she missed a step. She flailed for endless microseconds, her right foot landing hard on the wrong step, but regrouped. Legs pumping like pistons, she sprinted up the last set of stairs, rechanneling her concentration and breathing. A stitch flared in her side.

8:26.

Her phone buzzed again. *Forget the call. Forget Rif. Forget everything.* Her arms acted as counterweights, propelling her forward and upward. Five steps . . . three . . . one. She reached the top and slapped her finger on the timer.

8:57.

Her best time yet.

She rested against the white stone wall beside the stairs, gasping for air, blood pulsing through her body. She stroked Aegis's short coat, the dog already ready for more racing. Must be nice. Still, a painful euphoria filled her. Papa would be impressed. Maybe he was on deck, watching for her arrival at the top.

She straightened and looked down toward the lagoon. But the *Aphrodite* was no longer docked. Instead, its sleek lines were cutting through the water, headed out to sea. *What the hell?*

Her father had no plans to go anywhere, and he'd never leave her behind. She grabbed her phone. A private number had called twice, leaving no message. She hit the callback button, but it didn't ring through. "Come on, boy." Her legs felt like overcooked spaghetti as she stumbled down the stairs beside Aegis, pressing the call button again and again. Nothing. The pounding in her ears wasn't from exertion now but, rather, alarm.

The trip back down the cliffside lasted an eternity. Her knees throbbed from the unforgiving cobblestone descent. She tried Papa's cell, but it bounced straight to voice mail. Unheard of. Her father had his BlackBerry cemented to his hip—he'd never ignore a call, especially from her. Aegis led at a brisk pace, as if he could sense her urgency.

The stitch in her side intensified. The *Aphrodite* faded on the horizon, disappearing in a haze of clouds. She pressed 1 on her speed dial. Hakan Asker answered on the first ring.

"Let me guess: Christos wants more cigars for the party tonight." He laughed. "My helicopter leaves in ten from Athens. I don't have time to shop, but tell him I'll help smoke the ones he has."

"I'm having a *humdinger* of a day," Thea said. Their code word for an emergency. She had to be careful, because she wasn't on an encrypted satphone. Her breath rasped as she barreled down the final flight of steps.

"How can I help?" His voice lost all frivolity.

"The birthday boy's playing shy—he's heading west on the water, and I'm losing visual contact."

"With his buddies on board?"

"Can't imagine they'd let him run off alone."

She exited the stairs, then sprinted along the wharf to where the yacht had been docked. She skidded to a halt. Piers was sprawled on his back, two holes in his chest, his eyes lifeless. Aegis ran to the bodyguard and licked his face. "Piers is . . . indisposed," she told Hakan. She tried to swallow the lump in her throat but failed. The South African had been part of her life as long as she could remember.

Piers's Glock still rested inside its holster underneath his windbreaker. She secured the weapon and scanned the area. No one around. The shooter had obviously surprised him—not an easy task. Although Piers had always treated her with warmth and kindness, he had the instincts of a killer. And her father's security team, handpicked by Hakan Asker, had thoroughly searched the docks last night when they'd arrived.

"Any other friends in the vicinity?"

She checked left and right again. The old woman was long gone. Three empty boats were moored. An eerie silence engulfed the normally busy wharf, the only movement a ghostly breeze. Everyone was probably home celebrating Christmas with family members. She eyed her father's Donzi. "No, but Aegis and I will follow the birthday boy until you arrive, make sure he doesn't go off half-cocked before the party tonight."

"Best take Piers along, despite his . . . indisposition. We don't want the other guests to worry," he said.

"Will do. I'll keep you posted."

"Don't break up the party until I get there."

"Got to run."

She hit the end button and tucked her phone away. Her hands shook. She steadied them and forced herself to concentrate.

Hakan would mobilize the troops, and they'd keep everything under wraps. Her father would want it that way. Papa knew Maximillian Heros, a Hellenic Police inspector general, as they were on a few advisory boards together and had traveled in the same circles for years. If needed, Heros could help cut through any red tape.

A roll of blue tarp rested on the deck of a fishing trawler. Thea yanked the plastic sheet onto the wharf. Kneeling down beside Piers, she squeezed his callused hand. "I'll miss you, my friend." If only she could undo the last twenty minutes and bring him back.

She shifted Piers's body onto the tarp, gently supporting his limbs, and eased him down into the Donzi. She placed his body on the rear bench seat, then used the bailing tin to wash his blood off the wharf.

Voices sounded in the distance. Probably fishermen headed out to catch their Christmas dinner. Aegis hopped into the boat beside her, sniffing Piers's body. She searched underneath the dash, hoping Piers had tucked the keys in their usual spot. Her fingers connected with a flotation key fob.

She started the engine, untied the ropes, and headed west. She activated the GPS tracker on her phone to locate the *Aphrodite*—the yacht had a chip installed that allowed her father to keep track of its whereabouts when he wasn't aboard. For once, she was grateful for his controlling nature.

She accelerated to full throttle. Hakan would be there in less than an hour from Athens, riding in an Aerospatiale SA 360, which had a top speed of 170 miles per hour.

The brisk wind caused her eyes to water. She shivered, the sweat wicking off her T-shirt chilling her. Still, she didn't have the heart to take Piers's windbreaker.

As she sped through the winter chop, one question rattled through her mind. *Was Papa still alive?*

Chapter Five

As she closed the distance to her father's yacht, the silhouette of the *Aphrodite* became clearer. It bobbed up and down on the swells, engines off, drifting in the inky sea. She circled it, searching for signs of life.

The decks appeared deserted.

"Where is he?" she asked Aegis. He let out a low whine.

Hakan was at least fifteen minutes away. Her training demanded she wait for backup, but she had to board now, even if it was a trap. Seconds could count.

She texted Hakan the updated GPS coordinates. Her boss would be furious that she'd gone in alone, but he'd understand. He'd do the same for Christos.

Guiding the Donzi toward the starboard side of the *Aphrodite*, she flipped the bumpers over the transom, tied a quick reef knot to secure the boat, then killed the engine. She held Piers's Glock in her left hand and scanned the yacht's decks.

They looked abandoned. No signs of a struggle.

"Stay."

Aegis didn't look happy, but he obeyed, plopping down beside Piers's body.

Grabbing the stainless-steel railing, she pulled herself onto the deck and crouched low, Glock ready. She listened, but the whistling wind muffled any other sounds.

She edged along the deck. A small red dot stained the white helipad. Blood. She skirted the portholes, climbing to the upper level and skulking along the deck. The skylights were made from clear glass to allow natural light to flood the cabin. She stared through the forward one into her father's private quarters. Papa's wallet sat on the dresser, his freshly pressed clothes for the party hung on the oak valet, and a single red rose sat on the bedside table in anticipation of Helena's arrival.

She crawled toward the salon and looked through its skylight. *The New York Times* was folded on the table beside his reading glasses. Their empty espresso cups from earlier remained untouched. The humidor she'd given Papa still graced the table. Nothing seemed out of place.

A pinging sound came from the direction of the aft deck. She moved toward the noise, her knees scraping against the roughened fiberglass. The sound intensified. She scrambled forward, her frigid fingers clutching the gun.

She flattened to her stomach and inched forward. Her muscles tensed. She peered over the fiberglass lip—and exhaled. A mooring line had unraveled in the strong winds, and the metal end was tapping against the railing.

She twisted around and slid down the siding to the main deck. Pressed against the doorjamb, she scanned the interior of the salon. The cream leather couches remained pristine; the pale hardwood floors gleamed. All clear. She entered the room, back against the wall, searching for movement. The silence was eerie after the whipping wind. She steadied her grip on the Glock and inched forward. A foul odor made her nose wrinkle.

In her peripheral vision, she caught a flash of color in the den. Six crew members lay facedown on the plush carpet, two wounds in the back of each of their heads, execution-style. A professional job. No shell casings, undoubtedly no fingerprints.

Her father wasn't among the dead. Neither was Henri, the chef. Anyone else who had boarded the yacht had disappeared.

She sagged against the wall, knees rubbery. These men had been part of the Paris Industries staff for years. Who'd done this—and why?

She scoured the rest of the yacht. The *Aphrodite* was empty, Christos gone.

A loud sound, something thumping on the deck. She aimed the Glock toward the cabin's entrance.

Aegis stalked through the door on full alert.

So much for following commands. Used to hunt lions, ridgebacks could be ferocious. And they could leap over five-foot fences, so she wasn't surprised he could jump onto the yacht. It comforted her to have him close by now that he wasn't in any danger.

A beeping noise in the salon drew her attention. Her father's phone rested on the coffee table, a flashing red light indicating a new message. Having no idea what he used as a password, she tried his birth date, her mother's name and birth date, Helena's birth date, and a few other combinations. Nothing worked. After the seventh try, she gave it one last shot—BlackBerries were programmed to wipe clean after ten failed attempts, and if her final effort didn't work, she wanted to save the phone's data for the computer gurus.

She typed in ATHENA. The screen came to life.

A text message had arrived from an undisclosed sender.

Saepe ne utile uidem est scire quidem futurum sit.

It looked like Latin. But what the hell did it mean? As the foundation of so many European languages, she'd learned Latin long ago but hadn't used it in years. Why was the kidnapper trying to communicate with her in a dead language? It would take her some time to translate this message.

She was staring at the screen, willing it to give her an answer, when the rotor wash of a helicopter jerked her back to the present. Aegis barked.

Hakan had arrived.

Chapter Six

Special Agent Gabrielle Farrah craved a Gitanes, her favorite cigarette, but she'd have to wait until she left the firing range. Lebanese Muslim by birth, she didn't celebrate Christmas, so she figured she'd slip in some target practice while everyone was off enjoying the holiday. Even though she was outdoors and no one else was around, shooting and smoking just didn't mix. She needed her hands steady and her breathing still.

Lying on her stomach, propped on her elbows, she calculated the wind and assessed the shot. Five hundred yards away, the target perched in the field, almost taunting her. She'd hit the bull's-eye many times before from this distance, but the cool temperature and brisk wind presented a challenge today.

She blocked all distractions from her mind and inhaled deeply, her world shrinking as she stared through the sniper rifle's scope. Thumb down, safety off. Breathe in, hold. Her finger pressed the trigger. She exhaled.

The recoil of the M24 SWS engaged with her shoulder, the familiar feeling comforting her. She grabbed her binoculars. *Dammit.* The shot was just slightly left of the bull's-eye.

She rolled over and rested on her back, staring up at the gray sky, her breath crystallizing in the cold December air. The endless intel reports on her desk at the HRFC headquarters weighed on her mind, messing with her mojo.

Hostage Recovery Fusion Cell. The name made it sound like a biological experiment, and it kind of was, as the US government tried to cope with the changing face of kidnappings abroad and the horrific deaths of American journalists James Foley and Steven Sotloff, both beheaded on video by ISIS operatives. Those tragic deaths had created widespread public distrust in the government's ability to keep Americans safe at home or abroad in an age of rampant global terrorism.

Previously, federal agencies handling kidnappings had jockeyed for position, refused to share intel, and threatened to prosecute the hostages' families if they paid a ransom; the current administration had created a bipartisan, interagency group that could be a more effective force to bring hostages home and support their families. The government had issued Presidential Policy Directive 30, in addition to the current PPD 12, to establish guidelines to deal with hostages taken abroad. Given her intelligence background in the CIA and international experience in the State Department, Gabrielle had been offered a plum position in the new agency.

The briefing she'd received yesterday from the African desk demanded her attention. A faceless arms dealer called Ares was filling his coffers by backing the kidnapping of CEOs of multinationals involved in everything from mining and oil drilling to agriculture and banking. No middle-management grabs for this shadowy figure's teams—he went for the big money. In addition to kidnaps, Ares was delivering large numbers of Chinese weapons to various rebel forces.

Anything that affected the welfare of the US required immediate action, and natural resources were definitely of interest.
The political unrest and terrorist kidnaps overseas had cost US
companies billions, which was serious enough without a shadowy
player like Ares in the mix. Since abductions had tripled across the
globe over the past five years, her team was stretched to the limit—this
self-proclaimed god of war had to be stopped. The problem was, no
one could identify him. He was a ghost.

The chirping sound of her personal cell startled her. She
reached inside her shooting jacket for her phone. The screen
read PRIVATE CALLER. She hoped it wasn't the guy she'd had to kick
out of her bed that morning—she'd picked him up late the night
before at Kelly's, near Union Station, and hadn't bothered to
get his name. A nice enough guy, he'd wanted to have breakfast
together, celebrate the holiday, but she was having none of it.
If he was looking for a soul mate, then his dating radar needed
serious adjustment.

"Farrah speaking."

A hollow, mechanical-sounding voice echoed on the line.
"Christos Paris has been kidnapped."

"What? Who is this?"

"Santorini."

"Wait, what—?" A click, and the call flatlined in her ear.

Her fingers strangled the cell. Christos Paris, the billionaire oil magnate who'd been on the cover of *Forbes* more times
than she could count, kidnapped? Just yesterday, a bulletin had
crossed her desk about the upcoming negotiations in Kanzi. A
recent massive oil discovery in the impoverished nation could
shift the world's geopolitical balance. Japan, Iran, and Russia
had made overtures for the rights to extraction and refining, but
Paris Industries and the Chinese National Petroleum Company
were the only two players left at the table. If Christos Paris really
had been kidnapped, this could be an unmitigated disaster for
US interests.

She phoned the team that covered the HRFC desk 24/7. "Trace the number that just dialed my personal cell. Let me know the results immediately."

Man, she needed a smoke. She packed up her rifle and processed the startling phone call. Who had called, and was it true that Paris had been kidnapped? If so, was it too much to hope that it was a straightforward ransom case? Political kidnappings had the potential to hold a whole country hostage, causing massive disruption at home and abroad. Jimmy Carter's presidency had dive-bombed after the Iranian hostage crisis. An attempt to rescue American hostages being held in Lebanon had led to Ronald Reagan's Iran–Contra scandal. Somewhat more recently, Barack Obama's administration had come to grief over a political-prisoners exchange for Army soldier Bowe Bergdahl.

PPD 12 confirmed that the US government would not make concessions—politico-speak for ransoms—but made it clear for the first time that "no concessions" didn't meant "no communications." The government's position regarding ransoms had altered slightly—from not dealing with terrorists regardless of the circumstances to taking each hostage's case on its own merits. Now, paying ransom to a terror group might be considered if it would yield intelligence about the kidnappers, such as their identity, their location, or how they moved money. After all, the government's bigger goal was to gain information that would help locate and eliminate terrorists, capture them and bring them to justice, or cut off their financial networks.

A ransom could not be paid in a one-time deal just to free an American—there had to be a larger strategic purpose in mind. But that wouldn't be an issue if Christos Paris was the captive. The man's name was synonymous with the oil that fueled America. The higher-ups would do anything to facilitate his release.

Still, no way would she take some mystery caller's word for something this pivotal. She reached for her phone but hesitated over the keypad. The one person who could help her was the last person she wanted to contact.

What the hell? We're both adults. She dialed the number from memory, her CIA training staying with her.

"Maximillian Heros." The rumble of his baritone brought back memories of that night at the Hotel Grand Bretagne in Athens.

"It's been a while."

A moment of silence. "Gabrielle. I thought we were done."

"We are. This is a business call."

"Must you save all your empathy for your hostages? At least *pretend* you care how I am doing." Disappointment flooded the Hellenic inspector general's voice.

So much for them both being adults. She'd been up front about her lack of interest in a relationship when they first met, but one night after they'd bonded over a bottle of Scotch and despair over their sisters—hers had cancer, his had been in a bad car accident—he made it clear he wanted more. So she'd shut him down.

"How *are* you, Max?" She couldn't keep the sarcasm out of her voice.

"A good man could do wonders for your attitude. What do you need?"

"Information. Anything happening over there?" She quelled the impulse to bite her nails. Her hands itched for a cigarette.

"Perhaps you could be more specific."

"Kidnapping."

"In Greece?"

"Santorini," she said.

"Lots of extra security in Santorini this week because of Christos Paris's annual party—sheikhs, politicians, rock stars . . . *Skata,* who was taken?"

She had to give to get. "Paris. Unconfirmed." Max was wired in like no one else in Greece. If it were true, how could he not know about it?

"Christos Paris has been kidnapped?" Seconds passed. "This has the makings of a modern-day Greek tragedy—such irony."

"What?"

"Don't you keep up with *Who's Who in Kidnapping*, Gabrielle?" He was toying with her now, making her pay for having had the gall to reject the great Maximillian Heros. *Of course* he knew about the kidnapping.

"I see this call was a mistake," she said.

"Where is your sense of adventure?"

"It evaporated with my sense of humor. What's ironic?"

"Christos being kidnapped when his daughter is one of the top K&R experts in the world. Our families have known each other for many years. Thea Paris. Former DIA with a master's in international relations. Speaks seven languages. Known as Liberata, since a case in Sicily, when she freed a hostage from a mafia kingpin without paying a cent. No one knows how she did it."

Right, Thea Paris. She hadn't connected father and daughter.

"Also, Paris's son was kidnapped years ago, when the boy was twelve. Some families are just jinxed, I guess."

"The son came home?"

"After nine months of captivity in the bowels of Kanzi."

Where Christos was trying to close the biggest deal of his career.

"Can you nose around; see what you can find out? My facts are unconfirmed; my source is sketchy. While you investigate, I'll be on the next plane to Athens."

"'Sketchy source'? Come now. Smoke and mirrors are not necessary if you want to see me, Gabrielle."

"Focus on the kidnapping. Not everything's about you."

"That is where you are wrong. You could have called another contact in Greece, but you dialed my number."

"Because you're good at your job, or you used to be," she said.

"And good in bed."

"Don't make me regret calling."

He laughed. "Pack your red dress. See you soon."

She hung up. Max was the one guy she might've considered sharing a second night with—but she wasn't a relationship kind of girl. The firing range provided all the therapy she needed. Besides, getting close to someone meant risking her heart. She'd had enough grief with her parents' deaths and her sister's illness.

Family. Just the thought made her ache for her parents. Four years ago, they'd headed back to Lebanon for a holiday that had turned into a deadly nightmare. She still wasn't satisfied she had the full story of what'd happened, but she'd hit a brick wall when she tried to investigate further. Now the Paris family needed help.

If Christos had been snatched, this could turn out to be the case of the century, and the job would require all her attention. Time to have her team create a detailed dossier on Paris and his family. She slung her rifle case over her shoulder and headed for her battered BMW.

Chapter Seven

Thea brushed her long, dark hair, applied lip gloss, and slid into the black Anne Fontaine dress she'd picked out for her father's name-day celebration. Her mind whirled with the pretense she was about to play out. She'd booked a suite in the hotel directly across from the party location, thinking that she'd surprise her father with a post-bash soirée of his closest friends. But circumstances had changed. Now she had to address the party goers, manufacture an explanation for the guest-of-honor's absence, and use the time to scan all the faces in the crowd.

One of them could be behind Christos's disappearance.

She gave Aegis a big hug and a treat—he had been out of sorts since that morning, in tune with her mood. He also missed Papa. "We'll find him—don't worry."

After spraying herself in a mist of Creed perfume, she slipped on her Louboutins, wishing she could erase the last thirteen hours. Hakan's arrival, the debriefing, searching for witnesses—it was all a blur as they followed protocol, using routine to tamp down the panic bubbling under the surface. The golden window only stayed open so long: the first twenty-four hours were a critical period in any kidnapping, and they had so little to go on.

A quick check of her blood sugar, and she exited the hotel, traversing the courtyard to the Sphinx, the restaurant she'd booked for the party. Its view overlooking Santorini's stunning caldera was unforgettable. The tiny pinpoints of light on the cliffside worked with the stars to brighten the night sky. She wondered if her father could see the stars wherever he was.

Her stomach churned at the memory of the carnage aboard the *Aphrodite*, the crew's bodies lined up in a ghastly row. She'd make sure their families were taken care of financially, but no amount of money could ever be commensurate with their grief. As she well knew. All her father's considerable wealth hadn't done a thing to soften the blow of losing her own mother years ago. The death had left a gaping hole in their family that could never be filled.

After a thorough search of the yacht, she and Hakan had navigated the *Aphrodite* back to Santorini, towing the Donzi. Hakan had told Christos's trusted police contact Max Heros about the yacht, the bodies, and the bloodstain on the helipad. They had no idea who had taken Christos or why. Until they better understood the situation, containment was key, and Max was keeping the information on the down-low. Working openly with the authorities had never been her boss's modus operandi, and in this case she was willing to follow his lead.

Especially given the strange Latin text message that had been sent to her father's cell. She had eventually translated it: *Often it is not even advantageous to know what will be.* A quote from Cicero, it offered no clues, just a dark omen. She kept rereading the message, desperate for a lead. Although kidnappers usually transported their hostages to a safe house before calling in a ransom demand, this felt different. This felt as if they were being taunted.

She forced her mind back to the present, wishing she could've brought Aegis to the party for moral support. She stepped into the restaurant, surveying the Christmas wreaths decorating the whitewashed walls and the mistletoe suspended from the archways.

Waiters served Greek delicacies and poured Cristal champagne. Laughter infused the space. The men wore bespoke tuxedos, and the women paraded the latest designer couture.

She stopped to greet Ahmed Khali, Paris Industries' COO, a capable man who took his job seriously. He seemed harried. Did he know something about the kidnapping, or was he just anxious about his boss's party being a success?

Shaking her head to clear her mounting paranoia, Thea headed straight for the emcee platform. Every ounce of her energy was needed to pull this off. She nodded to Hakan. Before stepping up to the microphone, she squeezed her eyes shut, remembering happier times, wishing that Christos would magically appear to welcome his guests.

She opened her eyes, stepped up, and adjusted the microphone. "Good evening, everyone. Welcome to our annual celebration."

People turned to face the podium, and the noise tapered off. She scanned the faces, searching for a tightening of the lips, a quick glance away—any sign that someone here might be involved in her father's disappearance. But other than Ahmed Khali's quizzical look, only expectant faces glowing with good cheer gazed back at her. And no sign of her brother, Nikos, yet. She wasn't looking forward to breaking the news to him—Papa's kidnapping would probably unearth memories best kept in the past.

She forced a smile. "My family deeply appreciates your joining us here today." She leaned back from the microphone and cleared her throat.

Murmurs of approval buzzed through the crowd. Glasses clinked. The guests had flown in from all over the world: business rivals, dignitaries, sheikhs, executives from Paris Industries, politicians, rock stars, socialites.

"While nothing would give me greater pleasure than introducing Papa and kicking off his celebration, I'm afraid I won't be able to do that this evening."

A few groans. A voice in the crowd shouted, "Where's our man?"

She wished she knew. "A very dear member of the Paris Indus-tries team, my father's head bodyguard for the past twenty-two years, unexpectedly passed away this afternoon." Keep your lies as close to the truth as possible, Papa had always advised. "Due to this tragic loss, my father is with the man's family tonight. Christos sends his warmest regards and hopes you'll take advan-tage of the extra champagne available since he won't be here to imbibe." She lifted a glass in the air. "To Christos."

The ruckus in the restaurant intensified as people buzzed among themselves. The party mood quickly resurfaced. Sure, they were sorry they'd lost the chance to network with the man, but they wouldn't miss the opportunity to enjoy his fine food and champagne.

The guest list had been strategically assembled for months, every person handpicked. Although Christos had a sterling reputa-tion as a man of his word, he worked in a cutthroat industry where backstabbing and betrayal were de rigueur. And that made her job of looking for any unusual or suspicious behavior a challenge.

Her father's BlackBerry was clutched in her left fist, and she prayed for it to ring. Other than the trail of dead bodies and the Latin text, they had nothing to go on. Time was one of the kid-napper's most powerful weapons, keeping family members des-perate for any news. The game was all too familiar.

Surveying the crowd, she recognized sister and brother Quan Xi-Ping and Quan Chi from the newspapers. The delegation from China. Only her father would have the balls to invite his compe-tition in the Kanzi oil deal. Perhaps it'd be a good idea to intro-duce herself, see if the pair had anything to hide.

She set down her glass—no alcohol for her tonight—and stepped off the podium. Her legs were shaky from the stairs, the stress, and the stilettos. She wobbled on the last step. A strong hand steadied her.

She looked up. Rif stood in front of her.

"Your left eye twitches when you lie," he said.

"Sorry, no time to chat." She tried to step aside, but his large frame blocked her escape.

"Seems to be a pattern when I'm around, but tonight I must insist. My godfather wouldn't miss this party unless he was deathly ill or dead. Which is it?"

Always the tactful one. "Piers died. I wasn't lying." She met his gaze head-on. Rif had known Piers for years—Hakan and Christos had been close friends since before she and Rif were born.

The hard angles of his face softened slightly. "I'm sorry. I know you two were close."

"Thanks." She prided herself on her composure while handling the roller-coaster nature of kidnap cases, but this one was different. Her grip was tenuous. "I need to go."

"Not before you tell me what's got you rattled."

She reached up to gently push him away, his biceps hard underneath his tuxedo sleeve.

Before Rif could step aside, Hakan strode toward them. "Good, you guys are already on it."

"On what?" Rif asked.

"Son, we need your help with a situation."

"Not here." Thea stared at Hakan, her tone emphatic.

"Ah," Hakan said, nodding. "Let's take this meeting to the hotel."

He turned and headed for the exit. Rif gestured for Thea to follow. She remained still, her Louboutins rooted to the ground. He didn't need to know that she planned on talking to the Chinese contingent before joining them.

One of Rif's eyebrows arched. "Whatever it is, I can be discreet."

"But you don't always follow orders."

Chapter Eight

Rif trudged across the hotel courtyard behind his father. There was always that one person in your life—no matter how good your intentions, you couldn't do anything right by them. For him, Thea Paris was that person, and she had been ever since they were kids. Even back then, nothing he did to please her ever worked; most of the time, she just treated him as if he were a Neanderthal.

He told himself that he didn't care what she thought of him, but deep down he knew that wasn't true. In Nigeria, he'd gone the extra mile into enemy fire to bring her hostage home, then gotten reamed for not following orders. Hell, she liked her dog more than him.

Rif followed his father through the door to the suite Thea had reserved and left open for guests of the after-party.

Hakan placed his right hand on Rif's shoulder. "Christos has been abducted from his yacht. The crew members were all murdered, except Chef Henri, who is also missing."

Rif inhaled a deep breath, trying to process the news. "Any contact with the kidnappers?"

"Only a Latin text sent to Christos's cell."

"Strange." Rif rubbed a hand on the back of his head. "What did it say?"

"It was a line from Cicero. 'It isn't always advantageous to know what the future holds.' It's all we've got. What's your take on Thea's mood?"

Rif flashed on her announcement at the party about Christos's absence. "Given the circumstances, she's holding up well. She's a rock." If he were kidnapped, he'd want her on the case.

"Something doesn't feel right. . . ." Hakan murmured.

"Is there something you're not telling me?" Rif asked. His father was a labyrinth of secrets.

"It's just a feeling."

Yeah, right. "Don't play games, Baba. I need all the facts if you want me involved."

"Look—"

A knock sounded at the door.

"We're not done." Rif crossed the room and stared through the peephole. His breath quickened. Thea stood outside, a stormy look on her face.

Batten down the hatches. Incoming cyclone.

Chapter Nine

After Thea had spoken to the Quans—who seemed rather slick and somewhat dour but exhibited no overtly suspicious behavior—she had charged over to the hotel suite she'd booked for the after party. She kicked off her heels, dropped her purse on a nearby chair, and joined Hakan and Rif in the sitting area near the fireplace.

"So sorry about Christos," Rif said.

"Where are we?" She directed this to Hakan; she wanted answers, facts, anything to help bring Papa home, not Rif's sympathy. "Are we tracking every helicopter that's been in the area? That's the only way they could have whisked Papa off the yacht that quickly."

Hakan wrestled with the cowlick in his thick gray hair. "Waiting to hear back. The *Aphrodite* has been moved to a small port near Athens, where we're friendly with the customs officers. I've also updated Max Heros. Our forensics team is on its way to analyze the crew's bodies and other evidence—although I'm not optimistic. Everything indicates we're dealing with professionals. We're searching for that homeless woman you met by the stairs. She might've seen something. I also made a list of your father's enemies."

"Ambitious men scorch a lot of earth on their way to the top. Enemies are a natural by-product of the process," Rif said, looking over the printout Hakan had prepared.

Thea thought of Paris Industries—all the backstabbing and betrayals, the industrial accidents that had maimed and killed people, the ecological impact of Papa's holdings in several countries. The sheer number of potential adversaries unnerved her.

"Knowing Christos, he's probably busy negotiating his own release," Hakan said.

"Yes, maybe it's the kidnappers we should feel sorry for," she said.

They all laughed, but the joviality was hollow.

"Seriously, if the kidnappers' goal was purely financial, the easiest move would've been grabbing Helena—or me or Nikos—and demanding a large ransom. Papa would have been free to move money around and pay them off. This isn't a cash grab."

"Couldn't agree more." Hakan scribbled some notes. "Thea, you were the last person to see your father before he was taken. Did he mention anyone or anything unusual—maybe something small that was bothering him?"

The espresso they'd shared that morning seemed like a lifetime ago. "He wanted a tail on Peter Kennedy, the CFO of Paris Industries, but I'm not sure he was serious. I'm meeting Peter for a drink in half an hour at Club 33. I'll fish around, but he's a numbers guy. No way does he have the connections and resources to pull off an operation like this."

"Unless he has powerful partners." Rif paced beside the fireplace. "I had lunch with Christos two weeks ago, and he expressed concern over a recent negotiation in Venezuela. The Minister of the Environment had a connection with another oil magnate, and Christos lost the contract. Peter could be sharing insider information. . . ."

Her neck muscles twitched hearing about the lunch. Rif and Christos were close—the soldier's über-masculinity appealed to Papa, and being Rif's godfather meant something to him. Maybe Rif's reckless abandon reminded Christos of his younger self. "Then why kidnap Papa? If he already had the information, there'd be no need. And the COO, Ahmed Khali, would also have access to that information. Should we look at him as well?"

Hakan circled a name on the list. "Everything is conjecture, because we have so little information. But it gives me another lead to check out. Thea, there's something we need to—"

"If you think you're taking me off this case because it's too personal, forget it. I won't sit on the sidelines while Papa's missing." If their roles were reversed, her father would be relentless in his search for her.

Hakan sighed. "I know better than to suggest that. What concerns me is that you might've been on the *Aphrodite* when it was attacked. We don't know if they waited for you and Aegis to leave, or if they just missed you. Until we learn more, I want you under protection."

"I'm more than capable of looking after myself."

"I know, but your father would never forgive me if something happened to you. Rif is by your side twenty-four/seven until further notice."

She refused to give Rif the satisfaction of reacting. Still, her back muscles tensed. To keep Hakan happy, she'd go along with having a babysitter. It'd be easy enough to ditch him when she needed to. "What about Henri? He disappeared with Papa, so he's either another hostage or an accomplice. Any evidence linking him to the kidnapping?"

"I've brought in Freddy Winston from the London office. He's researching Henri's background. Also bank and phone records. Maybe we'll get lucky."

Freddy was one of the most senior London-based response consultants, and she was relieved he was on board. He'd just successfully wrapped up the case in Sudan for Beltrain, so he was free to help. "Freddy's a good choice. Can you keep me posted on any other additions to the team?"

Sweat dotted Hakan's tuxedo shirt. "When I can, I will. Look, we need to make decisions quickly. Christos's life could depend on it. Lines are being blurred, and this is different from our typical case. We'll need to have Freddy do a family-member interview with you. You may be one of my best nego-tiators, but you were also the first point of contact for the kidnappers. Anyone would have difficulty remaining objective in your situation."

"It's not like you're impartial either."

"And that's why I'll do everything I can to bring—"

A loud knock sounded on the door to the suite.

Rif moved soundlessly to the entryway, a Glock materializ-ing in his hands. "Who is it?" he challenged. After a quick look through the peephole, he opened the door.

Christos's wife, Helena, stood on the threshold, her strawberry-blond hair disheveled, mascara smudged under her eyes. Hakan had broken the news about her husband's kidnapping earlier, interviewing her to see if she could provide any helpful informa-tion. "You wanted to know when Nikos's plane landed. It arrived two minutes ago."

"Thanks for the update. You doing okay?" Hakan asked.

"I will be when you bring my husband home. I'll be in the cha-pel if you need me. I trust you'll brief Nikos." Helena glided back out the door.

A palpable tension filled the air. Nikos. Always the elephant in the room. Hakan and Rif would undoubtedly argue to keep him in the dark—for many reasons. But Christos was his father too, and no matter how troubled their relationship, her brother deserved to know what was going on.

"What about Helena? She's relatively new to Christos's life and has access to his schedule," Rif said.

Thea shot him a look. "Not a fan?"

He shrugged. "They haven't been together long. Maybe her sweet exterior hides a rotten core. She has a billion-dollar motive. It'd be crazy not to consider her."

"Everyone is under scrutiny," Hakan said, tapping his pen against his thigh. "As we know, Christos was about to sign the deal of his career in Africa, making Paris Industries the largest oil provider in the world. Wouldn't the Chinese have the most to gain by making him disappear?"

"Maybe, but maybe not. I just introduced myself to the brother and sister who head up the Chinese negotiations team. Kanzi could postpone the negotiations altogether if one of the major players was missing, and that wouldn't help the Chinese. Every oil company, both national and private, wants to get its hands on Kanzi's resources." The initial field of competitors had included many more than the final two bidders.

"Oil is a geopolitical labyrinth," Hakan said. "We need to look at all the players, national oil companies as well as the private ones."

The NOCs had the financial backing of their governments, access to political favors, and countless other advantages. Paris Industries was a private oil company, and that meant it had to fund all its own exploration. It'd been Christos's probing that had led to the discovery of massive quantities of oil in Kanzi. But the bulk of the oil was in an area that Papa hadn't negotiated rights to yet, opening the discovery to other bidders. But oil was only one potential motivation for the kidnapper.

"We also can't discount the guerrillas and politicians who exploit the oil wealth in their countries. And that list should include General Ita Jemwa and Prime Minister Kimweri." Her stomach twisted at the thought of Papa at the mercy of a Kanzi militia, possibly cold, wet, beaten, locked in a cage somewhere. A wave of dizziness caught her off guard. She reached into her purse and grabbed an energy bar.

"Anyone want one?"

"No thanks," Hakan said.

Rif narrowed his eyes, as if he couldn't believe she was thinking of eating at a time like this. Only three people knew about her diabetes—Papa, Nikos, and her doctor—but Rif was observant, intuitive. *Was* it possible he knew? Her hands trembled. She peeled back the wrapper and dove in.

"If Paris Industries bows out of the Kanzi deal, who gets in?"

"Russia's oil company, Rosneft, was a close third, given its geographical location. I'll ask Ahmed for the Paris Industries research on it," Hakan said.

"They'd certainly know people capable of a professional kidnap," Thea conceded. "Still, we can't point fingers without proof. What about Ares and some of the other prominent kidnap groups? We need to look at every angle. Sometimes the most obvious explanation isn't the correct one. Someone smart taught me that," she said.

Hakan frowned. "That someone doesn't feel very smart today. All these emotions are a distraction,"

"Agreed. You know what the experts say—a lawyer who represents himself has a fool for a client. So, should we really be handling this case?" she asked, knowing there wasn't an alternative. One more bite of the bar, and the room righted, the sheen of sweat cooled on her skin, and her focus returned.

"No one cares more than we do; no one has as much insider information—information Christos would never want revealed to others. Besides, I could never forgive myself if I outsourced this and something went sideways."

Her phone buzzed with an incoming text from one of their analysts. "The Latin message on Papa's phone was sent from a burner cell purchased in Athens. Untraceable."

"No surprise. I'm going to check in with Freddy, see if he's come up with anything," Hakan said.

She glanced at her watch. "I'm meeting Peter Kennedy in ten. I'd better go. Do you mind feeding Aegis?" She handed Hakan one of her room keys.

"Two ravenous bachelors having room service. Sounds like a plan."

"Thanks." She strode across the room.

Rif joined her at the door. She turned to Hakan. "Is this really necessary?"

"I need your mind focused on figuring out who took Christos, not protecting yourself. If something happened to you, your father would never forgive me," Hakan said.

Chapter Ten

Rif escorted Thea down the cobblestone path outside the hotel. Shadows from the olive trees wavered in the brisk breeze, playing tricks on his eyes as he scanned ahead. Nothing would happen to Thea on his watch. Not that she couldn't look after herself; she was correct about that. But right now she was vulnerable, maybe more than she realized. Christos had been snatched while she watched, unable to help, an eerie parallel to when Nikos had been taken twenty years ago.

"Let's be clear," she said. "This is my interview. Do what you do best. Intimidate through silence."

The edges of his lips turned slightly upward. "That's almost a compliment." Given the recent tension about Nigeria, it was practically effusive.

She stopped walking and faced him, her eyes brimming with emerald fire. "I'm just as keen as you are about your new babysitting gig, but our animosity about Nigeria can't get in the way of finding Papa. That's all that matters."

Our animosity? Right. She reminded him of that porcupine they'd run into on the mission, all quills and attitude. No thanks for saving her and Johansson's asses, no thanks for taking extreme personal risk to find her hostage, no thanks for putting her needs above his.

"Lead the way."

She strode toward Club 33, her long legs handling the stilettos with authority. He caught up to her in a few strides, reaching the entrance at the same time. "Please, allow me." He stepped into the dimly lit club. White marble floors, funky lights attached to a curved ceiling, and loud music—it was one of the premier nightclubs in Firá. A lone bartender dressed in black served whiskey to two wobbly figures perched at the bar. Too early for the dancing crowd to arrive.

A blond man commandeered the rear booth as if it was his private palace. Peter Kennedy, Christos's rising star, complete dickhead, and total ETC—empty the clip—candidate. In Kennedy's case, Rif would empty it twice.

He'd met Peter several times at Paris Industries functions, and the kindest thing he could say about the guy was that he was *Rain Man*–smart with numbers. Climbing his way to the top of Paris Industries, he had left his designer-shoe imprint on countless backs. Given Christos's disdain for Nikos, and Thea's lack of interest in joining her father's company, either Peter Kennedy or Ahmed Khali could be the heir apparent. And if Rif's godfather didn't survive the kidnapping, Peter would be one step closer to the top.

He'd call that motive.

He stepped aside to allow Thea to slide into the booth first. Peter started to stand, but she waved him off.

"Thanks for meeting us so late." She smiled, but it was forced.

"Sorry to hear about Piers. He had a heart attack?" Peter asked.

The CFO was divorced with two kids, and Christos had confided in Rif that Peter's speech had been slurred during a morning meeting recently. That was why Rif wasn't surprised that his eyes were glassy now, as if he'd had one too many Rusty Nails. His gaze dropped to Thea's cleavage, and Rif ached to punch him.

Her expression darkened. "We'll miss him keenly. He was with our family for twenty-two years."

"Can I assist with the funeral service or help in any other way?" Peter asked.

Sycophant.

"I appreciate your kindness, but Piers came from a small town in South Africa, and the service will be for family and close friends only. Meanwhile, Papa asked me to be a conduit between him and the business for a few days so he can put away his Black-Berry and spend time with Piers's family. Hopefully nothing pressing is on the horizon?"

Peter's eyes widened, perhaps skeptical that his workaholic boss was taking five minutes off work, let alone a few days. Still, he had no reason to suspect Thea. Also, she had an air of innocence that made her a skilled liar. Perfect for negotiating.

"Business is always hopping, but we can muddle through for a few days without him. I'll handle any necessary decisions."

Rif's gut told him something was rotten. What about the Kanzi oil deal? Didn't Peter think it important to mention a multibillion-dollar opportunity that would put the company at the top of their game?

"Actually, I'd like you to double-check with me before making any important decisions. Until my father comes back, you understand," she said.

The CFO cleared his throat. "Does this mean that you're considering your father's offer to join Paris Industries?"

Of course Peter worried more about Peter than anything else. If Christos's favorite child came on board, the CFO's aquiline nose would shift out of joint, and he'd possibly be out of a future at Paris.

"Kidnapping captures my interest right now." Her jaw tightened.

"There's a board meeting the morning of January second. He'll be back for that?"

"Sure hope so. I wouldn't want to sit through that painful experience for him. That's over and above the call of duty," she said with a light laugh.

"Believe it or not, I find them interesting. But your job trumps everything. Any good hostage tales to share?"

She didn't miss a beat. "We recently recovered a teenage girl in Colombia who had been taken en route to school. Turns out her chauffeur was involved. Talk about a violation of trust."

"Terrible." Peter's pale face became slightly pink, a physiological response indicating potential guilt. But was it from a deceitful business move, or was the CFO involved in the kidnapping? Or could it simply be the alcohol? Give Rif five minutes with Peter in a dark alley, and he'd get the answer, but Thea always wanted to play it straight.

A text message alert from her father's phone emanated from her purse.

"I need to take this; it could be work," she said. "Please excuse me."

"Sure, sure. I'll keep you posted on any developments."

Rif stood, letting her slip out of the booth. A slight tremor in her knees was the only sign of her tension, and he only noticed because he knew her so well. She strode toward the door. He leaned down inches from Peter's face and looked him in the eye. "You're hiding something, and I'm going to find out what it is."

Peter's skin darkened to deep pink.

Chapter Eleven

Thea stepped outside the club into the cool night, desperate for fresh air. Rif stood beside her, surveying the deserted street and the shadowed overhangs. Diligent, as always. Good thing, as her brain was wrapped in layers of fog.

"Let's go." He had his hand on her back, guiding her down the alley.

A war raged inside her. She ached to know the kidnappers' next move but dreaded potential bad news. Whoever was behind this had already left a trail of corpses. She couldn't bear the thought of Papa being one of them. No way could she wait to read the message. She fumbled in her purse for her father's cell.

Before she could pull it out of her purse, Rif's fingers dug into her arm. She looked up. Four figures dressed in black had encircled them. Two held knives, one had a crowbar, and the fourth brandished a chain.

She dropped the phone back into her purse and slung the strap across her body to free her hands. Instinctively she and Rif positioned themselves back-to-back. She slipped off her Louboutins and kicked them aside.

Two men charged her while the other two pounced on Rif. Her sensei's voice filled her thoughts. *Unless they are highly trained, people don't work well in packs. Use their disorganization against them.*

She moved to the left, forcing them into the nearby alcove. The first attacker approached. A flash of steel drew her attention. She stepped aside, hooked her wrist around his forearm, and stepped into the hold. Crack. She broke his arm and shoved him into the other man. The knife clattered to the ground. She spun around.

The second attacker pushed the first aside and came straight for her. She turned to avoid the chain. Too late. The heavy links lashed her back, battering her right kidney. Pain shot through her body.

She was reeling when a solid weight tackled her onto the ground, followed by a punch that rattled her teeth. She rolled away, coiled her legs, and unleashed the bottom of her right foot into the man's solar plexus. He collapsed, a loud wheezing sound escaping his throat. She scrambled to stand, the rough cobblestones scraping the bottom of her feet.

Movement registered in her peripheral vision. Rif fighting his assailants. Grunts, blood, the sound of a crowbar meeting flesh.

A metallic taste flooded her mouth. Before she could recover, the second attacker came for her again. The chain swung around. She tried to scramble out of the way, but the heavy links crashed into her shoulder, slamming her to the ground again. Her head collided with the cobblestones, leaving her in a haze. She tried to shake it off. The man stood over her, chain in hand.

She blinked, trying to clear her double vision. Her sensei's advice again flashed in her mind. *Chained weapons have a downside, leaving their users unbalanced.* She protected her head with her arms as the metal links crashed into her.

After absorbing the blow, she grabbed the chain with both hands and used a quick shift of her body weight to pull him off balance. The attacker stumbled forward. A beefy, barrel-chested man, he could easily overpower her in close quarters.

She needed the knife. On all fours she scrambled for the weapon, but his meaty fingers grabbed her left leg and pulled her toward him before she could reach it.

He flipped her onto her back and straddled her torso, forcing the air out of her lungs. His hands closed around her throat, tightened. She couldn't breathe. Her vision swam.

No, she had to fight. For Papa, Aegis, Nikos.

Her hand felt along the ground and found one of her shoes. She tightened her grip on the stiletto and swung hard, driving the heel into her attacker's neck. He grunted, mouth slackening. His fingers loosened around her throat and went to his own. He slumped on top of her. Dark blood spurted onto the cobblestones.

Seconds later, Rif ripped the massive man off her. She gasped for air. Sirens sounded in the distance. Three of the attackers limped into the darkness. The man with the stiletto lodged in his neck lay still.

"You okay?" Rif helped her to a sitting position.

She nodded. "I had it covered."

"Killer heels." Rif removed the man's ski mask, revealing his bullish nose and olive skin, and snapped a few photos with his cell.

The wailing of the sirens intensified.

"Let's get out of here." He yanked the stiletto from the man's neck. Blood had soaked through the delicate fabric.

"Ugh. It's not like I'm going to wear them again."

"Yep, but we don't want the local cops to come looking for Cinderella." His sharp features were marred by streaks of blood.

He helped her stand. Her head throbbed from its pounding against the cobblestones, so she leaned against him as they hurried down the street.

The squeal of nearby tires startled them. Hakan pulled up in his rented Renault and thrust open the door. His dark eyes widened at the sight of her and Rif. "I heard about a disturbance on the police scanner and knew you were headed in this direction to meet Kennedy. What the hell happened?"

She'd never been so relieved to see her boss. Sliding into the backseat beside Rif, she slammed the door, and Hakan tore away.

"Looks like Christos isn't the only one the kidnappers are after." Rif wiped blood off his forehead.

"Should I take you both to a clinic? You don't look so good." Hakan's eyebrows knitted together.

"The hotel, please." She sucked in a breath.

"I'll get one of the local docs to come to your room." Hakan weaved around the corners at warp speed.

"We can't waste time being questioned by the police. First thing tomorrow, I'll head for Athens, where we can set up a temporary base of operations." Her stomach lurched. The message. She searched for Papa's cell with its flashing red light, indicating a text.

Her hand trembled as she read out loud: "*Corruptio optimi pessima*. The corruption of the best is the worst."

"Another riddle—and no fucking ransom demand." Rif's voice was tight, clipped.

Hakan swerved into the parking area in front of the hotel, barely missing a stationary taxi. In kidnappings, the hostage takers were in charge, and they knew it. The family was at their mercy. That was why it was so important to understand whom you were dealing with, deciphering what they wanted—but it was challenging when they refused to be identified. "By the way, Nikos is at the party."

Thea struggled to swallow, not sure if her difficulty was due to the aftermath of being choked or the thought of the turmoil in her family.

Rif squeezed her hand. She pressed back, her way of saying thanks. If she'd been alone tonight, it would have gone very differently.

Chapter Twelve

Ares slipped through the rear gate of the Sphinx restaurant and climbed the stairs two at a time. The din of music, laughter, and clinking champagne glasses filled the night air. He had an invitation to the party via his other persona, but that didn't mean he was welcome. Not that that had ever stopped him before. He reached into his pocket and felt the reassuring presence of the music box. Almost time.

He paused in the shadows and surveyed the crowd he'd been around most of his life. Socialites flirted with Arabian princes, a female rock star gyrated against a business mogul, models with hungry stares waved away waiters carrying trays of food. Spotlights glittered off rock-size jewels, creating a strobelike effect. He inhaled, breathing in a mixture of expensive perfumes and colognes. Quite a party. But tonight he had no desire to play social games.

On the surface, he fit in well, his Italian tuxedo cut from the finest cloth, his dark hair fashionably styled just below his collar. However, unlike the spoiled people here, his hands were rough. Calluses covered his palms, and a scar from a knife fight slashed across his thumb. Unlike him, no one in this pampered crowd would survive five minutes in the desert without food or water, surrounded by scorpions and other predators—and that included Christos Paris. Ares scanned the room again. As suspected, no sign of the host or his new wife, Helena. Had he really been kidnapped? His men were on full alert, scouring for any clue to Christos's whereabouts.

A lithe Asian woman in the far corner of the room captured his attention. Quan Xi-Ping. The first time he'd seen her name, he'd had no idea how to pronounce it, but then he'd learned that "Xi" sounded like "she," and from then on, he'd thought of her as She-Wolf. She lived up to the nickname.

A slight pursing of her full lips told him she was aware of his presence. Smart, tough, confident—good qualities for his main arms supplier. She chatted with three men vying for her attention, her slender fingers clutching a champagne glass. Her pale gown clung to her curves like a second skin. Lady Godiva holding court.

His gaze connected with hers. He glanced toward the stairs. She squeezed the arm of the man closest to her and smiled. Seconds later, she headed in Ares's direction. He turned away, helping himself to a canapé from a passing waiter. The scent of jasmine flooded his nostrils as she brushed by him and sashayed down the stairs.

He waited for a few minutes, then descended the steps two at a time. The secluded bathrooms of the Sphinx were nestled on the lower level of the restaurant beside a private dining room. Inconvenient for most guests but ideal for his purposes.

A dim light glowed from underneath one of the bathroom doors. He twisted the knob and entered, locking the door behind him. "No sign of Christos. You didn't mess with our timing, did you?" Xi-Ping pushed at his chest with open palms, pinning him against the wall.

"Handle your end, and I'll handle mine." He pulled off her hair clasp so her long, dark tresses covered her bare shoulders. He kissed her hard. Goose bumps rippled down her sleek arms.

"Don't tell me what to do," she said. "I'm the boss now." She dropped to her knees and unzipped his tuxedo pants.

Hardly. But he played along with the game. He ensnared a handful of hair and pulled her close. Her silky mouth enveloped him, her tongue snaking down his shaft. Heat pulsated through his capillaries. A fine sheen of sweat covered his forehead.

But the call he'd received earlier kept running through his mind.

Had he been foiled so close to the endgame? He'd planned so carefully, considering every possibility—except one.

Xi-Ping licked hungrily, devouring him with her full lips. Still, he felt a slight softening.

Whatever had happened, he'd find a way to exact his revenge. He was Ares, and Ares was unstoppable.

He ground her face into his pelvis. Thrusting into her mouth, he hardened again. She grabbed his glutes, sinking her nails through his pants, digging into his flesh. He flexed as he stabbed faster and faster, blocking out everything but the euphoria of the moment.

He ripped her head away and yanked her to her feet. Excitement mounted inside him.

She slapped him. He grabbed her wrist, slamming her body against the door. Her fingers clawed at his shirt. He pushed her away, spun her around to face the sink, hiking the long skirt above her waist. He ripped off her lace thong and plunged inside her.

His muscular arms wrapped around her body, and his fingers twisted her nipples hard. He lost himself in her intoxicating scent. A loud moan escaped her lips. He pounded harder, starting to crest the wave.

She bit his arm, hard. *Bitch.* He tightened his hold and clamped a hand over her nose and mouth. Sounds in the bathroom next door distracted him. He couldn't afford to be caught with her.

He pinned her against him. Unable to breathe, she squirmed and bucked beneath him. White light flashed in his vision as he reached a crescendo. He remained silent, controlled, like a sniper in his hide. The waves of pleasure slowly rippled away, bringing him back to awareness.

The toilet flushed in the other bathroom, and the occupant departed. Ares removed his hand from Xi-Ping's face. Her desperate inhalation made a loud, rasping sound. She sank to the floor, chest heaving. Her hair was a tangled mess, her makeup smeared, but the corners of her full lips turned upward in a smile.

He rinsed off in the sink, zipped up his pants, and straightened his bow tie.

"Where's Christos? I thought we were securing him at the negotiations in Zimbabwe."

He assessed her face, trying to determine if she'd had anything to do with the premature grab, but her unfathomable gaze held no answers. "Everything is fine." Then she looked at him intently and sighed. "That was the best yet. It's never been like this with anyone else, Nikos."

Xi-Ping was one of only a handful of people who knew about his two personas: Nikos, son of the great Christos Paris; and his alter ego, Ares, an arms dealer and kidnapper who was on a first-name basis with revolutionaries from war-torn countries on three continents. A calculated risk, as she had more to lose than he did by divulging his secrets.

Chapter Thirteen

Thea's bloodstained stiletto rested on the hotel room desk, a grisly memento. Extensive hand-to-hand combat training could never fully prepare anyone for the raw desperation of a real fight: intense, primal. She'd had to make a choice: kill or be killed.

Rif seemed less affected by the attack, his demeanor calm. The time he'd spent in Afghanistan, Iraq, and Africa had hardened him to violence. When they were children, he'd been an adventurous, rambunctious boy, exploring the outdoors, hiking and fishing wherever he could. That carefree side of him had been extinguished by his experience in Chad, and a darkness seemed to ride his shoulders now.

Thea walked into the bathroom, slipped out of her torn dress, and stepped into the steaming shower, the powerful jets battering the knots in her shoulders. The last twenty-four hours had been hell—Papa's kidnapping, Piers's murder, and the street fight. She could still see her attacker's dark eyes, intent under the balaclava, his strong hands clamped around her neck, tightening. She rubbed her neck, her throat bruised from those powerful fingers.

She couldn't fight off the overwhelming dread of what might happen to Papa. Captivity was the worst form of mental torture, the hostage constantly thinking: Is this the day I'll die? Of course, Christos Paris was made of titanium and had limitless patience. That part of a kidnapping he could handle. The problem would be his inability to let others dominate him. His independence and stubbornness had played a big part in his financial success but had also made him plenty of enemies along the way. No doubt about it, he could be a difficult SOB if his mind was made up about something.

Being uncooperative in business negotiations was one thing, but as a captive, you had to play the game of yielding to the kidnappers' authority, or you might not survive. Bottom line: if something went horribly wrong, the easiest move for the kidnapper would be to kill the hostage and bolt. She told herself that Papa was way too valuable a captive for that to happen, but then, this wasn't a typical hostage situation.

He'd always been there for her. Even though his business had been all-consuming, he'd attended every important event of her life—school plays, tennis matches, graduations. He'd been delighted when she finished her master's degree in international relations—probably because he'd wanted her to join the family business—but he'd graciously congratulated her when she'd accepted a job with the Defense Intelligence Agency instead. And when she'd left the DIA for Quantum, he hadn't been happy, but he'd supported her decision.

Exhaustion and grief overcame her, and she sagged against the shower wall, sliding down the tiles until she sat huddled in a ball, arms hugging her knees. She released all the pent-up emotion in a crying jag, her tears lost in the rivulets running down her face, her body shaking with each sob.

The shower had always been her sanctuary, the one place where she could lower her defenses. Crying wasn't approved of in the Paris home—Papa considered it a sign of weakness, and

Nikos never cried. Her brother had once been compassionate and caring when she was afraid or upset.

Until he'd been taken.

Thea's childhood bedroom in Kanzi had a looming four-poster bed and vaulted ceilings with swirling bamboo fans, the blades casting eerie shadows on the stucco walls. Her stuffed-animal collection perched on a bookcase, the faces becoming lifelike as darkness dominated the room. During the rainy season, the heavy downpours battered the bay window, and the hardwood floors creaked with the gusting winds. Dark, stormy nights always brought nightmares of losing her mother on the sailboat all over again.

A vigilant sentry, Nikos would hear her sobbing through their bedrooms' connecting ducts and come support her. He'd prepare a makeshift fort for her, using the daybed on the far wall, a large comforter providing the roof. Tucked into the fortress, Thea felt protected, safe. He then often crashed on her four-poster, on guard until the morning light broke through the bay window, dispelling her fears. He'd wind up her music box so she could hear the soft notes of "Tie a Yellow Ribbon" as she drifted off to sleep.

Once, after a particularly loud rumble of thunder, she'd cried out for her brother. In seconds, he'd rushed in and carried her to the daybed on the far side of her room.

"I saw Mama in the water again." Their mother had disappeared in the sea while sailing in rough weather. Her body had never been recovered.

"She's up in heaven, happy and safe, watching over you." Another flash of lightning slashed the sky, followed by booming thunder. The windowpanes reverberated, making Thea's teeth chatter. Nikos pointed to the sky. "That was Mama telling you to get some sleep so you'll ace your spelling test tomorrow." He hugged her tightly.

She relaxed in his protective embrace. "Quiz me. Ask me anything."

"Triskaidekaphobia."

She scrunched up her face. A tough one. "T-R-I-S-K-A-I-D-E-K-A-P-H-O-B-I-A."

He frowned. Her heart sank. Then he started laughing. "You nailed it, Athena the Brilliant. Now, let me get some rest, or I'll get the strap for falling asleep in class tomorrow."

Tall for his age, Nikos was confident, regal. He tucked a blanket around her, and she snuggled into her cocoon of safety, watching him climb into her four-poster, where he'd remain for the night, guarding her dreams.

"I'm ten steps away if you need me."

She burrowed under the blanket and settled in. Having him nearby cast all the ghosts and monsters away. Happy dreams awaited, and she drifted off.

Later, a sound woke her from a dead sleep. Soft footsteps in the room. The storm had moved on, and a slight glow from the moon shone through the large bay window. A warm breeze blew the drapes aside. The floor creaked, making her tense. Then she remembered that Nikos was in her room—maybe he'd visited the bathroom.

She glanced over at the bed. Nikos was still there. More footsteps. A large shadow loomed over her brother. She blinked, wondering if she was imagining the monster.

The figure clamped a cloth over Nikos's mouth and nose. Her brother bolted upright, but strong arms held him in place. She opened her lips, wanting to scream, but no sound came out. She remained breathless, frozen.

Nikos kicked and squirmed but he was no match for the dark figure. A soft, mewling sound escaped her brother's lips, barely above a whisper. The monster clamped down harder on the cloth covering Nikos's mouth and nose, silencing him.

Was this a bad dream? Wake up, wake up.

Nikos stared at her, his eyes bulging, desperate, pleading. His limbs flailed, lashed out against the man, but it made no difference. She ached to help, but fear immobilized her. Her heart jackhammered inside her chest.

Seconds later, her brother slumped like a rag doll. The monster tossed Nikos's limp body over his shoulder and stepped through the open window, disappearing into the night.

Her entire body shook. A warm wetness soaked her pajama bottoms. . . .

Thea jolted at the knock on the bathroom door. She shook off the horrible memory and forced herself back to the present. The water that flowed over her body was now cold. Goose bumps covered her skin.

"You okay in there?" Rif asked.

She tried to steady herself. "Fine. Out in a minute."

Twenty years ago, she'd been powerless to help her brother, but she was no longer that frightened child. Her father needed her, and she'd be there for him. She turned off the faucet, grabbed a thick white towel, and dried herself off.

Back in her room, a quick blood sugar check told her she was a little low. She slipped into jeans and a black T-shirt, munched on an apple, and cuddled on the couch with Aegis while she scanned her e-mail, hoping for a lead. Her inbox held nothing new.

After drying her hair, she knocked on the adjoining door to Hakan's suite.

"Come in." Father and son sat huddled over a laptop. Aegis trundled across to them and plopped down, rolling on top of their feet. Rif scratched the ridgeback's belly. The dog always deserted her when the former soldier was around. *Traitor.*

"You okay?" Hakan sipped his coffee.

She glanced at the photo on the screen. Her dead attacker. "Better than him. I've been thinking. If they wanted to kill us, it would have been cleaner to send a team armed with silenced handguns. The crowbar, the chain . . . it felt like more like they wanted to deliver a good beating—but then it went wrong."

"Excellent point. Maybe a warning from the kidnapper to back off? I ran the photo Rif snapped through our facial recognition software. Meet Illy Natasha. Russian hood for hire, former FSB agent, fired for unknown reasons—but you could guess. Has an arrest record for assault and battery, rape, and—here's the kicker—illegally exporting ivory from Kanzi."

So her father's disappearance *could* be linked to the deal in Africa. "Any updates on Henri?"

"Not really. When I originally did his background check, five years were unaccounted for. Henri admitted that he'd dodged a manslaughter charge in Italy by escaping into the French Foreign

Legion. I recommended against hiring him, but Christos decided he couldn't live without Henri's *pain au chocolat.*"

"Could Henri be involved? He seemed so devoted to Papa." She pressed the home button on her father's phone. No more texts.

"Either he's complicit, or he's a hostage."

Rif stood, Aegis jumping up to join him. "These Latin messages, are they a stall tactic?"

"Maybe, or maybe we just don't understand the implications yet," she said. "Who has the most to gain by taking Papa right before the Kanzi deal? If Christos doesn't show up for the summit in Zimbabwe, what happens? Will the negotiations be canceled? Does another company usurp the place of Paris Industries? Or would the Chinese win the rights by default? Peter would know. . . ."

"If that bastard's involved, he's going to pay." Rif's hands clenched into fists. "I placed a bug inside his phone to monitor his calls."

Hakan looked at her with concern. "You're pale. Sure you don't want to see a doctor?"

"I'm good, just worried about Papa. He . . . he doesn't take orders well." She turned toward the fireplace to hide the pain in her eyes.

Chapter Fourteen

Rif finished his final set of one-arm push-ups on the floor of Thea's hotel room while fending off the affections of Aegis, who kept nudging him. Exercise helped him sift through the facts and figure out what mattered. The Latin texts bothered him. The provocative behavior felt personal. He didn't dare suggest it to Thea, but he wouldn't put it past Nikos to orchestrate something like this.

After a long night of drinking a few years back, his godfather had confided in him that after Nikos had returned home from captivity, his behavior had become erratic and explosive. Christos had felt ill-equipped to deal with his son and tried to get him help. Nothing worked. According to Christos, the shrink had seemed ambivalent about his son's chances of repairing the damage he'd suffered. Meanwhile, he'd warned Christos to expect further outbursts of violent anger as Nikos tried to heal.

Still, no matter how badly her brother acted, Thea couldn't see the monster inside. Even when he blew up at family gatherings, even the time he had stormed off for hours on Christmas several years ago, she never seemed to change her opinion of him. In her mind, Nikos remained the twelve-year-old boy who had protected her as a child and paid for it dearly. *Survivor's guilt.* Nikos's presence was a constant reminder of what could have been her fate. From his own experiences, Rif could empathize.

He pushed himself off the floor and glanced at his Stocker & Yale P650 watch: 3:00 a.m. *Damn, they'd better get some sleep.* A last check of his e-mails. He turned to Thea. "A former Legionnaire I knew in Afghanistan is investigating Henri's background in the Legion."

She glanced up from her computer, dark shadows circling her eyes. She'd had the same haunted look after Nikos's kidnapping twenty years ago. She'd been eight, Rif had been seven, Nikos twelve—children caught in a nightmare.

He wanted to comfort her, but that would likely get him the business end of the SIG Sauer he'd procured for her a couple of hours earlier. After the attack in the alley, he wanted them both properly armed. *Screw the rigid Greek gun laws.*

"You want to talk about what happened in the alley?" he asked.

"Absolutely not." She started typing, her gaze shifting back to the computer screen.

She was more like dear old Pops than she'd probably admit. Smart, resilient, a survivor. Qualities both father and daughter had. Christos had used them to climb to great heights professionally and personally. He'd been a good godfather and mentor to him, too. In fact, Rif wouldn't even have been born if Christos hadn't saved his dad's life. During the 1974 Turkish invasion of Cyprus, Christos, then a Greek soldier, had found Hakan alone, bleeding out in a barn. Despite being enemies, Christos had helped the young Turk survive, donating his own blood to replenish Hakan's. Rif didn't think his father would ever consider that debt paid.

"What about the latest text—any thoughts?" he asked, knowing better than to hope for a glimmer of suspicion about Nikos.

"Kidnappers usually get straight to the point, and the point is usually money or other demands. Waxing philosophical in Latin is an absolute waste of time, which could be deliberate. They

might be keeping us engaged while they transport Papa somewhere. Once the story is leaked, it'll be on every news station, so
they'll want a remote location to hide him."

"The oil negotiations start in a couple of days. Of the potential scenarios, it seems most likely that someone doesn't want
Christos there."

"That's what my gut tells me. Dammit, we took every precau-
tion with Papa—all members of his staff had intensive kidnap-
prevention training."

"This isn't your fault, Thea."

A loud knock sounded. He moved toward the door, Glock in
hand, but Aegis beat him there. Who the hell was visiting at this
hour?

"Thea, open the door."

Aegis's tail wagged, but the familiar voice sent bolts of tension ricocheting down Rif's spine. He released the chain on the
door and forced himself to point his Glock downward, aiming at
the floor. He couldn't treat this man as his enemy. Not overtly.

Nikos strode into Thea's hotel room. His world had turned bright
red, mottled with anger, and he struggled to regain control of
himself. Aegis's enthusiastic licks helped ease the pressure in
his head, but even the ridgeback couldn't totally dispel his rage.

He tossed the Greek newspaper at his sister's feet. *Eleuthero-
typia*'s headline read: *Oil Billionaire Kidnapped.* "When were you
planning on telling me?"

The fact that Rif was in her room irritated Nikos even more.
Soldier Boy was always hanging off his sister, using any excuse
to play the role of protector. But no one cared more about Thea
than he did. Their blood bond was stronger than any friendship
or past history with Rif.

His sister picked up the paper. "It's true. Papa has been taken.
I was going to call you, but then Rif and I were attacked in a
nearby alley this evening. I have no idea how the papers found
out about his abduction."

Nikos inhaled deeply, studying the bruises covering his sister's neck, her pale skin. She was obviously shaken. "Are you okay?"

She nodded, but he wasn't convinced. It took a lot to unsettle his sister. He kept stroking Aegis, soothing himself.

"Your sister can look after herself just fine." Rif, an unwelcome presence at the best of times.

"She has to—it's not like she can rely on you." Nikos couldn't resist taunting the man.

Rif moved toward him, the muscles in his jaw clenching.

Thea raised her hands. "Stop it, both of you. I'm sorry, Nikos, you have every right to be upset."

He refocused on his need for information. "What have you heard from the kidnappers? Do they want money?"

"We've received two Latin texts, quotes from Cicero. No ransom demand." She tucked her hair behind her right ear, fully exposing the scar, a gesture she used whenever she was in battle mode.

He felt bad about the accident that had caused the scar, but it had been Rif's fault for goading him. The interloper had gotten too close to his sister, the two of them thicker than thieves. He'd felt shut out, alienated.

"A philosopher-kidnapper? Papa has all the luck. Perhaps they're sipping sherry and discussing the merits of the Socratic method in modern interrogation."

"Don't joke. His entire crew—with the exception of Chef Henri, also missing—was executed on the *Aphrodite*." She placed the newspaper on the desk.

Hmm. Whoever had done this was serious—meticulous, bold, and willing to kill, if necessary. The kidnappers would be hard to track, but he needed to find Christos before Thea did. "Any leads?"

"We're working every angle. Nothing so far."

"There are countless potential kidnappers. You could be at this for a while."

"Nikos, this situation can't be easy for you—it could bring back memories." Her voice tapered off.

He wouldn't discuss this now, not in front of Rif. He'd never been able to talk about his kidnapping to anyone other than the shrink and Papa, and look how that'd turned out. He'd also told Aegis, but only because a dog couldn't talk back. "The coincidence hasn't escaped me, but don't worry about me. Papa's the one who needs our concern."

Before she could answer, her cell rang. "Thea Paris." She listened, her face turning a chalky shade. "Thanks for letting me know."

"What is it?" Nikos asked.

"I saw a homeless woman on the wharf just before Papa was kidnapped. Apparently her body has washed up on the shore."

"So she *did* see something," Rif said.

Not much of a lead. Nikos needed *useful* information if he was going to find their father before his sister did.

"Please forward me those texts. While you two lament the fate of those less fortunate, I'm going to give the kidnapping some thought, see if I can help determine who might have an ax to grind." Other than him, of course. The only shared passion he'd ever had with his father was animals—Aegis was as close to neutral ground as they could reach. And there'd been his polo horse, Martino, a gift from his father for his sixteenth birthday. He'd loved that stallion more than life itself. But during a match, he'd pushed too hard, and Martino had fatally injured his leg. His father came with him to say good-bye to the horse, and they'd even had a drink afterward in Martino's honor. But the détente hadn't lasted long.

Nikos gave Aegis a last head-scratch and strode out the door, but not before he heard Rif say to Thea, "I think he's starting to warm up to me."

Interfering little prick. At least the ex-soldier might be of use playing bodyguard to Thea. Nikos couldn't take care of his sister—the only person worth protecting—while also hunting for their father, so it was good to know Rif's devotion could be put to use.

Chapter Fifteen

Just back from a run with Aegis and Rif, Thea stared out the Santorini hotel room window into the blinding morning sun. Paparazzi lined the cobblestone streets outside the main entrance, reporters pacing with microphones in their hands, piranha looking for prey. Media attention was a tricky issue during kidnaps.

She'd used the press strategically in the past, releasing tightly controlled information to trusted sources, but in most circumstances, it wasn't advisable to address the media, since it could raise the value of the hostage, skyrocketing the ransom. In the case of Christos, the kidnappers obviously knew they had a billionaire in their hands.

Media attention could also lead to a hostage transfer, where one kidnap group passed along or sold the hostage to another group, sometimes turning a financially motivated criminal kidnap into a political one. For example, if a terrorist group had Papa, they could sell him for a hefty price to al-Qaeda or ISIS. And giving away too much information in the press could invite unrelated scammer or nutjobs to claim they had the hostage, which could divert attention and resources away from the real case.

At this point, she had nothing to gain by talking to reporters. Besides, given the apparent sophistication of these kidnappers, she didn't think they'd be swayed by a plea from the victim's daughter. The press would just be a huge nuisance.

"I wonder who leaked." Rif joined her at the window.

"Hard to say. It could even be the kidnapper." She'd asked Freddy Winston to follow up with the Greek newspaper that had broken the story, but sources were zealously guarded, so they might hit a brick wall there.

The timing of the snatch couldn't be ignored. A multibillion-dollar deal that also had political ramifications was about to be decided. Most of the major oil fields in the world had reached their peak output, so their future capacity would only go down. A find like Kanzi could change everything.

She'd overheard Papa talking to top officials in the US government and knew that if he clinched this deal, his influence could reach new heights with the administration. The United States had for decades cozied up to the Saudis because of their oil reserves—just the kind of relationship Christos might enjoy if Paris Industries won the rights to the second largest oil field in the world. Her father's dream was to support the failing Greek economy through the capitalization of select banks with progressive policies, and this political currency could give him the leverage to do it. *Did someone want to stop Christos from saving his home country?*

A flash of bulbs and a cluster of microphones around a redhead caught her attention. Helena dodged through the crowds, hurrying into a nearby car. The limelight was probably too much to bear, given her reserved nature.

Rif sighed. "She looks like a scared rabbit escaping a pack of wolves."

"She has a strong core. I've seen the way she handles Papa."

Remaining on Santorini wasn't an option; Thea had only stayed overnight in case information came to light about her father's abduction, but the kidnappers hadn't left a trace. "We need to head for Athens. There's a back door we can use to escape the hordes."

Her phone beeped. She checked the message before explaining the news to Rif. "We have a line on the helicopter that might've been used to transport Papa from the *Aphrodite*. The pilot lives in Athens. I'll send men to intercept him."

A gentle knock sounded at the door. "Room service."

Aegis growled.

"Did you order something?" Rif reached for his Glock.

"No, but I recognize that voice." A quick check of the peephole provided confirmation. She opened the door while Rif remained in the shadows.

Peter Kennedy stood on the threshold, a room service cart in front of him. He smiled. "I ordered breakfast and got enough for both of us. When I heard about your father, I was worried about you."

Creepy. Who ordered room service and delivered it to another room? "Come in." She'd planned on eating a protein bar for breakfast to save time, but maybe Peter's arrival could be useful.

The CFO's smile faded when he noticed Rif and the ridgeback, hackles raised. "Oh, am I interrupting?"

"Not at all. Rif's here as my bodyguard."

"Nice of you to bring enough for me." Rif lifted one of the silver domes and snatched a piece of bacon for himself, giving one to Aegis. Peter stiffened beneath his Versace suit.

"Sure, of course . . ." the CFO stammered, blinking as Rif downed a slice of toast.

"Peter, we plan on leaving shortly. Would you like a lift to Athens in the Gulfstream?" she asked.

She wasn't crazy about spending time with Peter, but she hadn't felt satisfied by their discussion the previous night. If he knew anything—and she sensed that he did—they needed to get it out of him.

She moved toward the room service cart. "Thanks so much for breakfast. Let's see what else you ordered." She lifted the second silver dome.

"Your favorite—" Peter started, then stopped.

Her heart tripped. Instead of breakfast fare, the plate held a watch—her father's watch, the one he always wore, the one her mother had given him early in their marriage. Proof of life? Hope?

Thea slipped on a pair of vinyl gloves she kept in her kit and picked up the Santos de Cartier Galbée, checking the inscription on the back: TO OUR FUTURE. LOVE, TATIANA.

Rif crossed the room and pushed Peter against the wall, hand on his throat. Aegis's ears shot straight up, and he paced before the two men. "What the hell is this?"

Peter sputtered. "I didn't know it was there. I just ordered breakfast. I might've mentioned that I was taking it to Thea's room. . . ."

"Try again." Rif's voice was sharp.

"I swear on my life, I had nothing to do with this."

She considered Peter's reaction when she'd lifted the dome and heard his words trail off. When he'd seen the watch, his eyes had widened for a brief second, no longer, an indicator of genuine surprise. Now his face showed fear, not guilt. "Let him go," she said to Rif.

Rif released him, and he slumped to the floor, gasping for breath. Aegis looked as if he wanted to finish the job, so she called him to her side.

She spoke in a measured voice. "If you want to join us on the plane to Athens, pack your bags. We leave in twenty minutes."

Peter scrambled to his feet. "You know I'll do everything I can to help you." He backed out of the room, his uneasy gaze on Rif and Aegis.

Rif slammed the door after he'd left. "I don't trust him."

"Me either, but he was telling the truth about the watch."

Rif frowned. "He's hiding *something*."

"Of course he is, but threatening him won't work." Brute force wasn't the way to get through to a guy like Peter—she had to make him feel like part of the team, let him know that whatever he'd done could be forgiven. "You need to work on your approach."

"We have different styles."

"What do you call yours—unbridled testosterone? Torture?"

He stepped closer to her, his voice tight. "I'll do whatever it takes to find Christos."

She let go of the argument. They might have different approaches, but he cared for Papa and was doing everything he could to help. "If Peter comes along, I want you to play nice. Meanwhile, let's go question the kitchen staff."

Chapter Sixteen

Nikos strolled along the African savannah section of Athens's Attica Zoological Park. He sported a typical touristy polo shirt and khaki pants, a bag of peanuts in hand.

A tightness settled in his throat. Who had taken Christos—and why? All his meticulous planning, and what had happened? The one contingency he hadn't imagined.

The feeling of being thwarted grated on him, an old wound. Father and son had never been able to connect emotionally after his abduction in Africa, but he'd kept trying. Even graduating magna cum laude from Harvard Business School hadn't impressed his father, who had never offered him a position in the family business.

Despite his father's obvious lack of confidence in his abilities, Nikos knew he had the acumen and drive to create something special. He'd just had to think differently. He'd had to think outside of Paris Industries. And that he did, creating an organization with the same global reach but selling arms to the underdogs of the world, allowing them to rebel against unjust governments and voracious corporations like his father's. He also gave aid to the downtrodden, empathetic to their plight, funneling more than half of his income into helping children affected by war. They were the innocents . . . as he had been.

As he thought of his abduction and the long months he'd spent in captivity, his hands closed into tight fists, but he forced himself to release the deep-rooted anger. Emotions facilitated nothing. He needed to use his mind.

The beauty of his surroundings helped him regain his equilibrium. Seawater splashed in a nearby waterfall, tropical fish torpedoing around the basin. Early-morning sunshine cast fractured shadows of the acacia trees onto the grasslands, reminding him of the real Africa, his home.

The monkeys in their nearby habitat squawked at him, their intelligent gazes assessing the likelihood of his carrying treats. He tossed a handful of his peanuts into their cage. A mid-size monkey grabbed the nuts and divvied them up among the smaller creatures. Seconds later, the alpha of the group descended, pounded his chest, cawed a loud call, and pounced on the food. The other monkeys dropped their peanuts and scurried off.

Like monkeys, humans had their hierarchy. Christos had been the greedy, overbearing alpha for years, scaring everyone else off so he could plunder the spoils. But that was about to end. Thea needed to see their father in his true light—she had to be made to understand it was Papa's greed that had destroyed Nikos's life.

First he had to find Christos before his sister did. His most trusted men were scouring Santorini and Greece, and they'd discovered the identity of the pilot who'd flown the helicopter that had whisked Christos off the yacht.

Kidnapping a man of Christos's stature was no easy feat, and the brutality of the abduction, including the execution of the crew, demonstrated the commitment involved. Immersed in the kidnapping world himself, Nikos knew most of the major players. He just had to figure out who had taken Christos and why.

The image of his proud father in a cage like the monkeys, covered in his own filth—a far cry from his usual platinum-spoon lifestyle—almost made Nikos smile, even as his anger threatened to resurface. He wouldn't tolerate someone interfering with his plans for his father. Just as in a well-crafted chess strategy, it had taken a Herculean effort to get the pieces into place, and the timing was crucial.

The scent of jasmine wafted into his airspace, and suddenly Xi-Ping was standing a few feet away. She was a woman whose strength he respected. She'd turned to arms dealing as a way to separate herself from her domineering brother and had become incredibly successful at it.

The supplier wore dark jeans, and a white blouse hid the intricate tattoos adorning her arms and back. Her striking features were devoid of makeup—she didn't need any. Lustrous black hair fell halfway down her back. Beautiful yet deadly. That was his partner. *Or was she? Could she be behind Christos's abduction?*

"Should I call you Ares or Nikos?" A smirk played on her full lips.

"No time for games. We have business to complete."

"Your pilot asked me to give you this delivery." She passed him a black resin container slightly larger than a hatbox. "Something I should know about?"

"Family business." Just not his family.

"Speaking of which, I read the papers this morning. Why accelerate the plan?"

He studied her carefully, looking for evidence of complicity in his father's abduction. His original strategy had involved Christos arriving in Zimbabwe for the negotiations first. Was Xi-Ping behind a preemptive snatch? Her brother? The two of them were representing the Chinese in the negotiations, so they certainly had motive to kidnap Christos. Still, he didn't think she would double-cross him. He'd been her top customer for the black-market arms she sold, and he'd helped design a plan that would eliminate her biggest rival—her brother. He couldn't fault her for wanting to vaporize Chi; the misogynist bastard spoke to her as he might a personal slave. Nikos would never treat Thea in such a demeaning way.

"Everything's under control." He would never admit otherwise to her. Besides, after facing down Uzis and AK-47s as a child, not much fazed him. His father's kidnapping was just another minor obstacle. And once he understood who'd orchestrated it, maybe he could work it to his advantage.

"Your sister could still be a problem." Xi-Ping's lips tightened. "Thea?"

"My men roughed her up in Santorini. I wanted her temporarily out of commission so she wouldn't be nosing into the kidnapping, interfering with our plans."

Thea's bruises. Her close brush with death. How dare She-Wolf hurt his sister? "Don't ever lay a hand on Thea again." He stared at the delicate hyoid bone in Xi-Ping's alabaster throat, wondering how much pressure would be needed to snap it.

She shrugged, as if the attack was a casual misstep.

"Let me be perfectly clear. Thea is off limits to—" His cell chirped. He raised a hand to Xi-Ping, putting their conversation on hold. "Yes?" he said into the phone.

A raspy voice echoed on the other end. "It's Konstantin from the hangar. Everything is ready."

"Good work. Continue as planned."

"Of course. Thank you for your generous gift."

"There's more to come." Nikos pressed the end button.

Xi-Ping gave him a questioning look.

"We're on target."

"Can we meet later at my hotel?" She arched a seductive eyebrow.

"We'll have time for that later." *Or not.* "I need to head to Kanzi as soon as possible."

Disappointment shadowed her eyes. He glanced around. A few families had started milling around the exhibits. "Handle your end, and we'll have plenty to celebrate." He hefted the black container and headed for the zoo's exit.

Cocooned behind the tinted windows of his black Mercedes, he unlocked the latches on the box and broke the seal. Mist drifted out. Vapor from the dry ice. As the plumes dissipated, he stared into the dark eyes of Carlos Antiguez, the former FARC leader, whose greasy hair was now frozen in place on his severed head. He smiled. A renewed energy filled him. Definitely the right choice, backing the nephew.

Chapter Seventeen

Gabrielle Farrah paced beside the baggage carousel at Athens International Airport, waiting for her suitcase, an unlit cigarette in her hand. She usually traveled with just a carry-on, but this time she had no idea how long she'd be gone. Max had texted her before her flight, letting her know that Christos Paris hadn't shown up at his own party.

Whoever had made that mechanical call—her team had tracked it down to an untraceable burner phone—obviously had inside information. Hell, it could have been the kidnappers themselves. Now that the news about the oil baron's abduction had been announced in the press, the US government was in an uproar about the head of Paris Industries being taken captive. And her boss, Stephen Kelly, the deputy director of the Hostage Recovery Fusion Cell, had mobilized a full support team to back her up while he updated the Special Presidential Envoy for Hostage Affairs. If there was one thing that fueled the political machine, it was access to oil.

During the flight, she'd immersed herself in the Paris family dossier. The son's kidnapping had the same tragic feeling as the

Lindbergh saga, except Christos's son had been lucky enough to come home alive. Now in his thirties, Nikos Paris ran a Kanzi-based import/export business that funded a large charity for orphans that he co-sponsored with his sister. Not involved in Paris Industries at all. Wonder why not? Still, good to see that he'd recovered from his own ordeal and was helping children. Not every hostage was lucky enough to return to a functional life.

The patriarch of the family had a reputation as a ruthless, self-made tycoon. He'd lost his first wife in a sailing accident. After that, he'd been married four more times; currently he was in wedded bliss with a Frenchwoman named Helena.

Thea Paris, the only daughter, worked at one of the world's preeminent K&R firms as a response consultant, probably motivated to join the fight because of her brother's kidnapping. In her field, she was the only female operative, known for her ability to free hostages under the direst circumstances.

No one in the Paris household did anything halfway. A psychiatrist would have a field day with this family.

The bell rang on the baggage carousel, jolting her out of her reverie. *Finally.* Gabrielle scanned the bags, looking for her hard-case Samsonite. Inspector Maximillian Heros would be picking her up—and, knowing Max, he'd have updated information on the case. The last time they'd been together, she'd been working at the State Department, and he'd unearthed critical information that'd helped her clear her case. The celebration afterward had led them to the hotel room. One night only—that was her creed. And no pillow talk. Her sister accused her of acting like a guy in her encounters. Gabrielle took it as a compliment.

Grabbing her Samsonite, she headed for the exit. The double doors opened to reveal the Greek police inspector in question leaning against his sleek silver Aston Martin, a lazy smile on his face.

"Looks like the olive business is booming." She'd almost forgotten that Max was filthy rich, his family one of the premier olive oil producers in Greece. Well, he could buy lunch. She was on a government salary.

He stepped onto the concrete sidewalk and opened his arms. "I have a welcome present for you."

His familiar scent of tobacco and vanilla brought back vivid memories of their night together. She sidestepped his embrace, handing him her suitcase instead. "Christos Paris has been returned to his rightful throne, and I can enjoy an authentic Greek salad before returning home?"

He laughed, a deep rumble. "I see you have not lost your admiration of the *hoi oligoi*."

"I have the utmost empathy for kidnapped oil billionaires whose business my government relies upon." The corners of her lips turned upward, and she lit the Gitanes.

"You are a cruel woman—maybe that is why I cannot forget you." He stowed her suitcase in the trunk and opened the passenger door for her. She slid into the soft black leather seat.

He climbed in and fired the engine. The V12 erupted in a throaty roar.

"About that present . . ." She inhaled deeply, the cigarette delivering a much-needed nicotine hit.

"Paris was snatched from his yacht in Santorini. Had to be by chopper, but a helicopter has a limited range. Paris is a hero in Greece, so it wouldn't be safe to house him here. I checked the private airports, looking at flight manifests, and one plane stood out." He shifted into gear and passed her a Post-it note. "I got this from a friend via the Interpol I-24/7 line—it's the tail number. I'm taking you to the private airport where it refueled."

"The list of suspects is endless at this point," she offered. "We've had a huge surge in chatter from ISIS in the last twenty-four hours. Grabbing someone with Paris's wealth could yield a bounty that would swell their coffers for years to come." She didn't state the obvious: that he could also be used as a political bargaining chip. "Things could get very difficult for the man."

"I've known Christos for years. Same circles. He's tough—he'll be fine."

"Everyone has a breaking point. For his sake, I hope this is a criminal kidnap, not a political one. Theo Padnos had a hell of a time in captivity with al-Nusra." In political cases, the kidnappers were motivated by ideology. She remembered the debriefing report from the American journalist's case. Padnos had been beaten, kept in solitary confinement in a Syrian-run prison, exposed to extreme cold, and even buried alive for half an hour. When he first returned home, he barely ate or slept, his thoughts scattered, his emotions mercurial, swinging from elation to crying fits. If terrorists had kidnapped Christos Paris, he wouldn't come back the same man, if he came back at all.

"Padnos is lucky to be alive. I wonder if his captors knew about his book *Undercover Muslim*. The guy converted to Islam and studied at one of the most radical mosques, and his book might be considered apostasy in Islamic circles." Max shook his head.

"All hostages have secrets, and those secrets can get them killed."

"Going to tell me yours?"

"I'm not your hostage."

"You could be."

"Focus on the case, Max."

"Paris's daughter is in Athens. We'll go see her after we finish at the hangar."

Max's foot pressed the gas pedal, the force of the acceleration thrusting Gabrielle back against her headrest. She typed the plane's tail number into her cell and texted Ernest, the researcher on her team, asking him to procure all the information he could.

The Aston Martin threaded the corners, riding low to the ground. They drove to the coast, soaking in the scenic landscape and relentless sunshine. But Gabrielle's mood was dark—she didn't want to see Christos Paris in an orange jumpsuit being paraded on a world stage for political gain. There had been enough of those videos.

"We're here." Max's baritone brought her back to the present. They snaked along the paved driveway leading to the small airport. It was nestled on the coast, a perfect locale if someone wanted to transfer illegal cargo—or a kidnap victim—from a helicopter to a plane without drawing unnecessary attention.

He pulled into the closest parking space near the air traffic control building. She stubbed out her cigarette. Her phone chimed. An encrypted text from her boss: *The team ID'd three ISIS training camps in Syria. Unusual activity at one. Looking into the possibility of Paris being held there. Also tracking all ships and planes leaving Greece around the time of the kidnapping. Will keep you posted.*

Was it possible that Paris was being held by ISIS? She stashed her cell in her purse. Before she could open her door, Max was already opening it for her.

They hurried up the steps and entered the building. Max flashed his badge and smiled at the receptionist, and they were immediately ushered into a rear office. Photos of Santorini covered the hallway walls, the famous whitewashed church with the blue dome featured prominently. Hard to imagine a more beautiful place—definitely not your typical kidnapping site.

The airport manager had just finished his lunch and was wiping his gaunt face with a napkin. The scent of hummus dredged up memories for Gabrielle of her late mother's version of the dish.

Max identified himself in Greek and asked if the man spoke English.

He nodded. "Konstantin Philippoussis."

"This is Gabrielle Farrah from the United States."

"Yes, America." The cadaverous man had a heavy accent, and his eyes sparkled with intelligence.

"Have you visited?" she asked, trying to establish a bond.

"Never. But my daughter like big statue with crown."

"The Statue of Liberty, in New York City. A gift from France."

"We're interested in any information you have on this plane's tail number." Max passed him the Post-it.

Konstantin wrinkled his brow. "Yes, I remember. Nice legs."

Max laughed. "I never forget a pair myself. Who were these attached to?"

"Asian lady. She floated on high heels like exotic *petalouda*."

Gabrielle gave Max an inquiring look.

"Butterfly," he translated. "When was this?"

"Yesterday, after I start work. The plane fly away after she come."

"Was she alone?"

Konstantin nodded.

"Did she take a cab, rent a car?"

"A white limo pick her up." He pointed out his window. "I saw those legs when she got in."

"What about the plane? Did the pilot file a flight plan?"

"One minute." He trudged out of the office.

Max shrugged. "Might just be some wealthy Asian woman visiting the sights."

"Christos Paris was supposed to negotiate for the Kanzi oil rights later this week. His main competition is the Chinese National Oil Company."

"You see conspiracies everywhere. . . ."

Konstantin shuffled back in. "No flight plan. Either the pilot not file one, or it is lost."

Dammit. She was hoping for a lead on the plane's destination. They'd have to find the woman instead. Max would be able to discover her identity—there couldn't be that many white limos driving Asian women in Athens.

Her phone buzzed. She scrutinized the text from Ernest while Max continued questioning Konstantin: *Tail number belongs to a Belgian shell corporation connected with Ares arms deals. Will continue to dig.*

Gabrielle's palms dampened. Ares had a reputation for financing the abductions of prominent CEOs. Had he just landed the mother lode?

Chapter Eighteen

Nikos rappelled into a remote cave close to the Mycenaean caverns, a private place in which he held meetings with his subordinates. Located more than fifty miles southwest of Athens and a substantial distance from any tourist area, the cave featured Neolithic etchings on the walls, lending gravitas to his hideaway, and the surrounding lush forest provided the ideal camouflage for his secret entrance.

The dark and isolated location provided the perfect cover for his double life. He'd drop down the narrow opening and remain behind a triangular rock formation, his face hidden in the shadows as he dictated his instructions to his employees. Only one associate had dared to step deeper into the cave and attempt to have a face-to-face encounter; that man had never returned home.

One of his phones vibrated. Better grab it before he lost reception. He wrapped the rope around his arm, braced his feet on the side of the cave, and pulled out the cell he used as Nikos. The screen told him it was Father Rombola from Kanzi, the priest who helped him and Thea run the orphanage.

"Good afternoon, Father." He kept his voice professional, even.

"I wanted to thank you for your generous donation. It couldn't have come at a more opportune time. A group of youngsters was dropped off last night. Poor boys were half starved, shaken by their time with the warlords."

Nikos's goal was to eradicate the practice of taking child soldiers in Kanzi, one band of brutal guerrillas at a time. As horrible an experience as he'd had as a hostage, he'd been one of the lucky ones, eventually returning home. So many of the other boys never returned or didn't even have a home to go back to after their parents were murdered. The orphanage was one way he tried to help. As Ares, he instructed his men to scour the jungle, rescuing such children. As Nikos, he was the benefactor of the African charity. The two dovetailed perfectly. "My pleasure. It's important to give back."

"I hope you'll consider visiting again soon. We'd love to host a luncheon for you."

"I'd be honored. Perhaps after the holidays?"

"Yes, of course. I'm sure you're busy with your family."

More than you know. "It's that time of year."

"Well, I won't keep you, but please know you're in our prayers every day. Send my regards to Thea."

"Will do. Thank you."

Nikos tucked the phone away and continued his descent into the cave, like a bat returning to its lair. The darkness comforted him, cleared his mind, and heightened every sense. He breathed in the rank scent of stagnant water; it smelled like home. Although the light had faded, he sensed where the next foothold would be and worked his way down.

His men had come through, finding the pilot who'd flown the helicopter used in Christos's abduction and bringing him here to the cave. His name was Andel Raptis, and he was apparently an experienced member of the local coast guard. Interesting. He wanted to question the man personally, because Raptis might be the one person who knew the identity of the kidnapper—the person who'd beaten him to Christos.

Nikos's climbing shoes scuffed the damp rock. He landed on the limestone floor of the inner chamber, eager to meet this moonlighting pilot. He unclipped from the nylon rope, stepped out of the rappelling harness, and reached inside his North Face windbreaker for a mini flashlight. The lightweight, insulated jacket was vital: the temperature had dropped more than twenty degrees during his descent into the bowels of the cave.

Shining the light at a narrow opening, he slunk through the cave, ducking when the overhanging archways weren't high enough for his six-foot-one frame. Fifty paces later, he found the pilot exactly as he'd instructed his associates to leave him.

Bound to a bamboo chair, Raptis squirmed in his seat but couldn't loosen the tight knots. He reeked of excrement and body odor. Urine stained his pants. Nikos's men would have beaten him soundly, so a little mess was to be expected.

Nikos flicked on a camping lantern that hung from a protruding rock and turned off his flashlight. Raptis's eyes bulged with fear. Nikos leaned over and ripped the duct tape off the man's mouth, taking some of his salt-and-pepper stubble with it.

The pilot's mouth moved, but no sound came out. Tears rolled down his grubby face. Nikos reached into his backpack and grabbed his water bottle. Positioning it near Raptis's lips, he squeezed out the contents. The man gulped greedily, water dribbling down his chin.

While his captive slurped water, Nikos glanced at his watch. He needed to get answers quickly, then find Thea to see if she'd made any useful discoveries. Working both ends would pay off.

"You want to leave? Tell me where you flew the man from the yacht," he said in Greek as he tipped the bottle of water upright and let Raptis catch his breath.

"Y-you'll let me go?" the man croaked.

"Of course. I just need information." Hope was a useful motivator.

Smudges of blood were caked in the wrinkles around his eyes as Raptis managed a weak smile. Within hours, most captives reverted to childlike shadows of their former selves, and an aggressive beating helped expedite the process. Modern life had softened people, leaving so few warriors.

"Thank God." Raptis's head slumped forward in relief. "My family th-thanks you."

"No thanks are necessary. Who hired you?"

Raptis looked down at his shoes, his face darkening in shame. "I play the horses, can't seem to stop. I owe a lot. Thousands. The bookie told me my debt would be erased if I did this one favor for him."

"Pick up people on a yacht."

He nodded. "It seemed harmless enough. Two men who looked like bodyguards escorted Christos Paris—I recognized him from the papers—onto the chopper, and then off we went. I thought maybe he was having a secret meeting, needed to fly under the radar. Rich people can be odd."

"How did you know where to go?"

"I was given a helicopter and GPS coordinates, on standby for hours before the call came in."

"Did you see anyone else on board the yacht?"

"A smaller racing boat was moored to the side, and two men and a guy dressed like a chef were in it. They left before we took off. I didn't know it was a kidnap, I swear. I only learned about it afterward on the news."

"And you told no one about your involvement."

"Not a soul. My family wasn't even home. I'd told my wife to take the kids to her mother's place for the holidays, since I had to work."

Stupid man, revealing where his family was. "Who carries your debts?"

Raptis winced, squirming in the chair. "Alec Floros."

"Where did you take Christos Paris?"

"Corfu. A Dash 10 was waiting on the runway, and they took off from there."

"Any markings on the plane? Did you get the tail number?"

"No markings that I recall. I just did my job, minded my own business."

With a quick movement of his hand, Nikos reached down and grabbed the ten-inch hunting blade from a sheath strapped to his left calf. The razor-sharp edge slashed through skin and cartilage on both wrists before the pilot could react. A blood-curdling scream echoed in the cave, followed by a moan and whimper. Nikos wanted to be sure he'd gotten every last detail.

"Tell me everything, and I'll stop the bleeding. Last chance."

"B-but I already did. Please, help me." Raptis's eyes bulged as he stared at the blood pooling on the cave floor. "My family—you promised I'd see them again." His voice was reedy, desperate.

"Family is what this is all about. But mine comes first." Nikos slashed Raptis's throat. Blood spurted from the severed carotid artery, splattering the cave wall. He wiped the blade on the pilot's sleeve and replaced it in its sheath. Raptis's eyes were empty and unmoving.

His men could clean up the mess later. He hurried back to the secret entrance and collected his gear. Energized by the success of the interrogation, he scaled the wall with speed and skill, finding anchor after anchor, rocketing his muscular frame to the top. He needed to shower, change clothes, and track down the plane that had left Corfu.

And since it was Friday, he'd text Thea a photo. No matter where he was in the world, even if they were in the same country, he sent her a selfie, and she wrote a warm, loving note back. Thea was always there for him. He counted on it.

Chapter Nineteen

Thea and Rif strode into the Hotel Grande Bretagne in Athens. Time was ticking by, and the uncommunicative kidnapper remained in the shadows. Not knowing where the search would lead them, she'd asked Hakan to take Aegis to Quantum's London office. Helena wasn't a dog person, but Aegis was slowly winning her over. Peter Kennedy had begged off from the ride to Athens, saying he'd catch up with them soon. She wondered if he was trying to dodge her more insistent questions.

The familiar surroundings of the landmark hotel reminded her once again of Papa. She'd passed through the ornate lobby with him countless times—the Doric columns, coffered ceilings with stained-glass insets, gilded mirrors, sumptuous velvet couches, and intricately tiled floor were all as familiar as they were luxurious. Today, though, it felt hollow and empty without her father's presence. Papa stayed here whenever he visited Athens, paying a monthly stipend so the presidential suite would be available if he showed up unannounced.

Before she and Rif could take the elevator to the sixth floor, where the butler check-in desk was located, a familiar face greeted her. Stavros had been the hotel manager for more than twenty years. "Ms. Paris, I heard about your father. Is there anything I can do?"

"If you could kindly prepare the suite, that would be wonderful."

He reached into the breast pocket of his suit and passed her the keys. "It's ready for you."

"Well, thank you, but—"

"I figured you were on your way when this letter was delivered." Stavros handed her a manila envelope with her name typed in block letters.

She'd strategically chosen their usual hotel in case the kidnapper wanted to reach her. Or perhaps it was something from Hakan? Better to play it safe. She reached into her backpack and grabbed a pair of vinyl gloves.

She opened the envelope and pulled out a sheet of white paper.

CHRISTOS PARIS AND THE *DAMOCLES* ARE UNDER OUR CONTROL. DROP TEN MILLION EUROS IN UNMARKED BILLS ONTO THE DECK IN WATERPROOF CONTAINERS BEFORE MIDNIGHT TOMORROW. EVERY HOUR AFTER THE DEADLINE, CHRISTOS WILL LOSE A BODY PART, AND OIL WILL BE LEAKED INTO THE MEDITERRANEAN SEA. NO NEGOTIATION. NO CALLS.

Her hands trembled, but her mind kicked into full gear. The *Damocles* was one of Paris Industries' supertankers, carrying more than fifty million gallons of crude. Her father had shown her the blueprints over dinner a couple of years ago. Papa loved all watercraft, big and small, and he'd been proud of his latest addition to the Paris Industries fleet.

She handed Rif the note.

He leaned closer to Stavros. "Who left this envelope?"

"A young messenger boy. Not one of our regulars." The old man's brows knitted together. "Have I done something wrong?"

"Not at all. Do you think you could describe this boy to a sketch artist?" The messenger would've been paid a few euros for the delivery. It was doubtful they'd be able to identify who had hired him, but they had to try.

"Yes, of course. Remembering faces is part of my job."

"We'll have someone here shortly. I need to make a few calls. May we go up?"

"Of course. Sorry if I made a mistake." Stavros's face was pale.

Thea squeezed his hand. "Not at all. Please say a prayer for my father." Stavros was a devout man with a large family—he understood her pain.

The hotel manager tried to smile, but it didn't reach his eyes. "Absolutely. Let me know if there's anything else I can do to assist."

"Thank you."

Rif led the way to the elevator and remained silent on the ride up. Meanwhile, Thea activated the same GPS app that had allowed her to locate Papa's yacht. The entire Paris Industries fleet had trackers accessible to Quantum employees, because Quantum provided the company's security. She typed the supertanker's name, her pulse throbbing in tune with the flashing red light on the screen.

They entered the suite, and she paced the spacious living room until the location pinged. She waved Rif into the bathroom and turned on the shower to shield their conversation as much as possible from any hidden mics. "The *Damocles* is nearby, in the Mediterranean Sea. Not exactly a pirate-rich environment. And why are we only finding out about this now?"

"Who would normally be contacted if there was an issue with one of the supertankers—Peter?"

"Not sure. He handles the insurance, but as head of security, Hakan should be the point person. Something's wrong here. First we receive these strange texts in Latin with insinuated threats, and now a straightforward ransom demand. No proof of life, no negotiations. I'm not sure the messages came from the same person."

"Maybe Christos was transferred to a new captor?" Rif's black boots, combat pants, and unshaven look were incongruent with the lavish surroundings.

"Don't think so. The Latin texts felt personal, revenge-oriented. Suddenly the kidnapper wants cash in unmarked bills? The people on the supertanker may not even have Papa. Could be a phantom demand."

"And they left us no way to contact them, to negotiate," he said.

"Or secure proof of life," Thea said. "I'll see if I can reach Magnusson, the captain of the *Damocles*."

"Wouldn't he have notified someone if he'd been boarded?"

"If the operators executed a surgical strike, there might not have been time. The ransom turnaround time is tight. If this note is from the real kidnapper, he's not going to let a bunch of thugs on the deck handle ten million euros. We need to unveil the key player. I'm calling the *Damocles*'s bridge."

Abductions varied in sophistication, from a basic express kidnapping—where a random hostage, often a professional or a tourist, was forced to withdraw money from an ATM—to an intricate, well-planned abduction of a VIP. This kidnapping—storming a well-protected yacht and possibly taking control of a supertanker—was as complex as any she'd seen.

She turned off the shower and searched the Paris Industries database for the number of the bridge. After she dialed, she set her cell to record the call while Rif texted Hakan for more information about the supertanker and its crew.

The phone rang and rang and rang. She was about to hang up and try again when someone picked up.

"Captain Magnusson speaking." His voice was strong, but an underlying tension lingered in his tone.

"Thea Paris here, Captain. Has the *Damocles* been compromised?"

"Yes, ma'am, I'm afraid it has."

She sensed his shame. Her heart plummeted. Some part of her had been hoping this ransom note was a misdirection.

"Has anyone been hurt?"

"Not so far."

"Don't worry, we'll get you home to your family. I keep losing track—how many kids do you have now?" Magnusson was a savvy guy. He'd know what she was asking.

"Ten. That's why I spend so much time at sea."

Muffled voices sounded in the background. She couldn't tell what language they were speaking.

"That's quite a handful. Is my father on board?"

"Can't say for sure. I've been forced to remain on the bridge since they boarded."

"Can the kidnapper hear me?"

"Correct."

"Please put him on." She didn't want to place Magnusson in the untenable position of risking his life for what might be useless information.

"You have your instructions. Drop the money off, and Christos Paris will be returned unharmed." The voice was clipped, concise, with no hint of an accent.

"Who am I speaking to?" Get him talking, work for more information.

"Ten million euros by midnight tomorrow, dropped onto the deck in waterproof containers. In exchange, we return the crew and Christos Paris."

"It's impossible to gather that much cash so quickly. Give me a couple of days."

"Pietro Andreas can make it happen."

She reeled at the mention of Papa's personal banker. How could they know? "Let me speak to my father. We'll need proof of life before we make delivery."

"You have already received the watch."

She squeezed her eyes shut for a moment. The speaker's lack of contractions left her with the impression that English wasn't his first language. "Put Christos on. We need confirmation he's alive."

"Sorry, Mr. Paris is busy at the moment."

"We need proof of life."

Shuffling. A loud scream in the background. It sounded like Captain Magnusson.

"Midnight tomorrow, or Christos starts losing body parts, and we open the valves to blacken the sea. Your choice."

A click, then nothing.

She turned on the shower again, e-mailed the file to Hakan for analysis, then pressed the button to replay the entire conversation, listening closely for any further clues.

"My father says there's a twenty-four-man crew," Rif said.

"And we can assume ten kidnappers. Magnusson will do his best from his end. Usually kidnappers wax poetic about the horrific pain they're going to inflict on the hostage, trying to intimidate the family. This guy was more sterile." She rubbed her palms on her 5.11 Tactical Stryke pants.

"He did promise to cut off Christos's body parts." Rif's eyes narrowed.

"The man had no passion or swagger. I'm not sure who we're dealing with here." She paced the spacious marble bathroom. "We need to board that supertanker." She tucked her hair behind her ear. "Papa would hate for any of his company's oil to cause an environmental disaster. When the BP spill happened in the Gulf of Mexico, he was furious. He might be an oil man, but he's also the son of a fisherman. He went on a tirade about how the oil's strong scent interfered with sea animals, causing the babies to be rejected and abandoned, leaving them to starve and eventually die. He instituted safety measures on his fleet before they were legislated, built double-hull tankers to protect against spills even though it cost him a lot of money and time to do so. The Mediterranean is his home. He would expect us to act on this and prevent a spill."

"Where's the *Damocles*?"

"Forty nautical miles off Kalamata. Get the team ready. Johansson and Brown should be arriving soon. Hakan had them report for duty the moment Papa was kidnapped."

"Johansson's shoulder is fully healed?" Rif asked.

"The man's superhuman. Blueprints of the tanker are on their way?" she said.

"Absolutely." He paused. "Even if Christos isn't aboard, water-proof containers, a deck drop—we're not dealing with amateurs here."

She dialed Hakan's number and put him on speakerphone. "The team's set?" she asked.

"Mobilized. They'll be in Athens in a couple of hours. The banker's preparing the ransom. I started liquidating funds last night."

"Let's re-hijack the *Damocles*."

Silence extended on the line for a long moment. "Thea, you sure you want to take this risk? If your father's on board, they could kill him before you find out where he is."

"Just paying the ransom doesn't guarantee anything. We also can't let the crew down. We'll go in dark."

"I'm concerned the kidnappers have an inside track some-how. They sent you Christos's watch, had a team attack you, and they anticipated you'd be at the Grande Bretagne. How did they know you were coming to Athens?"

"I wonder the same thing," she said.

"Maybe it's an inside job," Hakan said.

"Why not have Freddy do a thorough check on the entire team at Paris Industries as well as Quantum, see if anyone might be hiding something?"

"Already on it. I'll keep you posted. You sure about this plan?"

"Yes." It'd be a hell of a gamble, given that they didn't know for sure that Papa was on board, but she had to try.

"Thea's right," said Rif. "Information like the existence of the watch could be leaked, traded, or sold, and this could be a copycat or phantom kidnapper. Hell, the actual kidnapper could even have hired these men to act as a decoy while he transports Christos somewhere else. Taking the offensive is the only way to get answers."

"It's your call to make. I'll arrange for the sketch artist, so we can try to find the messenger boy. The team will arrive with full gear. Anything else you need, let me know." Hakan's tone was committed.

If all went well, they'd recover Papa and the funds, but when was the last time anything went according to plan? She signed off with Hakan.

Honor, reputation, dignity—they were Christos Paris's mantras. He even had a public relations firm on speed dial to manage his image. He wanted to be seen as the angel of world energy; Paris Industries, the clean, caring company that stood out from the others. He had also taken great pride in the company's reputation as a philanthropic giant, setting up grants, scholarships, and charities, all showcasing him as someone who gave back. No way would he want to cause harm to the environment or others.

Her gaze met Rif's. "Tell me I'm not making a huge mistake."

"I can't, but your father would be proud of you."

"A lot of good that'll do if I get him killed." She straightened her shoulders. "Okay, time to plan the mission."

Chapter Twenty

Blackness cloaked Thea's team as they torpedoed through the water in two modified cigarette boats, each harnessing over one thousand horsepower. Stealthy and seaworthy, the racers had deep-V hulls that sliced through the swells like hot knives through butter. The inky depths of the Mediterranean and the muffled engines masked their approach to the *Damocles*. The VLCC—very large crude carrier—rode low on the water, bloated with several cathedral-size tanks, and was slow-moving, which worked to Thea's team's advantage. Dressed all in black down to face paint, they blended into the night. She captained one cigarette, Rif the other.

She adjusted her earpiece, waiting for the pilot's command. The low-flying Cessna was about to drop ten million euros in unmarked bills onto the deck of the *Damocles* in large waterproof containers. Timing was key. The ransom drop offered the perfect distraction for her seven-man team to board the supertanker undetected.

All of Paris Industries' crews had been trained to deal with piracy, but supertankers were especially vulnerable. Mostly automated, the bulky, slow-moving vessels had small crews. A crash-stop maneuver, taking the ship from full speed to full reverse, required fourteen minutes and nearly two nautical miles. And international law prevented the tankers from carrying weapons, so the men on board were sitting ducks, the perfect prey.

But Thea's team was ready to help the *Damocles* eject its hijackers. Brown and Stewart were responsible for eliminating the kidnappers' ability to leak oil into the Mediterranean Sea—Brown had a background in engineering, a useful skill set for this type of operation. Rif and Jean-Luc were assigned to disable the kidnappers' helicopter, leaving the two cigarettes guarded by Neil. Thea and Johansson were tasked with finding her father, if he was even on board.

She double-checked her blood sugar levels on her smartphone. All good.

"Operation Drop Zone initiated," the Cessna pilot rasped in her earpiece. She accelerated the speedboat toward the *Damocles*, headed straight for the rudder. The ship's curved hull blocked the kidnappers from spotting them. Somali pirates had perfected the use of this natural blind spot for boarding vessels undetected.

As the boats approached the expansive stern, they slowed to match the tanker's speed. Johansson crawled up the cigarette's deck and attached a powerful magnet to the *Damocles*'s hull, tossing a rope to Brown to hook onto the speedboat. Jean-Luc completed the same maneuver for Rif's boat.

The rattle and hum of the approaching Cessna masked their sounds.

Almost time for the drop.

Johansson, an avid mountain climber, scaled the hull using specially designed suction cups, the kind used by art thieves. A few minutes later, he dropped two rope ladders for the others to use. Neil stayed with the boats while the rest of the team slipped over the transom. With the bridge positioned at the stern, they needed to stay dark.

Crouched low, Thea and Johansson quickly scouted the area for any sentries, sound-suppressed MP5s slung over their shoulders. Light glowed from the bridge, and a lone silhouette stood inside. As expected, the arriving ransom was occupying the kidnappers' attention.

The Cessna's buzzing intensified as the plane swooped in for the drop. The team used the distraction to spread out and execute their tasks.

She and Johansson moved to the stern stairwell. If Papa was on board, he'd probably be kept guarded in one of the cabins belowdecks.

They padded down the stairs with measured steps. Six Quantum team members, twenty-four dedicated crew, and likely ten hostiles. As in FATS—firearm training simulator—drills, they'd have to determine in seconds if the people they came across were friend or foe.

Pale yellow light from an overhead bulb cast a sickly glow in the narrow hallway. The group inched forward to the first room. Thea eased open the steel door. Empty. She signaled Johansson, and they crept down the hall.

A sound. Scratching. Moaning. Her father?

Footsteps clattered down the stairs. Her hand tightened on her silenced MP5. She and Johansson ducked into the first room, leaving the door cracked open an inch.

A man dressed in black fatigues strode down the hall, AK-47 in hand. He stopped, listened. Another soft moan. Mr. AK headed for the noise.

They had to neutralize him quickly. She nodded to Johansson.

Chapter Twenty-One

Rif and Jean-Luc crept along the deck toward the heliport. This operation had been designed on the fly because of the tight time line. Three teams executing three different missions simultaneously meant three opportunities for fuck-ups. But oddly, the riskier the situation, the calmer Rif became. And the upside was, they still hadn't been detected by the kidnappers.

Even so, the deck was a covert operator's nightmare. Open and expansive, it left very few places to hide as they moved toward the helipad. Large pipes spanned the length of the deck, sectioning off the starboard side. They squatted low, scanning the area before moving forward into the night.

Several loud thumps kick-started Rif's pulse. The waterproof containers holding the ransom landed on the unforgiving deck as the Cessna buzzed by. They had to move quickly. Once the kidnappers confirmed the funds were enclosed, they'd load the containers into an incoming boat or the helicopter and take off.

Two soft beeps sounded in his earpiece. Team two, Brown and Stewart, identifying themselves. He waited. Three more beeps. Excellent. They'd rigged the pipes so the kidnappers couldn't leak oil into the sea. A temporary fix, but at least they'd neutralized that threat.

One mission down, two to go. The timing was critical. He didn't want to cause any commotion before Thea and Johansson had thoroughly searched the tanker. Hard to say whether Christos would be on board. It would've been easy enough to transport him from the *Aphrodite* to the *Damocles* in a Bell 206, but the billionaire could also be secreted in a faraway country by now. The whiplash turnaround of the ransom demand left little room for negotiation or investigation. Rif had been involved in enough of these operations to know that the kidnappers' tactics were rare and concerning.

With their job done, Brown and Stewart would be joining the search for Christos. Time to disable the ship's helicopter. He inched forward. Two dark shadows paced beside the Bell 206. Guards. Rif signaled to Jean-Luc.

Chapter Twenty-Two

Down below, Thea cracked open the stateroom's door again so they could scan the passageway. A slight squeak from the hinges echoed in the eerie silence. The gunman turned, his AK-47 ready for action. Johansson fingered the trigger on his silenced MP5, firing three quick bullets into the man's torso. He collapsed in a heap.

They dragged the corpse into the empty room and closed the door. She grabbed the kidnapper's radio in case he received a transmission from the men on the bridge.

Another groan. They moved down the hall and positioned themselves on either side of the door.

She signaled to Johansson with her free hand. He grabbed the handle and turned. She entered first, MP5 raised. Her gaze landed on a bound and gagged man in uniform. Blood from a head wound dripped down his face.

Captain Magnusson. She fought off disappointment. Removing the captain's gag, she undid the ropes binding his hands and feet while Johansson shielded them from the doorway.

"Ms. Paris, what are you doing on board?" Magnusson asked.

"We're here to help." Her blackened face and hands must be disconcerting.

The captain wiped blood from his eyes. "After we spoke, they beat me and locked me in here."

"Ten men, right?"

"All armed to the gills with Kalashnikovs, machetes."

"Is my father on board?"

"He wasn't with them when they boarded."

Her gut twisted. "What language do they speak?"

"Spanish."

Weird. Even though over sixty percent of kidnaps took place in Latin America, the *Damocles* was currently off the coast of Greece—far, far away from the usual kidnapping hotbeds of Mexico, Colombia, and Venezuela.

"Do you know where they're holding the crew?"

"Sorry, no idea."

She grabbed a QuikClot from her tactical pouch and staunched the blood flowing from his head wound.

Footsteps sounded in the hallway. Another guard, probably checking on the first one who hadn't returned. They eased the door back open. Johansson fired off two shots, but the kidnapper had ducked around the corner, scrambling down the hallway.

"We're blown. Let's move."

The dead kidnapper's radio buzzed. Yelling in Spanish.

She pressed the code to let the team know they'd been exposed.

A faint hint of smoke wafted up her nose, setting off her internal alarm.

"Fire." Johansson protected them from the hallway.

"Let's get you out of here, Captain." She helped Magnusson stand. He was unsteady, but the determined look in his eyes comforted her. She used a water bottle from her pack to soak some gauze. "Here, breathe through this."

They hurried into the thirty-foot corridor. Smoke billowed at them from the right.

"This way," Johansson said.

They retraced their steps, headed for the exit door on the left, but loud footsteps pounded down the stairs straight for them. Shouts in Spanish. Definitely not team members. They were forced to retreat toward the smoke. A piercing mechanical wail flooded the hallway. The fire alarm. Shots slammed into the steel wall near them. They dove behind the corner. Johansson signaled for her to find egress while he crouched low and returned fire with his MP5.

Thick, toxic smoke entered her lungs. She coughed, her bronchioles in spasm. The three of them were trapped.

Chapter Twenty-Three

Rif held the garrote in his hands and stalked the first guard. Jean-Luc loomed behind the second one. They attacked simultaneously. Rif snapped the garrote around the kidnapper's neck and tightened his hold. The man struggled for air, twisting and turning, his fingers prying at the wire, desperate to escape. Seconds later, the guard slumped to the ground, Rif softening his landing to avoid any unnecessary noise. Jean-Luc's target was already incapacitated, sprawled near the helicopter's tail rotor.

While his partner scanned the deck for potential threats, Rif slipped inside the Bell 206. Working quickly, he accessed the battery and detached it. Next he removed the tail rotor pedals and breakers. Now the kidnappers couldn't use this bird to get off the tanker—but they might have another boat headed for the ship.

One beep sounded in his earpiece. Thea and Johansson. Another long beep. An endless beep. *Shit.* They needed help. He crept out of the helicopter with the battery and tail rotor pedals in hand, searching for somewhere to hide them. He spied a nearby cubby, lifted the cover, and slipped the parts into the empty space for safekeeping.

Scanning for threats, he analyzed the layout of the tanker. Thea and Johansson were searching the cabins below for Christos. The closest stairs were located near the stern. He signaled for Jean-Luc to follow, then headed in that direction.

A loud alarm howled. Smoke drifted out of the staircase. What was happening?

Chapter Twenty-Four

Thea ripped off her jacket, wrapped it around one hand, and smashed through the glass to access the fire extinguishers. Smoke burned her eyes and lungs. The acrid taste of ash filled her mouth. Large bundles of what looked like burning laundry were strewn about the hallway. The kidnappers knew they'd been boarded, and they were trying to smoke out the intruders . . . literally.

Shots slammed into the opposite corridor. She tossed one extinguisher to the captain and grabbed the second one for herself. Pulling the pin, she sprayed the flaming piles of fabric while Johansson fended off their attackers with his M5.

Air—she needed air. She placed a hand against the wall and choked in a breath. Only two piles still burned. She blasted more fire retardant onto the flames.

She heard a loud grunt. Visibility was poor, so she moved down the corridor, keeping a hand on one wall, until she reached Johansson. A shot had pierced his left shoulder.

"I'll take over." She propped him against the wall and tossed him a QuikClot to slow the flow of blood.

"Fuck, do I have a bull's-eye on my shoulders or what? At least it's the left one this time."

She fired down the hallway, nailing an approaching kidnapper, then moved behind the corner for cover. "Not sure how much longer we can ward them off." With smoke on one side and gunfire on the other, they were in serious trouble.

Chapter Twenty-Five

In normal conditions, Rif would have slowed the pace, sniper-crawling along the deck to avoid detection, but Thea and Johansson had sent out a distress signal. Smoke billowed in large plumes from the nearby stairwell. They had to move quickly.

He and Jean-Luc traversed the starboard deck, one covering the other, moving in a leapfrog pattern. The most hazardous moment lay ahead: crossing to the stairs. Way too much open space between the gunwales and the stairwell for his liking, especially now that the kidnappers knew they'd been boarded.

They reached the spot parallel to the stairwell. He considered his options. *Fuck it.* Thea needed him, so he'd have to break radio silence to figure out what was going on.

"Team Tango, where are you? Over."

Seconds stretched with no answer. Then the sound of live fire greeted him. "Deck C, starboard. Surrounded. Fire blocking us from aft. Over."

"Coming. Out."

Scanning the deck, he signaled to Jean-Luc. Rif would cover his teammate, then cross solo.

Jean-Luc sprinted across the open space. Out of the darkness, four black-clad kidnappers brandishing Kalashnikovs surrounded the older man. Rif considered firing, but even if he eliminated two or three of them, the fourth man would execute Jean-Luc.

Instead, he became invisible, moving deeper into the shadows while the kidnappers frog-marched Jean-Luc toward the bridge.

He followed, a predator stalking his prey. Thea would have to wait a little longer.

Chapter Twenty-Six

Thea fired shots down the smoke-filled corridor. She was almost out of ammo.

Several grunts and screams pierced the air.

Silence. She waited, fingers tightening around her MP5.

"Friendly fire." Brown's familiar voice echoed down the hall. She snuck a quick look. Brown and Stewart were striding toward them.

"About time, gentlemen. Do we have to handle all the dirty work?" She coughed, the smoke a corrosive presence in her lungs.

Brown surveyed Johansson's bleeding shoulder. "Come on, mate, if you don't want to change the baby's diapers, you just have to say so."

"Screw you, buddy. I'll be a better one-armed parent than you would ever be with two."

"Hey!" She pointed down the hall. "We need to get back on deck. Grab the captain, and let's find Rif and Jean-Luc."

They rushed down the hallway, desperate for fresh air. They stepped over two bodies. She helped Johansson up the stairs. His skin was ashen, eyes glassy, but he was moving under his own steam. Brown led the group, searching for hostiles. Stewart helped Captain Magnusson, who was unsteady on his feet.

They hurried to the stern, meeting up with Neil, who was guarding their boats. They left him and Stewart in charge of getting Johansson and the captain into the relative safety of the cigarettes.

She and Brown returned to a shadowed overhang near the bridge. Movement caught her eye. Four armed kidnappers surrounded Jean-Luc, and the group was headed straight for the bridge. No sign of Rif.

One of their own, captured. A ransom drop was a dangerous time during kidnappings. Emotions skyrocketed; the kidnappers became paranoid and trigger-happy. If anything went sideways during an operation, all hostages were at risk.

Her gut told her Papa wasn't on board. But if these pirates were in touch with whoever was guarding Christos, they could easily end his life in retribution for her counterattack.

They needed to re-hijack the tanker.

But what about Rif? He'd told her he was headed belowdecks. Was he injured, hiding somewhere—or dead? Her stomach twisted. He wouldn't let Jean-Luc get captured without a fight. She sent out the signal to meet back at the bridge and waited for a response. Nothing.

She tried again, her finger trembling on the button.

A confirmation beep sounded in her ear. Relief flooded her body. Rif was alive.

Crouched under the overhang, she used hand signals to communicate with Brown. He gave the okay sign and faded into the darkness, positioning himself to attack the bridge.

Seconds later, a large shadow morphed into a man. Rif touched her hand, and their eyes locked. He looked away first, but not before she read him. *Shame.* She knew the feeling well, but now wasn't the time.

She signaled her plan, and Rif suggested a good adjustment. Looking him right in the eye, she used signals to confirm he wouldn't change the plan without communicating with her first. He nodded. She rarely doubted his battle strategy; like a chess master, he calculated every step ahead. She'd need to keep an eye on him, though. He was in warrior mode, at his most dangerous, and they needed to capture one or more of the kidnappers alive.

They moved into position. She and Brown trained their MP5s on the guards while Rif crept closer to the bridge, masked by darkness. She pressed the signal button. One soft beep. Then they opened fire on the guards, dropping one. Rif charged the bridge, flashbang in hand. He tossed the stun grenade inside. A loud blast erupted, obliterating their vision for about five seconds, causing a temporary loss of hearing and balance.

Rif rushed the door; she and Brown followed. The three remaining kidnappers were stumbling around the bridge, disoriented. She pounced on the one nearest Jean-Luc. The man was shaking his head. Before his equilibrium returned, she'd flipped him over and used tactical zip ties to restrain his hands and feet.

Rif and Brown had shoved the two other men against the port wall. Jean-Luc's face was battered, his hair soaked with blood, but he half smiled. "Nice of you to drop by. This asshole"—he indicated the man Thea had disabled—"was about to take me on a private date."

She sliced through Jean-Luc's restraints with her Ka-Bar.

Rif helped him stand. "And it's been such a long time since you got any."

"Very funny—although I wouldn't mind a little alone time with him." Jean-Luc spit on the floor, a mixture of blood and saliva.

"I got it covered." Rif grabbed the man by the throat and lifted him to his feet. "You and I are going to have a talk."

"Sí, sí, está bien."

Thea spoke fluent Spanish, and so did Rif, but they wanted the pockmarked man at a disadvantage, off kilter, having to converse in English. Besides, if the kidnappers thought they didn't speak Spanish, they might give something away. They needed to figure out who was in charge: the pockmarked man, the swarthy guy with a goatee, or the one who was so skinny, his legs resembled pencils.

"Where's Christos Paris?" Rif loosened his hold on Pockmark's neck.

"We no have him."

"That's obvious. Where's he being held?"

The man furrowed his brow. "I never see him."

Definitely not the man she'd spoken to on the phone—his English wasn't good enough. She gave Rif a small nod, letting him know the guy's face read that he was being honest.

"Where's the crew?"

"In bilge."

Brown stepped forward. "We stumbled on them while locking down the oil pipes but left them inside for their own safety."

"Take Jean-Luc and vet the crew members before releasing them. Check if any of them have been behaving suspiciously— there might be an inside man. If no one seems obvious, find out who was on watch when they were boarded."

Brown and Jean-Luc left the bridge. Thea had her MP5 trained on the three kidnappers.

"Let's try again. Where's Christos Paris?" She kicked Swarthy with one booted foot.

"*No lo sé.*" We don't know.

They didn't have the luxury of a long interrogation. "On your feet." She opened the door and indicated that the men exit the bridge. They shuffled forward, and she followed.

When they reached the chopper, Rif slipped his hand into a nearby cubby and extracted some helicopter parts. "Watch them for a minute." He entered the Bell, replaced the parts, and two minutes later, the blades whirred to life.

"Last chance to talk."

The men remained silent. Fine, if that was the way they wanted to play it.

"Get in."

The three pirates trudged to the chopper's door. She held them at gunpoint.

"Blindfold them. Somalia Six," Rif said.

She nodded, remembering the mission. She removed three bandannas from the pockets of her combat pants, tied them tightly around the men's eyes, nudged the kidnappers inside, then got in herself.

Rif climbed into the pilot's seat. Seconds later, the Bell lifted off from the tanker. He flew up and down, side to side, disorienting the men, then leveled out.

"Where's Christos Paris?" she asked the skinny one.

He remained silent.

She grabbed him by the collar and moved him near the door.

"Last chance."

Nothing.

She pushed him out of the helicopter, his screams quickly overpowered by the rotor wash.

Sweat rolled down Swarthy's forehead.

"You're next. Talk now or enjoy your final free fall."

Swarthy blanched, and his Adam's apple rose and fell in quick succession. "*Mierda!* I swear, we do not know about the oil man. We are FARC."

Bingo. She recognized his voice, the man on the phone. But FARC? The Revolutionary Armed Forces of Colombia was a Marxist-Leninist guerrilla group that specialized in kidnappings, including the infamous Hargrove case. But how did they get involved in this mess?

"Where did you get the watch?" she asked.

"I did not see the watch. They told us to say we sent it for proof of life."

"Who hired you?"

"Our leader Jorge sent us. We take over the ship, get the money. That is all."

"I don't believe you." She pushed him toward the door. His head and shoulders hung outside the copter.

"I swear, I swear."

Swarthy had no resistance left. And he didn't know anything. Chances were these idiots had never laid eyes on Papa. This whole ransom drop might have been a setup to distract them from the real kidnappers.

She gave Rif the okay signal, and he set the Bell back down on the helipad.

She ripped off the men's blindfolds. Their faces were chalky, but when they saw Skinny on the deck, pants soiled, maybe suffering a broken bone or two but very much alive, hatred filled their eyes. The copter had hovered twenty feet above the tanker, high enough for effect without much threat of death. Thea had wanted to keep them alive. Hakan would arrange for a full and possibly more effective debriefing they didn't have time for here. And her boss would pick up the ten million ransom and keep it handy in case they had sudden need of a large sum of cash.

She grabbed her radio and pressed the talk button.

"Brown, can you bring the crew up to the bridge?"

"Roger, right away."

"Get anything out of them?"

"Nothing substantive."

They'd take the crew in for further questioning as well. They'd probably get no more information, but she had to make sure.

The ship was a dead end.

Chapter Twenty-Seven

Frustration weighed down Thea's thoughts. Rif drove in silence back to the Grande Bretagne. They'd just wasted precious time and resources tracking down what looked like a feint by the kidnappers or a copycat who had inside knowledge and wanted to make a quick ten million euros.

Hakan had set up a hotline that had been flooded with reports of sightings, mostly from nuts looking for their fifteen minutes of fame. These were the shenanigans she'd hoped to avoid by keeping her father's abduction under wraps. Every year, more than forty thousand people were kidnapped across the globe, and the media rarely helped bring any of them home.

"I'd like to know who leaked Papa's kidnapping." She rubbed her eyes, trying to refocus.

"What about Helena? She might've thought the press could help."

"Possibly, but she told me she'd check in before making any moves. Hakan said a Greek radio show has some hack on saying Christos should have implanted a radio-frequency ID device in his body. Ridiculous. Papa would never surrender his privacy.

Let's face it, he tracks everything and everyone, but no one is allowed to track him." She glanced over at Rif, his face impassive as he drove. "Sorry, I'm ranting."

"I understand. The press doesn't care about a man's safety or the truth—they just want dirty laundry." He tightened his grip on the steering wheel.

She could feel his anguish. "Why are you so loyal to my father?"

"He's my godfather."

"It's more than that."

He hesitated for a moment, perhaps deciding if he should share. "Christos has never tried to change who I am."

"Unlike Hakan?"

"Father and son—rarely an easy relationship. Our worldviews are different."

"You should hear Hakan talk about you when you're not around—trust me, he's proud. So is your mom."

"Record it for me sometime." His lips quirked into a half-hearted smile.

"How's it going with the loving couple these days?" Rif's parents had divorced fifteen years earlier because Hakan traveled so much, but after two years apart, they'd started dating each other again. A heartwarming story.

"There's talk of them getting remarried, if you can believe it. Baba asked me to be his best man if they do."

"Lovely. You're lucky to be close to both our fathers. I feel for Nikos. Papa tears him down every chance he gets."

"Your brother is not the angel you'd like to think he is."

"What's your problem with Nikos—he's never done anything to you, has he?" She'd asked Rif more than once why he disliked her brother, but she'd never gotten the truth out of him.

Rif shifted into third gear on the final stretch to the hotel. "When it comes to Nikos, you lose all perspective. People talk about rose-colored glasses, but you have guilt-colored ones. It's not your fault he was kidnapped."

Everyone always said that, but the reality was much more complicated. "I often wonder how things would have turned out if I'd been the one kidnapped." For instance, it horrified her that she'd grown up with an overwhelming relief that she hadn't been the one taken.

"Hard to say. Given your mettle, you may have weathered it better than your brother."

They arrived at the front entrance of the Grande Bretagne. Rif handed the car keys to the parking valet, and they entered the vast marble-clad foyer. The hotel had breathtaking views of the famed Acropolis and Parthenon, the regal Constitution Square, the parliament buildings, the lush Lycabettus Hill, and the original Olympic stadium. History-steeped Athens felt like a second home to Thea, but right now her heart ached for her father.

Inside the hotel, a striking couple hurried toward them. She recognized the barrel-chested policeman who was helping Hakan with the forensics on the yacht, but she'd never seen the woman before. Rif stepped in front of her.

The man reached around him to shake her hand. "Ms. Paris, Maximillian Heros. I haven't seen you since that fund-raiser your father sponsored in Milan."

She clasped Max's hand. She remembered that evening: Maximillian Heros had worn a gold Rolex, a designer tux, and won the live auction for a limited-edition Ferrari.

"Olives, right?" Thea said, referring to his family's business. Papa had dinner with Max occasionally, two wealthy men sharing their fondness for Scotch and cigars.

"I'm also an inspector general with the Hellenic Police. This is Gabrielle Farrah from the Hostage Recovery Fusion Cell in Washington, DC."

The woman had large brown eyes and a strong jawline. HRFC. They did good work, but they had to paint inside the lines in a way that independent contractors, like QIS, didn't.

Thea indicated Rif. "This is my colleague Rifat Asker." She gave Gabrielle a firm handshake. "We're running late, so I hope you'll excuse us."

"Ms. Paris, can you give us a few minutes to discuss your father's kidnapping? All of Greece is in an uproar about his abduction, and we just saw a news report about you saving the compromised oil tanker." Max's dark eyes lingered on her face.

Her skin reddened. *Dammit, another leak. Could it actually be someone on their team?* "We appreciate your interest, but Quantum is handling the kidnapping. Too many cooks, and all that. I'm sure you understand." She turned to leave.

Gabrielle gently touched her shoulder. "I want you to know I'm here to help. And because you're in the business, I trust your discretion, which is why I'm sharing the following information. There's a SEAL team executing an extraction mission tonight somewhere in the Middle East. We have intel that there's a prominent American being held in the camp."

"What country? What makes you think it might be my father?"

"I'm sorry, I can't tell you more. But the moment I hear an update, you'll be the first to know."

Skepticism overrode hope. "Thanks. Why no negotiation? There are huge risks in extractions."

Gabrielle shook her head. "Classified, sorry. I used to be CIA stationed in the Middle East, and all I can tell you is that the decision for the mission is a well-reasoned one. I can't imagine the hell you're going through, but like I said, I'm here to help. Here's my card."

Thea glanced at it, then dug into her purse and handed the HRFC agent a card with her private cell number on it. It was probably too much to hope that the SEALs would rescue Papa, but even if they didn't—or if the captive they found wasn't Papa—Gabrielle's access to resources could still help bring her father home.

She would need to tread carefully. As courteous as these two law enforcement agents were, they also clearly had their own agendas. Her father's kidnapping would naturally be of great interest to both Greek and American authorities because of his financial support and connection to oil. The last thing Papa would want was to be caught up in a political maelstrom connected to his abduction.

The front doors opened, and a burst of sunshine blinded her around the contours of a familiar silhouette striding toward them. She blinked. *Nikos.*

Chapter Twenty-Eight

Nikos recognized the brunette standing next to Thea immediately. Gabrielle Farrah, his very own stalker. The Hostage Recovery Fusion Cell agent had recently been interviewed on CNN about the upswing in kidnapped CEOs. She'd mentioned her suspicion about Ares financing many of the abductions. Well, when life hands you lemons, make lemonade—unless he could figure out a way to squeeze lemon juice into this relentless woman's eyes.

In a few long strides, he joined his sister, who must've just returned from the sideshow at the supertanker. He was impressed by the way her team had neutralized Jorge's men. It made him optimistic about the future—if brother and sister worked together, they'd be unstoppable.

The diversion had given him time to head to Corfu, where he'd discovered that the plane transporting his father had been flown to Kanzi, landing on an abandoned airstrip on the southeast coast, near Zimbabwe. And that was where he was headed in about an hour. First he'd wanted to check in with his sister to see if the real kidnapper had made any further contact.

"This is my brother, Nikos Paris." Thea gestured to the brunette and her well-dressed companion. "You probably remember Inspector General Maximillian Heros from Papa's charity board. And this is Gabrielle Farrah, from the Hostage Recovery Fusion Cell."

Nikos leaned close and held Gabrielle's hand longer than necessary. "Pleasure to meet you."

He noticed a slight tightening around Max's mouth. *So, it was like that.* She did look like she'd be a tiger in bed.

He shook Max's hand, giving it a solid squeeze. The Greek inspector returned the pressure and then some. Nikos ignored Rif. "Any news about Papa?" he asked his sister.

"We were just getting to that," Thea said.

Gabrielle stepped closer. "The HRFC can offer your family intel, support, access to government databases."

"It's a multi-agency group, right?" Thea asked.

"Absolutely, which gives us the ability to compile information from many sources. We're following several leads, monitoring online chatter. Have you received a ransom demand?" Gabrielle's penetrating eyes studied Thea's face.

"No ransom."

No mention of the Latin texts. His sister's determined expression told him that Ms. Hostage Rescue wouldn't be getting her full cooperation. *Brava.*

"Well, keep me posted if you do receive any demands. We have access to resources that could help bring your father home."

"Please skip the sympathy. I don't mean to be rude, but I do this for a living." Thea's voice held a steely edge.

He was enjoying this—two strong-willed women trying to find out what the other knew. His stalker was wily and sharp, but his raven-haired sister wasn't known as Liberata for nothing.

"We respect your intimate knowledge of this industry, and we really do want to help. We've located the plane used to transport Christos out of the country. Max used his influence, and we discovered an interesting connection." Ms. Hostage Rescue let the words hang in the air.

"Don't keep us in suspense," Nikos said, knowing Konstantin had come through.

"Airports are meticulous about maintaining accurate records of flight plans. One plane at a nearby airport didn't have one. The tail number of the plane links back to a shell corporation that serves as a front for an international arms dealer called Ares. I'm sure you know he has a history of abducting prominent CEOs."

"He's a legend in Africa, supplying dissidents with arms to fight repressive regimes." Rif stepped closer to Thea.

"If the money's right, he'll sell arms to *anyone*," Gabrielle corrected.

Nikos bristled. *Not true.*

"And why would Ares want to kidnap my father?" he asked. Thea was no fool. He had to be careful.

"His agenda isn't clear yet, but he's rumored to be the puppeteer working the strings of the Kanzi government," Gabrielle said.

"Is your real concern my father, or is this more about making sure the Kanzi oil rights don't fall into the wrong hands?" Thea asked.

A large group of tourists entered the hotel, buzzing with excitement.

"Christos Paris is a prominent American citizen who has been kidnapped abroad. The HRFC wants to help bring him home." Gabrielle raised her voice slightly to be heard over the crowd. "Can you please join us in my suite so we can compare notes?"

"I need to make an important call. In twenty minutes?" His sister gave Ms. HRFC a tight smile. Thea worked best alone, a Paris family trait.

Nikos was tempted to invite Gabrielle for a drink later to make Max squirm, but he didn't have time for dalliances today.

"Room 604. Thanks for making the time. I'll order some food for us, as I'm sure you haven't had time to eat." Gabrielle headed for the elevator bank.

Max Heros grabbed Thea's hand and squeezed. "Your father is a memorable man and a friend. I will do everything in my power to bring him home. You have my word."

She gave the policeman a wary smile, like Aegis when he was trying to decide if he liked someone. Little Thea, never one to trust—except when it came to her brother. The irony didn't escape Nikos, but he appreciated her loyalty.

Chapter Twenty-Nine

Thea stood next to Rif in the lobby of the hotel, the two of them checking e-mail for any fresh leads. As she scanned her phone for updates, she processed the theory of Ares being involved in Papa's kidnapping. All kinds of stories floated around about the elusive arms dealer, an ominous shadow who hovered under the radar. Some factions looked at him as a hero, a modern-day Robin Hood, while others saw him as the devil personified. He was brilliant, wealthy, and had executed several high-profile kidnappings. And he was based out of Africa. A possible link to Ares was one more sign that the answers to Papa's kidnapping rested in that part of the world.

Max Heros and Gabrielle Farrah had taken the elevator upstairs, and Nikos had begged off, saying he needed to run an errand. She couldn't imagine the emotions her brother must be feeling, with accounts of his own kidnapping resurfacing in all the papers. One kidnapping in a family was newsworthy; two created a media frenzy. The press was eager to establish a connection between the events, even though twenty years separated them.

She turned to Rif. "What do you think about this HRFC operation in the Middle East?"

"When a man as influential as Christos is taken, the kidnapper needs to have extensive resources and connections. Could his abduction have to do with terrorists? Sure. There could be a link through the oil business to an OPEC nation, they could be fundraising for themselves, or maybe they're planning on making a political statement."

"But why not issue demands? It doesn't make sense to remain silent."

"ISIS, al-Qaeda—they don't always do the expected. Remember Peter Kassig's case? They sent his family an e-mail saying Peter was their guest. The only predictable thing about terror groups is that they're unpredictable."

Rif was being kind, not mentioning anything about political prisoners and orange jumpsuits. Her father would never be recorded denouncing the West. He'd die first.

She scanned the lobby, grateful for the soldier's presence. She had to admit she felt safer with him around. Her father's disappearance had left her distracted.

She pressed speed-dial 4 and spoke to Papa's chief pilot. "Please prepare the jet, destination Kanzi International Airport. I'll be there shortly." She hit the end button.

"What about the appointment with your new best friend?"

"I'll deal with her if and when she follows us to Africa. The jet will be ready in an hour."

"Guess there's an upside to being a Paris." Rif's gaze drifted over her face.

"Beats my usual ride." She spent more time in bare-bones former military planes than she did on her father's luxurious Gulfstream. Still, given that every hour counted, she was grateful for convenient transport.

"Let's—" Her phone rang. Helena. She held up a hand. "You okay?"

Her father's wife was breathless, agitated. "I know who did it."

"Did what?"

"Kidnapped your father."

Cold sweat dotted Thea's forehead. "Who?"

"I found Christos's Moleskine. You're at the hotel, right? I'll be there in two minutes. My limo is almost there. Meet me out front."

"Helena, wait—"

Her stepmother broke the connection before Thea could press for more information.

"She knows something?" Rif asked.

"So she says. Her limo's close. Let's find out what she's all worked up about." She strode toward the door. Rif caught up to her with his long strides.

"Be careful. This could be a trap."

"Maybe. But I'm not letting her out of my sight until I examine the evidence." She held the front door for Rif, knowing he'd want to scout the entrance area.

She lifted a hand, protecting her eyes from the setting sun dead ahead on the horizon, waiting for Helena to arrive.

"What'd she say, exactly?" Rif asked.

"That she found Papa's Moleskine and knows who took him. She sounded agitated, and she's normally even-keeled."

"Think this is for real?"

"We'll find out soon enough."

A black Hummer limo cruised toward Constitution Square. Undoubtedly Helena. She didn't have a license, so she always had a driver. Papa found it endearing.

Were they finally catching a break?

The limo stopped at the red light, Thea's gaze glued to its tinted windows. The light changed, and the vehicle started its sweeping turn toward the hotel.

She had started down the steps to meet the vehicle at the curb, when a concussive blast rocketed her backward. Every vertebra in her back screamed from the impact as she slammed against the stairs behind her. Rif dove on top of her, covering her body with his as white-hot heat surrounded them. Her breath escaped in short gasps. Pieces of the limo smashed into the façade of the hotel and rained to the ground around them. Screams filled the air, but they sounded far away. A doorman who'd been standing at the curb lay in a pool of blood, his empty eyes staring at the sky.

"You hurt?" Rif knelt beside her.

"Just dizzy." The ringing in her ears made it almost impossible to hear, even though she could see that Rif was shouting.

She rolled onto her side and sat up. Disoriented, she tried to shake off the aftereffects of the blast. Soot covered her face and was tangled in her eyelashes. The limo was a flaming black skeleton, scorched in places down to the frame. No way could Helena or the driver—or the Moleskine—have survived the blast.

Sadness filled Thea's heart. Her stepmother had been kind, the best thing that had happened to her father in a long time.

And now Helena's knowledge about the kidnapping had died along with her.

Sirens sounded in the distance, their penetrating wail competing with the hotel security guards' shouts.

Thea stood, regaining her equilibrium.

Furtive movement on a side street caught her attention. A charcoal Audi S8 inched forward, perpendicular to where they stood. At first she couldn't see the occupant because of the glaring sun. Then the car moved. She stared at the driver, who was holding a cell phone. No, it couldn't be. . . .

It was.

She pointed to the Audi.

"Henri . . . Papa's chef. It's him!"

Chapter Thirty

The loud explosion outside the hotel shook the windows in Gabrielle Farrah's room, reminding her of when she was stationed in Gaza. Without knocking, she yanked open the door to Max's adjoining suite. He'd insisted on treating her to a luxurious room, provided it was connected to his. It sure beat any accommodations she could have afforded on the government's dime—as long as she could lock the door from her side.

Max stood at the window, staring down at the street.

"What the hell was that?" She joined him, ice water running through her veins.

"Looks like a limo exploded." Sweat beaded his forehead.

Max had confided in her that his half sister, Laila, had been in a car accident, a horrible wreck that had burned her beyond recognition. This explosion probably brought back memories best kept buried.

"A white one?" She flashed on the Asian woman from Ares's plane.

"Black stretch Hummer—not much of it left, but I recognize the shape of the grille." His voice had a raw edge.

She stared at the smoldering remains blocking the street below, smoke billowing from the wreckage in large plumes.

A couple who had been sprawled on the stairs stumbled to their feet. "There's Thea Paris and her colleague!" Had someone tried to kill Christos's daughter?

Sudden movement caught her attention. Thea pointed down the street, then hopped onto a motorcycle with Rifat Asker behind her, the thin tires leaving a mark on the pavement as she peeled off. What had she seen? The bomber?

Tension settled in Max's jaw. "Let's go."

They hurried down the stairs, forgoing the elevator, rushing through the chaos in the lobby. Outside, the stench of burning flesh hung in the air. Gabrielle covered her mouth and nose with her scarf. Sirens wailed, lights flashed, and people cried. Police were already cordoning off the area with crime-scene tape. Paramedics scrambled to tend to the injured. Firefighters tamed the flames of the wreckage.

Max flashed his credentials at the lead detective. They spoke in Greek for a few minutes while Gabrielle scanned the hollowed-out limo. Whoever had placed the bomb in the vehicle wanted to make sure the occupants were *very* well done. This was no warning to them.

Max returned to her side, his eyes weary. "Helena Paris, Christos's wife."

Gabrielle raised an eyebrow. "The kidnapper wanted her out of the way?"

"Or perhaps it was a bomb meant for Thea. Either way, this is a nightmare."

Gabrielle's beeping cell interrupted the silence. She read the text. "Quan Xi-Ping."

"Who?"

"The woman in the white limo. She's staying at the King George Palace, right next door. Since Thea's gone, let's pay our neighbor a visit."

"Give me a moment." Max spoke to the lead detective in Greek again before rejoining her. "He will send me the incident report later this afternoon. Now for the butterfly."

Moments later, they stepped into the opulent lobby of the King George Palace. Chandeliers glistened in the expansive foyer, the marble floors sleek and modern, fresh gardenias perfuming the air. Max spoke to the front desk manager at the carved wooden counter, radiating intensity.

He translated for her. "Our butterfly fluttered away immediately after the explosion. Spooked or involved, it's impossible to tell."

"Feels like we're always one step behind."

He touched her arm. "Frustrating, but there is one upside to this whole situation. I get to see more of you."

One night only. And they'd had theirs.

Chapter Thirty-One

Thea cranked the throttle of the stolen BMW, using the motor-cycle's speed and agility to chase Henri's S8. She'd been exploring the streets of Athens since she was a kid; every street and lane was imprinted on her brain. The wind blasted her face, bringing tears to her eyes. Rif's arms tightened around her as she cornered hard.

Henri hammered the accelerator. The Audi rocketed forward, crashing into vendors' displays along the narrow street. T-shirts, knickknacks, and fruit spilled onto the pavement. She navigated the BMW around and occasionally through obstacles, leaning to maneuver the motorcycle. Rif followed her lead, and they moved as one.

The S8 screamed around a corner, narrowly missing a garbage truck trundling down the street. The truck's brakes squealed. Only a narrow gap remained open. Might be enough room for them to pass. Only one way to find out. She decelerated and threaded the opening, her right arm grazing the side of the truck.

She searched for the S8. As she'd hoped, Henri had made the mistake of turning right. The Audi hurtled toward a dead end and skidded to a stop. Thea hit the brakes, and she and Rif jumped off the bike, sprinting for the cover of a Dumpster.

The Audi's engine revved loudly.

She expected the car to reverse toward them. Instead, Henri raced the S8 to the far end of the alley, leapt out, knelt behind the car, and began firing at them. Bullets ricocheted off the Dumpster. Peeking out after a short silence, Thea caught a flash of movement and saw Henri speed off on foot down the narrow alleyway.

"Come on." Rif sprinted by her, his long legs covering serious ground. They turned a corner. Henri fired a few shots, but they merely peppered the walls of the shops along the lane. The crowd fractured, tourists and locals running for cover.

The entrance to the Acropolis lay straight ahead. Henri had no choice but to enter. He plowed through the queue and sprinted past the ticket collector. The security guard on duty tried to grab him, but Henri fired a head shot, killing him instantly. The crowd bolted from the commotion, people screaming. Pandemonium reigned. Even the stray cats and dogs that normally lingered around the Acropolis scurried away.

Rif and Thea followed his path up the hill, struggling to navigate the teeming crowds leaving the popular tourist attraction. Henri was surprisingly agile for a muscular man, but then, he'd been a French Foreign Legionnaire, expertly trained in combat.

Thea's breath burned in her chest, but she increased her pace and stayed focused on the chef's bald head. Rif was a few steps ahead of her. Training on the Santorini stairs seemed easy compared with this insanity. She wished Aegis was here to run ahead and bring the bastard down.

The mass of people slowed Henri's progress. She and Rif closed the distance to fifty feet.

"Go right, and I'll cover left," Rif said.

"Got it." The Acropolis was a large, flat plateau on a rocky outcropping hosting several ancient structures. By splitting up, they could cut off Henri's escape routes.

The stones were slippery and uneven, dangerous as a running surface. Thea stumbled. Her right ankle twisted, and sharp pain shot through her lower leg. She stabilized herself, grateful for her rubber-soled shoes, and continued running.

Henri knocked over two elderly Japanese tourists snapping photos. He turned and fired at Thea.

But nothing happened.

He'd emptied the magazine in his gun.

Henri tore through the Parthenon, then headed directly east. They were close to cornering him. Rif angled in to help. Thea's lungs were now on fire, but she kept her legs pumping.

The chef sprinted toward the eastern point of the plateau, where a flagpole had been planted beside the cliff. A Greek flag fluttered in the breeze. Rif trapped Henri from the north, Thea from the southwest, no escape route left.

Henri reached the flagpole and turned to confront Thea.

His face was blotchy; sweat dripped down his forehead. She was thirty feet away. Almost there.

Resolve flashed in Henri's eyes. He crossed himself, looked toward the sky, hopped the fence, and hurled himself off the cliff.

Thea's stomach plummeted as she reached the edge.

No, no, no.

She collided with the fence. Looking down, she ignored the Plaka—the old city—the ruins of the giant Temple of Olympian Zeus, and the Olympic stadium nestled in a pine-covered hill. Her gaze zoomed in on Henri's body on the rocks below, his neck and limbs twisted in death.

Tourists gathered near the fence. Rif joined Thea, taking in Henri's lifeless form.

"Fuck. Let's get out of here before the police arrive." He placed a warm hand on her shoulder.

She stumbled away from the cliff, a stupid history lesson from school in her mind. When the Germans had occupied Athens in the Second World War, the Evzone—a member of the Greek infantry—who guarded the Acropolis's Greek flag was ordered by the Nazis to take it down. The guard calmly did so, then wrapped himself in the flag and jumped off the cliff to his death.

She and Rif headed for the exit, trying to blend into the crowd, avoiding the security guards swarming the site. "Who merits such loyalty that Henri would rather die than risk revealing who hired him?"

"Or maybe he feared someone more than death."

"More questions. We need answers."

Her shirt was soaked with sweat, her skin coated with dust, her spirits dampened.

"Every lead is a dead end. *Actually* dead." The crew of the *Aphrodite* had been executed, the old woman murdered, Helena blown up, the oil tanker hijacked, and now Papa's chef, who had betrayed him, had died to hide the truth.

The body count would escalate until they figured out who had kidnapped her father. She needed to step back, sift through the information. Somewhere in this mess rested the answer.

Chapter Thirty-Two

Thea perched on a stool in the Hotel Grande Bretagne bar, sandwiched between Paris Industries COO Ahmed Khali and CFO Peter Kennedy. The large floor-to-ceiling windows showcased the spectacular Acropolis, but the view was ruined for her after Henri's suicide.

She nursed a glass of white wine. A single thread could unravel this blanket of murder and kidnapping—she just had to pull the right one. And that was why she'd asked for this meeting.

Every lead thus far had turned into a dead end. But Kanzi consistently resurfaced, so she planned to go there as soon as she finished here. Despite the news about her father's kidnapping breaking, the negotiations over the Kanzi oil rights had not been canceled after all. She would attend the negotiations in neighboring Zimbabwe to watch the power players—including these two men—to see if something or someone felt off.

Ahmed lifted a club soda to his lips and sipped. "Peter filled me in on the K-and-R insurance. Anything you need, just ask. We can easily liquidate more cash."

"Thank you. I wish it were that simple."

"Still no demands from the real kidnapper?" Peter downed the remnants of his second Scotch.

"No. Any idea who could be behind this?" She studied the executives as they struggled to respond to the blunt question. Between the two of them, she'd bet on Peter being implicated, because of his ambition. Still, she wasn't sure what lurked behind Ahmed's well-polished veneer.

"The Chinese or maybe the Russians could be involved. Both would benefit if they sent Paris Industries into a tailspin." Peter waved to the bartender and pointed to his empty glass.

"I'd look at the Kanzi military and political party officials. Fifteen years working in Africa showed me the corruption and greed inherent in the political system in Kanzi, from the national government on down." Ahmed's voice had a hitch to it, as if he was tamping down anger.

Thea toyed with the stem of her wineglass. "When we lived in Kanzi, tribal infighting played a prominent role in politics. Maybe this is about an internal power struggle?"

"You could be right. Can't ignore the timing," Ahmed said. "The locals are angry about the potential loss of jobs."

Peter turned to her. "Ahmed wants to import our entire labor force, but we can't do that. We need to train the Kanzi people, as Christos insisted we do. Otherwise, our bottom line, too, will be adversely affected."

"I'm the one who has to get the job done. You just want to cut costs," Ahmed said.

Turmoil in the C-suite. It could mean something, or it could just be business as usual.

The bartender appeared with Peter's refill.

"Let's worry about the details once we win this deal. The Chinese will be tough to beat. One of our main advantages is that Paris Industries is a family business. Christos is personally invested in the country's welfare. Of course, with him absent, it'll be difficult to use that angle now." Peter's hand trembled on his glass, his face puffy.

The opening she'd been looking for. "My father always believed that family was key to his relationships in Kanzi. Is there some way I could help?"

Peter wrinkled his nose, remaining silent.

Ahmed straightened his tie. "Would you consider making a short speech during our opening? Our communications people could help you write it."

Perfect. "I'll do anything to help make this deal happen in my father's absence. Count me in." It would give her a front-row seat to the action with only a brief detour from the search.

"Excellent." Ahmed glanced down at his watch. "Would you like a ride on the company jet? It's all prepped, and I'd like to arrive as early as possible. Wheels up in half an hour."

"I have to finish a few things first. I'll take my father's personal jet."

Peter finished his drink in one quick swallow. "Actually, any chance I could fly with you, Thea? I have some errands to run, so I could use the extra time in Athens."

"Sure, we have room. Let's meet in the lobby in three hours." She was happy to keep him close.

"See you both in Kanzi," Ahmed said.

They all stood, Peter quite wobbly. His eyes were glassy, and she wasn't sure it was just the alcohol. He didn't look well.

She texted the undercover security operative she'd stationed in the lobby. He'd tail Peter so she could find out exactly what the CFO was up to.

Chapter Thirty-Three

Thea sank into the cream leather couch on her father's Gulf-stream 5. Her body ached, her head throbbed, and her stomach growled. The last couple of days had taken their toll.

Brianna, the flight attendant, brought them sandwiches from the galley. Thea surreptitiously checked her levels, then ate a turkey and provolone on rye to keep her blood sugar levels stable. She reached for a sugar-free mint from her 5.11 Tactical SINK—survival insurance nightmare kit—which had everything *but* the kitchen sink in it. With all the international travel she did, often at a moment's notice, she never knew what equipment she might need. The kit also held medical supplies, everything from test strips to lancing devices.

Diabetes meant planning ahead, counting carbs, and keeping a close eye on her blood sugar. She'd been diagnosed at age ten, but her father hadn't babied her. He'd wanted her to take the illness seriously, be proficient in her own care. She'd practiced injecting an orange with a syringe over and over before she'd been ready to poke herself. Now needles were part of her life and didn't bother

her at all. She was more antsy about flying—not exactly her favorite activity, undoubtedly because she had no control.

To distract herself, she mulled over the intel Rif had shared with her before the flight. He'd been to Kanzi countless times over the years. In fact, he kept in contact with several former Special Forces friends working in Africa, so he had access to current security reports.

Since he took office three years ago, Prime Minister Kimweri had been filling the administration with his own family members. Nepotism was typical in African countries, where one's tribe and one's party were often closely aligned. General Ita Jemwa wasn't related to the prime minister but was reputed to be influential in the government. A steady supply of weapons from the arms dealer Ares reinforced the general's strength, in the desert and in the halls of power. The aging soldier might be looking for an opportunity to usurp Kimweri's authority.

Thea didn't want Kanzi to be yet another sad example of an impoverished African country depleted of its natural resources for the benefit of a wealthy minority while most of its residents remained destitute. Her father had done incredible work in certain regions of Kanzi, and if he won the contract, he had plans to build more schools, hospitals, and water filtration plants as part of the deal.

Peter Kennedy was currently knee-deep in oil negotiations documents. Her security operative had reported that, after leaving the lobby of the Grande Bretagne, the CFO had entered a large building housing various businesses, including accounting firms and medical offices. The operative hadn't been able to follow him inside without being made, so they didn't know his ultimate destination. She forwarded the report to Hakan in London. He and Freddy could investigate any connections between Peter and the tenant companies.

She riffled through her messenger bag for her computer, and a loose sheaf of unfamiliar, yellowed papers within caught her eye. The skin on the back of her neck prickled. Someone must have slipped them into her bag. But who?

She pulled them out and started reading.

Dr. Alexander Goldberg
July 4, 9:00 a.m.

INSTRUCTIONS

All clinical notes and records related to the patient Nikos Paris, including diagnosis and treatment, are to be released ONLY to the patient's father, Christos Paris. Hard copy only, no electronic release or mailed communications.

SUBJECTIVE

Christos Paris indicates that he had "always spoiled" his only son, Nikos, fulfilling his every wish and desire, up until the time of the boy's kidnapping. Nikos had grown to expect that he would be given everything he wanted and was accustomed to immediate gratification. Of particular note is the death of his mother in a sailing accident when Nikos was ten.

Nikos was kidnapped from his home in Kanzi, Africa, at age twelve. When he was returned after nine months in captivity, the father indicates that his son was moody, alternating between periods when he became withdrawn and uncommunicative and periods of uncontrolled temper outbursts, having little ability to enjoy many activities that would be normal for a boy his age. Nikos still had the expectation that his father and others should cater to his needs and desires with no exceptions. His moods are unstable, so Mr. Paris has a nanny watching over the children at all times. A new family dog seems to be helping Nikos adjust.

OBJECTIVE

Nikos is a well-groomed, intelligent boy who appears older than his stated age, in part due to his above-average height. He has no significant medical or health issues and no reported symptoms of pain, discomfort, or physical distress.

The patient's father was present for the entire intake interview. The father was also interviewed separately. The initial therapeutic contact occurred approximately two weeks after Nikos returned home from captivity and continued for several months. At first the patient did not disclose any pertinent details of his time in captivity, having a difficult time voicing his experience. It was only after additional sessions, the establishment of rapport, and with encouragement to write his story in his own words that he shared an account of those nine months of captivity. Nikos presented the usual, predictable resistance of a trauma victim to relive the ordeal, but after training in relaxation skills, he started the process of recording his experiences.

He generally demonstrated a flat affect and was for the most part fairly uncommunicative, allowing his father to provide much of the information regarding the history. On a few occasions, when being directly questioned about his captivity, he demonstrated some fairly extreme outbursts of anger, with both verbal (swearing, shouting, berating the interviewer) and physical (kicking the coffee table, punching himself on the leg) manifestations of emotion. These outbursts were followed by brief periods of complete silence, during which he made no eye contact.

ASSESSMENT

This almost thirteen-year-old, physically healthy boy presents as generally uncommunicative, with periodic outbursts of verbal and physical anger, making only infrequent eye contact. The provisional diagnosis is that of narcissistic personality disorder with antisocial tendencies, along with strong resentment toward authority figures. A contributing factor to his narcissistic features, including a strong sense of entitlement, may well have been instigated through extreme parental spoiling, whereas some symptomatology likely also emerged as a result of his kidnapping and the events of his nine-month period of captivity. Follow-up sessions will further explore these issues and diagnostic details.

PLAN

A trial of psychotropic medications and ongoing long-term psychotherapy are recommended. Individuals of Nikos's age, with his history, including that of trauma and captivity, and with his presenting symptomatology, generally require and may benefit from such long-term psychiatric interventions. However, it is noteworthy that individuals with a diagnosis that includes a personality disorder may have a guarded prognosis.

The story in the boy's own words:

TAKEN

My name is Nikos. This is the story of my kidnap. I'll warn you now, it ain't pretty. A lot of people died. Some deserved it, some didn't. I learned stuff, things some adults will never know. Like what a man looks like and smells like when he is dead. What it feels like when your mind is numb with drugs. What to do when no one gives a shit if you live or die. You want to hear my story? Be careful what you ask for. I really don't want to tell it, but my psychiatrist says I should, and Papa is pushing hard for me to finish. But I don't think he'll like what he reads. Maybe he just wants to see if my private education made me a good writer.

Well, here goes. . . .

THE GRAB

I couldn't breathe. My body tensed. I opened my eyes, confused. Looked around. Where am I? Thea's favorite teddy bear lay beside me on the bed. Then I remembered—I slept in her room because she'd had a night-mare about Mama dying. I tried to breathe again, but someone held a strange-smelling cloth tightly against my mouth and nose. I kicked, punched. Didn't matter. I wasn't strong enough. No choice. I sucked in air through the cloth. It made me feel weird. I looked over at Thea hidden in the fort I'd made her. She was awake, her eyes big and scared. I screamed to her in my head: "Help! Go get help!" Her mouth opened, but no sound came out. She didn't move. I felt dizzy. The room was spinning. Then it all went black.

The next time I woke up, it was still black. I had a hood on my head, rope around my hands, and a stinky rag in my mouth. Oil. Yuck. Puke came up my throat, but I swallowed it back down. My body banged against something hard. Felt like I was in the back of a truck. It hurt a lot. I tried to get free, but the rope was tied too tight. I was thirsty. My back was sore. My heart was beating fast, and I was wet and sweaty. Don't know how long I was riding, maybe hours.

I wanted to know who had taken me. Papa would find me, make them pay. He might even kill them. That would be good.

The diesel engine rattled and stopped. We were there. Not sure where. Someone opened the door. I felt the hot sun on my back as someone threw me over his skinny shoulder. I bounced around a lot, heard the creak of a door opening. Goose bumps on my arms. Cold. Air-conditioning.

The skinny guy dropped me onto something soft, maybe a couch. I sniffed in a weird smell, like dirt and moss, same as when we buried Grandpa in that deep, dark hole. Big footsteps. Someone yanked off my hood. Light hurt my eyes. I looked around. The room had scary African masks on the wall. A giant stared down at me. He smelled like Grandpa's grave too—death. I tried to be brave, but my teeth banged together.

The giant wore an army outfit and a camo beret. He was called "the General," and he bossed the skinny guy, Kofi, around. He had tribal scars burned into his cheeks. When we first came to Africa, Papa said tribal scars were from slave times, and free men scarred their faces so no one would think they were slaves. Was this guy going to make me his slave?

Kofi had a sneaky look in his eyes, as if he hated taking orders. They talked about some mix-up, the boy being in the girl's room.

Maybe they'd wanted to take Thea instead. Better it was me. Little sis is younger, smaller. She couldn't fight back. She couldn't survive. I could.

THE VILLAGERS

They kept me in a shed out back, so hot and dirty. That oil stink made me sick. The lumpy mattress was ripped, so I pulled out a loose coil I could use to draw in the dirt floor. I was good at taking stuff apart and putting it back together. Papa said I had good spatial intelligence, whatever that is.

Days went by slowly, and I used the coil to mark a line on the cement wall every time the sun came up. Eleven marks now. I smelled real bad, but when I asked for a bath, Kofi sprayed me with freezing water, so I used leaves to wipe the dirt off me instead. I had two buckets, one for water, the other for piss and shit. The water tasted funny. I think Kofi mixed up the buckets when he changed them. My stomach hurt down low.

So boring, being alone all the time. Kofi brought beans and rice every afternoon. He poked me with a sharp stick and laughed when I asked to come outside. I missed home. Was someone coming to get me? Piers would have to explain why he'd let this happen. He was head of Papa's security team. He might get fired after this.

On day twelve, the General showed up, still smelling weird, like dirt. He had a serious look on his face, like Papa did when he'd had a bad day. "Come."

I stood, but my knees wobbled. The bright sunlight hurt my eyes. I didn't move, 'cause I was scared. His big hand landed on my neck and pushed me toward a green Land Cruiser. Inside, I saw three rifles. Were they going to shoot me? Didn't Papa want me back?

Kofi drove, the diesel engine puffing out huge clouds of blue smoke. My hands shook. I straightened my shoulders, wanting to be brave. Papa had taught me that strong men put up a tough front. But I didn't want to die.

The Land Cruiser bumped along the dirt road. We passed acacia trees, cornfields, and lots of desert. Finally we turned down a path to a village with grass huts. Little kids with big bellies chased each other. Women crowded around a fire pit. They looked starved and sad. Old men stood nearby, letting flies buzz around their faces. These people had no hope. I got it. I didn't have much hope left either.

Kofi and the General opened the back of the truck and gave the villagers grain bags. People danced, smiled, and treated the General like some sort of hero. Two women dumped grain into a pot of water and started stirring. Everyone was suddenly happy. The General hugged the children, played games with them. When he called me over, I wasn't as scared. With all these people watching, he wouldn't kill me, would he?

It was weird. The villagers stared at me like I was an alien. They'd probably never seen anyone with white skin before. I still remember the question the General asked me.

"Have you ever been truly hungry—so hungry you would do anything for a scrap of food?"

I hated that horrible feeling of an empty stomach. If I didn't answer Papa's daily quizzes correctly, I'd be sent to bed without dinner. But I'd never gone days without eating, and I could tell what the General wanted to hear.

"No, sir." That was always my answer when I was in trouble. It usually worked.

The giant waved his hands in a big circle and told me that these people wanted to eat, but Papa kept buying up all their crops for something called biofuel, leaving them nothing to eat. I stared at him, confused. How could Papa be hurting these people when he didn't even know them?

At least I knew the answer to the next question about what Papa did for a living. That was easy. "Oil" was the one word I heard every night at dinner. Papa told me that my future rested in energy. But the General made it sound like a bad thing. That was why he was keeping me, to make my father stop taking away all the crops. I wasn't sure what to think, but I was kind of mad at Papa for making the General angry.

I asked when I could go home. For a second, the General's black eyes looked nicer, but then they got all mean again. He said Papa wouldn't agree to do what he said, that his work was more important than me.

I felt sick. The General must be lying. I was the only son, my father's favorite child. I was born in New York City, but Papa came from Greece, and the oldest son was the most important kid. One day, I'd take over his business.

Then I heard five big bangs. I almost jumped out of my skin. There was loud music and four Jeeps. All the villagers ran away. The General grabbed me and ran for the Land Cruiser, shoving me onto the floor. He picked up one of the rifles.

I peeked out through a rusty hole in the door. A tall man wearing a red bandanna stepped off one of the Jeeps. His name was Oba. The General shouted at him that he needed to go away, leave the villagers alone. But Oba didn't listen. He made his men load the grain bags onto his Jeeps and walked over to the Land Cruiser. I was really scared. The whites of Oba's eyes were yellow and red, like fried eggs cooked in blood. His pupils were huge.

"Get the kid," I heard him say to Kofi. Was Kofi working for him now?

Another loud bang made my ears hurt. Kofi shot the General in the leg. He said Oba paid better; then he laughed like a hyena. They opened the door to the Land Cruiser and grabbed me. I screamed and kicked, but it didn't matter. The General tried to stop them, but three of Oba's men held him back.

Kofi threw me over his shoulder and carried me to one of the Jeeps. I couldn't believe it. This crazy man Oba was going to kill me for sure.

NOBO

Bad news. Oba's camp was worse than the General's shed. Four mattresses full of lice, eight boys on each, their skinny legs all tangled. I huddled in a corner 'cause I couldn't sleep. This little kid Nobo curled up beside me at night, maybe to stay warm. I kinda felt sorry for him 'cause he was tiny and his two front teeth were missing. I shared my blanket with him because the other boys had stolen his.

Lice dug into my skull. My fingernails were bloody from scratching my head. Flies kept buzzing on my face and crawling on my arms. I'd given up batting them away. And the mosquitoes left blood marks and big bumps. The driver ants on the beds bit me when they weren't attacking each other. I itched everywhere.

I wanted to hide from Oba and Kofi and escape, but I was scared of the jungle more than them. One kid left, and they brought back his dead body, all torn up by lions. I could hear animal cries in the night, horrible sounds that kept me awake. I hoped Papa would find me, but as the days passed, I was giving up. Maybe he was too busy with his work to come. That made me mad.

I heard the bell. The boys ran for the outdoor shower, where the water was brownish. Nobo followed me everywhere. We had a quick wash—if you could call it that—and everyone lined up at the fire pit for breakfast. A large pot of the villagers' grains bubbled on the fire. I followed the crowd of boys, wanting to fit in, knowing I couldn't. They called me Mzungu. White boy. My skin color made me stand out like a zebra on a grassy plain. The boys always stared at me.

I dreamed of home, clean sheets on my bed, the smell of Cook baking fresh bread, the view of the gardens. I even missed Hakan's son, Rifat, who Papa said I had to play with because his father worked for him. Anything was better than this place.

One day, Kofi told all the boys to sit on the wooden picnic benches. Every boy got a rifle. He told us it was our new best friend and to keep it with us all the time. Oba stood in a corner watching. I didn't look at him. The guy was scary.

Kofi held an AK-47 in his bony hands and showed us how to take it apart and put it back together. The rifle was kinda cool. A big kid named Blado was the fastest. Poor Nobo wasn't good at all, his small hands too weak. I snuck a quick look at Oba, but his black eyes were all weird. I didn't want him to notice me, so I worked on my AK-47. But I was good, so Oba came over and watched me work.

Then he saw that Nobo had barely started. Oba grabbed the tiny kid by the ear and screamed at him.

"Five weeks, and you still can't do this?" He was so mad.

Nobo shook all over.

My mouth opened before I could think. "He's too small to do it. Why don't you get him to count bullets instead?"

All the boys were quiet. I knew I had made a mistake.

"Do we accept weakness in this camp?"

No one said anything.

"I asked if we accept weakness."

Total quiet.

*"The answer is no." Oba pulled out his gun, lifted Nobo into the
air, and shot him in the head. The loud bang made me jump. Blood
splashed my face.*

I felt sick. My heart skipped a few beats. I couldn't move.

*Nobo lay on the table beside me, his mouth open, showing his two
missing teeth.*

"Get to work. Now!"

*Oba hit me hard on the back of the head with the rifle. I saw
stars, wanted to puke. My hands were covered with Nobo's blood, but
I started working on the rifle. I didn't want to be the next person shot.
Still, I felt bad. I could have stripped Nobo's AK, tried to teach him. I
showed Thea how to do things at home. But I was too scared to help.
I had to do everything Oba said if I wanted to live. And the things I
did were bad.*

The yellowed pages of Nikos's story trembled in Thea's hands.
She sucked in a deep breath. Every benign thing she'd been told
about her brother's kidnapping had been a lie. Ripples of shock
reverberated down her spine. Who else knew what had actually
happened to Nikos? Hakan? Rif? Was she the only one who'd
been kept in the dark?

When Nikos had been held hostage, Papa had met with countless experts behind closed doors. A grave hush had fallen over
the household, as if no one could take a full breath until Nikos
came home. She remembered those long months when he was
missing, his kidnapping a tangible presence at every meal. Still,
she'd never fully understood what her brother had endured,
because Papa had always stuck to the same myth of where he'd
been—held as a bargaining chip between rival African tribes, a
little hungry and dirty but relatively safe.

Lies, lies, lies.

Empathy overwhelmed her. Nikos had been through sheer
hell, and perhaps her father had misguidedly tried to protect her
from the horrific truth. She'd participated in numerous hostage
debriefings. The horrors of captivity were never easy to handle,

but this one hit her especially hard. This was her brother, her rock after their mother died.

Nikos had never been the same after he returned. The first few days he was awkward and withdrawn. And really angry. Lots of doors slamming, yelling, outbursts. Allison, their nanny, had abruptly left two months after Nikos came home; then her brother had been sent away to a school in Utah for troubled kids.

Her world had become smaller and smaller as the people she cared about went away. She called her brother every Sunday, but she always got the feeling he was holding back from telling her how miserable he was. She'd wanted Nikos home with her full time. But when he'd return for holidays, he'd act withdrawn, dark, almost a stranger. Being around Papa seemed to set him off.

And the whole mess had started when Nikos had been kidnapped from her bedroom, in her place.

She wondered again who had given her this packet. Nikos himself? Possibly, but would he want to share that a psychiatrist had diagnosed him with a personality disorder? And all that torture . . .

Shaking off the shock, she turned her focus back to Papa. There'd be time later to sift through this avalanche of emotions, but not now. Nikos was back home, safe. Her father wasn't.

Papa's nightmare was only beginning. The man who revered power and control over everything had lost both. How would he cope? Captives often blamed themselves for their predicament. *If only I hadn't used that route to work. If only I hadn't let down my guard.* Especially with men, the inability to stand up to their captors and fight could lead to unbearable frustration, shame, a sense of inadequacy. A power broker such as Papa would struggle even more with this impotency.

Instead of taking action, hostages had to find a way to endure if they wanted to survive—to endure deprivation, psychological and/or physical torture, forced submissiveness, and not knowing if they'd ever return home.

Knowing Papa and his pride, he'd refuse to capitulate to the kidnappers, and that didn't bode well for him. Would he be tortured? Look at what had happened to poor Nikos.

She leaned over, head in her hands, trying to process the horrors her brother had endured. A strong arm rested on her shoulder. Rif's.

She quickly shoved the papers into her bag. Rif had never gotten along with her brother. Maybe he'd feel differently about Nikos if he knew the truth—or did he already? But she couldn't delve into that now. Peter was right there, for one thing, and she had no interest in sharing anything personal with the CFO. And Rif could barely tolerate him.

"You okay?" Rif asked.

"Just exhausted. Nothing that a shot of espresso won't cure."

"Why don't you take a hot shower? Relax for a bit." Peter placed his pen on the thick stack of papers in front of him.

Rif's fingers tightened around her shoulder.

"No thanks. We land in less than an hour, and I have plenty to do." She headed for the espresso machine. Before she could reach it, her cell beeped. She scanned the message. Freddy. "A team searched Henri's apartment, and they found an encrypted satphone," she reported. "The last number dialed was a location in Kanzi." Adrenaline jolted through her veins. Maybe she didn't need the caffeine after all. A potential lead did wonders to stoke the embers of her energy.

"The chef was in on the kidnapping?" the CFO asked.

Rif's lips tightened—he didn't trust Peter. Well, neither did she, but she wanted to gauge his potential involvement by assessing his micro-expressions when she shared non-critical information. "Looks like Henri might have been the inside man, or at least one of them."

"He seemed so devoted to Christos. It's hard to believe," Peter said.

"People have their motivations."

"I wouldn't know where to start if I wanted to kidnap some-one. I guess you'd need a large team to pull off such an elaborate operation as this abduction." Peter looked thoughtful.

"Definitely." It did take a large group, but probably not in the way Peter thought. There were usually several specialized cells that didn't know about each other: an abduction team, a transport team, a negotiation team, guards to look after the hostage, and a command center acting as the brain to coordinate everything.

"Is it structured like a corporation?" Peter asked.

"Kind of." More like a terrorist organization, really, with only the brain knowing the entire operation. That way, if any of the cells were compromised, they'd have no information about the others.

"Must be expensive."

"It is, but the payoff can be well worth the trouble. Kidnap-ping's become a lucrative business in many poor countries. Loads of displaced former military and police factions are resort-ing to it as a way to make a living. You ever had a close call?" She slipped in the question.

"No, I prefer to stay in the boardroom crunching numbers. I let the bodyguards handle my security." Peter doodled on his note-pad, then looked up. "If money is the main motivator, that's good news for Christos, right? He has plenty of K-and-R insurance."

Rif stood. "How do you know that?"

"Hel-lo, I'm the numbers guy. Who do you think arranges the insurance for all the top executives? For security reasons, the C-suite people are never told how much they've been insured for, in case they're taken and tortured. I made sure Christos had the maximum, a fifty-million-dollar policy plus excess coverage."

Peter sure had motivation to be involved in the kidnapping if he was looking for an early-retirement fund. But the real kidnap-per hadn't even asked for a ransom. *Yet.* She studied the CFO for any tells. So far, he seemed genuinely surprised, as well as curi-ous about her work.

"Why hasn't there been a ransom demand?" he asked.

"Every kidnapping is different." He didn't need to know details about the ten-million-euro FARC farce or the Latin texts. "Silence is common while the hostage is being transported to a new location—it buys the abductors time."

She made an espresso, adding a dash of cinnamon in her father's honor, weary of fielding Peter's questions. Waiting to hear from the kidnappers made her crazy. And that was exactly what they wanted.

"What can I do to help?" Peter asked.

"Tell me more about this oil deal."

"Sure. Paris Industries currently contributes about sixty percent of Kanzi's GDP through the purchase of biofuels, but biofuels were small change compared to the potential billions involved in fossil fuels. Our exploration led to the discovery of some very large oil fields. Some of the oil is in the land that we already have a lease on, but the majority of the find is tied to land not covered by our current agreement."

"And Papa's relationship with the prime minister wasn't enough to secure these other rights at a reasonable price?"

"Kimweri knows he's sitting on billions. Why not pit us against the Chinese National Oil Company to get the best deal? I would. Biofuels are a pittance compared with the money from the oil."

"Is there anything else we could use as leverage?"

"Up until this discovery, the Kanzi government has been disorganized, unable to supply the proper food, water, shelter, and stability needed for a healthy population in certain regions. The lack of water in the west has led to an internal refugee crisis. Tribes battle other tribes over watering holes and herds. Our proposal includes a plan to help all Kanzians establish a peaceful existence. Schools, firm borders between tribes, hospitals, places of worship. If they had the proper infrastructure, and everyone had enough of the necessities, they might avoid most of the current violence."

"I've always loved the natural beauty of the country, but even as a kid, I noticed the poverty and struggles."

"And the politics are a hot mess, typical for Africa. Prime Minister Kimweri and his brother-in-law, Bini Salam—the finance minister—were born in Kanzi's capital city, where tribal violence wasn't as much of a threat, whereas General Ita Jemwa, the security minister, hails from the west and understands the plight of the desert dwellers."

The General. She suddenly remembered Nikos's journal: the kidnapping stemmed from "the General's" desire to help the poor. That sort of thing might appeal to a soldier, but not necessarily to a politician. Kimweri seemed like a good man, but power-hungry dictators often projected an air of benevolence when necessary.

"Can you prepare a brief that covers all the players in the Kanzi deal? Maybe something in it will help me figure out who took my father." Kidnappings rarely resolved quickly. It could be days or even weeks or months before some vital piece of information came to light; Thea planned on finding out everything she could. Having Peter's insider analysis could be quite helpful.

"Gladly. Why don't we meet for dinner so I can fill you in?"

"Let's see how the evening unfolds." She had no interest in lingering over a bottle of Bordeaux with Kennedy. She just wanted the information. "I'm going to check in with the pilots. We're almost there."

She strode through the salon and knocked on the flight deck door. A voice called out to enter. She found the first officer alone at the controls, a fresh coffee from the cockpit's Keurig in his left hand. "Where's Captain Houston?"

"I'm afraid he must have taken ill—hasn't left the head in the last ten minutes. Maybe something he ate? Can you do me a favor and check on him?"

"Will do. How long before we land?"

"Thirty minutes. We're descending over the desert now." Sweat trickled down his temple, she noticed. Maybe he was catching something, too?

She peered through the windows at the endless stretch of sand. It brought back memories of happier times, her father racing a Land Rover alongside galloping camels, Thea and Nikos in the backseat. But that was all before her brother's kidnapping.

A sudden bout of turbulence interrupted her reflections. She braced herself against the bulkhead until they passed through the worst of it.

If only flying wasn't a requirement for her job.

"I'll go check on the captain. Be right back."

The first officer's shoulders looked tense, and his voice sounded a bit unsteady when he said, "Appreciate it."

She didn't like the fact that Houston wasn't on the flight deck. Redundancy comforted her, especially in the air. She turned to the lavatory door and noted the red flag that showed the cubicle was occupied. A light knock didn't receive any response. She knocked harder. No answer.

"Captain, you okay?" She didn't want to intrude, but what if he needed help? She lifted the cover on the lavatory sign and slid the door lock open from the outside. If people realized how easy it was to open an airplane lavatory door, they might not be so quick to join the mile-high club.

She found Captain Houston facedown over the toilet, arms limp at his sides. Vomit pooled on the floor. She tried gently shaking him. No response. She reached for his carotid artery. No pulse. She lowered him to the floor. His face had a blue tinge.

Dead.

The aircraft lurched again. She turned toward the passenger cabin, looking for Rif. He could fly anything from a helicopter to a jumbo jet, and she wanted him in the captain's seat keeping an eye on the first officer.

He was already headed in her direction.

"Captain Houston's dead. Looks like poisoning. Can you join the first officer?"

Rif ducked into the flight deck, and she followed. The pungent smell hit her hard. Vomit. The first officer groaned, and his coffee spilled on the floor. She leaned over to check on him while Rif buckled into the left seat, slipped the headset on, and grabbed the control wheel.

The first officer went limp. He slumped in his seat, only his shoulder harness holding his body upright. White froth leaked out of his mouth.

Thea searched for a pulse. Nothing.

"I need to start CPR on him." She reached for his seat belt, but a muffled explosion well aft of the flight deck sent a jarring shudder through the airframe. The instruments went wild, the lights dimmed.

"Sounds like something blew in the hell hole," Rif said in a clipped voice, shooting a concerned glance at her.

Hell hole: the unpressurized compartment beneath the vertical tail, where the batteries, hydraulic accumulators, auxiliary power unit, and other vital systems were housed and serviced.

"Strap yourself in. We're dropping fast. You can't help him."

"I need to try."

A needle on the instrument cluster took a disturbing nose-dive. Rif's left hand gripped the half-arc control wheel while the right one danced across the large display screen on the instrument panel, touch-tapping an array of menus, colored bars, and computer-generated dials.

"In the seat. Now."

The first officer was clearly dead. They were on their own. She folded down the jump seat in the flight deck doorway and buckled its lap belt.

"We're in deep shit," he muttered. "Losing hydraulic pressure, controls are already mushy. Hang on, I'm taking her down." He pulled the jet's twin throttles back to near idle and pushed the nose over, thumbing the trim switch on his control wheel to hold a steep dive angle.

"Here?" She swallowed hard, looking down at the endless expanse of sand filling the windows.

"Where else? Gotta get this bird on the ground before hydraulic pressure drops to zip and I lose control of the plane."

Peter and the two flight attendants, Brianna and Megan, needed to know what was going on. She grabbed the microphone. "Seat belts, please. Prepare for an emergency landing. Could be rough."

Rif's face was inscrutable; he held the control wheel forward in a steep, forty-five-degree descent, eyes flicking between the instruments and the desert rushing toward them. Thea gripped the back edge of his seat. Her stomach floated to her throat. She felt as if they were diving straight at the ground.

Rif pulled a thin boom microphone to his lips and pressed the radio transmission switch. "Mayday, Mayday, Mayday—Yankee Tango . . ."

She grabbed the intercom microphone again. "Brace for landing." Her ears popped as the plane's altimeter unwound at a dizzying rate.

Given her anxiety about flying, Thea knew every safety regulation by heart. She tightened her seat belt and lowered it to her pelvis. Every centimeter of slack in the seat belt tripled the g-forces on impact, and the strong bone of the pelvis handled those stresses better than did the fragile internal organs. She desperately needed a shoulder harness, but it was too late to drag the dead co-pilot out of his seat.

Rif was talking to himself. "Don't extend the landing gear. Sand's too soft, will flip the plane, rip off the nose. Belly landing's the only hope."

Their altitude plummeted. He worked quickly, his concentration intense. "Prepare for impact."

She bent forward, chest on her thighs, head between her knees, hands gripping her ankles. Her hair was scant inches from the switch-covered center console separating the pilots' seats. Seconds ticked by. The anticipatory dread heightened. They barreled toward the earth, wings rocking back and forth, the plane's nose wandering while Rif fought to keep the bird right-side up. Seconds later, the aircraft hit hard, bounced, then slammed back down to the earth, creating a tsunami of sand.

The fuselage swung sharply to the right as a wingtip sliced into a sand berm. Thea's body lurched forward, then whiplashed sideways. Pain wrenched her lower back. The Gulfstream shuddered as it torpedoed through the dunes, the windshield buried in reddish-brown sand, darkening the flight deck. They skidded sideways, the piercing screech of grinding metal penetrating her eardrums.

Every joint ached. White spots filled her vision. Her teeth rattled. The plane finally rumbled to a halt. Shell-shocked, she sucked in a deep breath and tried to orient herself.

A gash had appeared on Rif's forehead. Blood dripped into his eyes as he stopcocked both engines and ripped off his seat belt. "You okay?" he yelled above the moan of dying turbines.

She nodded. Her body was battered, but she didn't have any serious injuries. The alarming scent of jet fuel mixed with acrid smoke kicked her into action. "Out!"

Their quickest escape route was through the front, but they needed to help Peter and the flight attendants. Thick smoke filled the cabin. She pulled off her sweater and used it as a filter to help her breathe. She rushed toward the main cabin, Rif right behind her. Debris cluttered the floor. Coffee mugs, smashed glass, and a laptop computer rested near the first flight attendant's seat.

She stumbled over a duffel bag lying on the floor but caught her balance by slamming a palm into an overhead panel. The smoke limited visibility. Rif tried to open the exit door, but it wouldn't budge. The fuselage had twisted during the landing.

"This way," Rif told Brianna and Peter, moving on to the red release handle on the over-wing emergency escape hatch. He tossed the hatch through the waist-high opening, then helped the others step onto the sharply tilted wing.

Thea hurried through the cabin to find the second flight attendant. The woman's neck was bent at such an unnatural angle, she didn't need to check for a pulse. She stumbled back to the hatch, bending almost double to thread her body through the emergency exit. Rif offered her a hand, then led her off the wing's trailing edge.

They leapt to the ground and sprinted upwind from the crash. Seconds later, an oxygen bottle exploded, igniting fuel leaking from the breached wing tanks. A ball of orange flame laced with angry black smoke erupted, throwing a wall of heat and bits of burning aluminum in their direction.

Thea dove into the sand beside Rif, arms covering her head. A series of smaller explosions scattered debris and scorched the sand around the fuselage, ringing the jet's gaping wreckage with ugly black soot.

Thea pushed herself into a sitting position. Her lips were dry and swollen, her eyes irritated and burning. Tears streaked down her face. The broken jet was engulfed in a raging inferno, melting into the sand, forever grounded, a hollowed-out carcass. The bodies of the pilots and the other flight attendant had been cremated, their ashes lost in the unforgiving winds of the Kanzi desert.

Rif offered her a hand up. She accepted, grateful. Without his piloting skills, they'd all be dead.

Chapter Thirty-Four

Nikos's view of the arid dunes surrounding the airstrip was clouded by red earth kicking up as the Cessna Caravan touched down. The plane lumbered to a stop, and the grit hovering in the air dissipated. A Kanzi flag on a lone pole waved in the brisk wind—half red, half black, with a green circle in the middle, representing "through the mud and the blood to the green fields beyond." No green fields today, though: soaring temperatures and dry conditions had left any local crops desiccated. The surrounding area was a barren wasteland.

The Cessna had landed in the western region of Kanzi, where the harsh climate made the land inhospitable, though it provided the perfect location for a rebel training camp. Shots could be fired and grenades could explode without causing any alarm. The only people who roamed the surrounding desert were the nomadic tribes, and they knew better than to venture near this encampment.

"Welcome home." The flight steward opened the exit door while the co-pilot ran around the spinning propeller to unload Nikos's luggage. Four soldiers in fatigues stood armed with the newly supplied AK-47s beside a pair of Toyota Land Cruisers.

As difficult as the conditions were here, Nikos considered this country his home. He might have been born in New York City, but Ares had come into being in Kanzi. For years he'd kept his two identities separate, never merging. But now he was taking the ultimate risk, revealing himself. He planned on tricking one devil to exact revenge on another, fulfilling his destiny, bringing his story full circle after twenty long years.

He strode over to the lead truck and climbed inside, the airconditioning providing a welcome respite from the unrelenting heat. They headed for the camp, the truck bouncing up and down on the uneven terrain.

Fifteen minutes later, they entered the military encampment, and the Land Cruiser stopped in front of a large canvas tent with a sweeping overhang. A massive figure stood beside two young boys dressed in matching Nike shirts.

The General.

Nikos stepped out of the truck and came face-to-face with his former kidnapper for the first time in twenty years. The man walking toward him had been his abductor and his savior, but today they shared a common bond—a hatred of Christos Aristotle Paris. So when Nikos had reached out via encrypted satphone with his proposal, the General had agreed immediately.

At six foot one, Nikos was hardly a small man, but standing next to this giant, echoes of his twelve-year-old self resurfaced. Somewhere inside, his rigid self-control faltered for a second.

No, things were different now. *He* was the power player, the General only a pawn. The weathered warrior had gray hair near his temples, deep crevices etched in his ebony face, and his tribal scars had left his skin looking like the hide of a rhino. His immense bulk had softened, the buttons of his uniform fighting against his belly. He also had a slight limp from that long-ago firefight, when Kofi had betrayed the General and shot him in the leg.

In contrast, Nikos was fit and in his prime, a feared arms dealer who could order someone's death with a casual whisper into the right ear.

Nikos had become the giant.

The General waved his large hands toward the boys. "My grandsons—we're just spending time together before they head back home this afternoon."

The kids scrambled away, chasing each other around the Land Cruiser.

"You've certainly grown up." A faint smile lingered at the edges of the General's mouth. He proffered a meaty hand. "After all these years, we meet again."

Nikos hesitated for a second, then accepted the handshake. The General turned his palm downward, trying to maintain control. Nikos turned it back, reclaiming the dominant role. Just as he'd expected, the soldier wasn't interested in relinquishing his supremacy. That made him useful, at least for a while.

"The troops are in a strict training regimen in case they're needed."

"Excellent." If the oil negotiations didn't end well, they were poised for a coup to overthrow Kanzi's administration.

"I read about your father's kidnapping in the papers. Christos is now under lock and key?" A gleam in the General's eyes unsettled Nikos, but he didn't want to read too much into it. Why would the giant be involved in Christos's kidnapping? Why would he undermine Nikos's arrangements and risk the enormous wealth and influence he'd gain by working *with* Nikos—unless he had another endgame in mind?

"We're moving forward as planned." Nikos's stomach felt unsettled.

"Within a few days, Kanzi and all its oil wealth will be ours." The General smiled.

No, mine. All mine.

A familiar bang reverberated through the camp. Nikos looked around, searching for the source. One of the grandsons had discovered a guard's AK-47 lying on the rear seat of the Land Cruiser. The boy's small hands held the rifle, and he pointed the barrel straight at them, a thousand-watt smile on his face.

The giant's eyes widened. Fear. Not for himself, but for his grandson. The skinny youngster holding the rifle triggered Nikos's memory. He'd been no older than this boy when he'd used a Kalashnikov to kill on Oba's command.

Nikos strode over and squatted beside the child. He gently released the kid's tiny fingers from the weapon. "*Zuri mtoto, baya ridhe.*" Good boy, bad gun.

The boy giggled and ran after his brother, not realizing the danger they'd all been in. Innocence needed to be protected at any cost. That was why he funneled money from his arms deals into helping children in need. In their formative years, kids' psyches were established, and they became who they'd be for the rest of their lives. Every child deserved a chance at happiness, but many youngsters never had a hope in hell.

He touched the pocket where he kept the music box and glanced at the General, a look of understanding passing between them. Unlike Oba, the giant agreed with him that children should never be involved in war.

Chapter Thirty-Five

Sweat soaked Thea's cotton shirt. The relentless sun punished any exposed skin. The temperatures soared above 120 degrees, waves of heat rising from the desert floor. Trying to escape the unforgiving conditions, their small group huddled under an Apache-style *kowa* that Rif had created from nearby brush. Even with the shelter, the cruel rays reflected hotly off the sand.

Nothing had survived the massive explosion, leaving them with only the clothes on their backs. Because of her illness, Thea always kept two days' worth of insulin in the special insulated container Papa had given her, which was in her cargo pants. She also had a few protein bars stashed in her pockets. She'd already rationed out pieces of the first bar to everyone but was saving the others until later, since they had no idea how long they would be stuck out here. She was concerned. Diabetes impaired one's ability to sweat, and sweating was the body's way of cooling down. And when the thermometer on her insulin clocked in at eighty-six degrees Fahrenheit, it could render her medication useless.

Heat was not her friend.

She thought back to her survival training and the powerful rule of three, which could help prioritize your actions in an emergency. Three seconds without hope, three minutes without air, three hours in punishing temperature extremes without adequate shelter, three days without water, and three weeks without food—any one of them led to death.

They had the hope, air, and shelter covered, but they'd had nothing to drink for the last five hours, and dehydration was making her dizzy and weak. Searching for help in the desert would be reckless, likely fatal. Miles of endless sand dunes stretched across the bleak horizon in all directions. The safest plan was to wait for rescue. Waiting was an activity in which she usually excelled, but her and her current companions' lives weren't the only ones at stake. Every hour ticking by was an hour Papa might not have left to spare.

She had her phone and her father's cell, but there was no reception in the desert. Her satphone and SINK bag had blown up with the plane. Fortunately, Rif had radioed in the distress call during their emergency landing, so Kanzi officials should be looking for them. Smoke from the burning plane would be easily spotted by anyone searching the desert, but would their little group last long enough to be rescued?

Brianna's face was beet red; her body trembled. Rif crouched beside the flight attendant, comforting her. "Help is coming soon—hang in there."

"Look, I see water. I need a drink." Her eyes were unfocused, her lips dry. She pointed to the horizon and tried to stand. Rif gently pulled her back into the shade.

Thea glanced to the west. An inferior mirage floated in the distance—it appeared to be a lake. Too bad it wasn't real. "Don't worry, we'll get you some water soon."

The flight attendant was obviously in shock. It was painful to witness the deaths of co-workers and friends. Thea forced herself not to dwell on Captain Houston and the others. There was no room for negative thoughts in such a dire setting.

Their best tools were their brains, as survival often required more mental than physical skills. Keeping a rational mind helped you avoid making stupid mistakes. They needed to stay in the shade and avoid exertion to maintain hydration.

Drought had ravaged Kanzi the past few years. No wonder the country was ridden with strife. Local tribes struggled to find watering holes, herding their cattle into other tribal territories for survival. Deadly battles raged over both the water and the cattle. The desert was an unforgiving environment.

She'd undergone SERE training —survival, evasion, resistance, and escape—during her time with the DIA, and she was thankful that modern military training was more scientific than it had been early on in the Second World War. In North Africa, the US military command thought they could condition soldiers to survive with less water by progressively reducing the amount they drank during training. These experiments had led to hundreds of heat casualties. Humans needed water to survive, lots of it, especially in high temperatures. She would kill for a tall, cold glass right about now.

Peter wiped sweat from his forehead, his fair skin pink and mottled. "Christos demands impeccable maintenance of his planes. What the hell happened up there?"

"Sabotage." Thea hugged her knees. Her suspicions about Kennedy had lessened somewhat, given that he was on the plane when it went down. She still sensed that he was holding something back, though.

"What?" she asked Rif, whose face was a study in intensity.

His expression darkened. "Someone must've slipped a little C4 into the hell hole. A perfect spot, because the pilot wouldn't have seen it in his preflight visual inspection. We lost hydraulic pressure. And just to ensure we'd crash, both pilots were poisoned. Whoever was behind this was definitely thorough."

"Who was the target?" Peter asked. *Good question.* It could have been one of them or all of them. Given the other attacks, Thea was likely at the top of the hit list.

"I don't know. But whoever did this didn't count on us having another pilot on board. We're damn lucky we had Rif." She swatted away a fly.

"This heat is giving me a headache." Sweat poured down Peter's face. "And my legs are cramping." Headache, mental confusion, irritability, excessive sweating, weakness, and cramps were all symptoms of heat exhaustion.

Thea wasn't feeling well either. Her diabetes was going to be a major problem when they ran out of food or the high temperatures destroyed her insulin. But she wouldn't disclose her condition unless absolutely necessary. The others had enough to worry about.

The heat was their fiercest enemy. Ironic, given that in a few short hours, the sun would set and leave them with the opposite problem. Hypothermia. At night, temperatures in the desert could drop below fifty degrees, and they had no blankets or jackets for warmth.

Brianna seemed to be fading, her body language signaling defeat. "If I don't make it, please tell my son, my little Jimmy, that his mother loves him."

Rif held her hand. "You'll tell him yourself. Picture going home to Jimmy. What's the first thing you'll do?"

A spark reignited in her eyes. "I'll hug him and kiss him and then take him swimming."

Thea wiped her brow. "Damn, that sounds good. Can I come?"

They all laughed. But the situation wasn't really funny. Rif stayed close to the flight attendant, supporting her so she wouldn't give up hope.

He handled himself well in emergencies—always had. Thea thought about how long she had known him, and she traced the scar on her cheek.

Thea nestled on a chaise longue by the pool at their Meadow Lane estate in Southampton, sipping a glass of wine. She didn't drink much because of her diabetes, but she wanted a little something to take the edge off having to socialize with a few hundred people at the upcoming party.

Today was a happy day, as Papa was home after a long trip to the Middle East with Hakan and Piers. She reached down to stroke Aegis, who was curled up at her feet, snoozing as the sun dropped in the sky. Labor Day weekend, the end of the summer—kind of a sad time. Rif, Nikos, and Thea would go their separate ways. Nikos would leave tomorrow for Harvard, where he was doing his MBA, and she'd head to Georgetown for her sophomore year.

Rif had been accepted into West Point—one of the few international students enrolled—and Papa was hosting a party for him to celebrate the news. Christos was proud of his godson and wanted everyone to know it.

The sun dropped below the horizon, and the torches around the pool flickered on the water's surface. Staff worked in formation to set up for the party. Rif stopped to help one of the waiters, who was struggling with a large box, then joined Thea on the next chaise. Aegis stirred, immediately abandoning her for the future officer.

"You just can't find loyalty today." She laughed.

Rif reached into his pocket and brought out a treat. "Like most men, he's a slave to his stomach. He knows I'm a soft target."

"You must be excited about West Point and the training you'll be doing."

"Well, I need to defend myself against your kung fu, Bruce Lee." He was always teasing her about her study of Jeet Kune Do.

"You'd better work hard. But let's face it: I'll always be older, wiser, and tougher than you."

"Yeah, eleven months' worth. I can never catch up," Rif said.

Nikos stumbled down the path toward the pool, a crystal tumbler in his hand filled to the brim with bourbon—and from the look in his eyes, it wasn't his first.

"What are you two conspiring about?" He laughed, but it was forced. Her brother and Rif were an incendiary mix. Rif tensed beside her.

Aegis ran to greet Nikos, and her brother gave him an enthusiastic head-scratch.

"We're just chilling before the party. Have the guests started arriving?" she asked.

"I think they're all marching in now—in West Point fashion. Can't believe we're hosting a party to celebrate Soldier Boy joining the drone factory for American imperialist aggression." Nikos downed a large gulp of bourbon, swaying where he stood.

"They teach you those big words at Harvard?" Rif asked.

Nikos stepped closer to Rif. "And then some. Should I speak in plainer language so you can understand?"

"Down, boys." She should be giving Aegis that command, not these two young men.

Rif stood. He was an inch or two taller than Nikos.

Aegis paced by the pool, sensitive to the tension. Thea's palms dampened. Trouble was brewing, and she didn't want a fight to ruin Rif's special day.

"Prepare yourself for a life of simple pleasures, because that's all you'll be able to afford." Nikos's eyes narrowed.

"I'd rather be a patriot than a man who's only loyal to money."

"Better to make money the old-fashioned way than watch it being flushed down the toilet of the military-industrial complex. Oops, am I talking too highbrow again?"

"You call inheriting the old-fashioned way to make money? Your father made money the old-fashioned way, starting with a mop in his hand and working his way up. The only effort you've made is to keep that silver spoon firmly clamped in your mouth."

Not good. She should intercede, but each man would feel she was siding with the other.

Nikos's voice lowered. "If you like being told when to eat, sleep, dress, and shit, the military is the perfect place for you. You'll be taking orders, just like your father, for the rest of your life."

Rif straightened his shoulders. "And you'll be leeching off your dad's millions for the rest of yours."

"Don't push your luck. The help can always be replaced," Nikos said.

"You really want to do this?" Rif's tone was measured, controlled.

Oh, God, it was like watching a traffic accident. She wanted to do something, but she was frozen.

"You don't intimidate me, G.I. Joe." Nikos tossed his bourbon toward Rif's face, but Rif sidestepped, the liquid splashing onto the deck.

"Last chance to back off," Rif said.

Her brother drew the heavy crystal tumbler back and hurled the glass. Rif ducked. The glass sailed by him and hit Thea squarely in the face, shattering.

A large shard carved into her cheek.

Stars. Sharp pain. A scream. Hers. She reeled from the blow. Blood streamed down the right side of her face.

Rif grabbed a towel and pressed it against her cheek. "Are you okay?"

"See what you've done now?" Nikos glared at him.

Papa and Hakan sprinted out of the house at her scream. Aegis nuzzled close, licking Thea as if to comfort her. Rif drove her to the emergency room, and twenty-two stitches later, they'd missed the entire party. Papa blamed Nikos, but she couldn't. Not entirely. The night her brother had been kidnapped, she hadn't done anything to help. Life gave you the same lessons in different forms until you owned them. Well, she got it now. Take charge, and don't freeze.

She'd had a black eye and a permanent scar on her face. She could've tried plastic surgery, but the doctors weren't optimistic. So she bore it proudly, the scar serving as a daily reminder always to be brave, no matter what the cost.

And never to recoil from conflict.

"Look, look!" Brianna's voice cut through her memories. "I see something."

Another mirage? Movement in the distance caught Thea's attention. Dust kicking up on the horizon. She kept searching the endless desert. A caravan of vehicles was barreling toward them.

In this country filled with despots and warlords, she just hoped these arrivals were friendly.

Chapter Thirty-Six

Thirty minutes later, the distant haze on the horizon blossomed into a billowing cloud of reddish brown. Thea strained to identify five Toyota Land Cruisers racing toward them. Brianna was elated, her energy resurging. Peter's face relaxed.

In contrast, tightness settled into Rif's jaw. A similar trepidation hovered in Thea's mind. They were in the middle of a war-torn country—the last thing they needed was to be "rescued" by guerrillas or other hostiles.

The caravan finally reached the crash site, and the Land Cruisers parked one behind the other. Men wearing desert fatigues exited the vehicles, brandishing AK-47s. One of the soldiers opened the rear door of the third truck. A huge man climbed out, dwarfing the others with height and shoulders that could span the equator.

She shivered, recognizing General Ita Jemwa's large stature and scarred face from the newspaper articles about Nikos's kidnapping. Now looming large between her and rescue was the man who'd collected the million-dollar reward for her brother's return, the man who—according to Nikos's journal—had been his original kidnapper. She wondered who had put those notes into her bag in the first place. Who wanted her to know what had really happened in Kanzi?

The general nodded to two of his men. The soldiers opened the back flap of the first truck, unloaded a cooler, and handed out bottles of water and sandwiches. Peter and Brianna leaned against a truck, downing water. Rif's erect posture told her he was on guard. Thea twisted the cap off an icy bottle and guzzled the contents. The water quenched her thirst, but a pit of foreboding still lodged in her stomach.

The general surveyed the black carcass of the plane's fuselage, then zeroed in on her. "Ms. Paris, I believe. I've worked with your father over the years. Welcome to Kanzi. This must be your lucky day."

Hardly. "I'll consider myself lucky when I'm sitting in an air-conditioned restaurant eating a steak." She forced her lips into a tight smile.

The general laughed, a deep, rumbling sound. "I'll kill the cow myself if I have to—we don't want our guests to be disappointed."

Chapter Thirty-Seven

Rif calculated his options should things go sideways. There weren't many. The AKs pointed in their direction were difficult to ignore. He'd recognized General Ita Jemwa immediately from the files Hakan had on Nikos's kidnapping.

"Let's get you somewhere cooler. My camp is two hours west of here." General Jemwa adjusted his beret and snapped his fingers. The soldiers sprang into action, repacking the water and supplies into the Land Cruiser.

Rif and Thea rode with the general in the newer truck. The air-conditioning was heavenly after being stuck in the unforgiving desert for hours.

Sitting next to the huge soldier, Rif experienced a flicker of sympathy for Nikos. He couldn't imagine how frightened a twelve-year-old boy would be faced with this gigantic man as his kidnapper.

The Land Cruisers negotiated the endless sand dunes, targeting the setting sun. The general shifted his bulk to face Rif. "We intercepted your distress signal on our radio and realized you were close by. What happened?"

"Technical difficulties," Rif said.

"Of the most serious kind, apparently," the general said. "You're very fortunate to have survived that crash."

"The pilots died saving us." Thea was smart to say that. Keep your potential enemies in the dark about a teammate's aviation skills. She had a hell of a poker face. "We need to reach Victoria Falls Hotel in Zimbabwe by noon tomorrow. Can we arrange for a helicopter to pick us up at your camp?"

"Let's get you showered, fed, and rested. Tomorrow will take care of itself." The general smiled, clearly enjoying his control.

Rif sensed Thea's unrest, understood her impatience. She was torn up about her father. Every minute she was away from cell reception was a minute she wasn't searching for Christos. Perhaps they should take a closer look at General Jemwa. After all, he had a history of kidnapping as well as a past with the Paris family. Contrary to popular belief, it wasn't unusual for more than one family member to be abducted by the same person or group, especially if the family acquiesced to the demands too quickly. Soft targets made kidnappers greedy. These abductions were twenty years apart, but maybe the Kanzi oil negotiations had acted as a catalyst for Jemwa. A need for money? A power move?

"Your hospitality is appreciated, but it's urgent that we reach the hotel. Our negotiations start tomorrow," she said.

"We'll make sure you arrive on time. In fact, I'll be traveling with you—I've been consulting on security measures for the event, and I already have an advance team in place."

"Excellent, then it won't inconvenience you to leave tonight."

"We have a celebration planned for our soldiers this evening. But don't worry: as my guests, you'll be included in the festivities."

"How gracious." Her words hung in the air. "Any chance you have a satphone at the camp?"

"Absolutely. It wasn't working this morning, but we can try again tonight."

So, the general wanted to control their communications, but why? Was he an opportunist trying to use them as leverage in a business deal? Was he involved in Christos's kidnapping? Or was he kidnapping them?

The caravan pulled into an encampment surrounded by electrified fencing and armed sentries. For now, they were the general's guests.

Or, perhaps more accurately, his prisoners.

Chapter Thirty-Eight

Given that General Jemwa's training camp was in the middle of a desert, Thea was impressed by its creature comforts. Two soldiers brought hot water for the tub inside the permanent-feeling tent where she'd spend the night. After bathing, drinking another large bottle of water, eating two sandwiches, and injecting the insulin that still seemed sufficiently cool from her insulated pouch, she finally felt rejuvenated.

But concern weighed on her mind. She had Papa's cell phone, but it'd been all day since she'd had proper service. If the real kidnapper tried to reach her and was dumped into voice mail, who knew what he would do to her father?

She also needed to discover who'd sabotaged the plane and poisoned the pilots. How many people had had access to the Gulf- stream? Hakan would fly in a team to analyze the crash site and recover the remains of the flight crew. She was missing some- thing. No ransom demand, and every effort to investigate was met with violence. The killing wouldn't stop until they figured out who'd taken Papa and neutralized the threat.

With any luck, the plane wreckage would offer some new clues. If there was any useful evidence, her boss would find it. *Hakan.* He'd be so worried. She was rarely out of touch for an hour, let alone an entire day.

Another pressing problem troubled her. With only enough medication left to last until the next afternoon, she had to reach the pharmacy in Victoria Falls before midday so she could purchase more insulin and other supplies. Her stockpiles had blown up with the Gulfstream. With no access to medication and no outside communications, she felt naked, vulnerable.

Dressed in a colorful sarong the general had provided, she left her tent to find the others. The camp doctor had taken Peter and Brianna to the medical pavilion for a thorough checkup, as they were both showing signs of heatstroke. She explored the camp, following the row of torches lining the main thoroughfare. The beauty of the firelight was in direct contrast to the militarized setup of the place. Simple, structured, with one goal in mind: training killers.

The combination of the brisk wind and her wet hair sent a shiver across Thea's shoulders. With the sun gone for the night, the desert was cooling down.

A massive tent at the end of the row caught her attention. It was circular, and the heavy canvas looked durable, weathered. Spartan outdoor furniture huddled under a beige awning. No doubt the general used this pavilion as his quarters.

She strode over to the opening. "*Jambo,* anyone here?"

Silence greeted her. She paused for a moment, then tried again. No response.

It wasn't as if she could ring a doorbell. She pushed back the flap, peered inside, then entered the spacious tent. On the left, eight rattan chairs encircled a round table. A likely meeting spot for the general and his top lieutenants.

She moved deeper into the pavilion. The next room was a fully stocked kitchen with stainless-steel appliances supported by a generator. Off to the right was a fully outfitted office. She did a double-take. The desk, the chairs, even the lampshade—all the furniture mirrored the pieces in her father's former study in Kanzi. Right down to the crystal ashtray on the desk and the humidor beside it. What the heck?

Creepy.

She strode over to the desk, her nose wrinkling at a familiar smell. She raised the lid on the humidor and looked inside. Sure enough, Flor de Cano Short Churchills lined the box. She remembered sitting on the deck of the *Aphrodite* with Papa as he smoked these cigars. She lifted one to her nose and sniffed. Alarm ricocheted through her.

"Care to join me for one?" The low rumble of the general's voice jolted her back to the present. She almost dropped the cigar.

"Afraid they aren't to my taste. But, interestingly, they are my father's favorite brand." Not to mention that the whole office was a duplicate of her father's long-ago study.

Amusement showed on his bullish features. "A man of refined taste, your father. Perhaps you can both join me for dinner at my villa? I could educate you on the merits of the cigar's delicate flavors. That would be a memorable meal. As Raúl Juliá used to say, a cigar is as good as the memories that you have when you smoke it."

He had to be toying with her. But the fatigue, the pressure—they could be making her paranoid. "You must know that my father's been kidnapped."

The general's eyes widened, and his mouth opened. Gut feeling? His expression lasted slightly longer than genuine surprise. But that was only her intuition talking.

"Very sorry to hear that. I've been here training my men. We don't get much news."

"My father does a lot of business in Kanzi. Any thoughts as to who might want to abduct him?"

"My guess would be the Chinese, as they are quite keen on winning those oil rights, but it could be anyone. Billionaires and their families are always targets." He shrugged. "By the way, how's your brother doing? I don't know if you remember, but twenty years ago, I rescued him from a brutal warlord named Oba."

Rescued him. Right. It required every ounce of her self-restraint not to punch him. This giant was a master manipulator, a born liar. She glanced at the books lining the shelves of his office, everything from the classics to biographies. A sophisticated sociopath, he used his brawn as well as his brains to dominate others.

"Yes, that's right, you collected the million-dollar reward for Nikos's return. I knew you looked familiar."

"That money saved countless lives. We farmed land, grew crops for food. Your father became a local hero."

In Nikos's journal, "the General" had hated Papa because he'd bought all the crops for biofuels. Now the story had been rewritten, her father starring as the white knight?

"I was hoping to use your satellite phone," Thea said, needing this conversation to end.

"Of course, but please hurry. The men are eager to start the festivities." He passed her the phone. "Join us at the fire pit when you're done." He vanished as quickly as he'd appeared, light on his feet for such a large man.

She plunked down into the nearest chair, her mind swirling. Motive—what would be General Jemwa's motive for taking Papa? Money . . . power . . . oil . . . revenge? The possibilities were endless.

She dialed her boss's cell. He picked up on the first ring.

"Hakan Asker."

"My feng shui seems to be off today." Their code that the line wasn't secure.

A slight hesitation. "Where are you?"

"We had a unique landing in Kanzi. Rif, Peter, Brianna, and I are now enjoying the hospitality of General Ita Jemwa at his desert camp. Would be good to know who had access to the plane."

"You need air support?" It comforted her to hear his voice. Hakan would investigate, locate the wreckage.

"The general offered to transport us to Victoria Falls in the morning. But if I don't check in with you by eleven my time tomorrow, please send help. You can trace the GPS coordinates from the phone, right?"

"Definitely."

"We drove around sixty miles southwest of the crash. That should help you find the plane."

"Thanks. And text me when you arrive in Zimbabwe."

"Will do. How's Aegis behaving?"

"You don't want to know. Let's just say that my couch is looking rather unstuffed."

She smiled. "I told you he needs intense, daily exercise to keep the digging at bay."

"Don't worry, I'll have the newest recruit doing long runs with him every day now. They both need the exercise."

She shouldn't ask but couldn't help herself. "Anything new on your end?"

"Always. You know how busy I've been. Let's talk about it tomorrow."

"Perfect." Hope rose in her heart. Hakan had new information, maybe a lead.

"Send Rif my best."

"Will do. I should thank you for insisting we travel together. He's come in handy."

He laughed. "My boy has his charms."

"Let's not go overboard. Until tomorrow." She replaced the receiver and rested her head in her hands. The last thing she wanted to do was go to a party hosted by a sociopath, a man who could very well be holding Papa captive. After all, he'd already kidnapped one Paris and lied about it. Why not another?

And why stop at two?

Chapter Thirty-Nine

Rif sat by the fire, pretending to swig from the bottle of spirits that was being passed around the circle of men. General Jemwa's soldiers had traded their uniforms for traditional garb, their ebony skin glistening with sweat from the fire, white paint smeared across their cheeks and bodies. Spears and shields perched on the ground beside these warriors.

After they had enjoyed a meal of rice and goat on a spit, their dancing would start. Jaramogi, the general's second-in-command, would kick off the first performance. Rif had attended many native celebrations when he worked in Zimbabwe and Chad. Hell, he'd even admit to kicking off his shoes to join in the odd *mbende* step. But tonight, he needed to remain on guard.

They weren't among friends.

Peter's skin had deepened to a rosy pink, an indication that he was three, or maybe more like six, sheets to the wind. The CFO might be a whiz with numbers and contracts, but he had zero common sense. Stuck in the middle of the desert in a war-torn country, they were at the mercy of a dangerous man—getting drunk was a dumb-ass move. At least there'd been some good news. He'd checked on Brianna in the medical tent, and she was feeling much better.

He sensed the men's focus shift toward the lane leading to the tents and turned to see what had captured their interest. Thea glided toward the fire in an emerald sarong, the rich color highlighting her piercing green eyes. Her long, dark hair reflected the firelight. He regretted his part in giving her the scar on her right cheek, but the mark took nothing away from her beauty. It actually made her more striking—and human.

The men studied her with great interest. He could hardly blame them. They had probably been separated from women for months while posted at the testosterone-laden camp.

She slipped in between him and Peter, sitting cross-legged on the ground.

"I spoke to Hakan. He was startled to hear where we were," she said.

"Full circle from twenty years ago."

"Except this time it's Papa who has been taken. I wonder if our host is involved."

"Anything's possible," he said in a low voice.

"I found a humidor in the general's tent filled with Papa's favorite cigars, and his office has the exact same furniture as my father's former home office in Kanzi."

"Definitely weird. But why kidnap the man who could make your country richer than Saudi Arabia?"

The pounding of drums drowned out her response. The soldiers danced to the staccato beat, the sound and rhythm of the drums reflecting the heightened mood. As the men gyrated their hips and shimmied their shoulders, they merged into a circle. Each man took his turn inside the ring, often balancing on one hand, feet straight up in the air. Jaramogi stood out among the crowd, his tremendous strength and agility on display. The general's troops were a cohesive force—one might even say battle-ready.

A tremor of warning rumbled through Rif. He'd spent half his life in war-torn countries watching rebels plot to overthrow existing regimes. This camp in the middle of the desert didn't feel like a government-sanctioned training ground; it was more like the general's private headquarters. A barbed-wire fence surrounded the site, four armed guards were posted at the only exit, and the surrounding desert was utterly inhospitable; it was the perfect spot to "disappear" someone. Maybe Jemwa was biding his time to see how the oil negotiations went before he made a move. Nothing would surprise him.

Their host finally made an appearance, dressed in full uniform, the numerous medals pinned to his jacket covering only a small portion of his massive chest. He swaggered around the campfire, slapping backs with his bearlike paws, a cigar hanging from the left side of his mouth. The heady tobacco scent infused the air. Thea was right—it was Christos's favorite brand.

The drumming intensified, the earth thumping to the beat. Roasted goat, a hundred men who hadn't showered in days, the threat of scorpions and snakes. Best party he'd been to in a long time. *Right*. The last time he'd been in the desert, it had ended disastrously.

It had been a perfect night for a raid. A sandstorm shrouded the UN food depot in an ominous brown cloud. Rif continued patrolling the perimeter, a gust of wind blasting sand into his eyes. His lips were caked with dirt, so he spat out the gritty bits, then tramped past the spindly security gate in search of rebels. Standing orders were to shoot on sight. Everyone knew about the curfew, and they had to protect the refugees' food stores. The emaciated evacuees were already down to eight hundred calories a day. If they lost any more food, the gravediggers wouldn't be able to keep up with the bodies.

He'd spent the day hanging around the communications hut listening to reports of rebels moving in the night, defying the curfew. His unit was on high alert, protecting thousands of grain bags in the middle of the barren Chad desert. Sure, the rebel army also needed food, but he'd be damned if he'd let the bastards steal the supplies he was guarding.

The storm intensified, the gritty residue battering his exposed cheeks as he strained to see through his night-vision goggles. Damn things were useless in these conditions. He ripped them off and replaced them with clear-lens shooting glasses. They weren't much better.

What he wouldn't do for an ice-cold Coke. He thought of the local boy Kinshasa, an eight-year-old whose family lived in a neighboring village. The little guy was entrepreneurial, always showing up with cold drinks to trade for cash or food. This time of night, he'd be curled up inside his simple home, safe and sound.

Rif had spent his off-duty hours teaching the scrawny boy English. He'd broken his usual rule about not getting involved with the locals, but he had no regrets. Wasn't much else to do in the desert besides getting blotto on local beer, and he wasn't much for that. The kid's spunk inspired him, reminding him of Thea, who bounced back no matter what happened to her—witness how she'd pursued K&R work in response to her brother's kidnapping.

The glowing numbers of his Stocker & Yale P650 read 0200, four hours before the punishing sun would rise and Brown would relieve him. The crappy weather meant shorter night watches. A man could swallow only so much sand.

Sweat trickled down his forehead into his eyes, burning, impairing his vision. He removed one hand from his M4 and turned his back to the wind. Raising his glasses, he wiped off the sweat, but the gesture was useless. Gritty particles cut into his eyes like tiny blades.

Concerned about his weapon malfunctioning in the harsh conditions, he checked the firing mechanism. It still worked, but a layer of sand had accumulated on the barrel. He brushed it off in several quick strokes. His rifle had better not jam.

Bleary-eyed, he continued the patrol. The rebels' khakis would be camouflaged by the sandstorm, so he scanned the area for their signature red kerchiefs instead.

Movement to his right caught his attention. He held his breath, spun around, and caressed the trigger of his rifle, stopping just in time. A jerboa hopped past him. Damn rodent almost got its furry tan ass blown to bits. Weirdest-looking animal he'd ever seen, like a kangaroo mated with a mouse. His pulse thundered at the false alarm. He removed his finger from the trigger.

Time slowed to an agonizing grind. He tried not to think about the Coke. A week's wages for a sip—okay, maybe even a month's. In the middle of the African desert, he had nothing else to spend his money on.

A sound, like that of boots swishing through sand. Damn. The intel had been right. He caught a glimpse of red to his left. Another blast of grit kicked up and blinded him. Instinctively he pointed his rifle in the direction where he'd seen the red and squeezed the trigger. Bullets spewed from the barrel, the recoil hammering his shoulder.

A sharp cry filled the night, followed by silence. He waited, moving his rifle back and forth, ready for the second wave of soldiers. Nothing happened. Strange. The rebels always traveled in groups. He lowered his rifle and stepped toward the flash of red. Still nothing. Where the hell was Brown? Hadn't he heard the shots? Slowly moving forward, he raised his rifle. Another step, and the red fabric stopped him cold.

Kinshasa lay spread-eagled on his back, decked out in a red Coke T-shirt with what looked to be a twelve-pack of soda beside him in a threadbare canvas sack.

His heart jammed. Kinshasa moaned. A bullet had ripped through his tiny body. Oh, God. What the hell was he doing here in the middle of the sandstorm? He knew not to be out past curfew. Rif wiped at his cheeks. The little boy had probably snuck out, hoping to make a buck from the thirsty men.

Slinging the rifle over his left shoulder, he scooped up the weightless body in his arms. Kinshasa's eyelids fluttered, then closed. The boy's stillness was Rif's unraveling. He used his jacket to slow the blood loss.

What could he do? The nearby refugee camp—they had doctors. He cradled the boy in his arms and raced through the sandstorm, desperate for help.

Kinshasa had lived, thankfully, but the trauma of being shot had transformed the lighthearted boy into a quiet, serious young man. Rif still sent him and his family money every month, anonymously.

His team, his superiors, and later even Thea had told him his actions had been by the book, but . . . he'd shot an eight-year-old boy, a friend. He looked at his work differently now. More cautious about getting close yet more aggressive during maneuvers. He'd do whatever it took to make sure the people he cared about were safe.

Chapter Forty

Thea couldn't have been less excited to be flying so soon after the crash. But at least the Bell helicopter hovering over the mile-wide Victoria Falls gave her a spectacular view of the world's largest curtain of falling water. Mist surrounded the Zambezi River in the early morning, casting a haze over the lush greenery and red earth. The cataract, called *Mosi-oa-Tunya*—Smoke That Thunders—deserved its place on the list of the seven natural wonders of the world. As David Livingstone eloquently recorded in his diary in 1855, there were "scenes so lovely, they must have been gazed upon by angels in flight." But the giant sitting next to her was certainly no angel.

"My men are looking into the possibility of your father being held in Kanzi. If he's in my country, we'll find him," the general said.

Hardly comforting. The Kanzi dignitary was a proven kidnapper in his own right. And his doppelgänger office had given her shivers. For all she knew, he could be the one holding Papa captive. Still, no sense antagonizing him. "Thanks for your help and the ride." She was sitting behind Rif, so she couldn't read his expression. Brianna and Peter were in the second helicopter, following them.

Fatigue shrouded her shoulders. She'd had a sleepless night in her tent, tossing and turning, uncertain whether General Jemwa would come through on his promise to transport them the short distance to Victoria Falls. But the temptation of keeping his unexpected guests in limbo obviously paled next to being on hand for the negotiations about the billions of dollars in oil rights.

The Bell descended toward the Elephant Hills Hotel's helipad. Less than a minute later, they landed on the painted white circle. Four Hummers waited to transport them to the Victoria Falls Hotel, a few kilometers away.

She exited the helicopter and hurried to the Hummers, her mind already planning ahead. First she needed to speak to Hakan; then she had to ditch Rif so she could find a pharmacy. Being out of touch had been a frustrating purgatory—not knowing if the kidnapper had called, not knowing if Hakan had had a break in the case, not knowing if Papa had been hurt, or worse.

Thea, Rif, and General Jemwa slid into the first Hummer, and they set off for the hotel. The town was in reasonably good shape, given the devastation Mugabe had wrought amassing his own wealth. Still, the guarded, fatigued faces along the street reflected the wear and tear of a long-time dictatorship.

Her phone started vibrating in her pocket. They had cellular service again. Leaning forward in her seat, she scanned the messages.

A text from Hakan: *Call me ASAP. The blood on the helipad of the Aphrodite was the same type as Christos's.*

Rif stared at her. She shook her head. Not now. She'd fill him in at the hotel. And she was still waiting for her father's phone to pick up a signal—stupid BlackBerry. Ignoring the beauty of the ferns, palms, and liana vines, she scrolled through her personal messages. One from Freddy caught her eye: *Christos's personal calendar was erased from his computer. We're working on recovering the information. As soon as we do, I'd like you to review it. He had a phone call with someone the morning he disappeared. Maybe you can put names to the initials.*

Who would have access to her father's calendar? His assistant? Ahmed? Peter? Or maybe someone had hacked it. There had to be something incriminating on it if someone had gone to the trouble of erasing it.

A minute later, slightly delayed, her father's phone vibrated as well. A multitude of business e-mails downloaded, as well as several heart-wrenching messages from the now-deceased Helena. A single text popped up on the screen.

Pede poena claudo.

"Punishment comes on halting foot." Retribution may be slow, but it gets there in the end. A quote from Horace.

She shuddered. This was no conventional K&R, where the perpetrator simply wanted a ton of unmarked bills for the return of the hostage. They'd dealt with ransom cases, political ones, but this one was different. What did the kidnapper have to gain from holding Papa if he didn't want money or concessions? Yet the Latin expert wouldn't bother communicating with her if it was just a straight assassination. They needed to read between the lines, discover the subliminal clues to the identity of the mystery man or woman.

The Hummer's door swung open. They'd arrived at the hotel, the majestic colonial building boasting white columns along the main entrance. Two large palms stood guard over the historical landmark, the red roof and pathway contrasting with the crisp, light walls. African five-star hospitality awaited them.

"I hope you'll be my guests at the cocktail party hosted by Prime Minister Kimweri this evening," said the general. "It'll give you a chance to mingle with the respected leaders of our great nation—and your competition in the negotiations."

"We wouldn't miss it." Rif hopped out of the vehicle and offered Thea a hand.

"Until tonight." Jemwa strode down the pathway to the front entrance.

"What the hell is he up to?" she asked.

"General Ita Jemwa was Nikos's original kidnapper. It was never my confidence to break, but, given the circumstances, you need to know about the past," Rif said.

"How do you know this?" Was she the only one who'd been kept in the dark?

"I discovered the combination to my father's safe and read Nikos's journal. Christos had asked my father to keep the notes private, but I was a nosy kid."

"You know about Oba?"

"Yes. How do—"

"Someone slipped Nikos's psychiatrist's notes into my computer bag. Not you?"

"No, I haven't seen those pages in years."

"Does Nikos realize what you know?" she asked.

"He caught me ransacking the safe. I often wonder what he was doing in my father's study. Maybe he wanted his journal back."

No wonder Nikos felt so hostile toward Rif. Having the worst moments of your life exposed—especially to a younger boy, who'd snuck access to the information—couldn't have been easy.

As they headed toward the hotel entrance, a wave of dizziness washed over her. She needed insulin, food, and rest. Two out of three were essential.

"You okay?" he asked.

"Just worried. Let's check in." She nodded to the doorman, a tall man with a winsome smile dressed in a reddish-brown topcoat and hat. Everyone in the hotel exuded human warmth, creating an incredibly welcoming atmosphere.

"Fill me in. Did the kidnapper send a ransom demand?" Rif asked.

"No, another Latin text. I'm beginning to worry that all the money in the world isn't going to save Papa."

Chapter Forty-One

The lights in the 767's cabin dimmed as the meal service ended. Max had insisted on upgrading them to first class. Gabrielle had gone along with the luxury because she hoped to get some quality sleep before they arrived at the summit in Zimbabwe on the trail of Thea Paris. Besides, the food was a lot better up front.

While Max communicated with his office, she read the encrypted texts from her boss, Stephen Kelly, at HRFC. Disappointment flooded her. The SEAL team had recovered a bank executive in Syria, not Christos Paris. She tried to reach Thea with the news but had no luck, so she called Hakan instead. The owner of Quantum International Security was professional, intelligent—he had a good team on the kidnapping, and she hoped to find a way to assist, as the political pressure to bring the oil billionaire home was mounting.

While she normally wasn't mandated to carry a weapon outside the US, she'd contacted a friend who was a former CIA operative. He'd be kitting her up while she was in Africa. If there was trouble, she wanted to be armed and ready.

Two glasses of full-bodied Cabernet Sauvignon left her muscles relaxed, the plush blanket soft against her arms. She'd phoned her sister to check on how her latest chemo session had gone. "My hair is Marine-ready," Adriana had told her. "I'm going down to the recruiting office today." Her sense of humor and optimistic attitude while fighting stage three breast cancer were humbling. Gabrielle pressed the end button, hating to say good-bye.

"Your sister?" Max asked.

"On round two now. I should be there with her."

"But she disagreed."

"Exactly. I booked vacation days to look after her during round one. Maybe it was my cooking that put her off." She tried to smile but knew the mirth didn't quite reach her eyes.

"Even people who are very ill still need to feel independent sometimes. They already give up so much, they need some semblance of control."

He was right. Adriana was just trying to hold on to what she could. "How's *your* sister, Max?" She should have asked sooner, but they'd been so focused on the case.

"About the same." Pain shimmered in his eyes. It was rare to see a man so open about his raw emotions. "Although we didn't always live in the same house, we spent a lot of time together."

Right; she remembered that they were half siblings, sharing a mother. She squeezed his arm. "I'm sorry. It's horrible to watch someone you love suffer."

"Memories of you and me in Athens help get me through the pain." His powerful hand slid under the blanket and rested just above her knee. "I've missed you, Gabrielle."

Whoa. She peeled his fingers off her leg. "We live in different countries, have different lives."

"And that's why we need to make the most of every moment we have together."

His hand returned, sliding up her inner thigh. Excitement shot through her body. He made her feel animated, adrenalized.

She should resist, maintain her professionalism, but the wine had weakened her resolve. She wanted to say yes.

He pulled aside her lace panties. The cool air tingled on her exposed flesh. She shivered. He thrust two fingers inside her. She gasped.

The flight attendant arrived with a tray of drinks. "Can I offer either of you a nightcap?"

Gabrielle tried to maintain a calm façade so the attendant wouldn't know what was going on underneath the blanket. "No, we're good, thanks." *Better than good.*

"If I can get you anything else, just let me know," the flight attendant said, moving down the aisle.

"I have everything I need right here." Max's fingers eased in and out deeply while his thumb stroked her clitoris.

She arched her hips in response to his fingers. Her whole body ached for him. What was she doing? A top-level government operative screwing around on a commercial plane. If news of this ever got out, she'd be a laughingstock.

She searched for the strength to stop him, but a wave of pleasure drowned any lingering resistance. Oh, God, if he kept this up, she'd be frog-marched off the plane for screaming.

She was hovering on the crest of a climax; he pushed her over the edge. She stifled a moan as her body rode the waves of pleasure. He made her feel so good, and not just physically.

He leaned over and kissed the top of her head, a genuine smile on his face, but sadness lingered in his eyes. "You are special."

Dammit to hell. She didn't think she could stand it if he got all romantic on her. And had she technically broken her one-night rule if they hadn't had actual intercourse?

Chapter Forty-Two

Thea had ditched Rif while he showered so she could restock her medications and supplies. The local pharmacy didn't have her regular brand of insulin, but she'd make do. Time-zone changes, stress, and missed meals all wreaked havoc with her blood sugar levels, and stabilization was key to remaining healthy.

Back in her room, she studied the layout of the hotel. Knowing the ins and outs of the building boosted her confidence. Given the litany of recent attacks, she was determined to maintain her situational awareness.

She phoned Hakan.

He picked up on the first ring. "I spoke to Gabrielle Farrah. Disappointing news. The SEAL team recovered a banker who'd been kidnapped six months ago. No sign of your father."

Of course finding Papa wouldn't be that easy. "Thanks for letting me know."

"The press is going crazy with hypotheses about who abducted Christos," Hakan said.

"The media loves dirty laundry. I guess this situation is too tempting to resist."

"I have a team looking into the plane crash. Watch your back. Someone didn't want you making it to Kanzi." His voice sounded depleted, tired. She was sure he'd been awake around the clock, working every angle with Freddy Winston and the team at Quantum.

"Rif's piloting skills came in handy."

"My son works well under pressure. So do you."

"We're missing something. The answer's in my peripheral vision, but I can't quite see it." She was beyond frustrated.

"No ransom, cryptic messages, zero forensic evidence. The kidnapper's a pro. Henri used a burner cell to set off the limo explosion, but so far nothing to trace back to whoever orchestrated Helena's murder."

"She knew the kidnapper's identity but wouldn't tell me on the phone."

"And the Moleskine is gone. I have Paco working his connections in Colombia to analyze the FARC angle, but I agree with you—the real kidnapper had nothing to do with what happened on the supertanker. He's playing an intricate game and doesn't want to reveal himself yet. Could it be someone in our industry? It feels like they have the rulebook on kidnapping, making none of the typical mistakes."

"And always several steps ahead. We need to catch up before we reach checkmate."

"I'm worried about your safety. The attack in the alley, the plane crash . . . they keep coming for you. It makes me think they missed you on the yacht. The timing of your stair run might have saved your life," Hakan said.

"I lost all my belongings in the plane crash, so if they planted a tracker, that's out of the picture now. Rif and I are on full alert, so don't worry."

"I can't help but worry. We keep striking out chasing leads. I have the team working every angle, including ISIS, Ares, the Russian mob, General Jemwa, Prime Minister Kimweri, the Chinese . . . the list goes on."

"Don't discredit an event from the distant past. The planning involved in such a complex operation would take the patience of Job. It's also the twentieth anniversary of Nikos's kidnapping, coming full circle now that Papa has been taken."

"Speaking of which, have you heard from your brother?" Hakan had a soft spot for Nikos, maybe because he knew what had happened during his captivity.

"No. He wasn't pleased he'd been left out of the loop. Someone stuck his old psychiatric notes in my bag, the full story. All my life, I've been fed lies. Why didn't anyone tell me what he'd really endured?"

Silence echoed on the line for an endless moment. "Christos insisted. One child had been stripped of his innocence. Your father didn't want you to lose your childhood as well."

"What about when I grew up? Didn't I deserve to know the truth about my own brother?"

"That wasn't my decision to make."

"Was Nikos told not to say anything?" Her heart ached for her brother—she couldn't imagine living through such horrors, then having to hide it all.

"You'll need to ask your father about all of this."

And she would, but she needed to find him first. "Any leads on the latest text?"

"Sent from another burner phone, disabled immediately after it was used."

"You think the kidnapper hired the men on the *Damocles* to distract us?" she asked.

"When someone as wealthy as Christos is kidnapped, everyone comes looking for their fifteen minutes of fame, or ten million euros. It could be totally unrelated."

"FARC knew about Papa's watch."

"Things have a way of leaking out. They didn't have the actual watch; they just knew about it. I have the lab analyzing it for fingerprints or other evidence."

A knock on the door jolted her. "I need to go. The cocktail party hosted by the prime minister starts shortly. I plan on spending time with General Jemwa—I definitely don't trust him. And what about the plane crash?"

"I'm meeting with experts this afternoon."

"Please keep me posted."

"I'm on it."

"I feel lucky to have you in my corner, boss."

"Always."

Another knock. She pressed the end button and stared through the peephole.

Peter Kennedy. Just what she didn't need.

She tightened the sash on her robe and opened the door.

"I thought we should have a drink before the party starts, talk strategy about tomorrow's negotiations." He stood on the threshold, dressed in a cream-colored suit with a pale orange tie and matching pocket puff. With all their luggage lost in the crash, how the hell had he found such an outfit so quickly?

"How about we meet after the party, say, around ten o'clock? I'm not quite ready. I asked the hotel gift shop to send up a dress."

His gaze drifted to the neckline of her robe. It took an effort not to cringe.

He blinked a few times, his eyelids fluttering in a weird pattern. "Why don't we sit in the gardens? I don't want anyone overhearing us. When Christos returns—and he will return—I want him to be proud of what we've accomplished in his absence. This deal—it could change everything."

"Absolutely. See you at the party."

She closed the door and collapsed in the nearest chair, weary of presenting a brave front. Kidnappings were often prolonged, demanding infinite patience and a poker face, but none of her experiences had prepared her for this intensely personal and confounding case. Grief and worry were shaped differently when the stakes were so close to home.

She squeezed her eyes shut. Clarity tamed the chaos. Control was obviously important to the kidnapper, and she was about to rip it away.

The room phone rang. "Hello."

"Ms. Paris, your dress is ready. Shall I send it up?"

"Right away, please."

Time to take the reins.

Chapter Forty-Three

The plunging neckline on the gift shop's sapphire sheath revealed more cleavage than Thea was comfortable showing, but her options were few. The dress reminded her of Helena, who'd loved the color blue, redoing her father's home in the south of France in shades of azure, cerulean, and indigo. Thea's eyes stung. She wondered if Papa knew about his wife's death.

She brought herself back to the moment. The kidnapper was in her sights, and she would pursue him relentlessly. She brushed out her long hair, applied lip gloss, and headed through the arched hallways to the grandeur of the Livingstone Room, bracing herself for the night ahead.

Antique furniture and portraits of British royalty gave the large ballroom an old-world, colonial feel. A pianist danced his fingers along a baby grand, and white-gloved waiters served champagne and hors d'oeuvres. First class all the way. And so it should be—billions of dollars were at stake, and the Kanzi officials were about to enjoy a significant improvement in their lifestyle, regardless of who won those oil rights.

Peter was perched beside the bar on the far side of the room. *Surprise, surprise.* He waved at her, but she pretended not to see him. She'd deal with him later. Right now, she wanted to assess the players, see if anyone stood out as a potential kidnapper, specifically the Quan family, Paris Industries' direct competition for the oil rights.

She maneuvered deeper into the room, accepting a glass of champagne from a passing waiter. The colorful splashes of traditional African garb brightened the space. Many of the women wore elaborate headdresses befitting royalty. Standing in the receiving line for the prime minister, she scanned the room. Like the United Nations, it was filled with people of varied backgrounds, a thousand agendas being pushed forward.

When she finally made it to the front of the line, she was surprised by the compassion in the prime minister's eyes. "Ms. Paris, I've been trying to reach you. I wanted to see if I could assist somehow with your father's kidnapping. Many years ago, Christos helped my family during difficult times. I will never forget his kindness."

Her heart softened, thinking of Papa's charitable spirit. Sure, he was a hard-nosed businessman, but he always gave back to the community. But was the prime minister being sincere about his offer, or was it a cover? "Thank you. I'll definitely come to you if I need something. He'd be sorry to miss your lovely party."

The prime minister laughed. "Yes, I could always count on your father to be part of any celebration. Please remember my offer."

"Will do, and I promise that Paris Industries will stay on top of everything until he returns."

The receiving line surged forward, and people anxious to rub Buddha's belly nudged her out of the way. She headed for the back of the room to find a better vantage point.

In direct contrast to the colorfully clothed Africans, the Chinese contingent wore all black, tuxedos for the men, a floor-length evening gown that clung to the lone woman's svelte figure. Her jet-black hair contrasted with her pale complexion and red lipstick for dramatic effect. Thea recognized Quan Xi-Ping—and her brother, Chi—from Christos's party. They would be the main negotiators on behalf of the Chinese National Oil Company, bringing more than twenty-five years of combined experience to the table.

Chi was reputed to be a genius with logistics, while his stunning sister was the "closer," a woman who didn't take no for an answer. The general held her hand to his lips for an endless moment, as if transfixed by her loveliness.

A strong hand grabbed Thea's arm. Rif. There were storm clouds in his eyes. "Next time I shower, I'll handcuff you to the sink."

"I had errands to run. As you can see, I'm perfectly fine."

"Men attacked us in Santorini, our plane crashed, and we're about to start negotiations for a billion-dollar commodity in a war-torn country. You need to be extra careful."

Genuine concern had replaced his anger. He was right. She'd been irresponsible, unfair. "I'm sorry. I'm so used to traveling alone, I rarely think about it."

"I have no interest in being Big Brother . . ." He stared across the Livingstone Room as Nikos entered, decked out in a designer tux. "But now that I see yours is here, I'll leave you to the family reunion."

She strode toward her brother and hugged him.

He returned her hug, hard. "I heard about the plane crash from Peter. Are you all right?"

"I'm fine. Let's talk about you. All the hotels in all the towns in all the world, you walk in here?"

He smiled. "Here's looking at you, kid."

Her playful tone changed to one of concern. "What's going on, Nikos?"

"I was rude to you in Santorini. I'm sorry I lost my temper. To make it up to you, I wanted to offer my support. With Father missing in action, you shouldn't have to face everything alone."

"Thank you. I wanted to do whatever I could to support Peter and Ahmed in the negotiations—and I sense there's a connection here to Papa's kidnapping."

"I've come across the Quan family before. They don't play fair."

Papa would be aghast if he knew Nikos was here. Still, maybe this situation could mend fences in their family.

"I had a meeting canceled in South Africa. Being close seemed like kismet." Her brother's expression was earnest, beseeching.

General Jemwa headed straight for them with the Chinese siblings in tow. Nikos was about to come face-to-face with his kidnapper. How would he react? She braced herself for an explosion. Her brother had a terrible temper. She'd witnessed it more than once over the years and had a scar to prove it.

"Ms. Paris, good to see you again. We can arrange for that steak you wanted tonight. And look who's here, the brother I rescued from that horrid warlord many years ago." Jemwa turned to Xi-Ping and Chi. "Did you know about Nikos's kidnapping?"

"Maybe we should discuss the reason we're all here. I understand we'll have an early start in the morning." Thea wanted to avert her brother's infamous temper. Things were tense enough.

But Nikos surprised her. He merely gave Jemwa a curt, emotionless nod. "That's okay, Thea; if the general wants accolades about his heroism, he's welcome to share my tale of woe."

Chi gave Nikos a cold look. "Well, the general won't be reflecting on your shared history at the bargaining table."

Nikos smiled. "If I were worried about Paris Industries' competition, it wouldn't be because of you. I crossed paths with Xi-Ping a few years ago when I imported goods into China. She's a ferocious negotiator."

Chi had a flat affect. "It'll be me you'll see in action. My sister is just window-dressing."

Yikes, what a sexist! Xi-Ping stared at Chi in an unsettling way.

Thea ached to get away from the siblings—and to separate Nikos from General Jemwa, in case the situation soured.

"General, would you like to join me for a drink with the prime minister? I see he's finished the receiving line."

"Of course."

A subtle spark in the general's eyes told her that Kimweri wasn't the giant's favorite person. Still, he tucked Thea's hand under his arm. "Nikos, come see me later so I can hear how you've been doing. Always a pleasure to catch up with old friends."

Friends? Hardly. Only a slight wariness in her brother's gaze belied his enthusiasm for this meeting. Out of the corner of her eye, she caught Rif staring at her. She didn't blame him for standing alone in a corner. This was the cocktail party from hell, with more tension in the room than even she could tolerate. She glanced over her shoulder, almost expecting to see a knife aimed at her back.

Chapter Forty-Four

It had been a while since Nikos had had this much fun at a cocktail party. He only tolerated these events as a necessary evil when he was Nikos Paris. The best part about Ares was his ghostlike persona, since very few people met with him directly, and those who did craved the same anonymity.

And talking of façades, the General had demonstrated how adept he was at lying, which came as no surprise. Even Thea had proved to be a talented poker player. If he didn't know her so well, he'd have missed the subtle signals of panic she'd emitted as Jemwa approached them.

It meant she'd read the notes he'd slipped into her computer bag. Now that his past was out in the open, she would see the truth, that Papa wasn't some kind of hero. She needed to understand how much he'd suffered because of their father's greed. Hope sprung up inside him—that Thea did love him unconditionally. Together, they'd made a real difference with the African charity, but there was so much more they could do.

"You didn't tell me your sister was so beautiful," Xi-Ping said after Chi left to speak with one of Kanzi's dignitaries.

"Feeling threatened?" Nikos asked. Thea had won the gene-pool lottery, inheriting their father's dark hair and olive skin and their mother's emerald eyes, but it was her intelligence that set her apart.

"Never." Xi-Ping smiled, her tongue then stroking her lips. "Come to my room tonight—I'll show you how threatened I am."

He laughed. "I'm afraid I'll need my beauty sleep to be fresh for tomorrow's business."

"What are you talking about? You aren't involved in the negotiations."

He raised his eyebrows. "I need to refresh my drink. Excuse me."

"But—"

He headed for the bar. He might not know his father's location yet, but he would soon enough. The twists kept the game stimulating.

Chapter Forty-Five

Rif stood in one corner of the Livingstone Room, taking in the coffered ceilings, elegant sconces, and rich burgundy tapestries. Definitely a tonier venue than his usual, military-style accommodations. He'd ordered a tonic water from the bartender—no alcohol for him tonight, though he could use a stiff drink.

A few feet away, a circle made up of Thea, Nikos, and a striking Chinese couple—undoubtedly the opposition in the oil deal—had just broken up. Good thing, as he sensed from their body language that trouble was brewing. General Jemwa had his arms crossed and was leaning slightly backward, a position indicating opposition. Given the history between him and Nikos, Rif was not surprised.

In turn, Nikos maintained intense eye contact with the giant man, which in certain situations could mean positive interest. In this case, it probably indicated that Nikos had zero trust in the general and didn't want to lower his defenses. Still, there was something unsettling about the interaction between the two men that Rif couldn't put his finger on.

Chi, black hair slicked back with product, hadn't blinked once during the entire conversation—a potential sign of deceit. Thea's head and neck had been straighter than a steel rod, her shoulders rigid. People never tilted their heads if they were with someone they didn't trust or were afraid of.

He'd been about to rescue her when she'd led Jemwa in the opposite direction and Chi had turned away, leaving Nikos alone with the Chinese beauty. The woman's hungry gaze drifted from Nikos's eyes down to his lips. *Someone* was hot for Nikos. And this clearly wasn't their first meeting. They emanated a familiarity, standing way too close to each other to be strangers. He wondered if Thea knew anything about their history or had sensed it tonight.

A few suits drifted around the room. Rif recognized two of the corporate types as lawyers from Paris Industries—he'd met them briefly when he'd handled security at industry functions. Ahmed Khali was also there, pressing the flesh. With all the characters in place, these negotiations promised to be compelling. And somewhere in this complex web hid the answer to Christos's kidnapping—he'd bet his life on it.

He combed the perimeter of the room, scanning for threats, keeping a close eye on Thea. He'd taken a quick shower earlier, and she'd disappeared. She was aware of the potential threat, so she had to be up to something important to take any risks at this point. He'd check with the bellman later, slip him a tip, and ask if she'd taken a taxi into town. Although he hated to invade her privacy, he couldn't risk her safety. And *forthcoming* wasn't exactly her middle name.

As he negotiated the crowd, he came face-to-face with the general. "Quite an impressive camp you had in the desert. You expecting a war?"

The man's nostrils flared. "You expected child soldiers toting antiquated weapons? Sorry to disappoint. This region of Africa is a dangerous neighborhood; it's best to be prepared."

"I lived in Kanzi when I was a kid."

Jemwa blinked. "With Christos Paris?"

"My father coordinates his security."

"Well, then, perhaps it's your father who's antiquated. His methods didn't prevent Mr. Paris from being kidnapped."

Rif stood straighter. "Now that you mention it, your soldiers' weapons did look brand new. Chinese manufacture, if I'm not mistaken. Did those come from Ares?"

"Who?"

Rif could feel Thea's gaze on him but didn't look in her direction. "Your arms dealer. I bet you know more than you're saying about what happened to Christos. Weren't you the one who kidnapped his son twenty years ago?"

The general smiled, a big, broad, crocodile grin. "You must be mistaken. I rescued Nikos from the warlord who had abducted him."

"That's not what I heard." Rif stared deeply into the general's eyes.

"Spreading rumors can be dangerous, especially when you're in another man's neighborhood. Perhaps you should enjoy the festivities and leave your suspicions for another day."

Sudden movement across the room distracted him. Peter was stumbling in Thea's direction, obviously inebriated. Where the hell was his professionalism? Maybe it was acceptable to be half-sloshed at some business functions, but wouldn't it make more sense to keep your wits about you? And this was undoubtedly the most important negotiation of Peter's career; he was stepping up in a crisis to help close this deal. Being intoxicated now seemed foolish, even for him.

Rif left the general, wanting to intercept the CFO before he embarrassed Thea.

Too late. Peter bumped into a waiter, vaulting a tray of champagne glasses across the room. Crystal shattered on the floor. People turned to stare. The pianist stopped playing. A hush fell over the Livingstone Room.

Peter staggered forward, his pace slowing with every step. His face was mottled, eyes glazed. White froth leaked from his mouth. Seconds later, he collapsed on the hardwood floor.

Rif scrambled forward to help him, quickly feeling for a pulse. He couldn't find one. Thea joined him on the ground, preparing to start CPR.

A faint but familiar whiff of almonds drifted into his sinuses. He placed a hand on Thea's shoulder. "It's too late. He's gone."

Chapter Forty-Six

Thea stared at Peter Kennedy, wishing she could will him back to life, but his bulging, inert eyes left no hope. Minutes ago, he'd waved to her from across the room, his normally gregarious self. Now he was dead. Cyanide, by the look and smell of it.

Sirens sounded in the distance. The partygoers hovered around them in a scattered circle, muttering to each other. The room's festive, relaxed mood had turned sour. Now a corpse marred the gleaming marble floor.

Rif offered Thea a hand up. She accepted, her knees wobbly.

General Jemwa strode toward them. "Ms. Paris, my guards are sealing the entrances to the hotel until we determine what happened here. The local authorities are on their way."

Whoever had murdered Peter could easily have slipped something into his drink and had plenty of time to leave the party. Even if the killer was still here, finding any evidence would take time.

The general announced in his booming voice, "Ladies and gentlemen, please move to the far side of the room, and the waiters will continue to serve you. Nobody may go until the authorities arrive and release you."

From the expressions on the guests' faces, Thea surmised that the last thing they wanted to do was remain in a room with a dead body, but no one disobeyed the giant's orders. After all, he was Prime Minister Kimweri's head of security.

"Can your men collect any photos or video footage from tonight?" she asked. It was doubtful they'd catch the killer in the act, but it would be worth seeing if anyone had hovered near Peter at the bar. "I'd also like to interview your bartenders."

"Whatever you need." The general seemed genuinely distressed by Peter's demise.

Thea and Rif stood together near the CFO's body, waiting for the forensics team and medical examiner to arrive.

Rif's hand brushed the stubble on his cheek. "I wasn't a big fan of Kennedy, but he didn't deserve this."

"I feel so bad. His ex-wife, his kids. They're going to be devastated."

"This whole deal is cursed. So many people involved have died—and then there's Christos's kidnapping. It was the right decision to come here. It's all connected."

"I'd look closely at the Chinese. They have the most to gain if Paris Industries folds at the bargaining table. And you need to know . . ."

Nikos walked up and touched her shoulder. "You okay?"

"Far from it, but we'll get through this somehow." Her eyelids felt heavy, tired.

Ahmed joined their group. "I spoke to the prime minister. He's offered to delay the negotiations for a day or two, his way of showing respect for our loss."

Peter's extensive knowledge of the figures would be sorely missed, but Ahmed Khali was a genius at the negotiating table. Whoever was behind Peter's murder wanted this delay, so Thea hoped Ahmed wouldn't give it to them. They'd had enough setbacks. Ahmed needed ballast at that bargaining table.

"Are you still willing to move forward?" she asked.

"Absolutely." Ahmed touched his temple, as if warding off a headache.

"Perhaps it would help if we had both brother and sister at the Paris table, a show of family solidarity," Nikos said.

"I'll let the prime minister know that we'll be ready to start first thing. Nikos, come over and meet him." Ahmed and Nikos headed toward the leader of Kanzi.

Rif's glare made her uncomfortable.

"What?" she asked.

"You really think this is a good idea? Christos would be apoplectic if he knew that Nikos was anywhere near this deal."

"I'm tired of being reactive, and it's not as if Nikos and I will do the actual negotiating. That's Ahmed's job. It's more about showing how the Paris family stands behind the company. And we need to draw out the kidnapper."

"He might be closer than you realize," Rif said.

"What does that—"

Two people were making their way across the room. As they closed the distance, she recognized Gabrielle Farrah and Maximillian Heros. Was it too much to hope that they had information that could help?

Chapter Forty-Seven

Gabrielle stubbed out a cigarette and strode over to where Thea stood beside her bodyguard, Rifat Asker. Damn good thing she had extra protection. Dead bodies were piling up, and with the recent plane crash, it seemed likely that Ms. Paris was a target as well.

Over the last couple of days, she and Hakan Asker had been sharing facts about the Christos Paris abduction. Gabrielle had the HRFC analysts running the Latin quotes he'd given her through their filters, looking for any similar messages in other kidnaps. She wasn't hopeful on that score, as this case was clearly an anomaly.

"Dare I ask?" She nodded toward the dead body.

"Peter Kennedy, CFO of Paris Industries and one of the lead negotiators for the Kanzi deal. Looks like he was poisoned. From the scent of almonds, my guess is cyanide," Thea said.

"I'll make sure my team takes a look once the forensics are in." She could coordinate with the State Department, help them deal with the American businessman's death.

"I am sorry for your loss," Max said. "Will the negotiations be canceled?"

"Our COO Ahmed Khali will handle things, but it won't be the same without Peter."

Gabrielle admired this young woman. Her father had been kidnapped, her stepmother blown up, her plane sabotaged, and now the lead negotiator of Paris Industries was dead, poisoned—yet she soldiered on. "May I have a moment of your time?"

"Sure, what is it?"

"Over here, please." Gabrielle headed to a far corner of the room. Thea, Rif, and Max followed.

"Have you learned something about my father?"

"Hakan told you it wasn't Christos that ISIS was holding captive in Syria?"

"Yes, he did."

"More and more I'm thinking Ares could be behind this kidnapping. The arms dealer has such a strong presence in Kanzi, and there's talk among the local militia that he's involved. Max and I are exploring that angle. The HRFC team is scanning multiple communications channels, searching for chatter about your father's abduction. Criminals can't seem to keep their mouths shut—or, in this case, perhaps, their fingers still."

"I hope they find something."

Gabrielle's phone rang. "I need to get this. I'll catch up with you."

She turned on her heel, phone to her ear, leaving Max with Thea and Rif.

Max cleared his throat. "Ms. Paris, we have not found anything on your father's yacht that points to the kidnapper. Just a small amount of Christos's blood on the helipad. But the Hellenic police are still processing the *Aphrodite* for trace evidence."

"I appreciate the update."

Max checked his watch. "I have secured special permission to work the case here in Kanzi, and I am meeting my contact from the nearby Interpol office in Harare. I would be pleased to help coordinate the flow of information."

"We'll take any help you're willing to give."

"Has the kidnapper made any demands?" he asked.

She looked across the room at Peter's body, still shaken that he'd been murdered. Questions swirled in her mind. Had the CFO been involved in the kidnapping? Had he been a corporate spy? Or was he another innocent victim?

"This isn't a good time, Mr. Heros. Perhaps we can talk later. I hope you understand. I'd like to notify Peter's family of his death and assist the police when they arrive."

"Of course, I apologize. Please know that I am at your disposal if you need anything at all." Max shook her and Rif's hands and headed for the crowd of partygoers on the other side of the room.

Chapter Forty-Eight

Back in her hotel room after talking to the police and contacting Peter Kennedy's family, Thea wanted nothing more than to sink into the pillow-top bed and close her eyes for twenty-four hours. But she had a meeting with Ahmed Khali and the Paris Industries lawyers at 5:00 a.m. the next day to go over the speech she was to give and discuss any last-minute issues. But as she was removing her heels, she spied some yellowed papers resting on the bed, similar to the pages she'd found in her computer bag: more pages from Nikos's journal.

Before reading them, she carefully searched the suite, room by room. Empty. Whoever had been there was long gone. She called the front desk and asked if anyone had accessed her room. Only the maid, as far as they knew. But someone other than a maid had definitely been there.

Chances were it was Nikos. He'd been there in Greece and now here in Kanzi. Besides Rif and Hakan, who was a world away, who else would have access to the notes or want her to read them? The thought left her unsettled and sad. After all these years, her brother was ready to share the truth, but he couldn't just sit down and tell her? Traumatized by the memories, he might not be able to verbalize the horror of what had happened. Or he could be worried about rejection, stigma, disgrace. Well, she would stand by him, no matter what. His story could have been hers.

She double-checked the chain on the door, then sank back onto the mattress. It comforted her that Rif was in the adjoining room if she needed him.

Curiosity overrode her fatigue, and she started reading.

LAND MINE LINE

We played Oba's favorite game called Land Mine Line every week. We all got scores each week for how well we did shooting targets, completing chores, or performing combat drills. Oba hid one land mine in the field beside the camp, and the six boys who got the lowest scores had to hold hands and walk in a line across the field, trying not to step on the mine. If anyone let go, the whole game started over again.

Some weeks, everyone got across okay. Other times, a boy would be like a rocket shooting into the sky, all blood and body parts everywhere. Oba and Kofi would laugh and say the dead boy would have made a bad soldier if he couldn't even find a mine. My scores were always high. I worked really hard because I was too scared to play the game.

If any of the boys refused to walk across the field, me and Blado had to stand with our rifles pointed at them and make them do it. If they didn't play, we would have to shoot them, so I showed them I meant business, even though I felt bad inside.

The AK-47 was my new best friend, and I held it tight, my skinny arms getting stronger every day. The sun burned the back of my head, even though it was still morning. The rains were long gone, and now it was just plain old hot.

Blado shoved two bright pills he called candies into my hand and waited until I put them into my mouth. He jammed the barrel of his rifle into my gut. "You Mzungu, but I the boss."

I was tired of being called White Boy, but that was my name now. Blado said it looked like someone had erased my color, making me invisible. That's how I felt. Invisible. No one had rescued me, and after sixty-five days, I had given up counting. Papa wasn't coming.

I tucked the pills into the side of my mouth until I could spit them out. Whatever they were, I didn't want them. I'd seen what happened the last time Blado made the boys take them. They'd danced around, shooting their guns into the air like maniacs, screaming for blood.

After everyone took the pills, we marched in single file toward the field. I went to the back of the line, spit the pills into my hand, and stuffed them into my pocket. I ran to catch up to the others.

Red dirt covered my old boots and olive uniform. Just the thought of seeing Oba made me sweat—he'd been away the last week raiding villages to get new recruits, and it'd been quiet in the camp. That was about to end. The devil had returned to hell.

We stood at attention. We'd seen what happened to those who didn't, including that poor little kid Nobo.

"God has spoken to me." Oba raised a fist into the air. "You are the chosen ones, the soldiers who must eliminate the unbelievers." He paced up and down the line, inspecting our uniforms and studying our faces. My chest tightened. The pills made the other boys' fingers dance along their weapons, while their knees twitched. I copied what they did to fit in.

"Prepare yourselves for the holy war." Oba had told us lots of stories about the power of God and how important it was to defend his Christian beliefs. It seemed different than what they talked about at the Greek Orthodox church my family went to on Sundays, even though some things were the same.

Oba held a razor blade in his hand. One by one he sliced one temple on each boy, and then Kofi rubbed white powder into the cut. "You will now become men." I couldn't think of a way to avoid this poison, whatever it was. Waiting my turn, I didn't have to fake the wildness that was on the other boy's faces. My heart pounded against my ribs.

Blood from the cuts dripped down the boys' faces and mixed with their sweat. Oba moved down the line. My turn. A burning feeling hit me as the razor blade sliced my skin.

"I hear you're a good shooter," Oba said.

I stared straight ahead, scared to say anything. With Oba, there was no right answer.

"I heard you're very good."

I nodded and looked straight ahead. Every day, the guards took us to the garbage dump to practice shooting. I hit the bull's-eye most times.

"Keep practicing, and you can join my hunting team." Oba moved to the next boy.

Blood from my cut dripped onto my arm. Kofi rubbed the white powder in. I hated the skinny man. The General might have been a bully, but I'd been safe with him. These men were like rabid animals.

The powder didn't seem to work. Nothing happened. But then, all of a sudden, I felt hot. I saw things better, my brain spun faster, and my muscles flexed. Kofi's laugh sounded louder, echoing inside my head. The powder was magic. It made me feel like a god.

"Bring out the prisoners," Oba told Kofi.

Two dirty men with leg chains shuffled in front of the low stone wall at the end of the field. They had been so badly beaten, they barely looked human. One man wore all black with a white collar, and the other wore a uniform with the red, black, and green Kanzi flag stitched on the shoulder. My chest puffed out, and my muscles flexed.

"We need to punish our enemies." Oba stood at the end of the line, commanding us, his troops.

My mind raced. These men, what had they done to deserve being killed?

"Right shoulder arms . . . Present arms."

Obediently I swung my AK-47 into the firing position, jamming the butt of the rifle into my shoulder. It would be just like shooting targets, but now the targets were men. But wait. How could I think that way? Was it the magic powder? Had being here in this crazy camp stripped me of everything Papa had taught me about being good and honorable?

But I had to obey, or I would be forced to play the land mine game, or worse.

My breath was shallow. I lined up the sight.

"Ready . . . aim . . . fire!"

Our rifles exploded. The prisoners screamed and danced like jumpy monkeys as the bullets hit them. I pressed my trigger, the rifle banging my shoulder again and again. A smoky smell filled the air. Red dots covered the men's bodies. The bullets kept flying even after the men fell down.

I had fired above the targets. I just couldn't make myself fire into human flesh.

"Halt." Oba walked over to where the prisoners lay on the ground. The man dressed in uniform was still moving. Oba took the dagger from his belt and stuck the blade into the man's chest. The twitching stopped.

"Drag the prisoners to the fire pit and burn them," he ordered.

The boys hefted the dead bodies and marched off with them. My feet felt like concrete blocks.

"Mzungu." Oba's voice made me freeze. "Come here."

My throat felt tight. I made myself put one foot in front of the other. I held my breath. Did Oba know that I hadn't shot the men?

CRACK SHOT

I was starting to forget home. Papa's lessons, Thea's smile, my friends—all were becoming blurry in my dreams. I lived and breathed war. Oba had us practice ambushing, sniper-crawling, shooting—lots of crazy combat stuff.

Oba was very hard on me, kicking me and hitting me in the stomach with his rifle. He knew I'd chickened out at the firing line. I squeezed my eyes shut, wishing I could turn into a Greek god like Zeus or Apollo so I could save myself. I'd given up on anyone rescuing me. The jungle was too thick. No one could see us from the sky or land. If I wanted to leave, I'd have to find my own way out.

I was cleaning my gun when something smacked into my shoulder. Ouch! I looked down. Blado had thrown a rock at me. "Come on, Mzungu, you lazy idiot. Oba wants us."

I wanted to punch him, but it was too dangerous. Big Blado was the leader of our troop, and we had to do what he said. I stood, picked up my rifle, and followed him. He headed to the garbage area where we practiced shooting. I pinched my nose. The stink was horrible. I tripped over an empty Coke can.

Blado pushed my chest with both his hands. "What kind of soldier are you when you can't even walk straight?"

I wanted to push back but stopped myself. "I'm better at shooting than walking."

He made a fist, winding up for a punch. Footsteps sounded. Blado dropped his hand. "Jambo, sir."

Oba and Kofi walked toward us. Kofi carried a paper target in his hands. "Time for shooting drills."

Kofi hung the target on a tree about sixty feet away. Oba pointed to me. "You're first. And there's a prize. Whoever shoots better will lead the troops."

Heat rushed to my face. This was my chance to be Blado's boss. I could do better than the older boy if I stayed calm.

Oba took off his bandanna and wrapped it around my eyes. The cloth stunk, but I kept my body still, wanting to hit that bull's-eye. We'd practiced shooting blindfolded so we could learn how to reload and fire in the dark. There was talk of nighttime raids, and Oba wanted us ready. We had to close our eyes and keep our feet in the same spot, doing it over and over again until we could hit the target from ten feet, then twenty, then thirty. It was amazing how good we got without even seeing the target.

"Prepare to fire."

I dug my feet into the dirt, then lifted the rifle.

"Fire." Oba's voice echoed in my ears.

I held steady and pressed the trigger. Boom, boom, boom. After firing all five shots, I lifted the bandanna. I'd hit the small circle on every shot, but a little to the right. Not good enough. Blado smiled.

"Not bad. I'll give you one more try." Oba turned to Kofi. "Post a new target."

This was my last chance to beat Blado. I would be a better leader of the troops. Fear didn't earn loyalty—good leadership did. Papa said so.

Kofi pulled down the old target and kept it to compare with Blado's shooting. After he posted the new one, I lined up my feet and reloaded my rifle.

Last time, my shots went right. Not again.

When Oba blindfolded me with the bandanna, I stayed still and waited for his command.

Scuffling footsteps. A soft cry. Probably Blado trying to distract me. No way would the bully win. I entered the shooting zone, picturing the target. I could do this.

"Fire." Oba's voice sounded farther away, but I didn't care what he was doing. I wanted to win. I wanted all the bullets to land in one black hole. I squeezed the trigger, kept my aim steady.

The sound was different this time, like a hammer smashing a watermelon. What had happened? I'd kept my aim steady. I ripped off the blindfold.

Kofi and Oba held Blado in front of the target. A bandanna covered the boy's mouth. All five shots had hit a small circle in his chest, his tan shirt soaked with blood.

My body shook. Kofi laughed his hyenalike cackle.

Oba dropped Blado's dead body on the ground. "I told you the better shot would lead the troops. We already knew you were the best. Congratulations, you've killed your first enemy."

I sank to my knees. I couldn't speak.

Oba looked at Kofi. "Drag the body into camp. I'll tell the boys that Blado tried to run away and Mzungu stopped him. That will keep them in line."

I couldn't believe it. They'd made me a killer.

BABY BRANDON

Oba and I were on the hunt for food because the villagers' grains were almost gone. Charcoal and mud covered my face and body to make me dark so the animals wouldn't see me coming. My belly was growling. I'd only eaten one meal a day for the last few weeks. My ribs stuck out, and my arms were matchsticks. I needed meat.

I missed good dinners from home but tried not to think about all that. Thea and Papa would not be proud that Oba had tricked me into killing Blado. I said nothing to the other boys about what had happened, but they looked at me with scared eyes now. News travels fast in a camp.

I stepped carefully in the thick bush, trying not to make any sound. Branches cut my skin, but I didn't care, because I had eaten lots of candies and breathed in brown-brown—gunpowder mixed with the white powder. It made me feel so awake.

Oba froze and lifted a hand to tell me to stop. An animal? I could feel drool in my mouth. We'd eat tonight.

He pointed to the right, then stepped like a cat through the bush. I followed, heart thumping hard. He was just ahead of me. I saw light through the trees. The hot sun fried the back of my neck. An empty stomach, the heat, the buzz of the brown-brown. I felt dizzy and almost tripped.

Strong fingers dug into my arm. Oba gave me a mean stare. I shook my head, trying to get rid of that weird feeling. He was crazy enough to roast me over the fire if he got too hungry.

I heard a sound. Soft at first. Like a kid's laugh.

Oba ran through the trees. I hurried to keep up. He lifted his AK-47.

There was an open-air Land Rover with a sign on the door. I got closer. My head wasn't working right, but I knew it was Mr. Grantam, the park ranger, and his young son, Brandon. Me, Papa, and Thea had gone on safari with him last year. The two of them were standing on the driver's seat, and Brandon was pointing at two giraffes butting heads.

"Look, Daddy. Are they mad at each other?"

Mr. Grantam wore a brown uniform with a gun, binoculars around his neck. "Not really, Brandon, they're just trying to decide who's the boss. You know, like me and Mom do sometimes."

The little boy laughed again. His father messed up his hair. I was so busy watching them that I didn't see Oba get close. Mr. Grantam turned to see Oba with his AK pointed at them. The giraffes hurried away, as if they knew playtime was over. Mr. Grantam reached for his holster, but Oba had him cold with the rifle.

"The gun."

"Daddy!" Brandon scrambled into his father's arms.

"Stay calm. Just tell me what you want." Mr. Grantam looked at Oba and then at me. Didn't he know who I was? Maybe he couldn't tell because of the mud and charcoal.

"Take off the gun." Oba couldn't miss if he tried. He was only a few feet away.

Mr. Grantam held Brandon close and tossed the holster and gun into the red dirt.

"Whatever you need, I can help." Even though Oba had the AK pointed at him, Mr. Grantam seemed calm. I guess he was used to guns.

Oba stepped forward and grabbed the kid. Brandon squealed, "Daddy!"

"It'll be okay, son. Just take a deep breath."

Brandon kept quiet, but his blue eyes were huge saucers. It made me think of Thea the night I'd been kidnapped. She'd been so scared, she couldn't scream for help.

"You have food?" Oba held Brandon's neck to keep him from squirming away.

"In the bag." Mr. Grantam pointed to the sack on the passenger seat. "Take it all. Just let the boy go."

"Don't tell me what to do, white man." Oba turned to me. "Shoot him, and I will spare the boy."

"Let's just take their food and leave them be." I tried to process what was happening, but my brain was cloudy, fuzzy.

The man's face was really pale. Oba pulled Brandon closer, putting the barrel of his rifle against the kid's head. "Shoot the man," he told me.

"Calm down. I just want to take my son home." Mr. Grantam's voice was strong, brave.

"Do it." Oba was scary calm. I knew he meant it. "Or I shoot the kid on the count of three."

"Don't do it." Mr. Grantam looked right at me. Didn't he know I was Nikos Paris?

Oba started counting. "One . . ."

What to do, what to do? My head was all confused. Could I shoot Oba? No, the kid would die first. I remembered how Oba had killed Nobo. He never bluffed.

"Two . . ." Shooting Blado had been horrible, but he'd been a bully. This kid was young, like Thea, innocent. I couldn't let it happen. Papa *always told me to look after anyone younger than me. My hands shook on the rifle.*

"Three."

I fired straight at Mr. Grantam. Bang, bang, bang. Three red blotches dotted his chest. He slipped to the ground, reaching for his son.

Brandon screamed.

Oh, God, what had I done? I'd just shot the boy's father in front of him. I let my AK drop. My legs felt like big rubber bands. I leaned over and puked. Standing up straight, I watched Oba fire a bullet into the boy's head. Brain matter splattered the ground. Oba dropped the tiny body onto the red earth.

I ran over and knelt beside the boy. "No! You said you'd save him if I shot his father."

"Too young to fight. Don't need more mouths to feed. We're not UNICEF."

Oba walked over to the truck, grabbed the sack of food, and emptied it on the ground, opening packages, shoving food into his mouth. Apples, candy bars, sandwiches—everything I'd dreamed about for the last few months. But now I couldn't eat them if I tried. I was dead inside.

Thea's mind reeled as she placed the pages on the bed. The words were poignant, but they couldn't properly convey what had transpired. She'd had no idea he'd been turned into a child soldier, twelve years old and forced to kill. The damage that had been done to her brother's psyche was unfathomable.

An overwhelming mix of emotions filled her. Hatred for Oba, for forcing Nikos to commit such atrocious acts of violence. Another emotion surged from beneath the surface. Anger, red-hot anger, toward her father.

Papa had kept her in the dark. She understood how he might not have disclosed this sensitive information to her as a child, but why not tell her in later years? It wasn't as if she hadn't witnessed horrific situations in her job. But, no, Christos had chosen not to tell her what had happened to her own brother.

She agreed that it was smart to keep this information out of the public eye. Nikos already had enough celebrity as a former child hostage and scion of the head of Paris Industries. If the press discovered that he'd been a boy soldier, murdering people, he might never have had a chance at a normal life. She had to give Papa credit there. Still, why had he given up on his own child, excluding him from the family business, acting as if he was a leper?

It all started to make a sick sort of sense. Nikos might have been given everything he needed and more, financially, but he'd been forced to hide the brutality of what he'd experienced, forced to hide the truth of what had really happened, forced to live a lie.

Their father didn't require such silence purely to protect Nikos from the public. He'd also done it for himself. Papa had muted his son because he didn't know how to handle a damaged child. With no wife to help, he'd been overwhelmed, channeling his energy into his business, where he could flourish, instead of dealing with the difficult task of reforming someone who'd been so psychologically scarred. He'd sent Nikos away so he didn't have a daily reminder of the horror that had befallen his son.

Papa must have used his wealth and power to whitewash any mention of Nikos's activities during captivity. Most of the press coverage had been about the million-dollar reward he'd given General Ita Jemwa. Hush money. She wondered if there was even more she didn't know about.

Emotion overwhelmed her. She was saddened and angered by Papa's reaction to Nikos's ordeal, yet she felt guilty about that anger. For God's sake, he himself was being held captive now, locked in his own private hell.

And Nikos—how did she feel about him? "Complicated" didn't begin to describe it. Her brother had been taken in her place. She owed him in the most profound way. That guilt haunted her, too.

Still, reading about what Nikos had done filled her with fear. What was her brother capable of? Was it possible that he was behind Papa's kidnapping? Part of it made a sick sort of sense: swooping in to kidnap Christos right before the biggest deal of his career. The ultimate payback. But Nikos had seemed genuinely disturbed when he found out about the kidnapping. Could he really be that good a liar?

The story of her brother's kidnapping had opened her eyes, demonstrating that even the people she loved, her family, were capable of anything if pushed hard enough. In the field, she had killed to avoid being killed. Sometimes choices were taken away from you.

She turned off the lamp and crawled under the covers. She needed to shut off her mind, sleep for a few hours. Tomorrow the negotiations would begin, and she had to be sharp. Nothing could be taken at face value. Peter Kennedy's murderer was still at large, and presumably whoever it was had had a hand in Christos's kidnapping and everything else that had happened since. The general seemed smug, as if he knew something they didn't. And the Chinese were driven to win the contract at any cost. She would also have to face Nikos, her understanding of her brother forever changed, now knowing he'd been a child soldier, a killer.

Chapter Forty-Nine

The bright African sun pierced the crack between the room-darkening drapes in Gabrielle's room. She'd been up since well before dawn, communicating with the HRFC team, already cruising through her supply of Gitanes.

Her buddy and former CIA operative Rick Dennison had given her an off-the-books care package, including a SIG Sauer, a first-aid kit, GPS trackers, a few bugs, an M24, and a parabolic microphone, among other items. She smiled, surprised there wasn't a flame-thrower in the mix. Who knew what might come in handy?

Someone knocked on her door. She looked through the peephole. *Max.* She crushed her cigarette into the crystal ashtray and let him in.

"Any news?" he asked.

"Not really. Come in."

He glanced briefly at the mahogany bed in her suite. It hadn't been easy to say no to his attempts to break her one-night rule, but not for the usual reasons. She might actually like him, and that was a whole lot more dangerous than sex.

He looked disheveled, strained. "I've been working with Interpol, combing through leads coming in to their hotline. I will meet my contact from the Harare office later today."

She half smiled. "Our kind of work doesn't exactly lend itself to regular hours."

"Our kind of work does not leave much room for a life," he said.

"And yet we still do it." She took in his Cartier watch and signet ring. "Why even be an inspector for the Hellenic Police, when your family has more money than olives?"

"Justice. Everyone deserves it, rich or poor."

"Agreed." She wondered if his sister's accident was part of what drove him so hard. She'd like to ask more about what had happened but didn't want to pry.

"You understand me, Gabrielle." He stepped closer, his right hand stroking her cheek.

Her cell phone beeped, disrupting the moment. Part of her was relieved.

Two messages arrived from her analyst, Ernest.

Max reached for the bright blue box of Gitanes. "You mind?"

"I thought you'd quit."

"I just started again." He lit a cigarette, breathed in a lungful of smoke, and reviewed the messages on his phone while she did the same on hers.

Her first message detailed an intercepted conversation between the prime minister of Kanzi and his brother-in-law, Bini Salam. According to the information, Salam wanted to oust General Ita Jemwa from his position as head of security, but Kimweri refused. African leaders often appointed family members to prominent positions. With the promise of great wealth on the horizon, the prime minister's relatives would be jockeying for position. If Bini Salam went head-to-head with the general, she'd bet on the military man.

The second message kick-started her heart. The plane tail number Konstantin Philippoussis had given them had been traced back to a Belgian shell corporation, which had been the holder of an end-user certificate, or EUC—an internationally accepted document that allowed for the shipping of arms to legitimate recipients. And that EUC was linked to an Ares weapons deal in Syria.

It had taken several analysts to sift through many layers of ownership and link the shell corporation to an automotive manufacturing company, which had been sold two years ago to none other than Quan Chi, one of the lead negotiators in the Kanzi oil deal. Was this the link she'd been searching for?

She typed a brief response, pushing her team to follow the money trail to other shell corporations. Was it possible that the Quans had arranged an under-the-table arms deal with Ares? Had Ares kidnapped Christos Paris to help influence the negotiations?

It would make sense. The Stockholm International Peace Research Institute stated that while data on Chinese arms deals were difficult to confirm, it was common knowledge that China was one of the top suppliers of arms to sub-Saharan African countries. It was buying up minerals, oil, and natural gas, offering military aid or other assistance in exchange for the resources.

Or was one of the Quans actually Ares, working both ends?

Goose bumps ran down her arms.

China was especially influential in the murky world of small-arms sales—such as AK-47s and grenades—as they were easier to buy, sell, and use and were considered far more destructive, because of their ubiquity, than heavy weapons. Small arms played a powerful role in fueling bloody rebellions and encouraging civil unrest in Africa. Could Ares be working to supply arms to the Kanzi government in exchange for control over the oil rights?

She'd need to investigate further, collating the details in her mind. She glanced at her watch. "We'd better go; it's time for the negotiations to start."

Chapter Fifty

Thea finished her shower with a blast of cold water to revitalize herself, dressing in a navy suit, a crisp ivory blouse, and black pumps she'd purchased in town. She slipped her extra insulin into her jacket pocket. The two extra-large coffees she'd ordered with breakfast should give her the kick in the pants she'd need.

She'd conferred with Ahmed, Nikos, and six Paris Industries corporate lawyers in a private meeting earlier in the morning. Though Ahmed had agreed to have Nikos join them at the table, she was going to represent the family, handling the opening remarks on behalf of Paris Industries.

After her speech, she'd hand over the details to the experts. Ahmed had had a speechwriter send over a statement for her, and they'd reviewed the fine points. She was no oil executive, but she certainly had a lot of experience keeping calm in dicey situations. Kidnap negotiations required intense discipline and often unfolded over endless days. She wasn't worried about even a high-stakes business deal.

Thea entered the conference room where the summit would take place. Cathedral windows let in the piercing morning sunlight, the deep burgundy drapes pulled wide open. Two tables sat near the front, and ten chairs perched on a small stage, ready for the Kanzi dignitaries. The venue held the same opulent grace and elegance as the rest of the hotel. She greeted Ahmed Khali and the team of lawyers. The COO's demeanor was intense, his eyes studying the proposal like the nose of a pig hunting for the finest truffles. This was his big moment, his chance to shine.

The empty chair beside him should have been Peter Kennedy's.

They still had no idea who'd poisoned the CFO, but the local authorities were interviewing everyone who'd been at the hotel. With tourism the main source of income in Zimbabwe, having a foreigner murdered on its soil was very bad for business. Gabrielle had promised to communicate with the State Department regarding the details surrounding Peter's death. Quantum International would also do everything they could to discover who'd poisoned him. Just not now.

Today she'd stand in for her family. Papa might not be here in person, but he was certainly with her in spirit.

Even at this early hour, the region's heat nearly overwhelmed the air-conditioning. Thea slipped off her jacket and hung it on the back of her chair. The gallery brimmed with international press covering the negotiations, executives from other oil companies, and countless others—including Gabrielle and Max. Prime Minister Kimweri had insisted on making the opening remarks accessible to the public because he wanted to demonstrate that Kanzi had zero tolerance for corruption, unlike some of its neighboring countries.

A hand rested on her shoulder. She turned. Nikos.

"Sleep well, sis?"

"All things considered, not bad. You?" She surveyed her brother's crisp white shirt, black suit, and gleaming oxfords. Tall and fit, he looked the part of a confident, polished businessman, an image utterly incongruent with the lice-ridden, terrified boy she'd just read about in his journal notes.

"I'm looking forward to seeing how today unfolds." He sat down in the chair beside her. "As I told you yesterday, I've dealt with the Quan family before. They are masters of *guanxi,* spending a lot of time with the locals, building relationships. We don't know what they've promised the prime minister behind closed doors. But Papa has a long-standing relationship with Kimweri, so he should have that angle covered."

Guanxi—the Chinese cultural approach to business, which prioritized bonding with fellow citizens, rating the welfare of the group higher than that of the individual. After handling several kidnappings in Beijing, she understood how the intricate culture focused on hierarchy and trading favors.

Nikos was right. Ahmed had told her they'd hired investigators to research the Quans, following them when they visited Kanzi. Their team knew exactly which perks the Chinese had promised the locals.

Given the Chinese tradition of addressing all the issues in the negotiation simultaneously, in no apparent order, patience would be crucial to keep things on an even keel. Ahmed had also shared that he didn't want the Paris Industries team to be portrayed as stereotypically American—arrogant, risk-taking, and overly direct. That wouldn't work here. Adaptation was a negotiator's best asset. Today, Chinese traditions, African customs, and American business would collide—giving her a chance to study all the players in detail.

The Paris Industries table was positioned at the front left of the room, close to where the Kanzi dignitaries would soon file in for the opening ceremonies. The Quans headed for the Chinese National Oil Company table on the right, Chi in a dark suit and Xi-Ping sporting a black sheath that left little to the imagination. The Chinese beauty looked at Nikos like a piece of meat she'd like to devour. Well, by the end of the day, Thea hoped Xi-Ping would have lost her appetite entirely. Ahmed had a few surprises planned.

Nikos leaned close. "I'm sure Father offered a large signing bonus and royalties—we can easily match the Quans in that domain. But Ahmed will need to avoid getting bogged down in the details. Because Chinese children learn symbols rather than letters for language, they develop a strong affinity for big-picture thinking. We must not fail to see the forest for the trees."

Her brother's insightful presence comforted her. She'd developed good intuition thanks to her work in K&R, but Nikos offered a uniquely qualified perspective, given his international business achievements. Negotiating the release of a hostage was a different kettle of fish than securing a billion-dollar, multinational contract.

"The pipeline Papa designed is a major advantage for us." Paris Industries had the largest fleet of oil supertankers in the world, and her father planned to head west with the pipeline so he could use a port in Namibia to transport Kanzi oil to the world.

"Chi will counter that they have a more direct route through Zimbabwe." Nikos's gaze was intense.

"Zimbabwe is an unstable country. As in Nigeria, they'll experience rebel attacks on the pipeline," she said.

"The Zimbabwean government recently purchased a large shipment of military hardware from China, including a thirteen-million-dollar radar system, six Hongdu JL-8 jet aircraft, twelve JF-17 Thunder combat aircraft, and a hundred other military vehicles. I'd say they are securely positioned."

"Where did you get this information?" she asked. Her brother had a keen eye on African politics, but this was something else entirely.

"People talk. I wouldn't be surprised if Quan had visited President Mugabe and promised him the pipeline if China wins the bid. This relationship could be profitable for Kanzi, Zimbabwe, and China."

That made sense. China and Zimbabwe had a relationship dating back to the 1970s, during the period of the Rhodesian Bush War. Robert Mugabe had tried to garner Soviet support for his Zimbabwe African National Union, but the Kremlin—already supplying arms to Joshua Nkomo's Zimbabwe African People's Union—turned him down. Instead, Mugabe had partnered with Beijing. The relationship with China was vital to Zimbabwe; with Mugabe's record of human rights violations, no other international player would endorse an official relationship with the African nation. As a result, hundreds of millions of Chinese investment dollars poured into the country.

"Time for the opening ceremonies. Hope you had plenty of coffee." She gave Nikos a brief smile. Growing up, they'd lived in several African countries, and one key cultural difference between Americans and Africans rested in the way they perceived time. Monochronic Americans favored schedules, agendas, and detailed communication. Polychronic cultures such as Kanzi's chose to start and end meetings spontaneously, address several issues simultaneously, take ad hoc breaks, and use an informal approach of dialogue and information flowing freely. They would have to expect the unexpected and roll with it.

The Chinese would be up first, presenting their opening remarks and initial offer. A man wearing African robes glided into the room and positioned himself at the head table. He pounded a gavel, and a hush spread across the room. The Kanzi government bureaucrats filed in, including General Jemwa, Prime Minister Kimweri, and his brother-in-law, Bini Salam.

Let the negotiations begin.

Chapter Fifty-One

Rif hated that Nikos was at the head table. Christos would not like that at all. During long lunches with the oil billionaire, Rif remembered his ranting about keeping his son far, far away from his business. But now Christos was gone, and Nikos was swooping in.

Vulture.

Hovering near the exit, Rif kept Thea in his peripheral vision. She was poring over a large binder with her brother, the two of them looking way too cozy for his liking. Nikos was Machiavellian, capable of manipulating anyone when he wanted something or someone.

Such as Katie, Thea's friend from her final year in high school. Rif and Thea had been in their late teens, Nikos in his early twenties, when Thea met Katie, a pretty blonde. Nikos became infatuated, always urging his sister to bring her new friend to the house. Within a month, Katie had disappeared from her life. Thea had been disappointed to lose her friendship—she didn't understand what she'd done wrong. Years later, Rif ran into Katie at a bar. They'd talked for hours, and after several tequila shots, the twenty-eight-year-old had opened up to him.

Katie had been a virgin, a late bloomer, shy around boys, and at first when Thea's dashing brother paid her serious attention, she'd resisted, more than a little intimidated. But Nikos won her over with his charms, and he pushed hard for sex. Thinking she was in love, she gave him what he wanted.

She'd expected her first time to be loving, gentle, but Nikos was seriously rough. After he was done, he climbed out of bed, zipped up his pants, and told her she was the worst lay of his life, that he never wanted to see her again. Devastated, she avoided the entire Paris family. Katie had experienced Nikos's dark side, and she had no interest in being near him again. And she couldn't face Thea. Even years later, Rif could see that the experience still weighed heavily on the young woman.

He'd never told Thea. It wasn't his secret to share, and he wasn't sure Thea would've believed him. She never saw her brother for who he was. She'd let Nikos join her at the Paris Industries table for one simple reason: guilt. Nikos used it to jerk his sister around like a marlin on a lure. And Rif had never seen her brother so intent on insinuating himself into the family business.

Xi-Ping stared at Nikos with displeasure. His presence at the Paris table must be an unpleasant surprise to the Quans as well. What was he up to, exactly?

Time to find out.

With the proceedings meandering along, Rif headed for the hotel spa. He stripped off his clothes, stuffed them into a locker, and slipped on a plush white robe and a pair of ridiculous terrycloth slippers.

He hurried to the elevator and pressed the button for the second floor. As he'd suspected, the maid had already started cleaning the rooms. In fact, she was standing beside her cart two doors down from Nikos's room. Rif made a show of searching his robe pockets for his key.

"I must have misplaced my key at the spa." He shrugged and gave her a sheepish smile. "I'd ask at the front desk for a replacement, but it's a mob scene down there with all the reporters. I'm not really dressed for the public."

"It's against the rules." She frowned, her pert nose wrinkling, at war with herself—sure, it was against hotel policy to open doors for guests, but she also didn't want to burn up possible tips.

"Please, look it up on your sheet. The name's Paris, Nikos Paris." Housekeepers kept logs of guest names and checkout dates so they knew when to do a major cleaning and bedding change.

She hesitated. "Can you tell me what's in the room?"

Lucky him gets Betty Do-Right as the maid. Nikos often dressed in designer black suits with crisp white shirts, as if it was a uniform for Harvard MBAs. He was also a neat freak. "You'll find the room spotless, the closet full of black suits and white shirts."

She used her master key to enter the room. He followed her inside, and, sure enough, Mr. OCD still reigned. Every surface was free of clutter. Even the local tourist guidebooks the hotel normally left on a side table had been tucked away. She looked in the closet: black suits and white shirts. Bingo.

The maid smiled. "You made my job easy."

He pulled out the American ten-dollar bill he'd stashed inside the robe's pocket. Enough to make her happy, not enough to create suspicion. "I appreciate you saving me any embarrassment."

"Thank you, Mr. Paris." She walked toward the door, stashing the bill in her uniform.

He and Nikos were both tall Westerners with dark hair. Certainly not twins but close enough for an overall description. And if the maid ever realized she'd let the wrong man into the room, she wasn't likely to admit it and lose her job.

Closing the door behind her, he snapped on the vinyl gloves he'd brought and started with the bedside tables, looking for anything that might offer clues as to why Nikos was there and whether he was involved in Christos's kidnapping. He found nothing obvious. Not surprising—Thea's brother was a careful guy.

He searched under the wastebaskets. When Rif traveled, he often placed important documents in an envelope, taped them to the bottom of a wastebasket, and kept the can empty so the cleaning staff wouldn't move it. Nothing there.

In the bathroom, he examined the shampoo bottles and lotions. The tinted containers could be ideal hiding places for valuable items, but Nikos hadn't tampered with them either. Rif slid his hand under the mattress, careful not to disturb the pristine bed. Still nothing. He searched for "slips," hiding places that were easy to access but hard to find. Zip.

Next, the safe. People were naïve if they thought their valuables were secure inside a hotel safe, and Thea's brother was not a trusting person. But Nikos hadn't had time to store any critical items in the hotel vault because he'd arrived last night just before the cocktail party, and the negotiations had started first thing in the morning. Maybe he'd be in luck.

His left hand smacked the top of the digital safe while his right hand twisted the dial. The safe clicked open. A small motor pulled down the pin and allowed the bolt to slide. When he hit the top of the safe, the shockwave dropped the pin, and if he twisted at the right time, the door would open just as if he'd entered the code.

A cooler pouch filled with syringes rested inside. Rif flashed on Peter's poisoning last night. Cyanide? He sniffed the end of one of the syringes. No hint of the bitter almond scent. Instead, the fluid smelled like those rubbery Band-Aids they'd had as kids. Weird. What the heck was this stuff? Was Nikos hooked on drugs, or was this syringe meant for someone else?

Noises in the hallway jolted him into action. Maybe the maid checking on him? He placed the syringe back in the safe and closed it. The door rattled. No time to exit. He stepped into the spacious closet, closed the door, and masked himself behind

Nikos's freshly pressed shirts. He had a view of the room through the slats.

Soft footsteps sounded on the plush carpet. Nikos entered the room and closed the door behind him. Rif hoped he wasn't planning a change of clothes. And why wasn't he in the negotiations? Seconds later, a sharp rap sounded. Nikos opened the hotel room door.

"I told you we couldn't be seen together in public," he said.

"You're fortunate they called for a short break. It'll give you a chance to explain yourself. Why are you planted at the Paris Industries table?" Xi-Ping asked.

"'Planted' is the right word. I'm gathering intel on Paris Industries' strategy so we can outmaneuver them."

"Why didn't you tell me?"

"I don't report to you. Our arrangement remains the same."

"If I'm your partner, you need to keep me apprised," she said.

"Stop being such a controlling bitch. I like it too much."

She laughed, a husky sound. Christ, had he stumbled on a Psychos-R-Us support meeting? They'd better not start screwing. That'd be more than Rif could stomach.

"Do we have time?" Xi-Ping's voice was a purr.

"Later. If we play this right, we'll have all the time in the world."

So Thea's brother was hooked up with the Chinese competition. Sounded as if Nikos was playing by his own rules, as usual. He was definitely using this woman—but what was his endgame?

He had to warn Thea.

Chapter Fifty-Two

A short break was announced after Chi's opening remarks. Thea turned to Ahmed Khali. "The Chinese National Oil Company seems to have made substantial inroads with Prime Minister Kimweri."

"True, but Paris Industries has been doing business in Kanzi for decades, and we've worked hard to build schools, hospitals, and wells to help the people here. Hopefully our long-term commitment will pay off."

Papa had purchased biofuels for more than twenty years from Kanzi, working with three different prime ministers. Plus they'd already been studying and drilling on the land adjacent to this particular find, which was how the oil had been discovered. "My father would be very proud of the job you're doing in his absence."

Because of political instability, loyalty was a moving target in Africa, with the wealthiest company often hitting the bull's-eye. And proof of that was Prime Minister Kimweri's laughter as he chatted with Chi Quan. Thea looked around for Nikos, wanting to ask him for more information about the Quans, but her brother had disappeared.

She exited the conference room and scanned the hallway. No sign of Nikos, but Gabrielle Farrah blazed a path directly toward her.

"May I please have a minute?" the government agent asked.

"You have news?" Thea dared to hope.

The woman passed Thea a folded sheet of paper. "Not on Christos's whereabouts. But I agree that these negotiations seem to be directly tied to his abduction. To that end, we ran across something else. I hope it's helpful." She headed back into the conference room.

Thea studied the paper—an intercepted e-mail between Prime Minister Kimweri's brother-in-law and Quan Chi. In it, Chi detailed the exact percentage of production value Paris Industries planned to offer and promised two percent more—which translated into millions of dollars.

Her body stiffened. Very few people knew the intimate details of their closely guarded offer. How had Chi garnered such sensitive information?

A loud bell sounded, signifying the end of the break. The crowd headed back into the negotiations room.

Rif stormed toward her, an intense look on his face. "I need to talk to you privately."

An announcement over the intercom warned the delegates to reclaim their seats.

She glanced around—no one was within earshot. "I have proof about a leak in Paris Industries."

She passed him the paper, which he quickly scanned.

"Nikos could be the culprit—he's secretly meeting with Xi-Ping."

"Not this again. He already told me that he knows her through his import/export business."

"Did he mention that they're sleeping together?"

"What?" Could that be true?

Nikos suddenly appeared beside her. "We'd better get in there."

"We'll talk more about this later," she told Rif. Nikos couldn't be the leak, could he? He'd had zero access to Paris Industries' long months of preparations for the negotiations. Papa wouldn't let him near the company, let alone any sensitive documents.

"Be careful." The concern in Rif's voice worried her; he was not the type to overreact.

She hesitated. The three of them were the only ones left standing in the hall. A final announcement sounded on the intercom. The doors would be closing soon. They had to go in.

Nikos pulled at her arm. "Come on."

She reluctantly headed into the conference space, wondering how Rif had discovered this new information about her brother. A blast of air-conditioning hit her, and she shivered.

Chapter Fifty-Three

Rif watched the security guards close the doors on the negotiations room. He felt bad that he'd rattled Thea with the news of Nikos's involvement with Quan Xi-Ping. Still, she needed to know that her brother couldn't be trusted.

A sturdy bellman headed toward him with a Tumi hard case in hand. Rif was about to step aside to make room for him to pass when the bellman gave him a nod. He touched Rif's shoulder and said, "Excuse me, sir," slipping a folded paper into his pocket.

Rif headed for the men's room, entered a stall, and opened the note: *We have information about the man who died last night. One hundred American dollars. Come to Blue Zulu today.*

He recognized the name of a restaurant in nearby Victoria Falls. The information was worth a hell of a lot more than a hundred dollars if it led to whoever had poisoned Peter Kennedy, but the price tag was a commentary on the standard of living here. That amount probably felt like a fortune, given the minuscule daily wage here.

Since Thea was embroiled in the negotiations, he'd use the time to head to town. He was also curious about where she had disappeared to yesterday while he was taking a shower—maybe he'd discover what she'd been up to.

He was tempted to jog the couple of miles, but the baking sun dissuaded him. As soon as he stepped outside, sweat immediately coated his skin, and his lips were parched. The intense heat reminded him of his time in Chad, and he flinched at the thought.

As he walked, he distracted himself by watching bungee jumpers soar off the massive Victoria Falls Bridge, bouncing like human yo-yos above the Zambezi River. In town, warthogs dined on the short grass while a congress of baboons hounded tourists for snacks. The hotels on the Zimbabwe side of the falls had foundered for years because of the civil strife under Robert Mugabe's rule. Recently, though, tourism had surged again, and people in safari-wear kicked up the region's famous reddish dust on their way to the mile-long falls.

Rif passed a couple of banks and the post office, headed for the Elephant's Walk Shopping Centre. He entered the Blue Zulu restaurant, planted himself at the bar, and ordered a Tusker from the elderly bartender. He recognized the guy from the party last night—he'd been manning one of the bars.

Several customers were enjoying an early lunch in the restaurant area, but Rif sat alone on his stool. He placed a hundred-dollar bill underneath a beer mat, his hand remaining on the coaster.

The bartender opened the Tusker and placed it on the counter, assessing him with wary eyes. Rif sipped the cold beer and waited.

"I saw you trying to help the man who died last night. I asked my brother to give you the note."

"The bellman."

He nodded. "The police don't want the truth, but maybe you do."

"Let's hear what you have. If the information's good, the hundred's yours."

The bartender started wiping down the counter. "Been bartending for thirty years. I pay attention, who drinks what, who knows whom. The man who died was drinking Scotch, Glenfiddich, and he hung out at my station because I pour heavy."

"Then you'd certainly be popular with Peter."

"Early in the evening, I noticed a woman sipping champagne. But later she comes by my bar with a Scotch in her hand, places it down while she checks her phone. When I give the man his next Scotch, she picks up his drink and leaves hers there. This happened shortly before the man collapsed."

"And what did this woman look like?"

The bartender eyed the hundred-dollar bill. Rif shifted it over to him and removed his hand. The old man pocketed the money.

"Chinese. Tall, in a black dress, with very long hair."

Quan Xi-Ping.

Rif grabbed a twenty from his wallet and placed it on the bar. "Thanks for the drink, my friend." He stood, leaving the rest of the Tusker on the counter. That was when he spotted Max Heros near the back of the restaurant, drinking Zambezi beer with a local.

He strode over to their table.

"Mind if I join you?" He pulled up a chair and sat down. "Any updates on Christos?"

Max didn't look pleased to have the extra company, but he remained polite. "This is Epi Buganda, a member of Interpol Harare who is also responsible for Kanzi. He is helping us investigate Mr. Paris's kidnapping."

"Rif Asker, Quantum International Security. Also a close family friend of Christos Paris." He shook Buganda's hand and found it clammy and cold.

"My men are working the area, questioning locals to see if they've witnessed any unusual activity." Buganda slurped his beer.

Right, because lawless behavior was so unusual in this ravaged country. Grease a few palms, and silence was king. It'd be a great place to stash Christos, but why would the kidnapper want to keep his captive so close to the negotiations? It'd be too risky. "You learn anything?"

Max leaned back in his chair. "We are investigating all inbound flights over the past few days to see if we note anything suspicious, but several airstrips boast only a windsock, so it's hard to know who has flown in."

"And I'm sure President Mugabe is being his usual helpful self."

The Interpol agent's left eye twitched. People were scared of the dictator, since those who didn't fall into line usually disappeared.

Max glanced at his watch. "I have to get back to the hotel. Mr. Buganda, let me walk you to your car. Until later, Mr. Asker."

He could tell the Greek came from a wealthy family, used to brushing off any unwanted lint with a quick swish of his hand. No way would Rif be so easily dismissed. The inspector had to know more than he was sharing; according to Hakan, Max Heros was trustworthy. Which probably meant he'd done some dirty work for Christos. "We should meet for drinks later. I'll come find you."

Max frowned. Before he could answer, Rif stood and exited the restaurant, eager to get back to Thea with the news. On Park Way, he passed a pharmacy and a few high-end art shops. The town of Victoria Falls was a study in contradictions, the affluent dabbling in luxuries while the poor struggled to put food on the table. Everyone seemed used to it. As the saying went, TIA—This Is Africa. Sad but true.

A group of men in red soccer uniforms hiked down Livingstone Way. He hesitated for a moment, catching some shade beneath an acacia tree. Although soccer—or football, as they called it—was the most popular sport here, the locals didn't swarm the athletes. Instead, people walked away, looked down, avoided eye contact. Their fear was tangible.

Rif studied the men. Fit, with ramrod-straight shoulders. They carried equipment bags in their left hands, walking in a formation more common to a military unit than a sports team. Something wasn't right. Rif let them pass, then trailed them at a comfortable distance.

At the end of the street, an old yellow school bus spewed a cloud of diesel into the air. A man dressed all in black stood near the open door. The familiar face left Rif cold inside. Jaramogi, from General Jemwa's camp.

"How far now?" one of the men in the red jerseys asked.

"A ten-minute ride. Get in," Jaramogi replied.

The athletes boarded the bus in quick succession. Rif used the bushes as cover and positioned himself on the other side of the bus. His instincts told him to find out what the hell these men were up to—especially with the negotiations going on at the nearby hotel.

He removed his backpack, slid under the bus, and used the straps to help attach his body to the underbelly of the chassis. He gripped the undercarriage with his hands. Ten minutes, Jaramogi had said. How bad could it be?

As the bus lumbered down the bumpy road, Rif regretted his decision. He closed his eyes to protect them from the dust blasting his face. His hands clung to the axle as the bus jostled back and forth. He silently cursed Zimbabwean road builders as the vehicle lurched from pothole to pothole.

Chapter Fifty-Four

Gabrielle Farrah positioned herself on a rear bench inside the conference room in case she needed to exit quietly and quickly for a phone call. The morning dragged on and on, with more remarks from the Chinese delegation. They had just begun, and already she was bored. There was a reason she hadn't pursued business or law as a career: not nearly enough action. Her idea of a good time was going to the range and firing an AR-15 until her shoulder was battered and bruised.

The opening presentations were public, so she'd figured she'd attend. Hakan agreed with her that the oil deal was likely related to the kidnapper's plans. It didn't hurt to scout the room, see who was there, both participants and spectators. And she hoped to catch Thea during the next break to see if the information she'd provided about a leak had sparked any insights.

She scanned the gallery for Max, but he'd left earlier to check in with his local Interpol counterpart. Maybe they'd grab dinner tonight, catch up on the case and their lives. He was one of the only people she'd confided in about her sister's cancer. The last time they'd met up, it had really helped her to talk about her feelings, hear about Max's childhood on Mykonos.

Her cell vibrated. She glanced down. The buzz of the presentations faded into the background. A photo of Christos Paris stared back at her. Thea had been copied on the text.

She enlarged the picture for a closer look. The billionaire held a copy of today's *New York Times*, proof that he was alive, at least as of this morning. That is, if the photo was even real. She'd send it to the lab for analysis.

These days proof of life was often confirmed by an actual phone call with the hostage or by securing responses to personal questions only the hostage would know the answers to. Sending photos was old school.

Christos's expression caught her attention. She'd seen countless pictures of captives. Most looked weary, drained, shattered. Not this tycoon. His dark gaze burned with indignation, and his chin tilted slightly upward. Blood matted the right side of his head, but he looked resilient, defiant.

Paris sat on a cement floor in front of a gray wall, the backdrop offering no obvious clues about his location. She forwarded the photo to her team, marking the transmission urgent. Their forensics experts would scrutinize it for any information.

Interesting how the photo had been sent to her private cell. Maybe the kidnapper was the same person who'd phoned her on Christmas Day with the news that Paris had been taken. Strange. Thea had been the main contact so far. Now the kidnapper wanted Gabrielle involved. Why?

She uncrossed her legs, suddenly quite uncomfortable on the wooden bench. She scanned the room. Was someone watching her? No one seemed overtly suspicious; everyone was too engrossed in the proceedings. The Chinese National Oil Company representatives were still painstakingly plodding through their proposal while the prime minister and his team smiled and nodded.

Thea perched on the edge of her seat, focused on every word. Gabrielle wanted to attract her attention. They had proof of life for her father—presumably. Thea might have a sense of its legitimacy.

As Gabrielle watched, the kidnap negotiator reached into her jacket pocket and slipped out her phone. She must have kept it on vibrate. For a second, her body froze, but she quickly regrouped. She turned her head, meeting Gabrielle's expectant gaze. A slight nod. This was a breakthrough. Hopefully the big one they had all been looking for.

Chapter Fifty-Five

Nikos studied the Kanzi panel, reviewing in his mind the intimate details of the dossiers he'd compiled about each member. Everyone had a weakness, but some were more obvious than others. Prime Minister Kimweri had proven a challenge. A God-fearing man, he did his best to represent the people of his nation fairly. He worked hard, accepted no bribes, and led with dignity. It had required investigation, but eventually Nikos had found the man's kryptonite. But he'd only use it if absolutely necessary. If there was one thing Nikos had learned, it was that research and preparation were key. He'd spent lots of time studying his father's company, probing for insider knowledge and weak links—and had found both.

Chi was delivering his proposal to the panel, waxing on about how the Chinese could revolutionize Kanzi. The laborious speeches, freighted with references to the historic bonds between China and the region, would have been excruciating if they weren't playing such an important role in his tightening web.

Underneath the table, Thea pulled out her phone and stared at a photo of their father holding today's paper. Real contact from the kidnapper instead of those Latin texts. *About time.* Christos looked as if he'd taken a few hard knocks, but the tough bastard still projected insufferable arrogance.

Nikos caught Thea's attention and pointed to his own cell. She nodded. Seconds later, the photo appeared on his iPhone. He was tempted to make it his new screen saver so he could bask in Christos's distress any time he wished. He texted the image to his team, hoping for a clue that would lead to his father's location. Then he could make his final move.

It had to be an inside job, or the perpetrator had deep pockets and powerful, widespread connections. Abducting a billionaire with iron-clad security was no mean feat. He had a grudging respect for Christos's kidnapper. It had taken years for Nikos to find a vulnerable spot; whoever it was had pulled off quite a coup.

Still, Nikos knew he would triumph in the end. He'd questioned Alec Floros, the man who'd held the helicopter pilot's debts. And now, using his contacts in Greece's Customs Control, his men were pinpointing the destination of the plane that had taken off from Corfu. They were closing in.

Prime Minister Kimweri's head bobbed up and down like a PEZ candy dispenser in the hands of a five-year-old. Christ, this was boring. Chi was finally wrapping up his presentation, or so it seemed. He found the Chinese team's constant droning vaguely irritating and predictably open ended. Nikos had conducted enough negotiations in China to know that nothing was ever cemented, even after the ink on the contracts was bone dry.

He smiled at the memory of the endless negotiations he'd weathered to secure Xi-Ping as his arms supplier. She was as intelligent and ruthless as she was beautiful. He'd shared his dual identity with her but wondered if it had been a sage choice. There was a clock on the relationship, but the massive stockpile of weapons and ammo she had access to had kept it alive.

The gavel slamming down jolted him back to the present. *About fucking time*. Lunch break. He touched Thea's back and steered her out into the hall. Time to pump her for information.

And it looked as if his stalker from HRFC had the same idea, as she was headed straight for them. He hoped Gabrielle was paying attention. Ares was about to reveal himself.

Chapter Fifty-Six

Thea studied the image of her father on her phone. No doubt about it, Papa was sending her a signal.

Gabrielle approached her and Nikos. "Shall we find a quiet spot?"

"This way." Thea led them to the airy alcove she'd discovered while familiarizing herself with the hotel. Recon always paid off, and, given the situation, she needed any edge she could find. The three of them stood behind a large column so they wouldn't be visible to the crowds milling about in the main hallway.

"Christos is alive." Gabrielle's dark eyes emanated compassion.

"If the photo is real. Your team will also be authenticating the picture?"

"Already on it."

Thea considered her options. She could keep the information in the photo to herself, knowing the government analysts would eventually discover it. She inhaled deeply. Gabrielle had been patient, helpful. Maybe Thea should explore if they could be more effective working together.

"My father used to be in the military, so he's familiar with hand signals. He also attended a Quantum International Security kidnap seminar. All top-level Paris Industries executives have been instructed to share clues in photos and videos while being subtle enough not to get caught." She expanded the image on her phone so that only her father's hands were visible. "See his fingers? He's using military hand signals for the numbers zero and five. Now we just have to figure out what they mean."

"Any thoughts? You two know him best." Gabrielle stared at the photo.

Nikos's mouth tightened. Thea's heart ached for him.

"Five, zero—or is it zero, five? A clue to GPS coordinates? A lead to where the kidnappers are holding him?" Papa was trying to tell her something. She just needed to figure it out.

"Does the number somehow correlate to this oil deal?" Nikos asked.

Thea considered the reams of paper she'd gone through. "I don't think so, but I'll review the documents again."

"I'll get my people on it right away. Keep me posted if you figure out what Christos is trying to tell us." Gabrielle nodded to them both and strode down the hall.

Thea turned to Nikos. "Could Papa be referring to something that happened when he was fifty, ten years ago?"

"Nothing comes to mind. The fiftieth state, the fiftieth country?"

"We might not even be reading it the right way." Her head throbbed. Well, now was as good a time as any. "Are you sleeping with Quan Xi-Ping?"

He studied her for a long minute. "You never have to worry about my loyalty to you."

"Nikos, she's Papa's opposition in the negotiations."

"That part didn't bother me."

"Have you been feeding her inside information about Paris Industries?" she asked.

"Father never let me inside the business, so what could I tell her? Xi-Ping and I met during that import/export deal I told you about, the one involving Bucharest. It helped grease the wheels to have a personal relationship. I promise you, no wedding bells are on the horizon."

She believed him. No way would any woman be able to work her brother. Still, she sensed he was up to something. "I need a few minutes alone in my room. I'll meet you back here in fifteen."

He nodded. "Don't worry, sis, we'll find him."

A rush of empathy again filled her as she remembered Nikos's heartbreaking notes. She touched his arm. "Sorry. Papa's kidnapping must be stirring up difficult memories for you."

"Full circle from twenty years ago, except this time the father is kidnapped instead of the son. We can never escape our pasts, I guess," he said.

She couldn't agree more. Nikos's kidnapping had set her on a life path devoted to helping others. But her greatest fear was failing, yet again, to protect her own family.

Chapter Fifty-Seven

The bus squeaked to a stop, and the football players filed out. Rif released the straps securing him to the chassis and lowered himself to the ground. His mouth tasted like a dust bowl, and his shoulders were on fire from the strain of supporting himself for the entire ride.

He flexed his cramping fingers. Dropping down and flipping onto his stomach, he crawled toward the side of the bus now adjacent to a building and peeked out. Jaramogi and the other men entered an abandoned warehouse. White paint flaked off wooden planks, and fluorescent lights shone through rusty steel doors. He shimmied forward to get a better look.

Several open-air Jeeps sat in the dirt parking lot. The unmistakable sound of rifles being locked and loaded caught his attention. A few men wandered out of the warehouse. They'd traded their football uniforms and bags for fatigues and AK-47s.

Other men filed out. Had to be at least thirty of them.

"Load the equipment into the Jeeps," Jaramogi said to the troops.

Rif assumed they'd be heading for the Victoria Falls Hotel. Was General Jemwa planning a coup? As if the oil negotiations and Christos's kidnapping weren't enough to handle. He'd better warn Thea.

He tried to text her but had no bars on his phone. African telecom wasn't stellar at the best of times. *Dammit.* He needed to run back to the hotel, but first he had to escape unnoticed.

Parked about three feet from the warehouse, the bus was angled slightly so its front was closer to the wall. With Jaramogi's troops loading the Jeeps with arms and equipment, he'd have to time his exit carefully. Getting to the warehouse roof was his only egress. From there, he'd find a way down the back of the building.

He waited until the next group passed with their load. *Now.* He scrambled out from under the chassis and jammed one foot against the warehouse wall, the other on the side of the bus. He shimmied upward, using his arms for support. His boot slid down the wall with a slight scuffling sound. He stabilized himself and kept moving.

Voices sounded. Another group was coming out. He reached the roof as the men appeared. He rolled over the edge and lay flat on his back, his chest heaving from the effort.

"Did you hear something?" one of the men asked.

"Check it out," Jaramogi demanded.

Rif remained still, ignoring the pain of the roof's blistering tarmac against his back.

"Footprints. Someone's spying on us. Find him!"

So much for stealth. Rif jumped up and sprinted toward the back of the building while yanking out his belt and scanning for a way down. Seeing a large drainage pipe, he looped the belt around it and rappelled down the wall.

Once on the ground, he pressed his back against the brick and looked both ways. Clear. He moved closer to the propane tank that supplied the warehouse.

Fifty yards away, the open yard morphed into a heavily treed area.

He needed to reach the forest without being mowed down. He'd have to create a diversion.

Soft footsteps crunched on the gravel beside the warehouse. He rummaged in his backpack for a cigarette and lighter. Although he didn't smoke, he always kept a few packs with him when traveling. They were an international trading commodity and a handy detonator. He stuck a Camel into his mouth and flicked the lighter. A quick inhale, and the end glowed. He yanked on the hose connected to the tank, releasing propane, then flicked the cigarette toward the tank and ran like hell.

Voices shouted, but before the men could take action, a loud blast obliterated all other sounds. A wave of heat washed over Rif's head, burning his ears. He kept sprinting, zigzagging to make himself a hard target. He reached the forest line, two bullets punching into a tree right next to him. The near miss spurred him on, his legs pumping like pistons, his boots pounding against the forest floor.

He ran east, trying to determine the most direct path back to the hotel. Sweat soaked his shirt, and dust caked his skin. He had to reach Thea before it was too late.

Chapter Fifty-Eight

Gabrielle paced the hotel room, speaking on the phone to her lead analyst, Ernest. He had news about the Ares connection.

"I intercepted another communication regarding that end-user certificate. The content and originating location made me take a closer look." Ernest's voice was staccato—he always sounded like a machine gun on full auto when he had hit pay dirt.

"Tell me more."

"The message came from Victoria Falls. It mentioned that Belgian company we've previously linked to Ares."

"You're sure?"

"Yes. Not exactly a lot of traffic to decipher compared with, say, a place like New York City. Since you suspected the Kanzi negotiations were related to the kidnapper's larger mission, we've been monitoring all the chatter about it."

"So Ares is here?"

"Probably. And it's possible that Christos Paris could be held captive nearby. If Ares is behind the kidnapping and somehow enmeshed in the oil negotiations, he might want access to his hostage and the insider information Christos could offer. I had the team build a geographic dossier of Victoria Falls. They're monitoring the usual sources: satellite imagery, economic reports, and unusual traffic at transportation hubs. If we get any solid intel, we'll call in a team to help you unearth the hostage."

"I think we're on to something. Report any further transmissions immediately." She pressed the end button and spun around at the sound of the door opening.

"Good news?" Max stood on the threshold of their adjoining rooms.

"Potentially. It seems likely that Ares is here. The problem is, no one can ever describe the arms dealer; it's like he—or *she*, for that matter—doesn't really exist."

"My friend in Harare told me Interpol has been trying to track Ares for eleven years and has no hint as to his identity." Max entered the room and plunked down in the Queen Anne chair.

"Then why have we received two strong leads about him in a few days?"

"Perhaps he is distracted?"

"Possibly. Or maybe he's decided to come out of hiding for some reason."

"To make an entrance?" he asked.

"Our analysts have studied Ares's deals. He has this David-and-Goliath penchant, always selling to the underdog, even if he makes less money. That tells me he has a mission, a cause."

"We all do, no?"

She studied Max's face. "Yes, I guess we do. I wanted the truth behind my parents' deaths, but the Lebanese police gave me the runaround."

"Don't ever give up searching. For us, our families, our experiences . . . the pain scars us forever." His face was hidden in the shadows, but she could feel his anguish.

"What's wrong? Is it Laila—is she not doing well?"

He didn't answer.

"Max, you can talk to me."

He stood and kissed her gently on the lips. "I know. You are the one person I trust."

But instead of opening up, he told her he had to make a call.

After he left, she texted Ernest, asking for a status update on Max's half sister. The inspector general was getting under her skin, and she really wanted to find out more about him. As soon as she fired off the text, she regretted it. One night—that was her rule. Don't get emotionally involved. But maybe it was already too late for that.

Chapter Fifty-Nine

Thea shifted in her seat. The Chinese had finally exhausted every last excruciating argument about why their company was the only choice to handle the Kanzi oil rights. Most of it was spin, of course, but she was more interested in the players in the room, watching their faces for tells, looking for anyone behaving in an unusual way.

"Ms. Paris, we'll be able to fit in your opening remarks before the break," Prime Minister Kimweri said.

"Thank you. I'll say a few words before our COO Ahmed Khali takes over."

Nikos leaned over and whispered to her. "I believe in you."

The panel members' eyes had a glazed look. Even the prime minister seemed weary from the endless monologue. Time to shake things up. She stepped forward, then turned slightly so she was facing both the dignitaries and the crowd.

"My name is Thea Paris, and Paris Industries was built by my father, Christos Paris."

She paused.

Quan Chi's eyebrows rose an inch. Xi-Ping squinted. Nikos smiled at her.

"Although it is true that China has long held vital interests in this region, when you're deciding who you, your children, and your grandchildren would like to work with for the next hundred years, please remember that my father has been deeply and directly involved in Kanzi for nearly forty years."

The fog cleared from the panel members' faces. Even General Jemwa leaned forward.

"Christos Paris brought his family to your beautiful country. He invested his time, energy, and funds in the people of Kanzi, exploring the viability of producing local biofuels. To this day, many farmers subsist by providing Paris Industries with their annual crops.

"And when my father made promises, he kept them. Paris Industries built schools, hospitals, water purification facilities—all necessary additions to boost Kanzi's living standards. And he invested in the people by employing them instead of importing foreign labor. My father worked hand in hand with the people of Kanzi before most other companies knew this special place existed."

The prime minister nodded.

She spun around and headed for her brother. She stood behind him, hands on his shoulders. Ahmed had agreed with her suggestion to include Nikos and his history in her remarks. The COO was strategic, knowing that hitting the family note would affect many, including the prime minister, who was committed to his own kinfolk.

"This is my brother, Nikos Paris. When he was twelve years old, he was kidnapped and held in captivity for nine months. We were so grateful that we got him back." Her gaze locked with General Jemwa's. Under her fingers, Nikos's shoulder muscles knotted.

She returned to the front of the room.

"Even though his own son had been held hostage because of his business here, Christos maintained his close partnership with Kanzi. He loves the people, the land, the culture. And my father shares the same resilience as your townsfolk. He started life as a fisherman's son in Greece, poor and hungry. He built his company through hard work and sacrifice."

The prime minister straightened in his seat.

"And proof of our family's commitment is that Nikos and I are here today, representing our father, because he is going through a difficult trial. A few days ago, *he* was kidnapped. We're here to show you that Paris Industries remains dedicated to Kanzi even in his absence." She wasn't going to dance around the truth. "This is about family, and Kanzi has always been part of ours. Choose Paris Industries, and you'll continue to have that loyalty moving forward. Thank you for your time today."

She headed back to her seat, nodding to Ahmed, who stood and headed toward the dignitaries.

"Thank you, Thea." He cleared his throat. "Prime Minister Kimweri, board members, ladies and gentlemen, Paris Industries can offer something else that the Chinese National Oil Company can't—efficient and safe transport of the oil to the closest port."

The general's fingers drummed on the table; he was probably eager to escape the laborious proceedings. He was a man of action, not a corporate suit.

A soft creak. The rear door of the conference room opened, and a man dressed in fatigues stepped inside. Something about his rigid stance left Thea unsettled.

"Our company has a signed agreement from the government of Namibia, and . . ."

She stopped paying attention to Ahmed's speech and zeroed in on the soldier striding up the left aisle. A slight bulge on his rear hip set off warning signals. She slipped off her heels and kept him in her peripheral vision.

He closed the distance to where the dignitaries sat. Instinct made her move. She jumped up and knocked her chair aside, bolting toward him.

Seconds later, he reached for his hip, connecting with his weapon.

"Gun!" She lunged forward.

The soldier raised his pistol.

She sidestepped him, her fingers burrowing into his hand, nails hooked into his flesh. She twisted hard. The pistol clattered to the floor.

Before he could recover, she brought her hand down like a blade on his biceps. A loud snap. He screamed. She kicked his legs out from under him, knocking him to his knees.

The prime minister's bodyguards pounced on the soldier, cuffing him. She kept his gun at her side. Over a hundred pairs of eyes locked on her, the room suddenly silent. She turned to the prime minister, who looked shell shocked.

"We need to get you somewhere safe, sir."

Prime Minister Kimweri banged the gavel, ending the session. Chaos reigned as everyone charged out of the room. Thea grabbed her bag from the table, looped it around her torso, and ran toward Kimweri. She looked for the general, but he had vanished during the commotion. *Strange.* Why would the man in charge of protecting the prime minister disappear?

Movement outside the window caught her attention. Men dressed in fatigues swarmed the gardens. A volley of shots echoed in the courtyard.

The prime minister's bodyguards rushed to close the conference room's doors. Remembering the floor plans of the hotel, Thea guided Kimweri to the rear door, which led downstairs to the boiler room. She needed to get him to a safe location.

Chapter Sixty

Gabrielle slipped out of the conference room before Prime Minister Kimweri's bodyguards blocked the doors. Shots had been fired outside, and she needed to figure out what the hell was going on. But first she needed to procure the weapons in her room.

She scrambled up the rear staircase and sprinted to her suite, opening the door. After she punched in the safe's combination, the metal door opened with a long beep. Seconds later, her SIG Sauer was loaded and ready for action. She grabbed extra magazines and shoved them into her pockets. Opening her hardcase luggage, she quickly assembled the M24, slinging the strap around her shoulder, slipping the parabolic microphone, first-aid kit, and other items that her CIA contact had given her into her messenger bag.

A knock on Max's door. No answer.

She skirted the window to avoid becoming a potential target, then lifted the drape so she could survey the front yard. Soldiers surrounded the hotel, Kalashnikovs in their hands. A hulking figure commanded the men. General Ita Jemwa. As if things weren't crazy enough with Ares in the vicinity and Christos Paris kidnapped. Now what, a coup? She grabbed her cell and speed-dialed.

Stephen Kelly answered on the first ring. "What's the latest?"

"There's a bit of a complication. Looks like General Ita Jemwa is attempting a coup."

"That fascist. No way can we let him take over Kanzi. I'll mobilize some assistance. Take whatever steps necessary to keep the prime minister alive. Understood?"

"Absolutely. Last I saw, Thea Paris was protecting Kimweri."

"Roger that. Check in with me regularly."

She ended the call and tried texting Thea: *Where are you? Is the PM with you?*

Another quick knock on Max's door. Nothing. She tried calling him. Straight to voice mail. In the middle of a coup, it'd be helpful to have another trained officer by her side. Especially a friend.

Gunfire echoed through the courtyard again. The prime minister's bodyguards were going head-to-head with the rebels. No answer from either Thea or Max. When Gabrielle saw Thea last, the kidnap negotiator had been heading for the cellar stairs. Probably no reception there. Better make her way down, see if she could help.

She cracked open the door and peered into the hall. So far, so good. A rush of adrenaline and cortisol kicked her body into gear. She loved working in the field and hadn't had a taste of it in far too long.

She hurried down the corridor, stopping to check for sounds of movement. Nothing on this floor. The chaos outside had probably convinced any guests to remain hidden in their rooms.

A soft *bing* caught her attention. The elevator. Someone was coming up. She flattened herself in an alcove by the stairs and waited, hoping it would be Max.

Chapter Sixty-One

Thea shepherded the prime minister down the uneven stone steps that led to the cellar. "Stay behind me. We need to keep you safe."

A sound. Someone was already down there. She held her index finger to her lips and signaled for the prime minister to wait. She descended the stairs, careful not to make any noise.

At the bottom of the steps, she inched forward to see who was there. Could be a maintenance worker from the hotel, a guest hiding, or one of the rebels. She grabbed a plastic yellow *Wet Floor* sign and held it out beyond the wall.

Two shots punctured it.

She had her answer.

Pulling the sign back behind the wall, she crouched down and waited a few seconds. Then she tossed the plastic yellow sign at waist height into the air and rolled out on the ground. The soldier shot at the sign. She fired from her prone position. Two shots, and he collapsed on the floor. A quick kick removed the AK from his reach. She scooped up the assault rifle and surveyed the hallway for other threats, but only silence greeted her. It looked as if the man had been alone.

She pounded back to the stairs. "Okay, it's safe now, Mr. Prime Minister. Let's go."

"Call me Mamadou. You've saved my life twice in the last half hour, so I think we should be on a first-name basis." He gave her a tentative smile.

"Mamadou it is. In here, please." She pushed open a steel door.

They entered the boiler room, a noisy place filled with the sounds of soft hissing and gurgling water, with dim recessed lights stippling the ceiling. One wall had tools hanging on hooks; another was cluttered with buckets, mops, and other cleaning equipment.

The intense heat hit her like a concrete wall, but it was sanctuary for now.

She barricaded the door from inside using a workbench. "Sorry about the conditions, but until I find out what's going on, we'll have to enjoy the impromptu sauna."

"The heat doesn't bother me, my child. Everyone thinks I'm a city person, but I spent many summers on the plains tending cattle. I'm a bush boy at heart."

"Good, because we might be stuck in here for a while." Close-protection security meant keeping the subject, in this case the PM, tucked away in a safe location.

After the long morning, Thea needed to replenish her insulin. The blood sugar numbers on her phone weren't good. She reached inside her bag, then remembered she'd left the cooling pouch in her jacket upstairs on her chair. *Dammit to hell.* "I'll see if my colleague Rif knows what's going on. We need to figure out who's behind the coup."

"I can answer that. General Ita Jemwa. My spies reported that he was under the misguided impression that I'd be replacing him as head of security once the Kanzi oil deal had been signed."

"You'd have kept him on your staff?"

"Keep your enemies close. I didn't think he'd try anything before the negotiations finished, but I obviously misjudged him."

"My family has a history with the general, not a good one." She checked her cell phone. As expected, no reception.

The prime minister shook his head. "His ambition and greed have overwhelmed his good sense."

She respected Mamadou Kimweri's compassion, but it struck her as a tad naïve. Her experience in K&R had taught her that everyone was jockeying for power and money. Minerals, diamonds, oil—they brought out the worst of humanity, especially in a resource-rich continent like Africa.

She checked the handheld satphone she'd procured in town during her pharmacy run, but it needed line of sight to work. For now, no comms or support. With the chaos going on upstairs, they'd have to hole up for a while.

She searched for another egress in case they needed to leave. The only one that seemed somewhat manageable was the air-conditioning shaft. She moved a box underneath it, hopped up, and used a screwdriver from the tool wall to remove the vent cover. Good thing the prime minister was a lean man. Ten more pounds, and he wouldn't fit inside.

Sweat ran down her back. She jumped off the box and headed to the sink, splashing her face with cold water. After this, she was tempted to move to Iceland. As if the weather outside wasn't enough, the boiler room pushed the air temperature to a whole new level. And, unfortunately, heat only exacerbated her diabetes. A small cup sat on the counter. She filled it with water and passed it to Mamadou. "We'd better stay hydrated. I've no idea how long we'll be trapped in here."

"Thank you. Would you mind if I closed my eyes for a few minutes? It has been quite a day for this old man."

"Absolutely. I'll let you know if and when we need to leave. For now, this is the safest place for you." She grabbed a thick towel from the sink area, rolled it into a makeshift pillow, and handed it to Mamadou. "Maybe this will help."

He smiled and closed his eyes, his breathing deep and strong. She kept an eye on him for a few minutes, then dug into her briefcase to see if there was anything useful inside.

Another packet of familiar yellowed pages greeted her—along with the old music box she'd misplaced years ago, the one that played "Tie a Yellow Ribbon." It was a sappy song, but it always reminded her of the night her brother had been abducted.

Nikos must've slipped them into her bag during the negotiations. She needed to sit down and discuss the past with him—he obviously wanted her to know the truth. But first she had to survive this mess. She wasn't sure she wanted to read more. The description of his time in Oba's camp filled her with despair. Then again, she loved her brother and wanted to understand him better.

KILL COUNT

I killed and killed and killed. Instead of counting days, I started counting bodies. I was up to forty-eight. We raided villages, stole supplies, burned the huts. Oba, Kofi, and the older boys stuck their penises inside women, made them scream. Mothers begged for their children's lives, offering to "service" the soldiers. Oba said the women secretly liked the grinding, that it made them feel special.

The rainy season came with so many mosquitoes. I smeared mud on my body, but the bugs wanted blood even more than Oba did. I lay alone on the floor of my small hut that I'd earned as leader of the boys, but I could never fall asleep without my candies. Whenever I closed my eyes, Nobo and Brandon stared back at me. I hadn't protected them. I was sad they'd died. And I hated Oba more every day. All he did was bully everyone.

One night, a storm passed, water dripping through the thatched roof, big fat drops smacking me on the forehead. It was a hot night, and everyone had gone to bed early. No crickets, no rats, no sounds from the other boys. I was antsy. I had a feeling something was going to happen.

A warm breeze blew through the hut. The smell hit me. Earthy, stinky, like death. My body shook. I breathed in deeply just to make sure. I'd never forget that smell. I crawled to the opening of my hut and looked out. Men in olive uniforms were entering the camp. One huge shadow stood out because he walked with a limp. The General.

My mind spun. This was my chance. Oba's hut was hidden in the trees. There still might be time. I grabbed my knife, rifle, and machete, everything oiled and cleaned, ready for battle. Oba had trained me well. I snuck out of my hut and ran through the jungle. When I got to his hut, I slowed down. A figure moved in the shadows. Oba. The warlord knew his village was being attacked. Instead of fighting, he was trying to escape. Coward.

I knew where he was going to hide. The cave. I might be able to beat him there, but I would have to go into the swamp. I ran, using my machete to hack through the jungle. Branches scratched my body, blood all over my arms. The pain didn't bother me. All I cared about was making it to the cave first.

But I had to cross the swamp to beat him. I hoped the crocs were sleeping. I kicked off my boots and dropped the machete. Slipping into the slimy water, I held my rifle above my head. The water smelled nasty, made me feel sick. I breathed through my mouth and swam straight across.

Fifty feet to land. Forty. Thirty.

A sound. Something moved in the water. I looked right and left. Shadows and strange noises. My hand tightened on the rifle. My legs kicked harder. A soft splash. I swam backward, ready to shoot. I didn't want to warn Oba, but I didn't want the crocs to get me either.

Two ugly heads popped up. Then the crocs slid back under the water, disappearing. Scared, so scared. I kicked as hard as I could. Where were they? Something bumped into my back. I turned. Land, I'd reached land.

I stumbled out, fell onto my knees, and breathed hard. That was a close one. I put the shoulder strap of my AK-47 across my chest and checked to be sure that I still had my knife.

Hurrying along the path, I stopped to listen. Silence. I'd beaten Oba to the cave.

I crawled through the opening and reached back to brush away the marks my belly had made. I leaned against the wall and listened. Someone was coming. Oba. I climbed onto a ledge to be taller than him. Waited.

Footsteps. A figure stepped inside.

I cracked my rifle butt over his head. Oba lurched forward, dropped his AK, and fell to his knees. Before he could move, I jumped down, kicked the AK away, and aimed my rifle at him.

"Oh, it's you, Mzungu." He smiled, his teeth and eyes all yellow.

He was an idiot if he thought he could still boss me around with the General here. Now I had a way to get out of this hell. "Not Mzungu. I'm Nikos Christos Paris."

Oba looked at me as if I was crazy. His hand reached for his rifle. "Don't move."

He kept his hands still but didn't take his eyes off his weapon.

"What are you doing, idiot? We must hide. An enemy is attacking the camp."

"You are my enemy."

"Don't be stupid. I took you in, treated you like my son."

"You're not my father. You're a bully." I lifted my AK-47. "This one is for Nobo." I shot his left leg. He screamed and tried again to reach for his rifle. "This one is for Mr. Grantam." I shot his right leg.

Another yell. He twitched. Blood pooled on the ground. "Leave me be. We needed food." Spit shot out of his mouth. Oba had no honor. He always killed people weaker than him.

I stepped forward and pointed the rifle at his head. "This one is for Brandon."

I fired, and Oba was dead.

Noises sounded outside the cave. Soldiers hurried inside. I dropped my rifle to the ground. I'd done what I'd needed to do. The rest I didn't care about.

The General squeezed inside, holding Kofi by the ear. The skinny man's eyes were glassy and large. He'd bet on the wrong side after all. The General looked down at Oba, then raised his eyebrows.

"Let's get you home, boy."

Home. I wasn't sure what that meant anymore.

THE REWARD

I was going home today. I'd spent two weeks at the General's house letting my sores get better and eating boatloads of food. I threw up a lot, sick from fighting my need for the candies. I sweated a lot, and my stomach hurt bad. The General didn't lock me in the shed again, but I was never left alone.

I think the giant wanted to make me look better before sending me to back to Papa. A local doctor gave me cream to rub on my cuts. My body was covered in marks from leeches, and I had lots of bruises. I looked in a mirror for the first time since I'd been taken. At first I didn't think it was me. I could count my ribs. My eyes were different, my cheeks sunken in.

The General told me I had been gone nine months. I couldn't believe it. Was it really that long? I was so angry. All this time, and my father couldn't find me?

One morning the General gave me new clothes and a shiny pair of shoes. He dressed in his uniform with lots of medals, like he was going to a parade.

In the kitchen, a newspaper sat on the kitchen table. I read the top: HERO GENERAL RESCUES NIKOS PARIS; WILL COLLECT MILLION-DOLLAR REWARD.

The General was collecting a reward? He was the one who had taken me in the first place. What a liar. I thought about telling Papa as soon as I saw him but decided not to. I just wanted it all to be over. I wanted to forget.

We rode in the General's fancy Mercedes convertible, the seats covered in zebra hides. I sat in the back with my "hero," wondering what it'd be like to see Papa and Thea again.

"Tell your father about the villagers who are suffering. He must stop buying up all the crops for fuel."

"Why don't you give the million dollars to the villagers?" I asked.

"You know nothing of how the world works, boy."

"I know what I see. You live in a big house and feed your fat belly while your people are hungry. You're worse than my father." I wasn't afraid of the General anymore, or anyone, really.

"I did what I had to do to help my people. Your father is all greed. He only cares about money. I wonder what he would have paid if your sister had been kidnapped. That was my plan, but Kofi made a mistake. Maybe it worked out better this way. Oba would have loved Thea."

I got so mad at him. I thought about stabbing the General to make my kill count fifty.

"We're here." The Mercedes pulled into a small private airport where my father had parked his jet. Locals lined up on the road, cheering, holding signs. The General smiled and waved. This was his big moment. I hated him.

We stopped beside the Learjet with Paris Industries painted on the side. I glanced up. Papa walked down the stairs of the plane holding Thea's hand, smiling for the cameras. He looked healthy, like he hadn't missed a meal or a night's sleep. Thea's cheeks were rosy and pink, her eyes glowing with happiness. I was glad she was okay, that I'd protected her that night.

I climbed out of the car slowly, my body still sore. My father opened his arms for a hug. I stuck out my hand instead. Papa grabbed my hand with both of his and squeezed hard. Then he turned and smiled so the reporters could take a photo. Bastard. All he wanted was a story in the papers about his company.

I stood completely still, frozen like Thea had been that night.

I realized something—the General was right about my father. He only cared about making money.

REAL LIFE

It has been months since I've been back. I've been writing these pages for you, Dr. Goldberg. You wanted me to tell what happened. I showed the journal to Papa. After he read my story, he was quiet for a long time. Then he said softly, "You must never speak of this to anyone other than Dr. Goldberg, not even your sister."

I asked him why I shouldn't tell people what had really happened, and he said it would ruin my future, because people would be scared of me. I said, "But it wasn't my fault." And Papa said that sometimes that doesn't matter.

I was sent to a medical clinic for a while. I had to do all sorts of tests, and people watched me all the time. Finally they let me out. After that, I started doing whatever I felt like. Sometimes I saw Papa staring at me like I was a dangerous animal. He didn't talk about me taking over Paris Industries anymore. Now I'm going to a special school in Utah to "get help," but I know that Papa wants me out of his sight. He doesn't like what I did in the camp, but I just did what I had to to survive.

I will miss Thea. I'm taking her music box with me to Utah. Taking it apart and putting it back together makes me think about that night when my life changed. Papa said the song was about a man coming

home, looking for a yellow ribbon to see if his family still loved him.
There was no yellow ribbon for me.

That's fine. I won't let anyone bully me again.
No one disrespects Mzungu. No one.

The ink smeared on the final page, wet from Thea's tears. It was the first time in years she could remember crying outside the refuge of a shower. She touched the old music box, the familiar notes playing in her mind.

She pictured Nikos when he was younger, full of potential. The abduction had stolen not only his freedom, but his entire future. Instead of becoming an oil baron, he'd become a killer.

Prime Minister Kimweri stirred, opening his eyes and sitting up. "Are you okay, my dear? I'm sorry about your father's kidnapping. He's a good man."

He'd misunderstood her tears—or maybe not, as she had been crying for both men in her family: her brother, who'd suffered such hell, and her father, who hadn't been able to cope with his damaged son.

She wiped the wetness from her face and pulled herself together. "Have you heard any rumors about Christos's abduction? Do you think General Jemwa is involved?"

"I've heard nothing, I'm afraid. The general has a small army and a lot of influence in Kanzi, but I don't see him having the international reach or resources to kidnap Christos Paris like that."

"Unless he had a partner," she said.

"A powerful partner."

Thea stood and drank more water from the sink.

A loud explosion sounded in the hallway, shaking the steel door frame. A faint whiff of smoke wafted through the crack at the bottom of the boiler room door. She hurried over and placed her hand near the knob. Hot. They needed to get out. Now.

Chapter Sixty-Two

Rif sprinted the final yards to reach the hotel, his lungs burning from the exertion. Jaramogi and the general's men had already surrounded the building. Shots sounded from inside. He needed a weapon.

Using the recesses of the hotel's wall as cover, he closed the distance on a soldier posted outside the rear entrance. Only ten feet away. He waited for the man to pace in the other direction, then pounced from behind, his arm snaking around the soldier's thick neck. The man kicked and squirmed but couldn't make a sound. Rif dragged him into an alcove and tightened his hold. Seconds later, the soldier slumped to the ground.

He grabbed the Kalashnikov, extra magazines, combat knife, and the radio attached to the soldier's belt. He had a working knowledge of Swahili, so he might be able to intercept communications among the soldiers, figure out their plan. All indicators pointed to General Jemwa attempting a coup. Brilliant place to do it, as Prime Minister Kimweri had only his travel detail on duty, some of whom might be the general's men. Victoria

Falls was also relatively isolated, so assistance would be slow in coming.

He'd tried Thea's cell and new satphone several times but couldn't reach her. The best thing he could do to help was to eliminate Jemwa's men quietly and work his way inside. The longer he remained undetected, the better.

He'd counted thirty football players.

One down, twenty-nine to go.

Navigating the building's exterior, he detected the next sentry. He switched off the radio and stalked the man. This one would be tougher to surprise—he was more vigilant, alert.

Rif moved quickly toward the soldier, using the columns for cover. Knife in hand, he attacked. A quick swipe of the blade across the man's neck, and the sentry's spasming body fell to the ground, spouting blood and heaving wetly through the gash in his trachea.

A sound. He turned. Another of the general's men appeared from the shadows, lifting his AK-47 to fire. Rif dove to the ground, rolled away, and raised his stolen rifle. He'd probably get shot, but he'd go down fighting.

But the soldier didn't fire. Instead, the familiar crack of a high-velocity round being fired ripped through the air. The side of the man's head exploded, and he staggered forward and collapsed.

A sniper had just saved Rif's life.

There was another dog in this fight. Someone who didn't want the coup to be successful. But who?

Chapter Sixty-Three

Gabrielle snuck a quick look from the shelter of the alcove near the stairway entrance as the elevator dinged again. She held her SIG Sauer and prepared to identify: friend or enemy. *Please be Max.*

The doors opened to reveal a soldier dressed in British DPM fatigues—the same design as the man who'd attempted the assassination of the prime minister. He held an AK-47 in his large hands.

Definitely enemy.

She aimed her SIG, her finger hovering over the trigger. But a flash of movement stopped her from firing. Nikos Paris stepped out of the elevator behind the soldier, Glock in hand. Shocked, she hesitated. What was going on? Was Nikos part of the coup?

The soldier loped down the hallway, his gait relaxed. Nikos was clearly with him, the two men speaking in Swahili. She couldn't understand what they were saying, but she recognized the language. Nikos motioned down the hall. The soldier strode ahead of him.

Without warning, Nikos raised his Glock and fired point-blank into the back of the soldier's head. Blood splattered the white walls, the gunshot echoing down the corridor. The soldier slumped to the floor.

What the fuck? Was Nikos *pretending* to be part of the coup but secretly working against it? She wondered if Thea was somehow involved.

She peered down the hall. Nikos kicked aside the soldier's body, then rapped on the last door on the hallway. Seconds later, someone let him in. Gabrielle couldn't see who it was, but she'd swear from the voice it was a woman. Too bad the parabolic microphone her CIA contact had given her wouldn't work through walls. She decided to move closer. Considering what she'd just witnessed, she needed to know what the hell Nikos Paris was up to.

Chapter Sixty-Four

Rif ran across the courtyard and lay in wait for the next rebel patrolling the hotel's perimeter. He didn't know how long he'd go undetected, and he needed to take advantage while Jemwa's men were unaware of him. He'd been up against ridiculous odds before; the secret was remaining hidden and taking on one enemy at a time. Stay in the moment; don't do too much at once.

He turned the radio on low, hoping to intercept a communication. What was the general's endgame? Did he want Prime Minister Kimweri to surrender, or was this an assassination?

A burst of Swahili came from the radio. He recognized the word for "fire." Commotion on the east side of the hotel drew his attention. He scanned the immediate area. All clear. He sprinted toward the action, arriving at the southeast wall. He crouched low, catching his breath. Three soldiers smashed windows, tossing grenades and Molotov cocktails into the building. The stench of white phosphorus doused the air.

Flames erupted in the east wing. Explosions rippled across the hotel. *Screw the cloak of silence.* He needed to enter the hotel, make sure the prime minister, Thea, and any other innocents made it out alive.

He lifted the Kalashnikov to his shoulder, aimed, and canceled the first soldier, then a second and third. Six down, twenty-four left.

Time to get inside. He hoped the mysterious sniper would take care of any loose ends.

Chapter Sixty-Five

Smoke seeped into the boiler room, forcing Thea and Mamadou to leave their hideaway. They breathed through wet cloths while they prepared to leave. Most fire victims died from smoke inhalation rather than the actual flames. Lethargic, her blood sugar skyrocketing, Thea cursed herself for leaving the insulin upstairs.

"I hope you're not claustrophobic."

"The air vent?" the prime minister asked.

"Looks like our only way out." She slid her sat and cell phones into her bag and looped it over her shoulder. Then she grabbed the AK-47 she'd taken from the soldier and hopped onto the box. A wave of dizziness washed over her. She shook it off. No time for weakness.

"I'll go first, lead the way. You okay to crawl through the vent?"

"I might be old, but I'm limber." His eyes glistened like a mirage in the middle of a desert. She wasn't sure if the dampness was from smoke or emotion.

"Just follow me, and move quietly. I'll search for a vent that leads outside." The heavy vegetation and the falls due west of the hotel gave them the best chance of leaving the building safely until backup could arrive.

One last check for cell reception. No bars. Too bad. She could really use Rif's help about now.

Chapter Sixty-Six

Nikos sat with Xi-Ping and Chi in the sumptuous living room of their suite. The General had initiated the coup without waiting for his signal, but Nikos had anticipated this betrayal. It wasn't as though Ita Jemwa was a man to be trusted.

Explosions shook the building, the reverberations rattling the windows.

"Was this really necessary? Why wasn't it contained? And wasn't that a gunshot in the hallway?" Chi was on the edge of frantic, while Xi-Ping's gaze was more controlled.

Nikos smiled. "No need to worry. Prime Minister Kimweri is dead. I'll take you out the rear entrance. In a few short minutes, General Jemwa will be the new leader of Kanzi, and you'll be awarded the oil contract once order is restored."

"You'd better hope so." Chi leaned forward in the armchair, crossing and uncrossing his legs.

"We need to complete the wire transfer to the General's account." Nikos let the words hang in the air.

"We'll wait for the paperwork first. I want everything signed on the oil rights before we pay." Chi crossed his arms.

"I've known the General since I was a boy, when he rescued me from a warlord. That relationship is our biggest advantage. Do we really want to give him a reason to look elsewhere?" Nikos strode to the window and peered down at the courtyard. Two soldiers sprawled on the ground, blood soaking their shirts. Undoubtedly the work of his snipers.

Xi-Ping turned to her brother. "He's right. Hesitate, and the general could go with the Russians or Iranians."

"It's a lot of money," Chi grumbled.

"And we will make a hundred times that with this contract," She-Wolf said.

Nikos remained silent.

Seconds ticked by.

"Okay, we do it, but I want that contract by end of day," Chi said.

"I'll make it happen."

Chi grabbed his cell phone and punched in numbers. The transfer completed, he showed Nikos the confirmation number.

"Perfect."

More shots sounded in the yard. The soldiers were closing in. No time to savor the moment.

"This deal will immortalize you and the Chinese National Oil Company." Nikos pulled the soldier's pistol from his waistband and moved to where Chi was sitting. Before the other man could react, he shot him twice in the forehead.

Chi collapsed onto the right arm of the chair, brain matter and skull fragments everywhere.

"Ares" was now "officially" dead.

Xi-Ping strode to Nikos and kissed him savagely. "Thank you. You have no idea how much I hated my brother. Now, let's get the hell out of here."

He pulled her close in a tight embrace and, with her head against his chest, lifted the pistol and double-tapped two bullets into her heart. Shock froze her face as she fell backward onto the rug, clutching at her chest, legs kicking.

"You know too much."

He left the cell phone in Chi's hand. It was painful to sacrifice those millions, but he could afford it. The evidence trail would point to Quan Chi as Ares, infamous arms dealer, the payment indicating that Chi had hired General Jemwa to stage the coup.

The first half of Nikos's plan was complete.

He crouched over and dipped his hand into Chi's blood pooling on the floor, smearing it on his own leg and torso. Yes, more than enough for his purposes.

His phone buzzed—a text from one of his men stating that his father had been confirmed to be somewhere close by. *Good.* No one would beat him to the final punch. He called the chopper and ordered the pilot to stand by.

Plan for everything, count on nothing.

Chapter Sixty-Seven

Crawling through the claustrophobic ventilation system certainly wouldn't make Thea's top ten list of fun things to do. Her breath sounded heavy and raspy as it echoed against the metal structure. Ironic that an air shaft should feel as if it had no air.

She led the way with her cell phone's flashlight, Mamadou Kimweri following her closely. At the first junction, she turned left, then kept following the route that would take them westward.

Voices suddenly sounded from directly below them. She froze, flicked off her light, and strained to listen. The words weren't decipherable, but she recognized the familiar tones of Swahili.

A soft touch on her ankle. Mamadou letting her know he understood they needed to pause. Seconds passed like hours as they waited to see what would happen. Four shots were fired in the distance. The men in the room underneath them shouted at each other. Loud footsteps pounded as they exited.

It killed her not knowing what was happening outside.

She waited another two minutes to make sure the men were gone. Sweat from her forehead dripped onto the galvanized steel.

Okay, onward. She crawled away from the fire, searching for an external vent where they could slip out of the hotel unnoticed.

Intense thirst overwhelmed her, and she needed to pee. Not good signs. Her blood sugar levels were rising in the absence of insulin. She had to return to her room or the conference space and give herself an injection. But first she had to get the prime minister to safety.

They reached another bend in the ductwork. She considered the structure of the building. Her gut told her to turn right. This place was an absolute maze with all its twists and turns. She hoped like hell she hadn't gotten them lost.

Chapter Sixty-Eight

Gabrielle concealed herself in the alcove adjacent to the room Nikos had entered, and from there she could hear the sound of voices but not what they were saying. Then the sound of two gunshots, followed by two more. Then silence.

Who else was inside that suite?

Her phone vibrated in her pocket, startling her. She quickly checked her cell. Max. *Christos Paris is being held nearby. Meet me at the Victoria Falls Bridge.*

At long last, positive news. She texted back: *Hotel under siege. Will come as soon as I can.*

Movement. Sounds. The hotel room's door opened. She remained hidden in the alcove, where she had a view of the hallway. Nikos again. She hoped he was headed the other way. To her relief, he exited the room alone and hurried toward the rear stairs.

She waited a few moments to make sure he was gone. What to do? Curiosity overrode any hesitation. She raised her SIG Sauer and inched toward the room. The door was ajar. She listened, but only silence greeted her. Cautious, she pushed the door wider so she could look inside.

A metallic scent filled the room. A woman's body lay supine on the white carpet, blood framing her in a crimson blot. Quan Xi-Ping. A quick glance to the left revealed Quan Chi slumped across an armchair, also dead, his brains splattered on the chair and wall. Sister and brother, forever bonded in death.

She cleared the bedroom and bathroom. The suite held no other bodies.

A whiff of smoke flooded her nose. Time to leave. A cell phone rested on the floor beneath Chi's hand. She picked it up using a napkin from the table and scanned the screen. Locked. She slipped the phone into her pocket for examination later. It might hold answers to this unusual turn of events, and she didn't want it destroyed in a fire.

She exited the room, scanning the hallway, making her way toward the stairs. Nikos Paris had murdered the Chinese delegation vying for the same oil deal as his father's company. This took negotiating to a whole other level. Was he working on behalf of Christos, or did he have his own agenda? If he and General Jemwa were in cahoots to stage the coup and give the oil rights to Paris Industries, why did he need to kill the Chinese? And why had Nikos shot the soldier? Questions and more questions. Gabrielle tabled everything until later. She needed to reach the bridge and find Max.

Chapter Sixty-Nine

Nikos descended the stairs to the ground-floor exit. The General's men had started fires with incendiary devices on the east side of the inn. Before long, the iconic Victoria Falls Hotel would be consumed by hungry flames.

The General had brought only a small force, probably because they were in the sovereign territory of another country and he couldn't risk having their movement look like an invasion. That gave Nikos and his men an advantage.

Two sharpshooters targeted the General's soldiers from outside, while three of his operatives worked the inside. He'd assigned his best man the job of making sure Thea escaped safely. No matter how well trained the Kanzian platoon was, the men would be no match against his special-ops team.

Nikos exited the building and crept along the thick foliage nearby, then sprinted toward the General's Land Cruiser, which was parked at the far end of the hotel. The giant was issuing commands from the safety of the armored vehicle. This close to grabbing the throne, he wasn't about to put himself in jeopardy.

When Nikos was within range of the General's view, he slowed his pace and faked a limp. Chi's blood helped sell the story. His breath was raspy from running as he approached the Land Cruiser. "I'm hit. Kimweri's on the west side of the building, still alive."

The General assessed him shrewdly. He hadn't reached his position by being a fool. Deeply obsessed with his own safety, he never went anywhere alone, as evidenced by the two bodyguards sitting in the rear of the vehicle. But Ita Jemwa's paranoia was outmatched by his lust for power, which Nikos was depending on. More than anything, the General wanted to be the next ruler of Kanzi.

His radio buzzed.

"The prime minister's escaping. We need backup," one of Nikos's snipers shouted in Swahili, pretending to be a rebel soldier.

The General pressed the talk button. "Which way?"

"West."

"Go." The General gestured to his two guards. "Track down the old man."

"Through the jungle path." Nikos pointed. "You can catch him. The prime minister is old and slow."

"Kill Kimweri and anyone with him," the General instructed the guards.

The men exited the Land Cruiser and sprinted across the field, disappearing into the jungle. Rain pelted Nikos's face. He opened the driver's-side door. "The gods are angry today." He gestured toward the sky.

"Because they want me to lead Kanzi in a new direction." The General's eyes blazed.

"I'm afraid the coup is over." Nikos whipped out his Glock and pointed it at the General's temple. "Hands on the wheel."

Cold realization dawned on the giant's face. He'd performed too many double-crosses himself not to realize he'd been duped. "I should've known."

Nikos searched him for weapons, removed a knife and a pistol, dropped them to the ground and kicked them under the truck.

"People believe what they want to hear most. It's what helps men like you and I deceive them." He remained alert. The General was a seasoned warrior who wouldn't go down easily, and Nikos wanted to keep him alive for a little while longer.

"You need me. Don't be a fool."

"Get out, hands above your head. Make a move, and I'll shoot you in the leg like Kofi did all those years ago."

"And look what happened to him."

"I'm not Kofi."

The General slid his bulk out of the vehicle. Although his former abductor had aged, he still maintained his brute strength. Nikos remained far enough away that any attempt to escape could be stopped by a bullet to the giant's legs. He didn't want things to end quite yet, not before he'd had his say.

"Hands in front." He grasped the Glock in one hand while securing a thick zip tie from his pocket.

"This isn't necessary. We're stronger as a team." The General presented his hands with his thumbs together, palms facing downward, fists clenched tight.

"Unclench your fists, and turn your wrists inward." Nikos wasn't taking any chances the giant would squirm out. He yanked on the zip tie, making sure the thick plastic was tight around the General's meaty hands. "Kimweri trusted you, and look what happened."

"You're different. We're cut from the same cloth."

"Desperation breeds false humility. I've been there myself, thanks to you. Now we've come full circle. Move."

The General entered the thick bush at a lumbering pace. Nikos wanted him far from his Land Cruiser in case his bodyguards returned. No one was going to interrupt this long-overdue meeting.

"You're different from your father. Not so greedy. You care about the people of Kanzi."

"Don't misinterpret my deeds. I'm no communist; I just like to help the underdog. Head to the right." He'd hidden a few items in the jungle earlier in preparation for this moment.

"The people of Kanzi love and respect me."

"Fear does not equate to love and respect. I know this too well. My own father fears me, but any love and respect he had for me died after my kidnapping."

"I tried to protect you from the warlord."

"At twelve years old, my future was filled with endless possibilities. After nine months in the jungle, my life was irrevocably altered. My father could barely stand to look at me; my sister treated me like a broken doll. You took everything that mattered from me." Nikos kicked the tire that rested beside a nearby acacia tree. "Stop here."

"You're making a mistake." The General's voice faltered as he took in the tire and the gas can perched beside it. Necklacing was a horrific way to die.

"I can smell the fear on your skin, a wonderful change from the stench of oil I've been carrying around with me since you first locked me up." Nikos flashed on the smelly hood and the General's shed. "Now smoke, oil, and gasoline will fill your last breath."

Keeping the gun trained on the giant, Nikos filled the tire with gasoline. He stepped back, slipped the Glock into his waistband, and reached down to lift the tire with both hands.

The General raised both arms above his head, flaring his elbows, thrusting his hands downward into his own gut. *Snap.* The intense force ripped through the locking mechanism on the zip ties and cut bloody furrows into his wrists.

The giant barreled toward him. Arms wrapped around the tire, Nikos had only one option. He smashed the tire into the bigger man. Gasoline splashed, soaking them both, burning Nikos's eyes.

The General rallied, channeling his considerable weight into pushing the tire. Nikos tried to stand his ground, but the man outweighed him by at least sixty pounds. His feet slid along the muddy earth as he started to lose the pushing match.

He ducked, letting the tire sail over his head, and stomped on the General's right foot, cracking metatarsals. The giant grunted, encircling Nikos with his massive arms in a bear hug. Nikos tried to twist away, but the General was surprisingly quick—and strong. He squeezed like a giant boa constrictor, forcing the air out of his lungs. A couple of Nikos's ribs cracked, the crunch echoing in his ears.

Sweat and gasoline dripped into Nikos's eyes, blurring his vision. He blinked, face-to-face with the depths of the General's fury, then brought his head back and slammed it straight into the big man's nose. Blood gushed. The giant's grip loosened enough for Nikos to twist around and bring his knee up into the man's groin, hard. A groan. The General's grip faltered. Nikos planted his hands against the man's colossal chest and broke free.

He sucked in a deep breath. The giant shook his head and came for him again, arms wide. Nikos drew the Glock. Two quick shots, one in each leg. The General collapsed onto the ground, blood darkening his pants. Still he crawled toward Nikos, rage fueling him.

If the bastard wanted more, he'd give it to him.

A sharp kick under the chin snapped the giant into a seated position. The big man wavered, stunned by the blow. Nikos grabbed the tire and thrust it onto the man's enormous shoulders. He wiped his hand off on his shirt, reached into his pocket, and fingered the lighter. A quick flick, and he tossed the Zippo at the General. Flames ignited in a blaze of orange.

An animal cry, deep and primal, erupted from General Ita Jemwa as fire scorched his skin. Blood soaked his lower extremities, smoke engulfed his tribal scars, flames singed his eyebrows. The stench of charred flesh filled Nikos's nostrils. He inhaled deeply. There wasn't a horrible enough death for the man who'd stolen his innocence. This one would have to do.

His cell phone beeped.

Nikos read the text.

Time for his father's retribution.

Chapter Seventy

Thea crabbed forward in the air-conditioning shaft. A quick right turn, and she paused, hopeful. She turned off the cell's flashlight to make sure she wasn't seeing things. Light beckoned at the end of the tunnel. She scrambled toward the vent and fingered the slats, making sure it was real.

They'd been holed up inside the ventilation system for almost an hour, their progress painstakingly slow. She felt like a prisoner seeing daylight for the first time in years.

Ten feet below, an open field and the nearby forest beckoned to her. They'd reached the west side of the hotel, as planned.

Rain splattered on the pavement below. Fresh, moist air piped through the slats, which was a relief, but what she craved most was her true elixir: insulin. She checked her blood sugar on her smartphone: 421 mg/dL. Not good. Her temples throbbed, and she was beginning to feel nauseated.

Mamadou squeezed her ankle. He'd been a trouper, crawling through the narrow shafts without a whisper of complaint. She wiggled her foot in response to his touch and concentrated on opening the vent. The upper-left corner was loose. She pushed her head against the grille and scanned right and left. No one around.

Time for a little yoga. Lying on her belly in the cramped space, she lifted herself into a plank position, then brought her legs forward underneath her while arching her back. Her feet ultimately faced the vent.

Drawing her knees to her chest, she uncoiled her legs and pummeled the upper left of the grille with both feet. The metal fought to stay attached. She coiled her legs again and hammered once more at the grille. It finally slid down, hanging by only one screw.

Good enough.

She peered out the opening. A few dead soldiers were sprawled near the building, but otherwise no one was around. She would've thought the place would be crawling with sentries.

But the danger wasn't over. Gunshots rang out on the east side of the hotel. She dropped her bag and rifle, then eased her legs out of the vent, perched bent over in a sitting position. She dropped ten feet to the ground and rolled to absorb the impact. She grabbed the AK and scanned for the enemy.

All clear.

Mamadou Kimweri's head poked out of the shaft. She waved for him to come down. His eyebrows raised a fraction. He didn't have the flexibility to turn his long body inside the vent. Instead, he snaked his right arm up, grabbing the lip of the terrace above and pulling himself out of the shaft, shimmying his lower body and feet out of the air duct. He hung there for a few seconds, then fell to the earth.

She held her breath. The man had to be pushing seventy-five. Would his bones be able to handle the fall?

His feet connected with the ground. He dropped and rolled onto his right shoulder, tumbling over before coming to rest. She hurried across to check on him.

A smile greeted her. "Help this old man up, would you?"

"Well done." She offered him a hand.

The familiar crackle of automatic weapons fire spurred her into action. The relative safety of the jungle rested on the other side of a hundred-foot clearing. It'd be risky, but they had to chance it.

They crouched beside the hotel wall. "Run in a zigzag pattern to the trees. I'll be right behind you. If I'm shot, hide in the forest and call for help." She handed him her satphone. "Got it?"

His wizened face wrinkled. "Your father was right."

"How's that?"

"He told me that you were the bravest person he knew."

She grinned. "Well, let's go before I have a chance to prove him wrong." She gripped the assault rifle tightly, hoping for a little luck.

As she'd instructed, Mamadou loped across the clearing like a drunken gazelle. She followed, turned slightly so she could scan for soldiers. An overwhelming fatigue was beginning to weigh her down. She could almost feel her blood sugar rising now. *Just a little farther.*

Commotion sounded nearby. A loud yell. Two of the general's soldiers had rounded the corner. She'd been spotted. Bullets whizzed past her ear. She fired a volley of shots to provide cover. A muzzle flashed. Mamadou had almost made it to the jungle. She kept firing until she ran out of ammo. The prime minister disappeared into the foliage.

She sprinted straight into a tangled mass of bushes. Branches scratched at her face, and thorns clawed at her arms. Gasping, she slowed her pace, searching for Mamadou.

She stopped cold. A soldier in full camo and face paint had his hand clamped on the prime minister's mouth, an arm coiled around his body.

"Good to see you, Thea."

Johansson. She almost collapsed in relief. "About time you showed up."

"Hello to you too. By the way, you're officially godmother to my son."

"Congrats. Champagne later."

Jo removed his hand from Mamadou's mouth. "Sorry, mate, just wanted to make sure you didn't scream. Thea has lightning reflexes, and I didn't want another hole in my shoulder."

Leave it to Jo to joke around at a time like this. "Please take Prime Minister Kimweri to safety. Where's the team?"

"They're trying to save Rif's sorry ass. He's somewhere inside the hotel. You coming with us?"

"No, I have to handle something else first."

"You don't look so good."

"Just need some rest." And some insulin.

"Take this for good measure." Jo passed her a Glock.

Mamadou squeezed her hand. "Don't do any more jumps without me."

She smiled. "You're pretty tough for a prime minister."

"Once a bush boy, always a bush boy."

"You're in excellent hands now. Jo will get you back to Kanzi."

"Thank you, Thea. I wouldn't be alive without you."

"See you soon."

Looping around the main building, she searched for a way back into the conference space. Ominous black smoke rose from the eastern side of the hotel.

Chapter Seventy-One

Gabrielle ran down the main hotel stairs, her feet padding on the carpeted steps. On the landing, she came face-to-face with a rebel. He froze for a millisecond, a fatal mistake. She fired two quick shots into his chest.

She rushed outside, anxious to reach the Victoria Falls Bridge.

Her cell vibrated. She read the text: *Max's sister, Laila, wasn't in a car crash. She was severely injured in an industrial accident and died two years ago at the Heros family estate. Let me know if you need more.*

Two years? It had been eighteen months since she and Max had had their intimate conversation about their sisters, and he'd told her Laila was alive and suffering. An ache settled in her chest. Why would he lie to her, especially about that?

Chapter Seventy-Two

Thea's vision blurred, her head throbbed, and her mind churned. She'd only felt like this once before, and it meant serious trouble. A quick check of her smartphone. Blood sugar 437 mg/dL. Dangerously high.

Bone-weary, she plodded, one foot in front of the other, circumnavigating the hotel to avoid the few remaining rebels battling with the prime minister's guards. Except now, her special-ops team would give Mamadou's men a decisive edge. She hoped the team had found Rif. She wondered where her brother was.

A cry shattered her thoughts—it sounded like an injured animal in unbearable pain. Funnels of dark, greasy smoke billowed out of the jungle a few hundred yards away. What the hell was going on?

She had to get back inside and find her supplies. She couldn't help Rif, Nikos, or anyone else until she stabilized her blood sugar. The hotel was fifty yards away, but the distance felt more like five hundred. She scanned the area. No soldiers. The battle was raging on the other side of the complex.

Smoke from the hotel drifted with the shifting wind and mixed with pelting rain. She reached the door closest to the conference room they'd been in earlier. Her hand hovered over the doorknob, but her palm told her it was too hot to touch. She'd have to work her way around to the front, take her chances there.

She stumbled along the hotel's exterior, Glock in hand. The building was a fuzzy white block. The world felt surreal, as if she was Alice in Wonderland, falling through the rabbit hole. She could almost visualize sugar crystallizing in her cells.

One more corner to go.

Carefully she inched forward, checking that the coast was clear. A young soldier slumped against the wall, an AK-47 in his hands. Blood oozed from a leg wound. His eyes scanned back and forth, on full alert. A rat cornered.

She pulled behind the corner, trying to think. She had to get past him. What to do? She didn't have the energy to climb a water pipe to avoid him.

No time to waste. She raised her Glock and focused the sights on the largest exposed section of his AK-47, just above the trigger guard. Her hands didn't feel steady, but the distance was only twenty yards. She could make that shot.

Her finger caressed the trigger.

A sharp metal clang. Bull's-eye. The rifle bounced out of the soldier's hands, the ricochet nicking his forearm. He screamed. Glock raised for protection, she stumbled across the yard. His eyes widened in fear, but she held her fire. The kid wasn't a serious threat, given his leg wound, and she didn't want to kill him for nothing. All she could think about was securing that syringe. She stumbled to the double doors at the front of the hotel, holding on to the wall for support. Fumbling with a knob, which was cool to the touch, she managed to open one side.

A blast of smoke greeted her as she entered the lobby. She crouched low, lifting her shirttail to breathe through it. Fire licked the walls, singeing wallpaper. A wave of dizziness hit her hard.

She had to keep moving. Dropping onto all fours, she crawled toward the conference room. Ceiling beams creaked and groaned. She tried to hurry, but her limbs felt heavy, as if she were slogging through heavy muck.

The fire crackled, devouring the endless supply of wood in the structure. She entered the conference room and scuttled up the central aisle to the Paris delegation table.

A loud rumbling above, and a large beam crashed to the floor in a hiss of fire, landing between the two delegation tables and spraying debris everywhere. Still on her knees, she grasped for her jacket as smoke swirled around her. She fumbled for the thermal cooling pouch that held the syringes, her fingers slow and awkward. Removing one syringe, she grabbed a fold of skin on her belly, stuck the needle in, and squeezed.

Another beam crashed down, this one closer. She depressed the needle to ensure that all the insulin had been injected. Now she needed to get the hell out of there.

Through her mental haze, she heard pounding footsteps that sent a surge of adrenaline through her veins. She reached for her Glock, prepared to defend herself.

But it wasn't a rebel.

Rif stood above her, staring at the syringe in her stomach.

For a long moment their gazes met.

"Let's get you out of here." He squatted down, lifted her in his arms, and sprinted for the exit. Flames framed the doorway but he ducked low and burst through them, carrying them both out of the hotel.

Chapter Seventy-Three

Rif surged through the front doors, cradling Thea in his arms. Her breath came in rasps from the smoke clogging her lungs. He dodged behind shrubbery to protect them both from rebel gunfire and lowered her to the ground. The body of a dead soldier lay nearby. Rif ripped off the rebel's jacket and boots and handed them to Thea. "You'll need these."

She stepped into the boots and shrugged into the jacket. Both were large but certainly better than no protection. She found a knife in the jacket's left pocket and shoved it into her right boot for safekeeping.

Seconds later, Jean-Luc sprinted around the corner. The wizened Legionnaire assessed the situation quickly. "Medevac?"

"I'm fine." Thea coughed, her face streaked with soot.

"Just cover us so we can escape to the jungle." Rif lifted her back into his arms.

"Go." Jean-Luc cradled his M4.

Rif scanned the courtyard. No soldiers in sight. He sprinted across the clearing.

One final step, and he lunged into the relative safety of the trees. The thick underbrush jabbed through his fatigues, scratching his legs. He slowed his pace but kept moving. Some of the foliage had already been disturbed. They weren't the only ones who'd been here recently.

"Let me down. I can walk." She wriggled in his arms.

"Humor me. Your skin is the color of chalk, except for the soot." His arms tightened around her protectively. He considered what she'd been injecting into her stomach. No way could it be a drug addiction—it wasn't in her character. "Are you ill?"

She was quiet for an endless moment. "I have type 1 diabetes."

The news was a surprise but also made sense. She'd always been private, keeping him at a distance. Was this why? He considered her avoidance of desserts, her regimented eating patterns and fanatical exercise routine. Diabetes made perfect sense. He inhaled deeply, wanting to make sure his first words were supportive. "Thanks for trusting me with the truth."

She must have worn an insulin pump as a child, because he'd never seen her inject herself. But why hide it from the team? From him?

He considered their missions and thought he understood. Back when Thea first joined Quantum, many of the guys were skeptical about a woman entering their action-oriented domain. She had proven herself and then some. Still, the undercurrent of sexism arose from time to time with new male team members—until she outperformed them, and they ate a healthy serving of crow.

Even if she were a guy, their demanding world didn't tolerate illness or disease, because any weakness could be exploited. If their positions were reversed, he would've taken the same approach and kept the information on the down-low.

"Do you need anything?" he asked, wanting to help.

"I'll be okay. The insulin will kick in soon."

He remembered those syringes in Nikos's safe. Had that been insulin for Thea? Did Nikos know about her diabetes? He wondered how many people were aware of her condition. All these years, and he hadn't guessed. The woman was an enigma.

"Come on, let me down." She pushed against his chest.

"You win, but lean on me if you need to. The bush is thick here." He set her on her feet, making sure she was steady. A slight pink tone had seeped back into her skin. The insulin must be working.

He passed her his canteen. "Have some."

She swallowed several gulps. "Thanks."

"You could have confided in me. I told you about what happened in Chad." He kept his tone low, wanting her to know he could be a trusted confidant.

"And have you worry about me letting the team down?"

"There's no one I'd trust more to have my back. We're all human, fallible, but when you and I work together, we're unbeatable." He brushed soot from her cheek with his right thumb.

Her gaze was thoughtful, and more open than he'd ever seen.

She placed her hands on either side of his face and pulled him closer, their lips almost touching. His breath quickened.

The wind shifted suddenly, and a ghastly stench filled the air. They both drew back.

"What's that?" she asked.

He raised his M4. "Let's take a look."

Rain began to fall heavily as they cut through a clearing. A stronger whiff of that horrible stench hit them hard. Beside an enormous tree was something that shocked even a jaded soldier like Rif.

A large tire smoldered around a man's neck, his head and upper body charred to the bone. The fire had obliterated any facial features, but a quick assessment of the victim's size and uniform left no doubt.

General Ita Jemwa.

Thea held her hand over her mouth and nose. "Prime Minister Kimweri suspected that Jemwa was behind the attack. But necklacing? Someone had a serious ax to grind."

"Exactly. A quick shot to the head would've done the job." Rif had zero doubt about who was responsible.

Nikos.

Thea had to realize for herself that her brother was damaged and dangerous. She trusted Nikos too much and was overly protective of him. Rif hoped she wouldn't pay for her caring nature.

She was staring through a small opening in the bush showcasing the striking Victoria Falls Bridge when Papa's phone buzzed in her pocket. She read the text. *Alea iacta est.*

"What's up?" he asked.

"More damn Latin." She scanned her phone. "*Alea iacta est*—the die is cast. The kidnapper's latest text. Attributed to Caesar as he led his troops across the Rubicon, past the point of no return." She looked up. "Roll the dice, win or die. What's the kidnapper talking about?"

"The Rubicon was named for its color, from the red mud deposits."

"Zimbabwe has red mud and a giant river." She gestured to the Zambezi, then suddenly became animated. "Victoria Falls Bridge, the crossing over the kidnapper's Rubicon. Whatever was supposed to happen with the oil rights is irrelevant now. The kidnapper never asked for money or concessions. It was all about this moment, arranging a showdown." She turned in the direction of the bridge. "Let's go." She started an awkward jog, her footing uncertain.

He ran after her. Given the kidnapper's strange texts, her reasoning made a twisted kind of sense. Clearly General Jemwa wasn't the kidnapper. And given what had happened to the old soldier, he wondered if the kidnapper might be Nikos after all.

Chapter Seventy-Four

Thea and Rif hurried toward the legendary Victoria Falls Bridge, which linked Zimbabwe to Zambia via car, foot, and train. The steel girders arched proudly over the river's second gorge, the steady roar of the falls an ominous reminder of nature's power. Heavy canopied vegetation shrouded the area in shadows, and rain poured from the sky.

Though Thea still felt a little dizzy and weak, the thought of finding her father spurred her on.

"Can you head down into the valley, check the bridge from below?" she asked Rif.

"I'd prefer to stay together." Rain trickled down his face.

"If I get into trouble, I need you to be free to help."

He hesitated for a moment. "Okay, but no crazy moves. Let's keep in touch via our cells."

She stuck a bud into her left ear and called him. "Testing."

He adjusted his own earpiece. "Got it. See you soon."

Dark clouds commingled, gathering force. Wind gusted, blasting grit and sheeting rain into her face. Her sodden clothes clung to her body.

The sound of rotor wash caught her attention. A helicopter flew low overhead, headed toward Zambia. Who would be out in these conditions?

She made her way onto the main road. Rif skirted the footpath and headed for the underside of the bridge for a different vantage point.

She rushed to the outpost. Three border guards were slumped on the ground, eyes staring blankly at the darkening sky. Bullet holes leaked blood onto their neatly pressed uniforms.

Two figures stood in the middle of the deserted bridge, where the bungee-jumping platform was positioned. She recognized her father's unmistakable profile.

Alive!

Her spirits took a sudden nosedive, however: someone stood beside her father, gun in hand.

She hurried onto the pedestrian footpath on the bridge, closing the distance to her father, who teetered on the bungee platform. Seconds later, she recognized Maximillian Heros. The gun in his hand told her everything.

The Greek police inspector was Papa's kidnapper.

She flashed on her father's hand signals in the photo. Five and zero: 5-0. The police. Max Heros. She got it now. But why?

Max nudged Papa closer to the platform's edge. A gentle push, and Christos would plunge almost four hundred feet into the Zambezi River. If the fall didn't kill him, the rapids, rocks, or crocs would finish him off. An Australian woman in her twenties had once miraculously survived the fall when her bungee cord snapped, but she'd been young, healthy, and very, very lucky.

Thea moved closer to the center of the bridge, taking in her father's bedraggled appearance. Even so, his shoulders were squared. He hadn't given up—not even close.

"The bridge is rigged with explosives." Max's voice wavered, his left hand holding his cell in the air. "Stop where you are, or I'll blow us all to pieces."

A strong gust of wind rattled rain against the girders. She froze, noting the detonation cord stretched a few inches above the pavement. Another step, and she could've blown them all up.

A quick survey confirmed the inspector's words. The entrance from the Zambian side had been blocked by an eighteen-wheeler, so no one could access the bridge from the west, and he'd rigged explosives on the Zimbabwean side.

It was unbearable. Papa was so close, yet she couldn't reach him.

Rif's voice buzzed in her earpiece. "Keep him talking. I'll approach the bridge from below, try to find the bomb."

She looked at Max. "I won't come any closer. Please step away from the edge so we can talk." She remained still, but her mind kicked into gear. She had to remain detached, work it like any other case.

"You figured out the final text," Heros said.

"Help me understand what's going on, Max." Using his name would help strengthen their bond, and being up front in every statement was crucial. If he sensed deception, it'd all be over.

"Your father isn't the hero you think he is." He cuffed Christos in the head with the gun, hard. Papa stumbled, then glared at his captor. A strong gust of wind threatened to sweep them all into the gorge.

"What do you mean, Max? None of us is perfect; we all have flaws." She kept her voice even, calm. De-escalation was key.

"Christos hired me to fake his own kidnapping."

Gabrielle crashed through the foliage on her way to the bridge. She held her M24 in the ready position, the H-S Precision stock held against her shoulder. She wanted to be prepared if she ran into General Jemwa's soldiers. She worked her way along the tree line, visibility low in the drenching rain. Finally, an opening in the thick brush appeared. She could just make out three figures standing on the bungee-jumping platform: Max, with Christos Paris beside him, and Thea Paris approximately twenty feet away.

Max had found the billionaire. The police inspector would be a national hero in Greece.

She assessed Thea's body language. Her hands were open, as if she was trying to keep her emotions on an even keel.

But Max had a gun pointed at Christos. *He was the kidnapper!* But why? What the hell was going on?

She settled into hiding fewer than two hundred feet from the bridge. Two minutes later, she had set up the parabolic microphone from her backpack.

Max's baritone rumbled in her earpiece. "The bridge is rigged with explosives. Stop where you are, or I'll blow us all to pieces." Any remaining hope that this was a misunderstanding evaporated. His voice radiated tension, anger.

Gabrielle used the gun-shaped handle to wedge the microphone in a bush with the eighteen-inch dish facing the bridge. She tilted it like an antenna on an old TV until she'd trained the directional mic on the target.

She picked up her rifle. Adjusting the scope, she zoomed back to Max. He held a cell phone in his hand. Probably the detonator.

She couldn't let him set off the bomb.

Gabrielle ran through her checklist, calculating the wind conditions, rain, humidity. Max and Christos stood close together. It'd be a challenging shot. She'd need to pick her moment carefully. Christos was positioned at the open edge of the bungee platform, and she didn't want to lose the hostage over the ledge.

She entered the sniper "zone," breathing steadily, ignoring everything but the rifle and the target. The world narrowed; her senses heightened. She had to wait. Her crosshairs rested on Christos Paris's head, which now obstructed her view of Max. The oil baron looked determined, showing little fear. Christos shifted, dropping lower in her sights as he widened his stance. Then he tilted his head, very slightly and slowly, so that his gaze could scan the platform. He was searching for a way out.

Max moved into view. The anguish on his face cut to her soul. Framed in her crosshairs was the first man she might've broken her one-night rule for. *All the rules.*

This was the moment. She inhaled a breath and held it, flexing her finger. All she had to do was fire. His head was in her sights.

Do it now. Clean shots in hostage situations were rare, and snipers couldn't hesitate.

Her trigger finger trembled, but it wouldn't close.

She couldn't fucking do it.

She exhaled, berating herself. Max had become the enemy. She had the shot. Why the hell was she hesitating?

Max's voice rumbled from the mic. "Christos hired me to fake his own kidnapping."

What?

Chapter Seventy-Five

Rif clambered down a steep hillside, scrambling to maintain his footing. The bridge over the Zambezi River straddled Zimbabwe and Zambia, an impressive arch of steel girders joining the two countries. At the underbelly of the bridge, he discovered a makeshift wooden platform that day laborers must have abandoned because of the storm. After a quick search of their equipment, he tossed pliers, a blowtorch, and a few other tools into his backpack.

He hoped Thea could keep Max Heros talking long enough for him to neutralize the bomb. The police inspector had clearly arranged this bizarre situation because he had a message to deliver, but what, exactly, did he want?

Rif's fingers white-knuckled the slippery railing while he scanned the steel girders, searching for anomalies. He'd had some experience with ordnance, but it wasn't his specialty.

Max was both a cop and a rich asshole, so he would have the contacts and finances to create a complex device. If the bomb consisted of two separate compounds that needed mixing to be armed, the best way to defuse it would be to blow up the two compounds while they were still separated. But he didn't have any C4.

Given the circumstances, though, he hoped that Max would have been forced to improvise a more basic device. He remembered a Marine friend in Iraq encircling a bomb with shaped charges, using the technique to chunk out the device. But that wouldn't help here. Once the first charge blew, Max could simply shoot Christos.

A metal glint just underneath the bridge caught Rif's attention. He leaned forward for a better view. The bomb was placed in the most inaccessible spot possible. He scaled the girders, avoiding looking down at the plummeting depths of the river below.

Sweat and rain made him wish he had gloves. His fingers ached as they clung to wet steel. Thea's voice in his earpiece spurred him on. She was doing great.

He kept climbing. Almost there. The bomb clung to the inside of one of the girders, like a tumor adhering to bone. Most explosive devices consisted of one of four nitrates—ammonium, sodium, potassium, or calcium—along with whatever exotic mixture provided the desired outcome. Fire, projectiles, and explosive damage were among the most common. This was one of the latter varieties—there was enough C4 to decimate the bridge. If he could remove the primer from the volatile material, and if it wasn't hot-wired, it'd be a lot easier than defusing the detonator.

Especially this detonator, which was linked to a cell phone. Max, or even an accomplice, could trigger the explosion at any second.

One option left.

Chapter Seventy-Six

Thea couldn't quite process Max's words. Papa had hired him to fake his own kidnapping? *No way.* But Christos's defiant expression and the set of his jaw seemed to confirm it. She'd seen that look before.

Her stomach twisted, but her voice remained firm. "I believe you, Max. But why did my father hire you?"

"Oh, I've done lots of work for Christos over the years. When you like deals to go your way and can't keep your zipper up, having a police official in your pocket can be quite useful."

There was a ring of truth in all that. Papa was relentless when he wanted something, and she'd witnessed his womanizing streak herself.

"But why fake his own kidnapping?" she asked.

Max prodded Christos in the arm. "I think you should answer that one."

Papa spoke for the first time, his mouth bloodied. "Nikos was planning to kidnap me. I had to beat him to it."

Nikos? It couldn't be. "But . . . killing Piers? He was part of our family! All the staff on the yacht . . ." She pulled back. She couldn't afford to antagonize any party here. The situation called for de-escalation.

"No one was supposed to die." Papa glared at Max. "I trusted the wrong man."

Max's eyes narrowed. "Regrettable but necessary. It's a shame those people chose to work for a monster."

She turned to her father. "Why didn't you just confront Nikos?"

He didn't answer at first. Seconds passed. "Because I'm afraid of my own son. He wasn't just going to kidnap me. He wants to kill me. This was the only way to draw him out."

Max's face darkened. "Prince Nikos becomes a boy soldier, a killer. Now that boy is the world's most prominent arms dealer."

"Arms dealer?"

"Your brother is Ares—and Ares wanted to reclaim his rightful throne."

Nikos was the world's most infamous arms dealer, the one who kidnapped CEOs? Shock rippled through Thea's brain.

"Christos had me track your brother for years. I stumbled on something recently that revealed his alter ego," Max said.

"I did my best to help Nikos when he was a boy, but he was damaged beyond repair," Christos said. "As Ares, he sold arms to rebels, contributing to political unrest; he kidnapped and murdered people. Then I found out about this twisted revenge plot."

Goose bumps rippled along Thea's arms at the thought of how her brother could behave when someone interfered with his plans. She touched the scar on her face. Even with Max Heros holding Papa hostage on the bridge, she was more worried about Nikos.

Rif's voice murmured in her ear. "I'm cutting around the bomb so it'll fall into the gorge. Wait for my signal."

Rif balanced on a girder, twisting his body so he could access his backpack. The falls roared below, causing black vortexes of swirling water. If he survived this, he could always join the circus as a tightrope walker.

The conversation on the bridge sliced to the marrow. It didn't surprise him about Nikos, but what the hell had Christos been thinking, hiring Heros to kidnap him? Why hadn't his godfather come to him with the problem?

Shaking his head, he ignited the torch. Black smoke filled his vision. He waited for it to clear, then opened the oxygen valve. The blowtorch's white-hot flame began to chew at the girder. But would he have enough time?

Chapter Seventy-Seven

Thea blocked out her emotional pain so she could defuse the situation and get them all to safety. Only then could she sort through the implications of her father and Nikos's machinations. The sky had darkened even more. Thunder rumbled, reverberating through the gorge. Despite the rain, her mouth was gritty, dry. The cold gusts of wind on the bridge were chilling her bones.

She stared at the bungee-jumping platform and the coiled cords with their harnesses. She couldn't rush Max. It was crucial to listen, to ask open-ended questions, to let him vent.

"Why are you holding my father prisoner if he was paying you?"

"It's not about money. Christos treats his employees like chattel. Disposable." He rapped on the back of her father's skull with his Glock. Papa winced.

Thea was growing angry, but she kept her tone earnest and open. "Did Christos mistreat you somehow?"

"This has never been about me. This is all because of my half sister, Laila, a talented engineer who made the mistake of working for Paris Industries. She had safety concerns about the oil rig she worked on, and she voiced those concerns to Christos himself. He told her that they could discuss the problems over dinner. Bastard hit on her, a girl half his age."

Max was gesticulating, the gun waving. She wanted to lunge forward and disarm him but not before Rif gave her the go-ahead.

"Three weeks later, there was an explosion on the rig. My sister tried to save some of the workers and fell off the platform, breaking almost every bone in her body. Somehow she survived." Max turned to Christos. "She fell three hundred and ninety-three feet. This bridge is three hundred and sixty-three feet. I'm giving you a fighting chance."

Papa grimaced. "I never knew Laila was your half sister. And you're wrong. I had the team address her safety concerns right away. Human error caused the explosion."

"Shut up!" Max fired the gun, a bullet penetrating Christos's thigh.

Her father screamed, crumpling to the ground. It took everything Thea had to keep her voice even. "Please, Max. Tell me what happened." She needed him focused on her, not on her father.

The inspector's voice was leaden with anguish. "Laila lived for a while but with intense pain and disfigurement. She begged me to kill her." Tears ran down his face, intermingling with the rain. His voice faltered. "I smothered her with a pillow."

Thea exhaled. "I'm so sorry, Max." Papa pressed his right hand to his wound while his eyes searched the platform, probably looking for a weapon. She worried he'd do or say something to set Max off again.

"And now, before your father can seal the biggest deal of his career, he'll fall to his death." Grief had burrowed permanently into the lines around Max's eyes, and his words were laced with pain. His despair didn't bode well. He was hollow inside, with nothing left to lose.

"The plane crash, the limo explosion, Helena—that was all you?" Thea asked to keep him talking.

"I wanted Christos to lose you, Rif, Helena—everyone he cared about. I needed him to experience my pain."

Thea reeled. "What about the supertanker?"

Max shook his head. "I suspect Nikos was buying time to find Christos before you did. He and his people were on the hunt right away."

There was no easy way out of this. Max couldn't just walk off the bridge. He had to know he would spend the rest of his life behind bars. That was clearly not in his plans.

"Tell me about Laila."

Max glanced at Thea. "I know what you're doing, trying to keep me talking. We're done." His tone changed; his voice shook. He seemed to be spooling toward the end, and she didn't think he intended for any of them to survive this. She couldn't wait for Rif to take the bomb out of the equation.

She had an idea.

"If you push my father off the bridge, his suffering ends quickly."

Max's eyes narrowed.

She went on. "But Christos does have his kryptonite."

"What are you talking about?"

"Me."

Rif had sliced through the left side of the girder supporting the bomb and was halfway through the right side when Thea's voice stopped him.

What was she thinking? "I'm almost there." His hands steadied the torch. Sparks filled the air, the molten metal melting. "Thea, don't do this."

Offering herself as bait wasn't going to stop Max from killing Christos.

Heros would simply kill them in a different order.

Chapter Seventy-Eight

Gabrielle's hands gripped the M24. Laila's horrific accident and injuries, Max's agreement to end her suffering—these revelations explained the darkness in him. Her grief after her parents died was suffocating, but because she had no closure, no understanding of what had happened, she'd been obsessive in her quest for justice. If she did ever figure out who was responsible, it was possible she could be just as myopic in her desire for revenge. Maybe that was what had drawn her and Max together—the recognition of another soul in searing pain.

She spent her career assessing people, but with Max Heros her feelings had blinded her to the truth. Just her luck that she'd been attracted to a man on a full-on homicidal rampage. What Max, an officer of the law, had done in the name of payback had crossed every line imaginable. Innocent people had paid the ultimate price. And if she let him, he'd kill Christos Paris and his daughter, Thea.

Max would never relinquish his hostage. He might play with Thea, give her false hope while he used her for an audience, but he'd have his way in the end.

A raven cawed. She ignored it, entering the sniper zone. She inhaled a deep breath through the nose and held it.

The world became quiet, still.

Her eyes burned as the crosshairs settled on Max's face. She memorized the angular line of his nose, the cleft in his chin, the lips that she'd kissed.

"I'm so sorry, Max."

Chapter Seventy-Nine

Fog clung to the Zambian side of the gorge like a frightened child held on to a mother's skirt. Thea stepped closer to Max and Papa, careful not to cross the trip wire.

"For fuck's sake, stop this madness, Thea. I've almost cut through the girder." Rif's warning buzzed in her earpiece, but she ignored him. Papa was bleeding profusely, and Max was near the end of his tether. Rif was under the bridge, so he didn't understand how quickly the situation was spiraling out of control.

"Why not destroy what Christos loves most? I'm his only daughter, someone he has pampered and protected for years."

Come on, Max. You want to hurt me.

She raised her hands and tilted her head.

"You know too well how suffering can be worse than death. Let Christos experience what it's like to lose everything that matters to him."

"No." Papa's voice reverberated across the bridge, firm but scared. "Leave us, Thea. You have nothing to do with this."

Max stood a little straighter. Her words and Christos's reaction to them had triggered the logical, incisive mind of the police inspector. She'd presented an attractive alternative, a way to prolong his enemy's pain. How could he resist? Misery demanded company. She watched him, hopeful. *Come on, let me get inside your defenses. Let me close so I can disarm you.*

"The bomb's almost free . . . It might detonate on the way down." Rif's voice was tight, strained in her earpiece. "Don't take this crazy risk."

"Even better, I will just take all of us out together—that would be fitting." Max raised his cell phone and moved his finger toward the screen.

A loud crack penetrated the air. She recognized the sound and dropped to the ground.

Pink mist collided with the rain. Max's face was an angry red canvas after being struck in the T-zone with a high-caliber round. His head snapped back, and he stumbled, crumpling onto the cement.

She searched the horizon. *Who had shot him?*

"Max is down. Dump the bomb, Rif. I think he activated it."

On the Zimbabwe side of the bridge, movement on the grassy terrain below caught her eye. Gabrielle Farrah charged toward them, a rifle slung around her shoulder.

"Shit, you're right. It's been activated. Ten seconds before it blows. Almost there." The tension in Rif's voice was unmistakable.

No way could she get to Papa and escape the bridge in time. They had to count on Rif.

"Got it!"

Thea peered over the edge of the bridge, watching the bomb as it sailed down through the air. The blast rumbled through the canyon, its concussion knocking her to the ground. The bridge shuddered as the bomb exploded, the blast traveling in all directions in a sphere of debris and concussive waves. Her ears buzzed, and her eyes burned.

Papa clung to the guardrail on the platform.

"Rif, you okay?"

Nothing.

"Rif! Talk to me."

He didn't respond.

Then she heard a cough in her earpiece. Another one. "Dammit." Cough. "Remind me not to climb any more bridges."

Thank God.

The high-pitched whine of a small engine caught her attention. *What the hell?* She rubbed her face, then climbed to her knees.

Out of the fog hovering inside the gorge, a motorcycle bulleted toward them from the Zambian side, snaking around the truck blocking the bulk of the bridge.

As it closed the distance, she recognized a familiar silhouette. *Nikos.*

Chapter Eighty

Thea's mind reeled. Time slowed, like in those horrific nightmares where you're desperate to get somewhere but feel as if you're running through sludge. She staggered toward Papa, knowing this was no dream.

She couldn't match the motorcycle's superior speed. Nikos beat her to the platform, hopping off the bike before it came to a full stop. Sparks flared from the pavement and metal groaned as the motorbike slid across the harsh concrete.

He grabbed their father by the back of the neck, forcing him to stand on the very edge of the platform. Raindrops streaked Nikos's face, looking like tears, but his expression was flat.

Thea closed the distance, her pulse thundering in her throat. Together they stood on the precipice, the three surviving members of the Paris family, a blood war boiling over after twenty long years.

Nikos looked down at Max's corpse. "He let emotion get the better of him."

"Don't make the same mistake." Papa tried to writhe away from Nikos. "This is between you and me. Leave your sister out of it."

Younger, stronger, her brother overpowered Papa. "Thea has a decision to make. She finally knows the truth, how your greed led to my kidnapping."

Hope warred with terror in Thea's gut. "I want to hear your story, do anything I can to help. I love you, Nikos." Maybe she could find a way to stop him.

"More than you love him?" Her brother's eyes brimmed with pain.

"I'm the one who let you down." Her words were honest, raw. "If I'd been able to scream for help that night, you'd never have been taken. I'm so sorry."

"That's not the point. If you had been the one kidnapped, your life would've been destroyed, and all because of our father's greed."

"That night will haunt me forever. I know I can never make it up to you, but I've tried every day since."

"I never wanted your pity, Thea. I wanted love and acceptance from my sister and father. You gave me that. He didn't."

Papa's voice held remorse. "I did everything I could for you, son, but—"

"You considered me damaged goods from the moment you read my story. And we wouldn't want to sully the great Paris name, would we?"

"You're wrong, Nikos. I did what I could to protect you."

"And that's why you sent me to the loony bin. Then away to that school for troubled kids. Because you loved me so much."

Papa looked as if he was at war with himself. "You needed help."

"Help from strangers wasn't what I needed. I wanted my family to stand by me."

Papa's eyes bulged. "It wasn't safe to have you with us. For Christ's sake, Nikos, I covered up a murder for you."

Thea felt sucker-punched. "Murder? What murder?"

Nikos glanced at her. "Our nanny. She was a bully."

All the air left her lungs. Allison had been a stern, unforgiving taskmaster, not popular with her or her brother, but she'd never hurt them. The woman's sudden disappearance made a sick sense now.

"When I left Oba's camp, I had a mission in life: to restore balance in the world by destroying bullies."

"There are many ways to make the world a better place, but killing people is never the answer." Papa spoke slowly, as if to a child.

"Justice is a hard game. Playing by the rules doesn't work. Ares made a difference."

Ares? So he justified being an arms dealer as a way to fight *bullying*? It was as if he was still twelve and just back from his abduction. He was the hero in his own story, but his quest was twisted.

Christos's face reddened. "You're no Robin Hood, just a common criminal."

Nikos laughed, a short bark devoid of humor. "You're the epitome of greed and a bully. That's why I won't let you have Kanzi."

Christos snaked his hand into a coiled pile of cords and harnesses. "Too late. Kanzi is already in my pocket. Prime Minister Kimweri and I made a deal weeks ago. The negotiations were only for show."

Papa had faked his own kidnapping, but not because he was afraid of Nikos. He'd wanted to beat Nikos at his own demented game.

With all her insight and ability to read others, Thea had been blinded to the true character of the two people closest to her. She understood Nikos's damage. He'd been through hell and couldn't find his way back. Her father didn't have that excuse.

She needed to force her roiling emotions aside and de-escalate the situation. "We're family. We have to find a way to work this out."

Nikos's voice trembled with emotion. "Time to choose, Thea. Him or me."

The frustrated boy who'd felt abandoned by his father, the child soldier who'd had to murder innocents, the arms dealer who sold weapons to foment rebellion—could she appeal to the brother she loved, the one who'd always protected her?

"Who's the bully now, Nikos?"

But her brother was beyond that kind of self-reflection.

"Good-bye, Papa," he said. He shoved their father closer to the edge, but Christos dropped to his knees, spreading himself on the platform so it would be difficult to push him off. One hand grabbed the side railing; the other clutched one of the bungee cords.

Nikos kicked him hard in the side, then forced his legs off the edge. Christos lost his grip on the railing and grappled for the platform but couldn't quite reach it. He pulled the cord he'd grabbed with him as his body weight worked against him, dragging him over the side.

Thea dove forward, but her hands grasped air. Christos tumbled toward the Zambezi River, the bungee cord wrapped around his arm, the slack snaking off the platform after him.

While her brother leaned over the railing to watch, Thea shimmied backward, snatching a harness, securing it to her hips. Her gaze met Nikos's for a fraction of a second, a lifetime of memories passing between them as he saw the choice in her eyes.

"He's not worth it." Her brother lunged toward her.

Twisting away from him, she dove off the platform's open ledge into free fall. Inverted, she sliced downward, the air barreling past her ears, obliterating all other sounds. The wind whipped her hair as the river rushed toward her. Falling, falling, she scanned the water for Papa, but she couldn't find any sign of him in the deep, rushing river below.

The bungee cord reached its full extension. A strong jerk grabbed her hips and legs, and she bounced upward, weightless. Blood rushed to her head, leaving her disoriented. After a long moment, she fell toward the water again, then another sharp tug pulled her up. Up and down, up and down. *People enjoyed this?*

The yo-yoing slowed, and she swung at the end of her tether, studying the waters thirty feet below, searching for Papa. Finally, movement in the river caught her eye. Her father had survived the fall and was clinging to a rock. His head disappeared underwater and resurfaced again, bobbing like a cork as the rushing waters of the Zambezi tried to sweep him away.

Thea jackknifed her body, clutching the bungee cord with her left hand. She reached for her boot knife so she could cut herself free. Before she could remove the knife, something slammed into her right shoulder blade. Pain reverberated down her spine, and she lost her grip on the cord, spinning around and around upside down, like a top.

Dazed, dangling, she spotted Nikos bouncing beside her on another bungee cord. "You need to stop living Papa's lie," he shouted as he smashed into her again, his left hand grabbing a large clump of her hair. She turned her body sideways and crooked her right leg, uncoiling a vicious kick to his chest. A loud grunt. Sharp, stinging pain flared in her scalp as he swung away, taking a handful of hair with him.

He came for her again but swung past without contact. She scrambled for her knife. Her hand connected with her boot, but she couldn't lift her pant leg fast enough.

In the meantime, Nikos had encircled her so that their cords were now intertwined.

She rotated in the opposite direction to unlink the twisted ropes, but Nikos's fist hammered her jaw. She tasted blood. He spun around her again. The knife. She needed it now. In close quarters, he would overpower her.

Nikos swung toward her, but she arched out of the way, yanking up her pant cuff. His foot connected with her lower back. Pain shot deep into her left kidney; white spots blurred her vision. Their faces were inches apart. His lips curled in rage. "How dare you choose Papa over me?"

All these years, she'd never seen this Nikos. Love and guilt had blinded her.

His breath was hot against her cheek. The pungent stench of gasoline flooded her nose. She flashed on the General, his necklacing. She understood now—all this was payback.

She tried to twist away, but his hands closed around her neck, crushing her windpipe as they swung back and forth, awkwardly spinning above the river. She chopped at his arms, but his grip was impenetrable.

Can't breathe. Darkness descended. She curled her leg underneath her, her fingers connecting with the blade's handle. She pulled it out and sawed desperately at her cord.

Nikos drew her face to his, his hands still wrapped around her throat. "You were supposed to choose me. Not him. You were supposed to love me."

"I do love you," she gasped.

Snap.

Her full weight ripped her out of his hands and sent her hurtling toward the river.

The impact of the water hammered into her like a truck, and she plunged down, the cold river swallowing her. She clung to the knife as her body tumbled in the vicious currents.

The sound of roaring water hit her ears when she broke the surface. A deep gasp, and she coughed repeatedly. Her throat burned. Her lungs heaved, greedy for air. She looked right, left, trying to orient herself. Nikos was still in the sky, hanging from his cord. She scanned the water for her father.

Papa lay face up in a slower-moving eddy created by a collection of rocks near the shore. His left hand clung to an outcropping, but the swirling water could suck him down the rapids any second now.

She swam to him, keeping an eye out for crocs. His skin was pale, but he was conscious. He'd lost a tremendous amount of blood from the gunshot wound.

"Can't move my arm. Hurts." His teeth were clenched, his eyelids fluttering. His right arm hung a few inches low and wide—his shoulder had been dislocated from being yanked by the bungee cord, but it had saved his life.

"You're going to be okay." She looked around, searching for a way out of the water. Rif was scrabbling down the escarpment, followed by Gabrielle. She'd never been so happy to see him.

A loud splash caught her attention. She turned. Nikos had dropped into the river, surfacing not far from them.

Her brother wasn't giving up.

She waved her arm high in the air, yelling to Rif. "Take care of Papa."

Her father looked into her eyes. "Don't leave me."

"Rif is here; he'll help."

She swam away from shore, inserting herself between brother and father.

"It's over, Nikos. Let it go."

"Get out of my way." Her brother's powerful arms made short work of the distance between them.

"I'm not your enemy, Nikos. Neither is Papa."

"You made your choice." He reached out with one large hand and shoved her head underwater. She dove down and resurfaced to his right, slicing the knife deep into his shoulder. His right arm flapped beside his torso, pouring blood into the water. She kicked him in the gut, forcing them apart.

The current was carrying them toward the rapids. She looked for something to grab on to, watching in horror as two crocs slipped off the shoreline into the water, their powerful tails driving them forward.

Nikos closed the distance between them, swimming strongly despite his injured arm.

Blood poured from his shoulder, hatred from his eyes. His left fist slammed square into her nose. Her head snapped back. Dizziness threatened. She sliced at him again with the knife, only grazing his left biceps.

Seconds away from the rapids, the current accelerated, trying to suck them below the surface. Water splashed into Thea's face, mouth, and nose.

Nikos grabbed hold of her right wrist and twisted hard. She felt a bone crack, followed by intense pain. The knife sank into the water.

She tried to head-butt her brother, but he ducked to the side.

His full weight was suddenly on top of her, his left arm holding her tightly, forcing her underwater. The dark river turned her world black.

He'd expect her to panic, flail. But fighting would expend too much energy, and he could overpower her at close quarters. Instead, she'd use the river. She went slack, every muscle soft.

Her lungs burned, desperate for oxygen, but she allowed the undertow to suck them downriver. *Not long now.*

His hold on her loosened. She waited, desperate for air, riding the force of the water. Her energy was waning. She couldn't hold out much longer.

Suddenly the speed of the current quickened, water slapping her from every direction. They had hit the rapids.

In one quick movement, she brought her knee up to his groin, hard.

Instinctively he arched his back. She capitalized on the move, twisting so she was now on top. She surfaced and inhaled. Foaming river water slammed her face. She sucked in a mouthful. Coughed.

The powerful current carried them through the narrows.

A quick glance downriver. Her only chance.

Seconds from plowing into a small island of protruding rocks, she thrust her fingers into the deep wound in Nikos's right shoulder. His body buckled from the pain.

She twisted to the right as they hit the rocks, the back of Nikos's skull taking the impact, snapping his head forward. He lost his grip on her entirely.

His body shuddered, and he vanished underwater. She dove down, trying to find him, but only blackness greeted her.

She resurfaced, scanning for any sign of him. A quick breath, and she dove again, her arms sweeping underwater, hoping. But he'd disappeared.

The current swept her along, banging her into rocks. She tried to swim toward shore to avoid the next set of rapids, occasionally diving down, still trying to find her brother.

Voices sounded in the distance. Rif was sprinting along the shoreline, headed for her.

She searched the water for Nikos.

Gone.

Chapter Eighty-One

Thea opened her eyes and looked around. She recognized the dark wood panels and rich burgundy brocade of the bedroom on the Paris Industries corporate jet. She shifted in the bed. Sharp pain radiated from her ribs. Her right arm was in a cast.

A doctor hovered over her, adjusting an IV drip. "Her blood sugar levels are stabilizing, but she's still dehydrated. In another twenty-four hours, she should be as good as new—well, except for the fractures. I'll be back shortly to check her vitals."

The doctor was talking to Gabrielle Farrah, who sat in an armchair in a corner of the bedroom. Her dark eyes had lost their luster. Stress formed fine lines around her mouth.

"Papa?" Thea leaned forward, her body tensed in pain.

"He made it; we're going to see him now. He was airlifted to the nearest trauma center, which is in Johannesburg."

Relieved, Thea collapsed back into the pillows.

"Rif flew with him in the chopper."

She recalled that moment on the river, asking Rif to take care of Papa. For once, he'd followed orders. She almost smiled before the full memory of what had happened rushed back. "Nikos?"

"No sign of him yet, but he wouldn't be the first person to disappear into the waters of the Zambezi."

Sadness overwhelmed her, pain thrumming in her heart.

Gabrielle leaned forward in her chair. "Nikos was deeply fucked up. I still can't believe he was Ares, but in addition to illegal arms deals, we know he murdered Xi-Ping and her brother in cold blood, then framed Chi as Ares. And it looks like he executed General Jemwa as well. The effect this will have on international relations is immeasurable; the State Department will have its hands full for months untangling this mess."

If only she'd known how ill he was, maybe she could have helped somehow. All the hostages she had helped over the years, and the one who had needed her most was her own brother.

"We also found evidence in Xi-Ping's room proving that she poisoned Peter Kennedy."

She tried to concentrate on what Gabrielle was saying. "Killing the competition?"

"Actually, it looks as if Kennedy was the leak. Initially he shared proprietary details about the Paris Industries offer with her, but then he turned the tables and tried to extort her. He chose the wrong target."

Xi-Ping was beautiful and deadly—no doubt that was why Nikos had been drawn to her.

Gabrielle went on. "Kennedy probably saw this as an opportunity to cash in, but he had no idea who he was dealing with." Gabrielle sighed. "But we shouldn't be talking about all this now. You need to rest. You have two cracked ribs, a broken wrist, innumerable lacerations, bruising all over, including a nice shiner, possible concussion . . ."

And a fractured heart. Thea's bones would heal, but she wasn't sure about the rest. Her family had imploded. Papa had made some very poor decisions, and Nikos . . . His long-ago abduction had twisted his psyche, and his seething hatred of their father had made him a monster. And he'd come close to destroying them all.

She thought of Mamadou. "Is Prime Minister Kimweri okay?"

"Yes, he held a press conference a few hours ago. He declared the emergency over and offered amnesty to any soldiers who had participated in the coup and wanted to return home."

"Smart. I'm relieved he's safe."

"He also announced that Paris Industries won the bid for the Kanzi oil rights." Gabrielle gave her a sad smile. "Needless to say, the US government is pleased about that development."

"Papa told me he had the contract all along. The summit was just for show. And you know that he faked his own kidnapping—at least at first." She studied the cast on her arm. "Is anything as it seems? Anyone?"

Gabrielle shook her head. "I don't know. Look how I misjudged Maximillian Heros."

"I'm sure it wasn't easy to fire that shot," Thea empathized. "And thank you for saving us."

"I spent days with him and had no idea he was the kidnapper. I . . . I cared about him. It scares me that we can't see what's right in front of us."

"We all have our blind spots."

"Max was twisted enough to think he was doing me a favor, handing me Ares on a silver platter. And he manipulated Henri into helping kidnap Christos." She sighed. "Still, shooting him was one of the hardest things I've ever had to do."

"I'm so sorry."

The pilot's voice came over the intercom. "We'll be arriving in Johannesburg in fifteen minutes. Prepare for landing."

"I'd better get back to my seat. I have a car waiting to take you to the hospital."

"Thanks, Gabrielle—for everything. You're not half bad for a Fed."

She nodded, a sad smile on her face. "You're not half bad for a contractor, either."

Chapter Eighty-Two

Battered and bruised, Thea stood outside her father's room, grateful for the pain meds flowing through her bloodstream. Gabrielle had snuck her in via the rear entrance to avoid the hordes of press out front.

Machines beeped, nurses hovered, and endless bouquets dominated the room. Standing in the doorway, she could see Rif and Hakan at Papa's bedside, the three of them absorbed in quiet conversation.

Her father's body had taken an extraordinary beating—from the beatings from Max and Nikos to his fall off the bridge to his near drowning in the Zambezi. But the worst injury was the gunshot wound, which had become septic from the river water. All his systems were crashing when they first brought him in, and he'd nearly died. They were able to save him, but they'd had to amputate his leg below the knee. For such an active and dynamic man, the loss wouldn't be easy, and the road to recovery would be slow.

She hobbled into his hospital room. Rif stood, offering her the chair closest to her father.

She sat down and reached for her father's hand. "How are you feeling, Papa?" While part of her wanted to hug him, part of her wanted to strangle him. What the hell had he been thinking?

"I'm alive, and that's thanks to you, my child." His voice was thready, weak.

Christos's PR team had whitewashed the Paris family name. Every international broadcast, newspaper, and Internet site had carried the headlines with photos of Christos in his hospital bed. Quan Chi had been exposed as the arms dealer Ares, while Max had absorbed the full blame for the kidnapping. Her disturbed brother came out a hero, having died "trying to save his father from Max Heros." *Lies. And more lies.*

Other than Rif, Hakan, and a few key government officials, including Gabrielle and her boss back in the US, no one knew what had actually happened. Out of loyalty, Hakan and Rif would comply with whatever Christos wanted, and the US government would remain strategically silent to ensure that the United States would have a regular supply of oil. In the face of all that, the truth about her brother and his death didn't seem to matter to them.

Rif touched Hakan's shoulder. "Let's grab a cup of coffee, give Christos a break."

"We'll bring you dinner, something fabulous from the cafeteria. I'm sure they have caviar and champagne," Hakan said with a smile.

They all forced a laugh.

After the two men left, Christos beckoned Thea closer. "Don't think I'm unaware of what you sacrificed for this selfish old man. But please know that the Nikos we knew and loved died when he was twelve. The boy who came back was someone else."

"I know what happened, Papa. I read the journal."

He winced. "He was transformed by his time in that camp into a killing machine who used drugs and shot innocents. And he never lost his taste for it." Christos grimaced. "He strangled Allison with his bare hands. That was when I knew what he'd become."

All those years, she'd never understood why their British nanny had left so abruptly without saying good-bye. Allison had been strict and demanding, but Thea had never doubted she cared. She had been a decent and loving woman who set boundaries and standards for her charges. "That's why you sent him away?"

"Military school in Utah, highly structured. It was the only place I could think of that might help him. But he got into trouble there as well. Started selling drugs, beating up other boys, threatening teachers. He was a manipulator. And smart as hell—they could never prove anything."

"You should have told me about his past. I deserved to know the truth. And you let Nikos get away with murdering our nanny along with countless others by covering up for him."

"You're right."

"And when you found out he was planning to kidnap you, you decided to beat him to it? What were you thinking? Why didn't you ask for my help? Or Rif and Hakan's? Why *Max*?"

"Remember the day of my party, when I said I wanted to talk about Nikos? I was going to tell you. I'd planned on sharing everything after you finished running the stairs, but Max had a different plan. You know the rest."

"And we all paid the price."

"I'm deeply sorry that everything turned out the way it did. Please understand that I thought I was protecting you." He placed his hand on hers. She forced herself not to pull away. It would take a while to process everything.

"Did Hakan and Rif tell you about Helena?"

Her father looked down at his lap. "Max did. He planned to murder all the people I cared about before forcing me off the bridge. I hold myself fully responsible for Helena's death."

"I'm not sure anyone could've predicted Max's actions. He hid his resentment well." Still, her father had exhibited poor judgment. Trusting the cop as his co-conspirator had resulted in so many deaths.

"I guess it'll just be the two of us from now on." Papa's eyes were sad, heavy.

Yes, but Nikos's shadow would always be there between them.

Chapter Eighty-Three

Four weeks later

Thea stared into the retinal scanner at Quantum International Security headquarters in London. It beeped, letting her and Aegis into the war room. It was her first day back at work since the trauma on the Victoria Falls Bridge.

Bridges usually took you from one place to another, acting as a gateway to a promised land. But that was when you crossed them, not catapulted off them. The last three Paris family members had hurtled off the bridge. Only two of them had made it home alive.

While she recuperated, Hakan had led a team of local experts on an extensive search of the Zambezi River, scouring the area for any sign of her brother's body, but the only thing they'd found was a remnant of Nikos's shirt. The authorities had promised to notify her immediately if there were any updates. Her brother wasn't the first person to disappear in the croc-infested waters, and he wouldn't be the last.

She stepped into the situation room, Aegis rushing forward to greet Hakan and Rif. Six helium-filled *Welcome Back* balloons hovered over a massive tray of raw vegetables and dips. "We thought about getting you a cake but realized we'd be the only ones eating it," Hakan said. "You're going to make us all healthier."

They both knew about her diabetes now and had been incredibly supportive. It was a relief to be herself around the people she trusted, with no secrets to hide.

"Thanks. I just left Papa at the rehab center." Her father was having a special prosthesis made, and it looked as if he'd be able to walk again. "If you can believe it, he's already back in the pool. And he challenged me to a race in two months' time."

"You'll lose," Hakan said.

"I expect nothing less."

But the father-daughter relationship was far from healed. Too many secrets, too many lies. She turned to Rif. "I spoke to Father Rombola yesterday. He plans on opening the new orphanage in two months." Thea had taken over the African charity that she and Nikos had worked on together. When she'd talked to Rif about it, he was keen to get involved. The organization now also rehabilitated former child soldiers, largely in Kanzi. It was important work, something positive her brother had contributed.

"Just let me know what you need. How does it feel to be back?" Rif asked.

"I need to be busy. Recuperating gave me too much time to think."

"We're grateful to have you here. Lots of work to do," Hakan said.

Rif stroked Aegis's head. "Hey, we forgot to tell Thea. Remember that guy, the doctor in the three-thousand-dollar suit who was part of your last training group and headed to Mexico? Zegna, I think you called him? He got himself kidnapped during his first week there."

She flashed back to the prevention seminar she'd conducted for a group of doctors before Papa had been kidnapped.

It was hard to forget the well-coiffed guy who'd challenged every word that came out of her mouth. "Who handled his case?"

"Paco. The guy's boss, Annie, specifically asked for you, but you were a little busy."

"Is Doc Zegna okay?"

"He was fortunate: taken by pros who wanted cold cash. Paco had it wrapped up in less than two weeks." Rif poured her a glass of sparkling water. "And the debriefing showed he'd been a model prisoner. Looks like your words hit the mark. He even sent you flowers and a thank-you card."

She half smiled. "Seriously?"

Both men laughed. Hakan shook his head. "No, he wasn't a model prisoner, just a lucky one. And his lawyer sent us a letter saying he was considering suing the firm. Some people are just assholes, no matter what happens to them."

"I'm still relieved he's okay." It felt good to be back in the saddle—at the office, ready to work. "Please fill me in on the docket."

Hakan recounted the active cases, sharing all the available intel. She was eager to get started, and not just because she was getting bored of her own recovery. People out there needed their help. After what she'd been through, the job felt more important than ever.

When Nikos had been abducted, they'd held more than his body hostage. The General and Oba had stolen his peace of mind, his security, his future. She and her father had hovered in a horrific limbo for those nine long months, desperate for him to come home, while the rest of the world continued its normal routine. And when Nikos finally did return, a dark passenger named Ares came with him. The kidnappers broke something in him and gave birth to something new, and Nikos could never fully find his way back. And now he'd been lost in the murky waters of the Zambezi.

She touched the Saint Barbara medal hanging from her neck.

I promise to work tirelessly so this doesn't happen to another family, Mzungu. Please forgive me.

She stared at the display board illuminating the ongoing cases across the globe. Currently, forty-eight on Quantum's roster. Some only hours old, others ongoing for years.

You couldn't come home, Nikos, but others will.

ACKNOWLEDGMENTS

I'm very fortunate to have worked as the executive director of ThrillerFest, the annual conference of the International Thriller Writers, for the last several years. I'd like to thank my mentor, Liz Berry, for all her support and guidance—a brilliant lady and Disney guru. And Jessica Johns, my conference coordinator, who makes my life easier because of her hard work and positive attitude. All my staff and friends at ThrillerFest and the International Thriller Writers, you are spectacular, including Jennifer Hughes, Heather Graham, Amanda Kelly, Kathleen Antrim, Terry Rodgers, Dennis Kennett, Shirley Kennett, Taylor Antrim, Jillian Stein, Jon Land, Jeff Ayers, Sandra Brannan, Luzmarie Alvarez, Joe Brannan, Kara Matsune, Christianna Mason, Olivia Mason, John Dixon, Jennifer Kreischer, Lissa Price, Ursula Ringham, Jenny Milchman, Roan Chapin, Bryan Robinson, Elena Hartwell, Shannon Raab, John Raab, and so many more. It's a community like no other. A huge shout-out to the "other K.J.," the phenomenal K.J. Birch from the Grand Hyatt in NYC, who cheered me on as I juggled organizing ThrillerFest while writing. K.J., Allison Wied, and the entire Hyatt staff are incredible—it's like coming home when I visit.

During my time at Seton Hill University, I benefited from the guidance of some generous and talented authors, including

Patrick Piccairelli, Victoria Johnston, Felicia Mason, Tim Esaias, and other kind souls. And I appreciate the support of friends like Maria V. Snyder, Meline Nadeau, Heidi Miller, Jason Jack Miller, Ceres Wright, Jacki King, and so many others.

Kudos to Karen Dionne and Chris Graham for the incredible experiences at the Salt Cay Writers Retreat and to Kelly Meister for hosting us on the gorgeous Blue Lagoon Island.

Rogue Women Writers. These trailblazing women write international and espionage thrillers, and I'm proud to call them my friends: Gayle Lynds, Francine Mathews, Jamie Freveletti, Sonja Stone, Christine Goff, Karna Bodman, and S. Lee Manning. Drop by and visit us on our blog at www.roguewomenwriters.com.

I'm an avid researcher, and I wanted verisimilitude in the airplane scenes. William Scott, talented author and former test pilot, your unabashed enthusiasm for aviation was infectious, and I really enjoyed learning from you. James Hannibal, former stealth bomber pilot, you have way too much fun making things dicey in the air. I love it! And Dave Hughes, thanks for your amazing advice.

Donna Scher, your insights for Nikos's journal were brilliant, and the analysis of each character's psyche—including mine—has been a fabulous learning experience. Your support and kindness is forever appreciated. Wendy Chan, thanks for being such a warmhearted friend.

When I first decided to delve into the dark world of kidnapping, I had some generous people who patiently educated me. To real-life response consultant Dr. Francis D. Grimm, you have been instrumental in helping me understand how the K&R world works, the ultimate freedom broker. Clint Miles, your insights into the reintegration of former hostages have been sensational. Dr. Anthony Feinstein, thanks for your insights into a hostage's mindset. Peter Moore, you are one of my heroes, and I always enjoy our "cheese" adventures. I have the deepest respect for how you are helping other former hostages. Ken Perry, your advice has been brilliant, and I deeply admire how you take risks to protect others. I could listen to your stories all day. Adam Hamon, your tactical knowledge and helpful feedback have been phenomenal. I promise you a date with Thea—if you behave yourself. Rigo Durazo, thanks for passing along a small fraction of your incredible badassery for the fight scenes. Warm thanks to Mark Harris as well as Lorna Titley and Alison Singhall from Quaynote for making me feel so welcome. I also appreciate the help of Joel Whittaker, Andrew Kain, Jack Hoban, Betsy Glick, and many others who need to remain nameless because of security concerns.

Before writing fiction, I was a medical, health, and fitness writer. Over 371 million people across the globe have diabetes, and scientists are working diligently to find a cure. My character Thea Paris has type 1 diabetes, and three inspirational ladies helped make sure that Thea's experience was an accurate portrayal. Any mistakes are mine. Bethanne Strasser, thank you for your keen insights, sharing information about your full and active life with type 1 diabetes as an avid runner, a talented writer, and a mother. Laura Rogers, your year-long trip around the world, shipping medicines to different locales, taking on adventures, absolutely inspires me. And thank you to Devin Abraham from the fabulous Once Upon a Crime bookstore for her insights and suggestions. Also, kudos to talented author Brenda Novak, who works tirelessly to raise funds to help find a cure.

Mike Bursaw, George Easter, Don Longmuir, Larry Gandle, Michael Dillman, Ali Karim, Jacques Filippi—you've really been there to support me, and I thank you for it! And M.J. Rose from Author Buzz, a marketing genius. Tony Mulliken and Fiona Marsh from Midas, thanks for your phenomenal ideas. And Meryl Moss, your support is greatly appreciated.

Susan Jenkins—Empress of All Things Literary, you were an incredible mentor early in my writing career, teaching me that less really is more when it comes to words. I really appreciate your friendship. Todd Allen, I can't imagine having a more supportive and insightful critique partner. I can't wait to be at your first signing. Simon Gervais, amazing friend and fellow Canadian author, your steadfast support always bolstered me when doubts crept in. It's definitely better in the Bahamas. Linda Pretotto, I appreciate your eagle eyes and incisive mind. And thanks to Suzanna Zeigler, Robyn Strassguertl, Angela Trevivian, Linda Crank, Rachel Evans, and all my tennis friends for being such fervent cheerleaders. Cheers to Brian Henry for his brilliant classes and to Rick Weiler for his advice on African negotiations. Thanks to my parents, Anne and Chuck Jones, for providing such an international and adventurous upbringing. And thank you to Russ and Pauline Howe for their enthusiastic support.

Mentors are key for success. We all need people to inspire and guide us, and I've had incredible ones. Peter Hildick-Smith from CODEX, thank you for explaining how important the message of covers, titles, and back copy are—and for guiding me through the process. I can't thank you enough for your patience, time, and energy. Jaime Levine, your editorial advice was incredible, and I treasure our friendship. Thank you to Karin Slaughter for seeing something in my scribblings to recommend me to our phenomenal team at the Victoria Sanders Agency. David Morrell tapped into the motivation behind my book and encouraged me to mine deep into my characters. Rambo's daddy is one of the most perceptive people I've ever met. He also shared his sage advice about the investment of time—if you're going to spend a year (or more!) on a book, you should learn, grow, and become a wiser person from the experience. Lee Child taught me that writing is like music, and you have to get the rhythm right if you want the reader to dance with you—or Jack Reacher. And Peter James, thanks for being so encouraging, supportive, and kind—you are one of the nicest people I'll ever have the joy of knowing.

Christopher Schneider from 5.11 Tactical, who calls himself my number one fan, you have been supportive beyond belief. Thea will always wear the best gear in the business, and if you're ever kidnapped by a bevy of Amazon women, she will come rescue you—that is, if you want her to.

Steve Berry, the Great One, you have given me the best advice on writing, the publishing business, marketing, pretty much everything—and you also recommended me for the job at ITW. I'm not sure there are enough Curly Wurlys in the world to thank you for your kindness.

Victoria Sanders, the day you signed me was one of the best moments of my life, and your incredible team—including Bernadette Baker-Vaughn, Chris Kepner, and Jessica Spivey—treat me like family. You all believed in *The Freedom Broker* from day one, and I appreciate your relentless enthusiasm, wise guidance, and incredible hospitality during my visit to VSA headquarters. And thank you to The Gotham Group for working diligently on the film/TV opportunities.

To my dream publishers at Quercus, Headline, and Hachette Canada. Nathaniel Marunas, your sense of humor and extensive knowledge in so many unique arenas are greatly appreciated. Elyse Gregov, it has been an absolute pleasure getting to know you, and you are so gracious. Vicki Mellor, thanks for being the first to show interest in Thea and her gang—forever grateful. Amelia Ayrelan Iuvino, Amanda Harkness, Alex Knight, Jennifer Doyle, Kitty Stogdon, Mari Evans, Jason Bartholomew, Sara Adams, Millie Seaward, Jo Liddiard, Martha Bucci, Donna Nopper: I'm honored to be working with you all.

And RJH, you never stopped believing. Thank you.

ABOUT THE TYPE

Typeset in Swift EF, 10.75/15 pt.

Named for an acrobatic city bird native to Holland,
Swift was designed by Gerard Unger in 1985 to meet
the need for a typeface that could remain crisp and
clear after coming off the high-speed newspaper presses
of the day. For its original distribution as a PostScript
font, it was leased to German foundry Elsner+Flake.

Typeset by Scribe Inc., Philadelphia, Pennsylvania